CHERRY BLOSSOMS
in the STORM

A NOVEL

ROBERT AND GAIL KAKU

Genesis Finalist Award

MAJESTYHOUSE®

Cherry Blossoms in the Storm
Copyright © 2015 Robert and Gail Kaku

ISBN-13 978-0-9799903-4-2 (paperback)
ISBN-13 978-0-9799903-5-9 (ebook)

Printed in the United States of America
Library of Congress Control Number: 2014920623

Published by Majesty House® www.majestyhouse.com
Cover design by Lauren Kudo

This is a work of historical fiction. Names, characters, places, and incidents are the product of the authors' imaginations or are used fictitiously. Any resemblance to actual persons, living or dead is coincidental.

Real historical figures have been referenced in parts of this novel, including:

President Franklin D. Roosevelt
President Harry S. Truman
Lieutenant General J. L. DeWitt, US Army
Colonel Young Oak Kim, US Army (has a captain's rank in the novel)
General John E. Dahlquist, US Army
General Charles W. Ryder, US Army
Hirohito, emperor of Japan—reign 1926–1989
General Mitsuru Ushijima, Imperial Japanese Army
Chiune Sugihara, Japanese diplomat
Akio Morita, cofounder of Sony Corporation
Shigeru Fujii, Heart Mountain draft resister
Sen no Rikyu, tea ceremony master, sixteenth century
Nobunaga Oda, a powerful samurai warlord, sixteenth century
Hideyoshi Toyotomi, preeminent samurai warlord and imperial regent, sixteenth century

For additional information, see the authors' notes at: majesty.org/cb

We are forever grateful to the Nisei—second-generation Japanese Americans—who fought for the freedom and rights of Japanese Americans.

PROLOGUE

San Francisco – August 24, 1929

Thirteen-year-old Akira Omura swallowed hard, unable to grasp the reality that Mama was sending him away to Japan with his younger brother Tad. So what if his parents were born there. He was an American and didn't want to leave his friends, his home, and the sandlot baseball games he loved so much.

Angst twisted his gut like a wrung-out washcloth, and stinging tears burned his eyelids. He trudged up the gangway of the *Tokyo Maru,* its steel stairs clacking with each forced step. Pivoting, he viewed the San Francisco waterfront against a backdrop of hills dotted with tall buildings and colorful houses. Screeching seagulls soared in circles under a brilliant blue sky.

He looked back at Tad, whose face looked calm. How could he be so emotionless at a time like this?

"Hurry Akira. You're holding everyone up." Uncle Tetsuo propelled him forward with a shove on the back of his head.

Akira stumbled and gritted his teeth to keep from saying something that would draw stronger wrath. The thought of having to live at his uncle's house soured his stomach.

His six-year-old brother, Danny, sidled close to Mama and brought up the rear.

"Come on, the ship will be sailing soon." Uncle Tetsuo brushed past Akira to an open area on the deck and briskly waved his hand, beckoning them to come.

Mama stooped next to Akira and Tad. "Be good boys and mind Uncle and Auntie. Say your prayers daily," she said in Japanese. Her voice cracked, and a tear streaked down her powdered face.

Akira blinked, amazed to see Mama cry for the first time ever. A bit of hope flared like a lit match in his heart. "We don't have to go if it makes you sad."

His mother drew him into a hug. "It makes me very sad, but I've already told you that I can't support all three of you boys."

The match snuffed out. The sweet fragrance of her lilac perfume loosened his control, and fresh tears cascaded down his cheeks, soaking her soft silk kimono. She released Akira and pulled Tad toward her.

Tad moved away from her. He covered his eyes with his fists and started bawling.

"You're not a baby. Tadao, you're ten years old." Mama straightened and looked at them. "Akira, Tadao, boys must be strong. Don't cry."

Papa had told Akira that many times as well—the last time on his deathbed with eyes reflecting the excruciating pain of stomach cancer. The memories threatened to cause new tears, but Akira beat them back. He wouldn't dishonor Papa anymore. His father expected him to set a good example for his younger brothers, so he blurted out to Tad, "It's going to be okay."

Tad stopped crying and sniffled a few times.

The ship's whistle blasted. Over the loudspeaker, a man requested all visitors to prepare to leave.

Akira wished he could trade places with Danny. The little squirt would get to stay here and even had an American first name, while he and Tadao were stuck with Japanese names. He once asked his mother why, and she said Papa had planned to return the family to Japan one day. But a few years later, Papa decided America was home, so the last child received an American name.

It wasn't fair, none of it, but it was no use thinking about that now. Akira reached into a bag he carried aboard, and he pulled out a small wooden box, which he handed to Danny. "You can have it."

Immediately Danny opened the box and peeked inside. His jaw dropped. "Baseball cards! You're giving them to me?" He beamed as if he'd hit a home run.

"You don't have to give them to Danny," Mama said. "You love those cards."

Akira didn't look at her. He also loved listening to the games on the radio, and he wouldn't be doing that either. The way the 1929 season was shaping up, his beloved Yankees would have a tough time catching the Philadelphia A's anyway. "Danny can have them. I won't have anybody to trade with over there." The words flew out sharper than he had intended, and from the corner of his eye, he saw Mama wince.

"Gee, thanks." Danny thumbed through the cards with a glint in his eyes. His chubby fingers would fray them in no time.

Akira shoved his hands in his pockets to keep himself from snatching the cards back.

Tad hovered over Danny's shoulder and shot a glance at Akira. "You're even giving him your Babe Ruth and Lou Gehrig cards?"

"You don't like the Yankees, so I'm giving them to him."

Tad reached for the wooden box. "You better not lose them like you—"

"I won't lose them." Danny jerked away from Tad.

The whistle blasted again, and through the loudspeaker, a final announcement was made, this time asking all visitors to disembark immediately.

Akira checked his wristwatch, the one Papa gave him for his twelfth birthday. He would always treasure it as the last gift from his father. It reminded him that his time in America was rapidly dissipating like the smoke billowing from the ship's stacks.

He would always remember the good times he had with Papa. They used to play catch at the neighborhood schoolyard, fish for smelt in the sloughs that flowed into the bay, or challenge each other at *Go,* Japanese checkers.

His mother bowed to Uncle Tetsuo. She and Danny turned back toward the gangway.

Akira leaned over the foredeck rail and followed them with misty eyes. He wanted to be as strong as Papa, but when Mama turned around and waved again, he flailed his arms frantically. "Good-bye, Mama! Bye-bye!" His throat hurt as he yelled his farewell over the din of the well-wishers.

Crepe paper streamers were distributed to passengers, who threw them to the crowd below. Tad's green one cascaded through the air and floated on the gray water lapping against the dock. Akira clutched his blue streamer in his balled fist but refused to throw it, as though keeping the crinkled paper meant holding on to a last piece of America.

Mighty engines rumbled and onboard motors whirred as crewmen unlashed the ropes and secured the gangway. The ocean liner eased away from the dock with colorful flags fluttering on the rigging. At the end of the pier, two tugboats chugged in, ready to guide the ship out of the harbor.

Akira and Tad abandoned their uncle and rushed to the back of the ship to wave their final good-byes. Akira's eyes tracked the figures of Mama and Danny until he could no longer distinguish them. As he turned toward the front, the cool, salty air of the bay whipped against his face. In the distance, a blanket of thick fog started to roll in, as if it were welcoming him into the new, unknown life ahead.

He peered over the side of the ship as it cruised toward the Golden Gate. White sheets of water washed away into the wake, reminding Akira of leaving behind Mama and everything he loved so much in America—perhaps forever.

1

Banzai!

Kumamoto, Japan – December 8, 1941

Could the rumors be true about Japan bombing Pearl Harbor? In the twelve years Akira Omura had lived in Japan, he couldn't recall a more dreadful day. It was as if he woke up this morning in a different universe.

He chided himself for not returning home to America with Tad seven years ago. Now he'd be stranded in Japan indefinitely.

Americans wouldn't stand for such an attack on their soil, not without fighting back. Granted, California was some distance from Hawaii, but if the war spread to the mainland, Mama, Tad, and Danny would be endangered. Akira's stomach churned like a turbulent sea as he strode past high school boys in black paramilitary tunics and girls dressed in dark-blue sailor uniforms.

"*Ohayo gozaimasu, Sensei.*" The students greeted him with warm smiles.

"Good morning." Trying to mask his dismay over the attack on Pearl Harbor, he forced a half-smile. "I'll see you in the auditorium."

Three girls waited for him and winked at him coquettishly. Although it flattered him, he had told them to pursue boys their own age—not a twenty-five-year-old teacher like him. "Go ahead of me," he said. Today he didn't want to mingle with anyone.

A chill snaked up Akira's back when he spotted a new wall photograph of Emperor Hirohito bedecked with medals—a symbol of the new, militaristic Japan.

A queue of students, faculty and staff waited to file into Kumamoto Senior High School's auditorium. Girls scooted over, making an opening for him in line, but Akira politely declined. Animated discussions broke out about Pearl Harbor. One boy pantomimed diving airplanes with his arms, making a buzzing sound and mimicking explosions. *"Bokan! Bokan!"*

It reminded Akira of the time last summer when he had coached a baseball team at a ballpark near Ariake Bay. In the distance, the deep-throated drone of engines quickened to a high-pitched whine. He shielded his eyes from the sun's glare as six silver flecks dropped from the sky toward the glimmering waves of the bay. The diving warplanes flattened their trajectories and zoomed in. Red sun insignias were painted on the tops and bottoms of the wings and on the fuselages. They whisked toward four large barges docked at the end of the harbor. Players and coaches from both teams stopped to observe the aerial ballet unfolding above them, pumping their fists and shouting, *"Ganbare!"* as if the pilots could hear their encouragements. When the planes came within two hundred meters, they gained altitude and banked toward the sea. The next flight of six descended to attack the mock targets.

Practice had become reality.

Inside the auditorium, Akira set his briefcase under his chair in the faculty section and greeted the other teachers. A large map of Asia hung at the center of the stage next to a military flag with sixteen rays emanating from a red sun.

Principal Kurosaki stepped behind the podium with a high-voltage smile. He raised his hand and lowered it when the crowd grew quiet. "Early this morning, our brave naval aviators struck a decisive blow to the American navy at Pearl Harbor. At least a dozen battleships, cruisers, and other vessels have been sunk or severely damaged."

The principal's words confirmed Japan was officially at war with America. Nausea swirled in Akira's stomach. He wanted to gain three years of teaching experience before moving home to America in a few months. It would improve his chances of getting a teaching position back home, which was tough for Japanese Americans. He had already purchased his passage home aboard a ship. Now, Akira had no choice but to stay.

"Our forces have also launched multipronged offensives against Hong Kong, Malaya, Guam, the Philippines, and other islands in the Pacific." Principal Kurosaki tapped the map with his pointer. "For years, the British and Americans have kept us from our rightful place among the nations. They colonized major areas throughout Asia and took the spoils. But when we assisted the Manchurian government against the greedy Chinese warlords, the West cut off our supply of iron, rubber, and petroleum."

A murmur reverberated throughout the auditorium.

The principal's depiction of America contradicted what Akira remembered—a land of liberty, freedom, and justice.

When the crowd quieted, Kurosaki continued. "Early reports from the battlefronts indicate we are trouncing the foreigners. Once again, we have proven our soldiers are far superior!" he shouted, raising his volume to a crescendo. "The great crusade to rid Asia of the Western invaders has begun. Asia for Asians!"

On cue, everybody rose from their seats with arms raised above their heads and roared, "*Banzai! Banzai! Banzai!*"

Not wanting to be conspicuous, Akira stood up, raised his hands, and moved his lips.

At the conclusion, he exited the auditorium with a heavy heart. The moment he saw Hiroshi Yamada, a political science teacher, he wheeled around in the opposite direction. Akira couldn't understand why his colleague always seemed to be competing with him—on the athletic field, in faculty meetings, or at social gatherings. Everyone knew Hiroshi came from a rich family, graduated from a top university, excelled in sports, and had a muscular physique. What else did he have to prove?

With a quickened step, Hiroshi caught up with him. "Good morning, Omura-sensei. Wasn't that absolutely grand?"

"Good morning, Yamada-sensei." If Akira didn't respond soon, the situation could become awkward. He forced a neutral expression. "Yes, it was."

"At the rate we're winning battle after battle, we'll be in San Francisco within a few months." Hiroshi broke out into a grin as wide as his ego.

San Francisco? He had kept his American roots a secret from Hiroshi and his other colleagues. "Do you think victory will be that easy?"

"Of course. Western soldiers are no match for us." Hiroshi smiled smugly. "We proved it against the Russians forty years ago."

Akira couldn't let Hiroshi spew out such nonsense. "America isn't like Russia was back then. The government has the support of its people, unlike the way it was with the Russian czar. It would be a mistake to think this is the same situation."

The grin on Hiroshi's face gave way to a frown. "I'm surprised you underestimate the samurai spirit of our brave soldiers. Look how we crushed the larger Chinese army when they encroached upon our Manchurian allies. You sound so unpatriotic."

Akira's neck muscles tensed. He needed a quick recovery, and he had to be careful about what he said. People informed on each other to the *Kempeitai*, a very harsh military police that enforced the Peace Preservation Laws and arrested dissenters for *thought* crimes. "I'm just saying we shouldn't underestimate the Americans."

Hiroshi's nostrils flared. "If I were you, I'd watch what I say."

Resentment crowded out Akira's desire to be civil. He hoped it didn't show on his face. He glanced at his watch. "I have to prepare for class. Good day, Yamada-sensei."

A thin smile stretched across Hiroshi's lips. "Good day." He turned and stalked away.

On the way to his first-period classroom, Akira considered his predicament.

Am I Japanese, or am I American?

2

A Day of Infamy

Mountain View, California

The RCA Victor radio on the shelf whined and crackled as Tad rotated the tuning knob for the best reception. The important broadcast would begin any minute now.

Danny crowded in from behind. "Try KGO or KSFO. They're the clearest." He bumped Tad into the walnut cabinet, rattling the Japanese doll case.

"Hey, watch it!"

"Come on. It's going to start soon." Danny hovered over Tad's shoulder.

Tad swallowed his words and resisted the urge to fire back. Yesterday's news had put everyone on edge.

The melodic NBC chimes sounded. "This is KGO San Francisco, bringing you the president's speech from the House chamber in the Capitol building," an announcer's deep voice blared. Indistinct rumbling and murmuring came through the radio speaker, then abated.

"Mr. Vice President, Mr. Speaker, members of the Senate and the House of Representatives." The president's voice came through crystal clear over the airwaves. "Yesterday, December 7, 1941—a date which will live in infamy—the United States of America was suddenly and deliberately attacked by naval and air forces of the Empire of Japan."

Tad's nerves revolted at the opening words of President Roosevelt. They could only mean one thing—WAR.

His stepdad, Mas, hurried into the living room with Mama, and they settled onto the couch. Minutes later, his wife, Lily, plopped onto the other sofa.

Throughout the previous night, a centrifuge of anxieties and misgivings whirled about in Tad's mind. The attack on Pearl Harbor could spark a violent backlash against the Japanese community and his family. He lay awake, staring at the ceiling, faint moonlight sneaking in through the venetian blinds. The country of his ancestors had provoked a war America would fight, quite possibly against his relatives—maybe even against his older brother, Akira.

President Roosevelt continued. ". . . the Japanese government has deliberately sought to deceive the United States by false statements and expressions of hope for continued peace . . ."

The indignation in his voice seared Tad's heart like a red-hot branding iron. Now, the entire nation was aroused against Japan.

"I regret to tell you that very many American lives have been lost . . ."

Tad buried his face into his hands. All of his hopes for living the American dream vanished in an instant. He dropped his hands and listened as the president continued the indictment.

". . . since the unprovoked and dastardly attack by Japan on Sunday, December 7, 1941, a state of war has existed between the United States and the Japanese Empire."

Thunderous applause echoed throughout the House chamber with President Roosevelt's call to war—confirmation of what Tad feared.

The commentator broke in with a reprise of yesterday's events. Lost in his thoughts, Tad barely caught snatches of the report.

". . . sneak attack . . ."

". . . over fifteen hundred Americans dead . . ."

". . . outrage . . ."

". . . Japs! . . ."

His stepdad's voice broke his contemplation. "Tadao, please translate for us," Mas said in Japanese.

Tad translated the gist of President Roosevelt's speech.

Tears squeezed out of Mama's closed eyes. "Akira's there. I must telegram him to come home immediately."

Danny shook his head. "Mom, there's no way he'll be able to leave Japan. Not now."

"Akira shouldn't have stayed there. I feel sick to my stomach." Mama's voice faltered.

"Japan and America at war is like your mama and papa fighting each other," Mas said.

Tad's eyes traveled to the cross hanging above the fireplace mantle, then shifted to a family portrait below. Mama and Mas stood in front of the farmhouse, she in her formal, dark kimono, and he in a three-piece suit. Mas had married Tad's widowed mother, and they settled in the sleepy, agricultural town of Mountain View at the base of the San Francisco Peninsula. Life had been difficult for them—Issei—first-generation immigrants from Japan.

Next to Mas in the photograph, Lily stood in her favorite Bette Davis-style dress with her hair curled into a fashionable hairdo. Tad wore a tweed sports coat with dark slacks, and he held Lily's hand. In his high school letterman's jacket, Danny posed proudly with his arms folded. Akira was the only family member missing.

As a Nisei—second-generation Japanese in America—Tad considered himself to be every bit as American as anyone else born in this country. Occasionally, the *Hakujin*—Caucasians— spewed racial slurs like Jap, Nip, Chink, or Chinaman at him. Yet he had many *Hakujin* friends in the community. Whether they were still friends was an open question.

* * *

Lily buttoned up her wool coat and marched down Castro Street, her heels clicking with each rapid step.

The downtown area buzzed with people, more than on a typical Monday. Near the drugstore, sidewalk newspaper racks were all empty. A familiar face appeared a few yards ahead of her. She quickened her pace and smiled. "Hello, Mrs. Miller. How are—"

"Get away from me, Jap!" The middle-aged woman slapped Lily's face, jerked her head away, and stalked off.

Lily stood on the sidewalk stunned for several minutes, mulling over what had just happened. Mrs. Miller was so friendly when they worked together at the arts and crafts fair two years earlier. She never expected this kind of reaction, not from Ann Miller. It didn't make sense.

Just because I'm Japanese?

Blinking back tears, she hurried down a side street to buy material at Trudy's Fabric to make costumes for the Christmas pageant. As she approached the store, Lily peered through the window and saw Trudy Jenkins, the proprietor, glaring at her with narrowed eyes.

Trudy rushed to the door, locked it, and flipped the sign to "Closed" before Lily could turn the doorknob.

Rapping on the door, Lily uttered, "How can you be closed? It's three in the afternoon."

Trudy acted like she didn't hear or see her.

Just two days earlier, Lily had no trouble with the town's *Hakujin* people. Now the Caucasians despised her.

Lily wanted to go home, but she had some items to pick up at the Japanese grocery market. She rounded the corner, and her heart jumped when she saw the words, "DIRTY JAP" painted across the hood of a sedan. The car was parked on the street with slashed tires and shattered windows.

Her lips quivered. How could a person do something so hateful? After a moment, Lily marshaled her inner courage and continued on. She couldn't wilt because of this.

About twenty-five feet from the Japanese market, she halted abruptly and covered her mouth. Plywood boarded the large window that normally displayed advertisements of sale items. Above it, a large sign declared, "I AM AN AMERICAN." Next to it, someone had scrawled in red paint, "GO HOME JAPS!"

Her heart caught in her throat. She stepped inside and found the store devoid of customers. Last week it had bustled with housewives—Japanese, Caucasian, and Mexican. She shuffled down an aisle where canned goods were strewn everywhere. Mr. Mori was hunched over, restocking a shelf.

He nodded at Lily and turned away with a grimacing face. "Some punks smashed the window with a brick. They came inside, stole stuff, and made a big mess. Before they left they shouted, 'Remember Pearl Harbor!' "

"That's terrible. I'm so sorry. Don't they know we had nothing to do with that?"

"We have a Japanese face and a Japanese name. It's all the same to them."

She looked at the boarded window that darkened the produce counters. "It's so unfair."

"That's not all. This morning I phoned my suppliers, and they're refusing to sell to me. And it's not because I don't pay my bills on time." After a moment, he perked up and smiled. "Anyway, how can I help you?"

"I'd like two pounds of pot roast, a small sack of *azuki* beans, and some *mochi*."

"Sure. I'll be right back."

Before Mr. Mori returned, Lily restacked two rows of cans on the half-empty shelves.

"Don't worry about that, Lily. My son, Dave, will be here soon. He left school early today, because some kids threw rocks at him."

Lily gasped. "Ouch! How mean. Is your son hurt badly?"

"He has some cuts and bruises, but he'll be okay. It's a good thing his teacher broke up the fight."

"From now on we're going to have to be extra careful."

"That's for certain." He bagged her purchases, gave her change for a five-dollar bill, and thanked her.

As she exited, Lily looked down the street and then back at Mr. Mori's store. A slap on the face, an indignant glare, and the vandalism was evidence that the world had indeed changed.

* * *

Tad squeezed his cloth napkin into a tight ball as Lily recounted her experiences. He pounded his fist on the table. "I can't believe that woman slapped you!"

"I can," said Danny with a deadpan expression. "Her son was on the football team with me, but he's a year older. After graduating, he joined the navy, and I heard he was stationed at Pearl Harbor."

"Still, for her to slap Lily for something we had nothing to do with. I don't know, the world's gone crazy." Tad looked at the downcast eyes of Mama and Mas.

Mama rose from her chair. "Let's pray for this war to end quickly and that nothing bad happens to Akira or the relatives."

The family rose and bowed their heads. In their own words, they prayed to God for solace and peace in a world erupting in death and destruction.

That evening, Tad and Mas took different sections of the *Valley Times*. Tad sat on the sofa, while his stepdad eased himself into his favorite chair.

The front page carried an oversized headline—JAPS BOMB HAWAII—with a large photograph of sinking navy ships ablaze in Pearl Harbor. The lower section contained a smaller headline— FDR CALLS FOR WAR.

Lily entered the living room and deposited herself next to Tad with a novel in her hand.

Seated in the rocking chair, Mama held her knitting needles and clicked away with a rhythmic tempo. A white-and-pink-mohair shawl began to form.

After a half hour of perusing produce ads, Mas dozed off with his head against a doily-covered headrest, newspaper neatly folded on his lap.

Danny emerged from his room, wearing his blue-and-gray letterman's jacket. "I'm going out for a while."

Mama peered over her reading glasses. "Danny, you shouldn't go out."

"I can take care of myself. Remember, I was a linebacker on the football team. And I'm a judo black belt." He put on his shoes and left through the front door.

The truck's engine fired up. With all the troubles in town, it'd be better if Danny stayed home, but Tad couldn't tell him that.

Later that night, as the grandfather clock chimed eleven o'clock, rapid pounding at the front door jolted them.

"Who can that be?" Lily sprang up.

Tad rose and approached the door. Someone hammered at the door again.

"Who is it?" Tad asked.

"FBI."

3

Emiko

Kumamoto, Japan

Akira stared blankly out the window as the streetcar whizzed by storefronts in downtown Kumamoto. He gripped the overhead strap to balance himself as the crowded trolley trundled over crossing tracks.

People around town shouted in jubilant huzzahs, but for Akira it was no celebration. The prospect of being marooned in Japan, possibly for the duration of the war, devastated him. Worse yet, he could be drafted into the Japanese army and forced to fight his own country, maybe against his own brothers.

As the streetcar screeched to a stop, his body pulled forward with his arm tethered to the ceiling strap. Several passengers disembarked, making room for new riders.

A slender young woman with large, arresting eyes and a light complexion stepped into the tram. Her lustrous hair swept into a fancy knot. She wore a deep purple kimono with embroidered pink cherry blossoms below the *obi* sash. A cream-colored wrap covered her shoulders. In one arm, she carried a fabric bundle. He caught the sweet scent of wisteria as she squeezed past him looking for an open strap. Akira released his strap. "Excuse me, miss. You can use this."

She flashed a winsome smile that made his heart quicken. "Thank you, but you won't have one."

"I'm fine. I can brace myself against the ceiling. Please, I insist."

"Well then, thank you." She graciously bowed and took hold of the strap.

Seeing no ring on her ring finger, he assumed she was single, but a woman like her probably had someone special. His eyes poured over her lovely features.

The purple in her kimono against her almost perfect alabaster skin was like a beautiful painting that took his breath away. Not that looks meant everything to him, but there was something special about her.

Her graceful movements combined with her captivating smile somehow caught his attention more than anyone else ever had. Despite the hundreds of times he rode this trolley line, he had never seen her before. Certainly, he would have noticed her. He wanted to speak to her again, but she faced the other way, and he didn't want to appear too forward.

The streetcar continued past several stops, but time stood still for Akira. He closed his eyes and thought about what he would say to make her smile again. The trolley jolted to an abrupt halt, and he nearly lost his balance. Akira peered through the window to see what had happened.

"*Baka!* Idiot!" shouted the driver at an errant bicyclist.

He lowered his gaze to the young woman, who was crouched down, trying to recover the items that had spilled out of her bundle.

"*Gomenasai*, I'm sorry," she said to the people standing nearby. Passengers around her helped pick up the fallen objects. She graciously thanked everyone who was helping her.

Akira stooped down and wrapped his hand around the base of a heavy, round weight with metal spikes. A couple of steps away, he picked up a pair of shears, which appeared to be used for *ikebana* flower arrangement.

He rose and handed her the items.

"*Arigato-gozaimasu*," she said softly and smiled, while her cheeks radiated a rosy blush.

"You're welcome. I see you're interested in *ikebana*."

"I teach it. I'm returning from an exhibition."

He tried to think of something clever to say about being a teacher, but history wasn't anything artistic like traditional flower arrangement. He wanted to keep the conversation going, but when their eyes met again, no words came out of his mouth. She seemed to be at a loss for words, too.

She looked up at Akira. "I'll be getting off soon. Again, thank you for your help. You're so kind."

His destination was also coming up soon. The thought of never seeing her again sank Akira's buoyant mood. He wanted to say something more but hesitated.

At the next stop, the young lady stayed onboard. Maybe she was going somewhere close to where he lived.

Soon, the streetcar eased to a halt in front of the ruins of Kumamoto Castle. The young woman moved toward the exit. *She's getting off at my stop!* Akira let an elderly couple go ahead of him, while keeping his eyes on her. As he stepped onto the pavement, Akira spotted her about ten meters ahead.

The crush of people getting off and on came between them, and he lost her in the crowd. He quickly searched the vicinity. No sign of her. He drew a deep breath. The thought of never seeing her again dampened his spirits.

Akira ambled along the boulevard toward his apartment. His stomach growled, reminding him that he hadn't eaten anything since dawn. He turned down a quiet side street where several eateries came into view.

"Come on pretty girl, let's have a drink together," a man said in a slurred voice.

"*Hanashite!* Take your hands off me!"

"What's the matter? Don't you like me?"

"No! Leave me alone. *Tasukete!* Help!" she cried out.

Akira turned his head toward the commotion, surprised to find the young woman he had seen on the streetcar. Instinctively he charged toward them. The drunken man was tall like him but must have outweighed Akira by about twenty kilograms. Perhaps strong words would dissuade him. "Let go of her!"

The drunk sneered at him. "Mind your own business."

Akira set his briefcase down and pushed himself in between them. "Miss, run!"

The drunk released her arm and wobbled backward.

Strangely, she didn't leave. Her safety was paramount. He had hoped she would have escaped while he held off the attacker.

The drunk closed in, standing nose-to-nose with Akira, glowering at him with bloodshot eyes. "Get out of the way." He shoved Akira on the shoulder.

Akira staggered back a pace. He didn't want to get into a fight. He turned toward the woman when a hard fist caught him in the mouth, dropping him to the ground.

The woman screamed.

"I told you to mind your own business!" The drunk leaned toward Akira with clenched teeth, then reeled around and grabbed the woman by the arm again.

Akira rubbed his aching jaw. He thrust himself onto his feet and dashed toward them. Lowering his shoulder, he barreled into the drunk, causing the man to release her.

The drunk rotated and swung at him. Akira ducked. The man took another swipe and punched nothing but air.

Akira hooked his leg behind the drunk's and sent the man tumbling to the ground with a thump. Then he whirled around toward the young woman. "Come on. Let's get out of here before he gets up. Please, let me help you carry this." He picked up her bundle and his briefcase.

The woman lifted the hem of her kimono and hastened her steps. When they were two blocks away, they stopped and rested. Visible plumes exhaled from their mouths as they caught their breaths.

"Are you okay?" Akira asked, between gulps of air.

"I was so scared, but I'm relieved now," she said, panting. "Oh, you're bleeding." She pulled out a handkerchief from her kimono sleeve and dabbed the corner of his mouth.

Even though his lip stung, he smiled at her concern for him.

"I'm sorry you were injured because of me. I feel badly about this, but I'm very grateful to you for rescuing me." Her eyes sparkled under a streetlamp. "I'd like to buy you dinner as a small token of my appreciation."

"That's very kind of you, but you don't have to repay me. Please don't worry about it."

"It's the least I can do to thank you."

Even though custom said otherwise, he couldn't refuse her invitation. "All right then. By the way, I'm Akira Omura." He bowed.

She returned the bow. "My name is Emiko Takata. I'm pleased to meet you."

Akira turned toward the main street. "I know a little café nearby that serves great *nabemono* dishes and specializes in *yosenabe*. It's reasonably priced too."

Emiko let out an effervescent smile. "Hot pot food seems perfect on a cold night like this. Let's go."

Pleasant seafood scents wafted in the air as they entered the bustling cafe. The woman proprietor bowed. "Welcome!"

"Good evening, Midori-san. You're busy as usual."

She smiled warmly at them and showed them to a table.

Akira set down the bundle and briefcase. He held Emiko's hand as she took a seat. Then he seated himself across from her.

The proprietor asked, "Two *yosenabe?*"

After receiving an affirmative nod from Emiko, he answered, "Yes, please."

When the food arrived, Emiko nibbled on a piece of sea bass and some chopped vegetables. "This food is absolutely divine. I didn't know such a place existed." She caught the proprietor's attention. "Madam, your *yosenabe* is delicious!" Emiko continued to eat as Midori-san bowed and acknowledged her compliment.

Akira grinned. "So, besides liking the same type of food, what else can you tell me about yourself?"

Emiko set down her chopsticks. "My mother passed away when I was eight, and I live with my father. I not only teach flower arrangement, but also tea ceremony and piano." She let out an impish smile. "All right, now that I've told you about myself, how about you?"

"I've been teaching history at Kumamoto Senior High School for the past two years."

"Oh, you're a teacher. I've always enjoyed history. Tea ceremony, as we know it today, has its roots with the tea master Sen no Rikyu in the sixteenth century."

"Yes, he had ties to the political leaders of that time—Oda Nobunaga and Toyotomi Hideyoshi."

"Too bad, Hideyoshi ordered Rikyu to commit suicide."

Akira nodded. "It's a shame to lose a genius prematurely. By the way, where did you go to school?"

"Aoyama Gakuin for high school and Tsuda College in Tokyo."

He had heard of these private schools. Tsuda specialized in English education. Akira opened his mouth to speak some English but stopped himself.

After they finished their meal, Akira looked at his watch. "Let's leave this crowded place." He asked for the bill.

The proprietor placed the bill in front of him. Emiko quickly took it before he could claim it. "No, I insist. Please let me."

He bowed slightly. "All right. Thank you."

As they strolled along the street, Emiko asked, "Where is your family from?"

Something told him he could trust her. He scanned the area to see if anyone was in earshot. "Actually, I was born in America, and my family lives there now."

Her eyes widened. "What? You're an American? But you speak Japanese perfectly."

"I learned the language in the twelve years I've lived here. After my father died, my mother sent my younger brother and me for schooling here when I was thirteen. I lived with my uncle and aunt until they died two years ago in a car accident."

Her smile disappeared. "How terrible. I'm sorry to hear that. So, do you live with your brother?"

"No, Tadao returned home to America after five years."

She lowered her gaze then looked up. "Now with the war, you probably can't—"

"Go home?"

"What will you do?"

"I don't know. I'll just have to see what happens with the war." While the thought of not being able to see or communicate with his family saddened him, meeting Emiko exhilarated him.

She stopped in front of a large house behind a substantial stone wall and wooden gate. Her family appeared to be wealthy.

Emiko bowed deeply. "Once again, I thank you for helping me, not once, but several times today."

Akira returned the bow. "It was my pleasure." He handed her the bundle and lingered for a moment. He couldn't let her go without a promise of another visit. "Takata-san, if it's all right with you, I'd like to see you again. Perhaps for a meal, tea, or something."

Emiko gleamed. "I'd like that very much."

"How about this Sunday around two? I'll pick you up here."

"That would be fine," she said, before stepping through the gate.

He kept his eyes fixed on her until she disappeared into the house. Akira couldn't wait to see her again and his heart somersaulted. His toes and heels tapped rapidly, and he twirled around, emulating a tap dance he had once seen in a Fred Astaire movie.

Akira inhaled a deep breath of the cold night air, but the chill traveling down his throat couldn't extinguish the spark that kindled in his heart.

4

Enemy Aliens

Mountain View, California

The voices outside sounded unfamiliar to Tad. He glanced back at Lily, whose narrow eyes ballooned. Maybe they really were FBI agents. "Is this some type of joke?"

"No joke buddy," the gruff voice blared. "We have a search warrant. Now open up or we'll bust the door down."

Tad cracked the door open.

Two men wearing nearly identical gray trench coats and black fedoras flashed identification badges in Tad's face, then shoved their way in, sending a chilly breeze inside.

Mas awoke and reached for his glasses. "What's all the commotion?"

The shorter man moved toward Mas and pulled out a document. "I'm Special Agent Oswald, and this is Special Agent Fredericks. We have a warrant, signed by the president of the United States, to locate and detain enemy aliens."

"Enemy aliens?" Tad shuffled forward a few steps. A bitter reminder that even after three decades of living in California, his stepfather was still regarded as Japanese—not American.

Oswald turned his attention to Mas. "Are you Ma-say-oh No-goo-chee?"

"Yes."

"We're taking you into custody," Oswald said.

Lily gasped. "Why?"

"What has he done?" Tad asked.

"It's for questioning." Oswald reached inside his suit jacket and pulled out handcuffs. He stepped toward Mas and made a circling motion with his hand. "Turn around." Oswald jerked Mas's wrists and cuffed them.

The confusing whirl of actions and words seemed surreal, like a nightmare to Tad—only he wasn't waking up. "This isn't right. Why are you treating him like a criminal?"

Oswald's lip curled into a contemptuous smile. "It's because we're at war with the Japs, and we want to make doubly sure he doesn't help them."

"Help them?" Tad's mouth went dry. He took a step toward Oswald. "He had nothing to do with what happened at Pearl Harbor. I demand that you tell me what he's being charged with."

Fredericks blocked Tad and shot him a scathing look. "First of all, you're in no position to demand anything. Second, he's not being charged, only questioned."

"You can't just drag people off like that," Tad said, stiff-arming Frederick's shoulder.

Fredericks's face twisted grotesquely. He grabbed Tad's arm and wrenched it behind his back. "You're obstructing justice. We're taking you in, too."

Lily's face blanched. "No! You can't do that," she shrilled.

"Watch and see, lady." Fredericks's eyes blazed like fiery coals.

"Don't yell at my wife."

The agent gyrated back to Tad. "You shut up!" Fredericks slapped cold steel cuffs on Tad's wrists.

Mama wobbled into the living room in her robe and let out a shriek. She hurried over next to Lily. "What is happening?"

With teary eyes, Lily huddled around Mama and filled her in.

Crossing the living room, Oswald lifted the radio off the cabinet shelf, examined the backside and bottom and turned it on and off. He set it down and his eyes settled on the bookcase against the back wall. Then he pulled out books with *Kanji* characters on the spines and tossed them on the floor. "Fredericks, bring the cartons out of the trunk. We're taking these

Jap books as evidence. After you return, keep an eye on them while I search the house."

The front door opened, and Fredericks exited.

"Evidence?" Tad wanted to yell. "Those are my stepfather's novels and history books. Be careful with them."

"That's what you say." Oswald frowned. "Those books might be secret codebooks for all I know. We'll have our experts look at them."

Fredericks returned with cartons and began dumping books into them.

Oswald started down the hall. He stopped at the first door and entered Danny's room. The lights went on. Metal objects clanged. Probably Danny's sports trophies. Good thing he wasn't home.

Lily stepped toward the hallway, but Fredericks cut in front of her. "Where do you think you're going?"

"I only wanted to ask him to be more gentle."

The agent shook his head at Lily. "Stay right where you are."

"But—"

"I said no!" Fredericks bared his teeth like a snarling dog.

Tad twisted his head toward Fredericks. "My wife's politely asking you guys to be more respectful of people's property."

Fredericks pointed his knobby finger at Tad. "I told you to shut up!"

With his frustration mounting and adrenalin racing, Tad would have punched Fredericks if his hands weren't cuffed.

Oswald emerged from the room without finding anything. He took two steps and grasped the doorknob of Tad and Lily's room.

Dresser drawers squeaked open and slammed shut. Lily lifted a hand to her mouth, her face reddening. One glance at her told Tad how humiliated she must have felt. Moments later, the door opened, and Oswald exited with Tad's camera and binoculars.

Tad stared slack-jawed. "That's my stuff!"

"They're on our confiscation list. So, shut up." At the end of the hall, the agent opened another door to Mas and Mama's bedroom. More ransacking sounds traveled down the hall.

After five minutes, Oswald returned to the living room. "Hey, Fredericks, look what I found." He held the lacquered scabbard in one hand and the embroidered, purple-and-gold hilt in the other. He pulled them apart, revealing a flashing reflection from a steel sword.

"That's my father's," Tad said. "It's been in the family for three centuries. Handle that with care!"

Oswald smirked and pushed the sword back into the scabbard. "Are there any other weapons in the house?"

Tad couldn't believe his ears. "That's not a weapon; it's an heirloom."

"You can kill people with it. It's a weapon."

"This is nuts. We have no reason to kill anyone—"

"Save it! Now answer the question. Are there any other weapons on the property?"

"No," Tad said through gritted teeth.

Oswald motioned to his partner. "Take these boxes into the car, and look around outside. But make it quick. We have to be at the detention center by 1:00 a.m."

"How long are you going to keep my husband and father-in-law?" Lily asked.

"As long as it takes." Oswald scowled.

"What does that mean?" Tad took a breath to unleash another verbal assault on Oswald but bit his lip instead.

"Ready?" Oswald asked.

"Let's go." Fredericks herded Tad and Mas toward the door.

Lily rushed over with two jackets. The agents stopped long enough for her to place a jacket over Tad's shoulders, then Mas's.

The agents led them out to a sedan, opened the rear doors, and shoved Tad and Mas inside. Fredericks cranked the ignition and revved the engine.

Tad craned his neck and looked through the rear window. He could see the silhouettes of the ladies' frightened faces. As the car drove away down the gravel driveway, Lily and Mama faded into the darkness.

5

Sakura

Kumamoto, Japan –March 22, 1942

For the past three months, Akira had been meeting Emiko every Sunday, even when it snowed. All this week, he had waited in eager anticipation to see her. He interlaced his fingers with hers, and they strolled through the park near the ruins of Kumamoto Castle.

Cherry trees lined the gravel pathway, heavy with ice-pink and white florets. They paused to view the collage of early spring colors and take in its delicate fragrance.

Emiko tilted her head toward the treetops where the thickest clumps of blossoms were. *"Sakura wa tottemo kirei desu ne."*

"Yes, the cherry blossoms are absolutely gorgeous." He picked up a broken cluster and handed it to her. "But their loveliness pales in comparison to you."

She blushed shyly.

Akira's pulse pounded in his ears. Sharing the magnificence of the full bloom with Emiko brought out a tender side of him that he didn't know existed.

A cold zephyr blew in from the sea, showering thousands of cherry blossoms onto their path. These delicate flowers had such short lives, falling to the ground at the height of their beauty before they wilted, only to be blown away like chaff. It reminded him of a verse he had heard in church recently.

With his meager salary, he couldn't afford the theater or nice restaurants. Most days they'd wander through the park, talking about life and their dreams. No topic was off limits with Emiko, not even the taboo subject of questioning the ever-expanding war in the Pacific. Japan was flush with recent victories in Singapore and Hong Kong. He believed that Pearl Harbor had awakened a sleeping giant in America, and soon his home country would release its full fury upon Japan. But as long as he could be with her, it didn't matter if the world around him was falling apart.

Emiko drew the collar of her silk kimono around her neck and gazed at Akira. "You must miss your family a lot."

He offered her his coat. "Yes, I do. I last heard from them in September, when they sent photos of my brother's wedding."

"Oh, yes. *Rie-rie-san* looked so beautiful in her white lace gown, and her bridesmaids wore such pretty dresses. American weddings look like so much fun."

Akira recalled going to a traditional Japanese wedding of a female colleague last year, who wore a white headdress and black kimono heavily brocaded with chrysanthemum flowers. Quite a contrast from Lily's wedding dress.

"*Rie-rie-san* seems like a friendly woman."

"You can tell that by looking at her pictures?"

Emiko nodded, flashing a demure smile. "It's just a feeling."

"Her name is pronounced, 'Li-ly.' "

"*Rie-rie.*"

Akira shook his head and chuckled.

"*Karakawanai de yo. Hidoi.*" Emiko jerked away from him and pouted.

"I'm sorry. I didn't mean to make fun of you." Akira chided himself for his insensitivity.

Like many Japanese, Emiko had difficulty pronouncing Ls. If he lived in Japan for the rest of his life, maybe he'd lose the ability as well. He came beside her, hoping to make amends and see her lovely face beam again.

As she turned her attention to the *sakura* again, her pout melted into a smile, as if the white and ice-pink clusters had washed away his offense. "When I was a little girl, I dreamed I would someday live in a foreign country."

"Perhaps you will."

Emiko brushed strands of silky hair from her eyes. "What is it like to live in America?"

"America is a big country with wide, open lands where in some places, no houses or buildings can be seen. Many people are tall, with blond or brown hair. Also there are many nationalities and races there."

"Why didn't you return to America with Tadao-san?" Her mood turned pensive. "It may be a long time before you see your family again."

"It was a difficult decision. In America, most Japanese Americans are relegated to menial jobs, even with a college education. Here I had the opportunity to attend college and become a teacher, and I wanted to gain some work experience before returning home. Then, I'd have a better chance of getting a good job. Had I returned earlier, I would have had to work on my stepfather's farm."

"You haven't seen your family in twelve years? Couldn't you have visited for a short time?"

"It takes nearly three weeks to cross the Pacific, four with a stop in Honolulu. And then I'd stay for at least a month. That's three months away. I couldn't afford that."

"A job is more important to you than your family?"

Her innocent words sliced into him like a razor. She had a habit of asking difficult questions, especially about his values and family. Akira hung his head. He remembered all those dark nights he was homesick and cried himself to sleep. "Actually the real reason is I thought my mother had abandoned me."

"Abandoned you? But your mother had no choice."

"It took me a long time to accept that and forgive her. I had a difficult time overcoming the hurt and rejection I felt as a kid."

"I see." She placed his hands in hers.

The rhythmic stamping of boots on the pavement interrupted their conversation. Up the hill, a procession of soldiers rounded a corner. A stone-faced officer led the way in a brown Imperial Army uniform with red collar tabs, wearing a peaked hat. Two foot soldiers in khaki field caps followed with rifles on their right shoulders.

Behind them a close-cropped, young man dressed in a ceremonial kimono marched in step with the soldiers. He wore a headband marked with the *Hi-No-Maru* rising sun in the center. Japanese characters on the sides praised the emperor.

A shaven-headed Buddhist monk in a flowing robe followed, accompanying a middle-aged woman, who dabbed her eyes with a handkerchief. A group of students waving miniature Japanese flags brought up the rear.

"I know that boy," Akira said, pointing. "Kiyoshi Takagi—he was one of my students last term. He's been drafted."

"He's so young. I hope nothing bad happens to him."

Akira called out to him. The boy turned his head and smiled.

Boots slapped the pavement in a steady cadence, and the soldiers marched down the hill out of view.

His thoughts returned to Emiko's difficult question. Seeing a blanket of fallen blossoms by his feet, he squatted down. With his hands, he cleared a small area of the pavement. Taking a pile of blossom petals, he began to fashion a curved shape.

She leaned over. "What are you doing?"

Without a word, he continued to move more and more heaps of petals into the shape, rounding the edges.

Emiko's eyes widened. "It's a heart. You've made a heart."

His eyes locked on to hers. "It doesn't matter whether I live here or in America. My home will always be where my love lives." He rose and took her hands and placed them over his chest. "Emiko-san, I give you my heart."

Her eyes floated in tears.

Akira hadn't planned on declaring himself yet, but the moment seemed right. He had a simple checklist of three things he looked for in a future wife.

First, she had to be willing to live in America, as he planned to return home someday.

Second, he wanted children, and Emiko had expressed that desire during one of their long walks.

Third, he ideally wanted a Christian. Emiko wasn't one, but he had a feeling that she'd eventually become one.

Akira drew her close to him and took her into his arms. "*Aishtemasu.*" His heart thudded as he waited for her response. He thought he had read affection in her eyes, but now that he had told her he loved her, fear battled with hope.

Emiko nestled her head upon his shoulder. "I love you, too."

Suddenly, all his fears vanished. Closing his eyes, he gently kissed her forehead.

When he opened his eyes, a stiff gust swirled around them and scattered the petals of the cherry blossom heart and began to disintegrate it piece by piece until all of it was gone.

6

Rights

Mountain View, California – March 23, 1942

Lily reported to her part-time job at the department store. It didn't pay much, but every little bit helped, especially since her husband and father-in-law had been taken into custody.

As soon as she set up for business at the jewelry department, her manager, Mr. Peterson, approached her. He handed Lily an envelope. "You've been terminated. Here's your final paycheck."

"Mr. Peterson, why? Have I done something wrong?"

"It's for security reasons." He pivoted and walked away.

One by one, her Nisei friends had been losing their jobs, and she had an inkling this might happen to her. She burst into tears, not so much for herself, but for all the Japanese who were fired.

* * *

Ever since that fateful day of December 7, 1941, Lily grappled with fear and worry. Three months had passed, and Tad and Mas still hadn't been released. Only one letter arrived from Tad, postmarked Fort Missoula, Montana, with no return address. What could have happened?

In her dreams, Tad's muscular arms enveloped her in warm embraces, but when she stirred awake each morning, she'd find the empty half of their bed greeting her.

Tad's Christmas gift still waited for him on their dresser. She lifted the present, his favorite cologne, and set it back down after dusting. Whenever he dressed up, he'd dab the spicy scent to both sides of his clean-shaven face. His gentle eyes twinkled whenever he smiled at her. The memories brought fresh tears to her eyes.

After she finished dusting, she entered the kitchen, poured herself a cup of coffee, and blotted her wet eyes.

Mama walked into the kitchen and hung fresh dish towels. She glared at Lily. "You can't just sit there and cry."

The rebuke stung like a slap in the face. "Mama, I miss Tad so much, and I'm worried."

Mama's hard expression melted like butter in a warm pan, then she placed her arm over Lily's shoulder and squeezed her. "Trust God," she said, leaving the room.

Lily admired her mother-in-law's strength.

A half hour later, the kitchen door slammed behind Lily as she was packaging strawberries.

Danny poured himself a glass of water and sat at the kitchen table. "I'm beat. With Tad and Mas gone, I can't keep up with all the farm work. Can you help with the deliveries to the local markets?"

"Sure."

"Of course, there's not much to deliver. Most of our *Hakujin* customers aren't buying from us anymore."

Lily nodded. "Today we received a letter from Mr. Baker."

"Who?"

"Mr. Baker's a lawyer in San Francisco who hired my dad as his gardener. He was nice enough to call people he knows in the FBI. But they told him normal procedures and due process have been suspended because this is a military emergency."

"This country is supposed to be a democracy. But the government hauls Mas and Tad off without even charging them with a crime—"

A knock on the front door jarred Lily's thoughts. She glanced at Danny. "I wonder who that could be."

They rushed to the living room and Danny opened the door.

Lily shrilled, "Tad's home!" She leaped into his arms. "Oh, honey, I'm so glad you're back home. Were you in Montana?"

"They had about six hundred of us locked up in a prisoner-of-war camp, including some women who taught Japanese. Later some people were transferred to other locations."

Lily's jaw dropped. "Prisoner-of war?"

"Yeah, but I couldn't write about that since they censored our mail."

"Where's Mas?" Danny asked.

"They're still holding him there."

Although it relieved Lily to have Tad back, the thought of Mas remaining in custody left her with a hollow feeling. "For how long?"

"I don't know."

"How did you get home from Montana?"

"They gave me money for my train ride, and I walked from the station since the phone was disconnected."

"The police cut off our phone service shortly after the raid," Lily said. "There's also a curfew in effect that only allows us to travel five miles from home unless it's for work."

"We're not dangerous criminals," Tad said through gritted teeth. "Where's Mama?"

"She's delivering produce to the struggling families, and at the same time recruiting workers in exchange for food," Lily said.

Danny crowded in, his deep-set eyes fixed on Tad. "What happened during the past three months?"

"The first week, we were kept in jail and about eight days later, we were shoved into an old rickety train with mostly Issei from Los Angeles and Santa Barbara. The train made stops along the coast and we picked up more men in Portland and Seattle."

"Whatever happened to the Constitution, Bill of Rights, and all that stuff they made us study in school?" Danny lashed out. "Why are they holding Mas?"

"They said it was because he's a deacon at church."

Danny screwed his face. "Huh? What does that have to do with anything?"

"The FBI rounded up Japanese community leaders, pastors and priests, businessmen, people who made donations to Japan,

Russo-Japanese War vets, or anyone who had influence over the community and could organize people."

"What baloney." Danny sneered.

"I know, it's crazy."

"So, why did they let you go and not Mas?" Danny asked.

"I wasn't on their list, but they took me because I tried to stop the FBI from taking Mas. No other Nisei were held. They also held a Chinese man by mistake, who kept telling them he wasn't Japanese. We were released on the same day."

"If they figured that out, why did they keep you for so long?"

"They knew I went to school in Japan. They asked me over and over which country I was loyal to. I kept telling them America, of course. But they didn't believe me."

"Did you tell them you only stayed through junior high school?" Lily asked.

"Didn't matter. They wanted to know what I studied, what sports I played, and if I was part of any paramilitary groups."

"Honey, how did they treat you?"

"Like a criminal. Boy, they sure knew an awful lot about us, even about Akira living in Japan."

Lily gasped. "What did they say about him?"

"They wanted to know what he was doing there. Why hadn't he come home. How often did we write him. For a while, I thought they were going to search our house for his letters."

Her shoulders tensed like a tightrope as she reflected back on the FBI's roughshod search of their house. "So, what happened?"

"I answered all their questions, and they never brought up his letters again."

The tightness in Lily's shoulders released.

"What about your camera, the samurai sword and other items?" Danny asked.

"They're holding them as evidence."

"Figures." Danny smirked. "We'll probably never see them again. Maybe we'll never see Mas again."

Concern washed over Lily. "How can you say that? We don't know what happened."

"Well, we don't know," Danny said.

"Let's not jump to any conclusions." Tad glared at him. "Mas didn't do anything wrong, so we have to hope for the best."

"Tschh . . ." Danny turned his back to them.

"Poor Dad. We'll pray for his safety." Lily glanced at her watch. "It's close to noon. You must be hungry. Let's eat."

"Yeah. That jail food was horrible."

Danny spun around. "You're talking about food? You act like nothing happened. Didn't you tell them they can't hold you without charging you with a crime?"

"I did, but it didn't matter."

"I wouldn't have let them get away with it. I—"

"As if we could really do anything about it," Tad said in a heightened volume.

"I would have demanded to speak to a lawyer."

"They wouldn't let us talk to anyone. Not even to our own family."

Trying to douse the flames, Lily stepped in between them. "Come on, let's talk about it later. I'm just glad Tad is home."

Danny's eyes shot daggers at her. "I'm not going to stand still while the government takes away our rights." He stormed toward the front door and yanked it open.

Lily peered through the living room window. "What's wrong with him?"

Danny's truck door slammed, and the engine roared to life. Tires spun, gravel crunched, and clouds of dirt kicked up as he peeled down the driveway.

She turned to Tad. "I sure hope Danny will be okay with all the anti-Japanese riots and violence erupting everywhere. A Japanese man was shot and killed in Stockton the other day. The *Hakujin* hate us so much now."

7

Omiai

Kumamoto, Japan – April 11, 1942

Emiko stepped inside the foyer, surprised to see her father. *"Otō-san,* you're home early." The wall clock read 5:00 p.m. Her father never came home before 9:00.

"Emiko, we have a guest. Prepare some tea and snacks, and come to the parlor."

"Who is it?" She stepped up into the house and put on her slippers.

"Just come quickly." He accentuated the order with a nod toward the kitchen, spun around on his short, bowed legs, and disappeared into the hallway.

She was curious who the guest could be. Emiko filled the water kettle and set it on the burner. She opened the gas valve, struck a match, and lit the burner. Retrieving a package of *manju* sweet bean cakes from the food cabinet, she wondered why her father was so brusque. He never treated her like that, except for the rare occasions when he scolded her.

When steam plumed from the kettle, she poured the hot water into a small porcelain pot with tea leaves. She placed the teapot on a tray with cups and small dishes with the *manju* and carried the tray to the parlor entrance.

Setting the tray on the floor, she knelt down to open the sliding door. Muted light seeped through the door's translucent paper. Her father and his guest were laughing and engaging in jovial repartee when Emiko reached for the recessed door grip.

"By the way, Takata-san, it's time your daughter married. I have someone in mind who would be perfect for her."

A bombshell exploded inside Emiko. She couldn't marry anyone selected by her father or anybody else, especially since she was in love with Akira.

"Iwamoto-sama, nothing would make me happier than to see my daughter married. She's twenty-three years old and not getting any younger. Who is he?"

"My nephew Hiroshi Yamada. He graduated with top honors from Kyoto University, and he's a clever young man."

Emiko's hand fell limp from the door grip, and her head sagged. With every fiber of her being, she wanted to spring up and run far away. She recalled her father saying Mr. Iwamoto was a government official, influential with business and local military leaders. For her father's sake, it would be essential to treat this guest with utmost respect.

Knowing she couldn't delay any longer, she slid the *shoji* door open and entered the room with the tray. She knelt down again, closed the door behind her, and swiveled around to face the guest. Mr. Iwamoto looked vaguely familiar with his distinctive white goatee and piercing black eyes.

She bowed to the man who sat cross-legged on the *tatami* floor. "Welcome, Iwamoto-sama."

Emiko served the snacks and tea to the guest and took a seat next to her father.

Mr. Iwamoto returned a slight bow to her. "Emiko-san. My, you've become a beautiful young lady. The last time I saw you, you were just a schoolgirl in pigtails."

Trying to hide her dismay about what she had overheard, Emiko smiled briefly at Mr. Iwamoto, then averted her eyes.

Mr. Iwamoto sipped the steaming cup of tea. "Emiko-san, I was telling your father there is someone I would like you to meet. He's twenty-seven years old and comes from a good family. You would make a great match for him. He's currently teaching at Kumamoto Senior High School, but I'm going to find him an important position with either the city or the civil defense forces.

He's going to be very successful, and he'll be able to take good care of you."

A knot formed in her throat.

Her father coughed, his way of hinting he wanted her to respond, but she couldn't. He cast an admonishing glare at her. "Emiko, *rei o iinasai*. Tell Iwamoto-sama how much you appreciate his offer to introduce you to his nephew."

Even if she didn't agree to meet the young man, it would be rude not to thank Mr. Iwamoto. She bowed low to their guest for an instant, then lifted her head. "Iwamoto-sama, I'm flattered that you would think so highly of me, and you are always so kind, helping my father with his business."

Broad smiles appeared on both Mr. Iwamoto's and her father's faces. Her father turned to him and nodded several times in obsequious fashion.

Her heart pumped rapidly as she measured her words. While she didn't want to hurt her father, she couldn't consent to this arrangement. "Iwamoto-sama, while I appreciate you thinking of me, I cannot agree to the meeting."

Her father's eyes bulged, and his face reddened. "Emiko! How dare you refuse Iwamoto-sama's kind offer. Apologize to him immediately."

Mr. Iwamoto's smile disappeared, and he leaned toward her. "Emiko-san, may I ask why?"

"This has nothing to do with you or your nephew. I do not wish to be"—she swallowed—"married." Emiko knew she wasn't telling him the whole truth. She'd happily marry Akira, but not this man whom she'd never met.

Her father scowled at her. "Emiko, why don't you want to marry? Who will look after you when I'm gone?" He turned to Mr. Iwamoto with droopy eyes. "Iwamoto-sama, I don't know what to say. She's always like this. She's refused every marriage offer that has come her way. I'm so sorry."

Emiko believed she could only marry a man that she met on her own and whom she loved. Many arranged marriages weren't happy. Perhaps the many romance novels from Europe and

America she had read in her youth shaped her thinking. And now there was Akira.

Mr. Iwamoto directed his attention to her. "Emiko-san, my nephew would make a perfect match for you. Think this over."

She remained still, blinked back tears, and noticed both her father's glower and Mr. Iwamoto's unsmiling expression.

Mr. Iwamoto glanced toward the door and rose. "I'd better be going."

Her father fawned after him. "Don't worry, Iwamoto-sama. I'll have a talk with my daughter."

After their guest left, her father returned to the parlor and sat across from her on the floor stone-faced, staring at the teacup. "Emiko, why don't you want to marry?"

She wiped away tears with her fingers. "Father, I'm sorry. I wasn't truthful. It's not that I don't want to marry. I'm in love with another man."

He lifted his head with round eyes aimed at her. "Who is he?"

"It's someone I met about three months ago. He's also a high school teacher."

"You never told me this. Whose family is he from?"

"His family lives far away." She couldn't tell him Akira's family lived in America. Father would certainly disapprove of that, and if word slipped out to someone like Mr. Iwamoto, Akira could be in grave danger. Also, the fact that Akira had no close relatives here, let alone anyone with money and influence, would not garner any favor with her father. "He's a really nice and considerate gentleman."

"Enough about that. Emiko, you know how important Iwamoto-sama is to my business. I'm close to signing a large contract to supply the army with thousands of uniforms. He introduced me to the procurement officer and helped me set up the deal."

"Father, I'm sorry—"

"Why can't you at least meet him? If you don't like him, then you don't have to marry him." His eyes darted from side to side and lowered to the floor as though he were uncertain about the last part.

Her father had built his business from nothing and became successful. Their family lived comfortably and happily in this large house and nice neighborhood, and he was able to send Emiko to private schools. But all that changed a few years ago with the worldwide economic depression. He began to drink too much, and his business suffered.

Emiko did what she could to bolster the family's finances with her teaching and tutoring, but her contributions were paltry. Now he'd been given the once-in-a-lifetime opportunity to redeem himself.

With her sight blurred by tears, Emiko bowed to her father. "All right, I'll meet him."

* * *

Brilliant green leaves flocked the trees in the park that only two weeks ago had been covered by white and pink cherry blossoms. Akira's step quickened when Emiko appeared.

At their rendezvous place, he looped his arm around her tenderly. She held him tighter than usual. When they separated, she wore a faint smile, and a faraway look appeared in her eyes. Something wasn't right. He took her hands in his and studied her facial expression. "What's wrong? Are you not feeling well?"

She glanced up. Her smile disappeared. "I'm fine."

"I can tell something's wrong. You're not your usual self. Tell me what's wrong."

Emiko pressed her lips together as if she tasted something bad. Her eyes glazed with tears. "I'm going to an *omiai*."

"What? A marriage meeting?" His breath rushed out as though someone punched him. "I thought we pledged our love to each other."

"I'm sorry. I do love you, but I must."

"But why?"

"For my father's sake. It's important for him."

"For him? What about us?"

"My father asked me to just meet the person. I don't have to marry him."

"You're supposed to meet this fellow and then say no? I don't believe it." All the hopes and dreams that had formed in the last three months collapsed like a sandcastle wiped out by a powerful wave.

She dropped her gaze and clasped her hands.

"Emiko-san, I don't like the sound of this. Tell me again why you have to go."

"The *omiai* was arranged through my father's business contact. If I don't go, my father could lose a large contract."

Akira grasped her shoulders and drew her close. She had told him that her father's business was failing. He understood what she said but couldn't accept it. The cost was too great. "Don't go through with this."

Emiko sobbed. "I'll find some way to turn down the marriage proposal, but I have to go to the first meeting."

Many marriages in Japan were like business transactions between families. He knew she was torn between her love for her father and her love for him. "So, who is this person?"

"He's the nephew of my father's business contact, from a prominent family here in Kumamoto."

Concerns and misgivings closed in as he held her. Akira was a low-paid schoolteacher with no family in Japan. It sounded like this person was everything he wasn't. "What does he do for a living?"

"He's a high school teacher like you."

Akira backed away, holding her at arm's length. "Really? What's his name?"

"Hiroshi Yamada."

His temples throbbed, and he let out a grunt. "I know him. He teaches at my school. The guy is so full of himself."

A thin smile formed on Emiko's lips. "Then it should be easy for me to turn him down."

"When is the *omiai*?"

"Next Friday."

He took her in his arms again. Knowing Hiroshi's bullheaded personality, Akira wasn't so sure she could turn him down. Perhaps it was God's way of pulling Emiko away from him since she wasn't a Christian. He'd wait to see what would happen.

8

Uprooted

Mountain View, California – May 20th, 1942

Danny dropped Mama's letters into a mailbox. He glanced through the post office window, and the words JAPANESE ANCESTRY caught his attention. He opened the door and stepped inside for a closer look.

WESTERN DEFENSE COMMAND AND FOURTH ARMY
WARTIME CIVIL CONTROL ADMINISTRATION
INSTRUCTIONS
TO ALL PERSONS OF
JAPANESE
ANCESTRY
LIVING IN THE FOLLOWING AREA . . .
All Japanese persons, both alien and non-alien, will
be evacuated from the above designated area . . .

The dreadful notice had arrived. It was just a matter of time before they would be evacuated.

People of Japanese ancestry living on the West Coast had been warned to move to the interior states or be evacuated. Already a few had moved on their own to places like Salt Lake City, Denver, and Chicago.

Some had been hauled away to prison camps, including Lily's parents, family friends and relatives as early as February. Most people waited for the inevitable.

His jaw dropped and his body tensed with every word he read. How could the government, who promised freedom for all its citizens, force them out of their homes?

The notice was signed, "J. L. DeWitt, Lieutenant General, US Army Commanding."

What a betrayal! Danny ground his molars so hard he could crack a walnut.

A fluttering American flag flashed across Danny's mind. He remembered placing his hand over his heart and reciting the Pledge of Allegiance in school. America, land of the free and home of the brave.

So much for that fairy tale. It was no different than the Indians being herded into the reservations.

He ripped the sign off the wall and bolted out of the post office.

Across the street, several other shops displayed the same poster. Danny ran to his truck and gunned the engine. He choked the steering wheel so tight, his knuckles whitened. The engine screamed as he floored the gas pedal and raised the speedometer needle past forty-five, blasting through the intersections.

Bursting through the front door, Danny hollered, "Tad!"

"What's going on?" Tad emerged from the family room.

Danny thrust the notice into Tad's hands. "This."

Tad scanned the cardboard poster and blinked hard. "We have to leave by May 26th? Although we've been preparing for this, it gives us little time to pack."

Mama and Lily scurried in, carrying baskets of laundry. Tad explained to them what was happening. Mama dropped the basket, sending the clothes tumbling onto the floor.

Lily took the poster from Tad and began to read: "Evacuees must carry bedding and linens (no mattress) for each family member . . . toilet articles . . . sufficient knives, forks, spoons, plates, bowls . . ."

Danny pounded the back of the sofa with his fist. "They can't do this to us! We're American citizens, for crying out loud."

"But maybe it will be safer there," Lily said.

Danny couldn't believe how naive she was. "Safer for whom? We don't know what these prison camps are like."

Tad grasped Danny's shoulder and spun him around. "What do you suggest we do? Not go?"

He shoved Tad's hand away. "We ought to fight this. Are we just going to roll over like you did when you were in custody?"

"Danny!" Tad's face turned lobster-red, and his lips splayed wide.

"Stop! Please, let's not fight." Lily stepped in between them and held out her hands to keep the brothers apart.

Danny blew out hot air and jerked away. "I can't stand this!" he shouted and fled out the back door.

Chest heaving, he gazed with misty eyes at the ten acres of strawberry plants and blackberry bushes arranged in neat rows, then at the leafy apricot and cherry trees covering the remaining twenty acres of their property.

Beyond that, the faint silhouette of the golden hills on the other side of the bay reflected the brilliant orange sunset.

Desperately seeking to release his fury, Danny clutched a two-by-four leaning against the shed and heaved it as far as he could into the field. It landed harmlessly between the third and fourth rows of the blackberry bushes with a thud.

He dropped to his knees and pounded the dirt with his fist. "God, where are you? Why don't you do something?"

* * *

For the past few days, Tad's head spun in a tizzy, trying to figure out which possessions to sell, give away, or take with them.

Today, he backed his 1939 Buick Century out of the driveway and parked it in front of their farmhouse with a "FOR SALE" sign on the windshield. He buffed the gleaming gray hood and polished all the chrome adornments.

People examined the car, kicking the tires and checking under the hood. A few took it for a test drive, but no one wanted to pay the asking price of two hundred dollars. Instead, they offered five, ten, twenty dollars, or some other ridiculous amount. With an eight-cylinder engine that purred like a well-fed cat and nary a scratch anywhere on the body, it was a steal even at five hundred dollars.

His neighbor, Bill Johnson, strode toward him with his dog. "Hi, Tad. Any word about Mas yet?"

"Good morning, Bill. Not a word." Tad squatted down and petted the collie's long soft hair. "Hiya, Duke."

"These are crazy times. Innocent men like Mas arrested, and families like yours uprooted. You folks worked so hard to make this place what it is. It's a crying shame."

Mas had worked as a sharecropper twelve to fourteen hours a day, six days a week for twenty-five years, so he could buy this thirty-acre farm. The property was deeded under Tad's name because laws prohibited Issei from purchasing land and forbade them from becoming naturalized citizens.

Tad rose. "We're all scrambling, trying to figure out what to pack, what to store, and what to sell."

"How are the sales going?"

"We're only getting pennies on the dollar. Ten bucks for a new washing machine, five bucks for the refrigerator, and thirty for the truck. Now, Mama's thinking about selling her china hutch, and Lily's been selling most of our wedding presents."

"That's ridiculous." The veins in Bill's temples bulged. "Sorry I can't help you with money, but I'll look after your property and get it rented out until you return. You can store your tractor and plow rigs in my barn. I've got extra room."

"That's so kind of you. I'm overwhelmed. I don't know how we'll ever repay you. Thank you so much!"

"It's the least I can do for all the years you and Mas helped me out. You lent me equipment and pitched in with the cherry harvest when I was shorthanded. Your family kept me from going bankrupt. Swing by later today, and let's talk about how we can keep your farm going."

"Okay. I'll be there."

Five minutes later, a middle-aged Caucasian man crossed the street with a limp. "I'll give you fifty bucks for the car."

"Fifty dollars? For a Buick Century? You got to be kidding."

"Take it or leave it."

"This car is only two years old, and it's in mint condition. I paid twelve hundred dollars for it brand new."

"I wouldn't know about that. But one thing I do know is you folks are being moved out soon and you have to sell everything."

"For that kind of money, I'll keep it."

The man shrugged. "Suit yourself." He turned and shuffled away.

Time was running out. It pained Tad to let this beautiful car sell for so cheap, but he had no choice. "Hey!" Tad shouted. "All right, you can have it for fifty."

The man whipped out his billfold and counted two twenty-dollar bills. "Looks like I'm a little short. Will you take forty?"

"Just go home and fetch ten more dollars."

"This is all the cash I've got, and the bank won't open until Monday. By then you'll be gone."

What an insult. Tad had half a mind to say no, but they needed the money. Maybe the man could send it to him later, but he didn't even know where they'd be sent. He bit the knuckle of his forefinger. "Yeah, okay." Tad blinked hard with regret and retrieved two copies of the bill of sale and title from the glove compartment. Taking a ballpoint pen out of his shirt pocket, he wrote in the sales amount and signed the forms. His fingers almost refused to release the keys.

The man handed Tad the money. "Thanks." He limped over to his new car and opened the driver's door. Before getting in, he looked back and surveyed the Omura property. "Got anything else you want to sell?"

"W. . . wh . . . what? I thought you said you only had forty bucks."

"Yeah, you're right. Just asking."

9

Engagement

Kumamoto, Japan – May 23, 1942

Emiko wrung her hands as she sat looking in the mirror at her red, puffy eyes and unruly hair. She was nowhere near prepared for the event that would change her life forever.

Aunt Fumiko entered the room, carrying an elegant black kimono with a white floral print on the lower portion that Emiko was supposed to wear for the engagement party. She gasped. "Emiko-chan! What are you doing? The car is coming to pick you up in less than an hour." She set the kimono down on the futon and scampered to Emiko's side.

"Auntie, I don't want to go." Tears spilled out of her eyes.

Her aunt patted Emiko's eyes with a tissue, then started to apply liquid foundation on her forehead. "Don't be silly. You can't back out now. All arrangements have been made. Gifts and dowries have been exchanged. How can you think of not going through with it?"

She had been counting on her aunt's support. "I don't want to marry Yamada-san."

Aunt Fumiko smoothed the makeup on Emiko's cheeks to cover the streak marks left by tears. "Why not? He seems like a fine young gentleman."

No! Not her aunt too. Hiroshi Yamada may have impressed her father and uncles with his educational credentials and prowess in judo and kendo, and even charmed her aunts with high-browed manners and glib conversation skills.

Not Emiko.

Aunt Fumiko dipped the lipstick brush and painted Emiko's lips ruby red. "You're fortunate to find someone like him."

Emiko's insides screamed in sheer terror. Her aunt had no idea what he was really like.

At the *omiai,* Hiroshi had boasted about the famous schools he attended and flaunted his family's affluence. He hinted that the daughters of Kumamoto's leading families vied for his affection and wanted to marry him.

Emiko wanted to vomit. The way he ogled her with his suggestive eyes made her very uncomfortable. When he touched her shoulder and took hold of her hand, she pleaded with him to let go, but it had no effect. She pried his strong fingers off, but he quickly recaptured her hand and forced her into an embrace with his lips reaching for hers. That's when she threw *saké* into his eyes and dashed out of the restaurant.

Now she was about to become betrothed to him. Her aunt put the lipstick brush down, blotted Emiko's lips with a tissue, and examined her work. "There, that looks good. With a little rouge, you'll be all set." She picked up another brush and swished it in the container, then highlighted Emiko's cheeks.

"Auntie, don't you feel it's important to love the man you marry?"

The woman paused and stared at Emiko momentarily. "Love?" She arched an eyebrow and resumed with the rouge. "You'll learn to love your husband."

"I can't. Not him." Fresh tears sprang into Emiko's eyes. Her thoughts drifted back to that appalling meeting with Hiroshi. Between his narcissistic ramblings, she told him repeatedly that she wouldn't marry him, but he ignored every word she had said.

"Emiko, stop crying. You're ruining the makeup." Her aunt grabbed a cotton ball to even out the new streaks that raced down Emiko's cheeks. She dabbed on more rouge. Aunt Fumiko's expression softened. She brushed back Emiko's hair into a stylish upswept hairdo and fastened it with a *kanzashi* ornamental pin. "Your father told me that he petitioned Iwamoto-san several times to get you released from this marriage. That awful man threatened your father with breach of contract and possible criminal punishment."

"What? Father could go to prison?" Emiko gasped. She knew that the contract was important to her father but hadn't realized there would be such dire consequences from canceling it. "How can that be?"

"Because it involved a critical military procurement."

"Was my marriage a condition of fulfilling the military uniform contract?"

"I'm afraid so." A tear rolled down her cheek.

"Father didn't tell me that." Emiko had pleaded with him, but he rebuffed her, telling her sacrifices had to be made for the business. In her disappointment, she had lashed out at him, but now she knew the truth. "Auntie, I don't know what to do."

It was either imprisonment for her father or imprisonment in a marriage to a man she detested.

* * *

The limousine arrived in front of the Royal Takara Hotel forty-five minutes late. The driver opened the rear door and helped Emiko and Aunt Fumiko out.

The doorman bowed and held open the polished glass doors for them as they stepped into the expansive lobby. Even during wartime, the rich could celebrate lavish events such as this.

Her father rushed over in his formal kimono. "Emiko, you're late. Everyone is waiting for you."

"I'm sorry. It took me longer to get ready than I expected."

He looked away and dropped his chin.

Emiko couldn't be sure, but she thought she caught a pang of regret in her father's eyes. He nodded quickly and cast his glance away from her. Perhaps this was his way of apologizing to her. Knowing what she knew now, Emiko couldn't be so angry with him anymore. He had made some poor decisions, but he was her father after all.

He pivoted and headed across the lobby toward the banquet hall. Emiko and her aunt followed.

Luscious bouquets of white chrysanthemums and pink carnations tastefully placed in various spots bedecked the banquet hall. Distinguished-looking men, some wearing military officers' uniforms, and their elegant ladies sat at a dozen or more tables, perhaps a hundred people. They were probably relatives and friends of the Yamada family. Emiko identified a few of her relatives.

After she took a few steps into the room, the chatter around the banquet hall ceased, and everyone's eyes fell upon her. The maitre d' escorted Emiko toward the front where a huge marquee read: Engagement of Hiroshi Yamada and Emiko Takata.

She choked out a sob. Just to save her father from prison, she'd have to marry this man. It was like being trapped in the web of a venomous spider, waiting to be devoured.

When Emiko arrived at her table, Hiroshi smiled at her admiringly. "Good evening, Takata-san."

Emiko glared at him, then turned away. Out of the corner of her eye, she could see him gazing at her for what seemed like an eternity. Then he whirled around to have animated conversations with his male friends.

Three tables away, Mr. Iwamoto chatted with her father. She hoped he wasn't making more demands on him. Squeezing her hands into tight fists, she summoned all the self-control she had to keep from rushing to their table and scratching out the eyes of the man who ruined her life and threatened to destroy their family.

The wait staff brought abundant servings of dark-red tuna *sashimi* and sumptuous portions of sea bream, lobster, and abalone, all beautifully presented on porcelain ware with hand-painted, colorful carp designs. The guests partook of the fine cuisine and conversed with their table companions. Emiko barely touched her food.

Nearly an hour into the dinner, a few guests, drunk from the liberally poured *saké*, broke in to loud, off-tune renditions of

Japanese folk songs, syncopated by slow claps. She let her mind drift away and relived the scene at the park where she and Akira had confessed their love for each other. He looked strikingly handsome, his large dark eyes sparkling every time he smiled. The corners of her mouth turned upward as she recalled the heart Akira had shaped out of cherry blossoms.

The very next instant, the heart image vanished when Mr. Iwamoto rose from his chair and made his way to the front and stood behind Hiroshi and Emiko. Her stomach seethed at his proximity.

"Ladies and gentlemen, honored guests. My name is Shunsuke Iwamoto. I have been appointed by the Yamada and Takata families to say a few words on this joyous occasion. First, the families thank you for taking time out of your busy schedules to attend this special event. My nephew, Hiroshi—"

A door banged open and echoed throughout the banquet hall.

"No!" shouted a man's voice from the shadows in the back. "Emiko-san, you can't marry him!"

The crowd murmured as a figure came into view.

Emiko gasped and covered her mouth with her hand. It was Akira. Concerned that it would be too much for him to bear, she purposefully had not told him about the engagement or the date and venue of this party.

"Seize that man! Call security!" Hiroshi hollered.

Two officers captured Akira and pinned him to the back wall.

Something inside Emiko burst. Gone was all sense of propriety. She leaped out of her chair and addressed the audience. "I'm sorry everyone, but I cannot marry Hiroshi Yamada!" She pointed to the back. "I love that man you're holding, and I will only marry him!"

With that, she rushed toward Akira as fast as her restrictive kimono would allow. She grasped his waist and buried her head against his chest. Unable to control herself, a fresh torrent of tears broke free.

The persistent murmur throughout the hall grew louder. The clacking of chairs and heel clicks compounded the noise.

"Emiko!" Her father's scolding voice accompanied a firm shaking of her shoulder.

She held fast to Akira, determined not to let anyone separate them again.

"How could you do this? You've humiliated Hiroshi-san and his family. You've doomed our family—" He gasped several times as if he were drowning.

Emiko released Akira's hand and spun around to see her father clutching his chest. His complexion purpled, and his eyes rolled back as he began to topple to the floor.

Akira leaped out and caught him in his arms.

She shrieked, "Father!"

10

Santa Anita

Arcadia, California – May 27, 1942

After an exhausting, all-night train ride on hard wooden seats to Southern California, Tad and his family, along with numerous other Japanese Americans, slogged to their new "homes." Men in suits carried suitcases packed tight. Women in hats and nice dresses followed with children in tow, each carrying smaller bags.

Wispy cirrus clouds highlighted the clear blue skies over the San Gabriel Mountains. Palm trees along the grandstand swayed as if waving a welcome to the throngs of new arrivals to Santa Anita Racetrack.

Setting down two heavy suitcases, Tad pivoted and observed his new surroundings. Lily halted next to him, struggling with two small duffel bags, while Mama and Danny trailed behind.

About thirty soldiers wearing helmets from the Great War carried rifles and stood guard around the barbed-wire perimeter. "What's with all this security?" Tad muttered. He lifted his bags and followed a procession of people to the registration area.

Four Caucasian men sat at a long table in front of signs hanging on the wall with large block letters: A–F, G–L, M–R, and S–Z.

Tad waited in the appropriate line with his family. A distinct odor of mimeograph ink wafted from the papers piled on the table.

"Next," the registrar said in a gruff voice.

Tad removed his hat as he approached the table. "Good day."

"Name?" The overweight man with sharp, beady eyes glared at him through horn-rimmed glasses.

"Tadao Omura." He extended his arm toward his family. "This is my wife, Lily, my brother Daniel, and my mother, Haruko Noguchi."

"Spell your name." The corners of the registrar's mouth turned downward.

"O-M-U—"

"No, I know how to spell that," the man said harshly. "Your first name."

Tad's face muscles tightened. He was only trying to comply. No need to be rude. Setting aside the snub, he spelled the first names of his family.

The registrar scanned the list and checked off each name. "You're assigned to 57-12. You'll be taking your meals at the Red mess hall at designated times. There's going to be six mess halls, but some are still under construction."

"Just one room?" Tad asked. "The ladies would have a fit if we crammed into a single room."

The registrar scowled. "There are over eighteen thousand of you at this facility. I can't give you another room. Now, move along."

"Is there someone else in charge that I can talk to?"

The man slapped his hand on the table. "Now, look! As far as you're concerned, I'm God. Got it?"

Blasphemous fellow. Tad blew out steam. The thought of his family being crowded into one room for who knows how long prompted another question. "Do you know how long we'll be here?"

"It's temporary until the permanent facilities are built." The man craned his neck and looked past him. "Next."

Lily set her bags down and tugged at Tad's sleeve. "I wonder how my parents are doing at the Tanforan racetrack. I've only received one letter from them in the two months they've been there."

"It's too bad we couldn't go visit them because of the curfew."

"I hope they'll be all right. At least my brother's with them."

Tad drew her close to him and wished he could do something for her family. Then they dragged themselves along the base of the grandstand and followed the signs to their quarters, passing rows of barracks covered with black tar paper.

Danny met his friends and stayed behind to talk.

At the entrance to their room, Tad stared openmouthed. "I don't believe this." Resentment and humiliation burned inside him.

Lily stood bug-eyed and gasped. "It's a horse stall!"

Mama covered her mouth with her hand.

Opening the door, Tad entered the dark, empty stall. The stale odor of horse manure, oats, and leather filled the air. It couldn't have been more than twelve feet long and twelve feet wide.

No windows—only a broad, two-piece door with upper and lower halves that opened and closed independently. The stall contained a kerosene lamp and five army cots. Each cot had one blanket and a canvas bag they were told to fill with straw for their mattress.

Lily stepped inside and burst into tears. She immediately rushed out, pinching her nose. "What did we do to deserve this? I don't know how I'm going to sleep in there."

Tad followed her out but didn't know how to respond. Having worked on the farm where they used to have plow horses, somewhat accustomed him to the smell. But his city-girl wife was a different story. "Honey, I'll see if we could move to one of the shacks we passed." He started to walk back to the registration tables.

She grabbed his arm. "No, it's all right. If we don't stay here, some other poor family will." She left her suitcase outside and stepped back inside.

Danny arrived shortly after. "We're not horses! How could they do this? Even the horses are treated better since they only assign one horse to a stall." He looked to Tad as if he had some answers.

"They're not going to do anything, so you might as well get used to it." Tad stuffed a canvas bag, knowing it would only make a lumpy and uncomfortable mattress. Out of the corner of his eye, he saw a middle-aged lady stop in front of their stall.

The woman looked toward the entrance and pinched her nose. Then she fixed her gaze at the Omura family and bowed. "Hello, I'm Yuko Tagawa. It looks like I'll be sharing these quarters with you."

"We're staying here," Danny said. "There must be a mistake."

"The man at the desk told me since it's just me, I'd be sharing a room with another family," Yuko said.

Danny's eyes blazed like bonfires. "We have to share this stall with someone we don't even know? I'm not going to stand for this." With clenched fists he stomped away.

* * *

Tad combed back his pomade-slicked hair, while eyeing his reflection in a small mirror that hung from a nail on the bare wood wall. "Come on, Lily, let's get in line for breakfast. I don't want to wait ninety minutes like yesterday, when the line wrapped around two buildings."

She looked at her watch. "We won't have time to eat. Besides, the canned foods and curled-up bologna they serve are terrible." His wife nudged him aside to take control of the mirror. "Sorry I didn't wake up sooner, but I was itchy all night and couldn't fall asleep until early this morning." Lily applied eyeliner to her eyes, making them appear larger.

"I didn't get a good night's sleep either," Tad said. "The neighbors made such a racket at four this morning."

Lily brushed mascara on her eyelashes and curled them upward. "The neighbors were probably scrambling to take showers before the long lines."

A moment later, Yuko approached Lily. "Can I borrow the mirror after you? With a two-day notice, I didn't have time to pack a lot of things."

"Of course you can." Lily straightened the collar of her blue chiffon dress, then scooted over for Yuko. "If you need anything else, please don't hesitate."

"Thanks Lily."

Tad gazed at Lily with a smile. "You look very pretty." Women had their priorities. Even with the limit of one suitcase and a smaller bag per person, Lily found a way to pack a few of her best dresses.

"Thank you." Her face lit up. She tried to smooth the wrinkles out of her dress. "I wish we had an iron."

"I couldn't pack a heavy iron in our luggage," Tad chuckled, adjusting his necktie.

"What? A big, strong man like you couldn't handle a little iron?" Lily fluttered her eyes.

Tad smiled and shook his head.

She placed her matching veiled hat on her head. "I wish I didn't smell like a horse." Lily sniffed her sleeve and scrunched her nose.

"Don't worry about it. We all smell like horses around here."

Lily made a sour face. "Some more than others."

He chuckled and slipped on his suit jacket.

"Can you fetch a bucket of water for me later today?" Lily asked.

"Sure, honey."

"I hate it when the guards aim the searchlight on me whenever I walk back to the barrack after taking a shower at night," Lily said. "Going to the lavatory during the daytime is bad enough, since there are no partitions in the shower room. I'd rather wash my hair inside here with a bucket."

"They're not going to build partitions around the showers since they use them to wash the horses," Yuko said with a glum expression. "I've already asked. Nor are they going to build doors on the toilet stalls."

Lily's jaw dropped. "We've been showering where they clean the horses? Yuck!"

Mama returned from breakfast, and a few moments later, Danny shuffled into the stall dressed in khaki trousers and a T-shirt, chewing on an oat stalk. He went to his cot and reached underneath to retrieve a couple of horseshoes.

"Aren't you going to get ready for church?" Mama asked Danny.

"Nah, some friends of mine are organizing a horseshoe pitching contest. Go without me."

"Danny, you don't want to skip church," Mama said with concern.

"I just don't feel like going. Look, we're cooped up in this stinky stable." He spit out the oat stalk. "And we have to share it with a stranger. We've had our rights and freedom taken away. I don't have much to be thankful for these days—"

"Remember the Bible story of Joseph?" Tad chimed in. "He was innocent but sold into slavery. Then Potiphar's wife falsely accused him of assault and had him thrown into prison, where God blessed him and prepared him to become a ruler of Egypt."

"You don't have to tell me all that. I went to Sunday school, too."

"So what's the problem?" Tad asked.

"Where is God right now? Why isn't he doing anything?"

"Just because we're going through hard times doesn't mean God isn't with us. He promises to never leave us."

"Honestly, I don't see how you can keep talking about God this and God that." Danny turned his back to him.

Tad rounded up Lily and Mama and left the stall. As they walked toward the makeshift church, his anger began to dissipate.

Lily nudged Tad's arm. "Honey, go easy on Danny. He's very hurt and upset like everyone else here. Just give him time."

"We pray for Danny," Mama said.

Concerns weighed Tad down about how this war was tearing apart the fabric of his family.

White Paint

Kumamoto, Japan – May 31, 1942

Akira stood in a long line waiting to pay respects to Emiko's deceased father. At the front of the room, a Buddhist altar sat on top of a table next to a framed photograph of Mr. Takata with black ribbon draping down from the top corners. A smaller table in front held a smoldering incense burner.

People stepped forward one by one, pinching incense powder with their fingers and sprinkling it into the cast-iron burner. They pressed their hands together with *ojizu* beads and bowed.

The rite reminded Akira of rosary beads he had seen while visiting his childhood friend in a Catholic church in the States.

After praying, they turned to Emiko and bowed, then returned to their seats.

With palms moist with sweat, Akira considered what he would do. Perhaps, for the sake of ceremony—and Emiko—he should perform the ritual. Besides, revealing his Christianity could get him into trouble with the authorities who viewed it as a decadent Western faith.

Just before Akira approached the altar, Mama's words from his memory seared his consciousness. *Never forget the most important commandment. 'Love the Lord thy God with all of thy heart and with all thy soul, and all thy mind. Do not bow before other gods . . . worship them or burn incense.'*

He pictured his mother readying him and his brothers for Sunday school. That memory dissolved into images of drying himself after being baptized, turning toward the audience, and seeing his mother's glowing face elated with tears of joy.

Mama's words echoed loud and clear once again, and his pulse quickened as Akira approached the altar. At the very last moment, he rotated left, bowed only to the photograph of Emiko's father and did not take part in the sprinkling of incense.

"Why isn't this man paying his proper respects?" someone muttered in the front row.

Although he didn't participate in the ritual, his condolences were genuine. Akira pivoted and faced Emiko. "I'm so sorry about your loss," he said, bowing low to her.

She focused her attention on him and graciously thanked him for coming.

Through the look in her eyes, he could see a pool of tears, and how deeply wounded she was.

* * *

A knock on Akira's door prompted him to grab a presentable shirt from the dresser. He tucked in the tails as he approached the entrance of his flat. "Who is it?"

"*Gomen kudasai,* I don't mean to intrude, but I need to speak with you."

Akira's heart pulsated at the sound of Emiko's voice. He quickly unlatched the door and opened it. "What a pleasant surprise."

She rushed into his arms crying, and he gently placed his hand behind her head and held her. Emiko had never been inside his apartment, and for her to be here right after the memorial service was unexpected.

"Here, let me take your coat. Please, sit down and let's talk."

She handed him her coat and sat on the *tatami* floor. "I feel so guilty. I killed my father." Her words choked with sobs. "Nobody says anything to me, but I know they're all thinking that if I had gone through with the engagement ceremony, my father wouldn't have died. I didn't know where else to turn."

"Darling, it wasn't your fault. Don't blame yourself." He grabbed two teacups from the hutch and started to heat up the kettle. "The arranged marriage was wrong to begin with. If Hiroshi Yamada and his uncle hadn't forced you into this, your father would still be alive today. So don't blame yourself. It's not your fault."

"But I'm such an unworthy, selfish daughter. Buddha is punishing me."

"I don't know about Buddha, but God is gracious. He would never force you to marry someone you don't love."

"Is that your god—the Christian god?"

"There is only one God." They had spoken about Christianity before but never in such a personal way or in a crisis situation like this.

As Akira was speaking, a heavy stone of regret weighed him down in the pit of his stomach. Yesterday morning when he studied the Bible, a verse leaped out at him that convicted him to marry only a Christian. He wrestled with the idea and somehow knew God was speaking to him about his relationship with her. He was in love with a girl who didn't share his faith.

Although Emiko had attended a Christian high school, she *only knew* about Jesus but didn't know him personally or believe in his divinity. But he was already too deeply involved in this relationship, and it would be nearly impossible to break it off. However, it was time to set the matter straight with her and within himself. Either he was going to lead her to Christ or abandon his love forever.

"Not even your god can forgive me for what I've done."

"That's not true. My God is merciful. When you invite Jesus into your heart and choose to follow him, you begin a brand new life of destiny, and your sins are forgiven."

"I don't understand. How can it be that simple?"

"Emiko-san, tell me what you know about Christianity."

She drew in a deep breath and let it out slowly. "Well, I studied it in high school."

"Yes, but what are your thoughts about it?"

Emiko stared at the ceiling in contemplation, then focused her eyes on him. "It seems the same as Buddhism," she said in a tentative voice. "It's doing kind things for less fortunate people and not doing evil things. Jesus was a great teacher like Shakyamuni Buddha, except Jesus was killed, even though he never committed any crime."

Akira weighed his response and tried to keep his explanation simple. "Some elements are similar, but I wouldn't say they're the same. Because of sin, we're separated from God. But he bridged this gap by sending Jesus to earth to die in our place."

Hearing the teakettle whistle, he rose to fetch the tea. After he returned, he took a seat next to her and poured piping hot tea into her cup on the low table. "Please help yourself. I'd serve some *sembei* rice crackers, but I don't have any."

The comment brought a smile to her face.

It heartened Akira to bring her out of her gloom even for a moment.

"Don't worry, Akira-san. Thanks for the tea." She blew the steam and took a sip. Her eyes searched his. "What is sin?"

"It's any type of wrongdoing like lying, stealing, or worse."

"I don't understand. If we do something that is wrong in God's eyes—shouldn't we be held accountable?"

"Yes, but Jesus paid the penalty when he died for us."

"Why would Jesus do that?"

"It's because God loves you."

"Love?"

"Yes, like a father who loves his children." As soon as he spoke these words, Akira realized any mention of the word *father* might send her into despair. But she seemed fine with it.

Emiko nodded as though she understood.

"You're precious to God, and he sent Jesus to die for your sins, so you can be forgiven and spend eternity in heaven."

"I can be forgiven even for my worst crime?" She raised an eyebrow.

"Yes, the blood of Jesus cleanses us from our sins when we ask him to forgive us."

She pondered his words for a while. "But how does that apply to a good man like you? You haven't committed any crimes."

"Oh, but I have. A sin is a sin, whether it's something big like murder and robbery or a little thing like telling a white lie or speaking harsh words. I'm as guilty as a man who has murdered or robbed."

"*Eh?* How could murder be the same as speaking harshly to someone?"

A long, silent minute passed. A mental picture presented itself to him. "God only likes pure, white paint."

She angled her head to one side and crinkled her nose. "*Eh?*"

"If you add a different color to white paint, even if it's just a drop, you no longer have pure, white paint, correct? Sin is like that other color."

"I think what you're telling me is God is pure, and he wants us to be pure, too, right?"

"Correct." Emiko never ceased to amaze him. She had already made the connection that God couldn't tolerate any sin. So far, so good. "That's right. But when you choose to worship and follow Jesus, you can be forgiven for your sins. It would be like receiving a new bucket of pure, white paint."

"In Buddhism, there is no forgiveness like that."

"It's very different. For one thing, Jesus is a man, but he is God as well."

Emiko squinted. "A man and God at the same time? How can that be?"

"Yes, I remember a verse in the Bible that my mom had us memorize when we were children. 'What is impossible with man is possible with God.' "

She nodded slowly. "Shakyamuni never said he was God. He was just a great teacher."

He knew that already. "Then why do Buddhists worship someone who isn't God?"

Emiko's brows wrinkled slightly. "We pray to be one with Buddha—to live according to his teachings and meditate on pure thoughts. It's not easy to do, but we continually strive to achieve enlightenment."

"Interesting. But until you achieve perfection, am I correct in my understanding that after you die, you come back as another person or creature? If I believed that, I'd probably come back as a grasshopper or toad." He chuckled.

Emiko giggled and covered her mouth. "Stop. You're making fun. The point is we must continue to improve ourselves until we are fully enlightened. That is our heaven."

"Christians believe heaven is a real place, not just a state of mind. It's a kingdom ruled by God. Moreover, you can't do anything to work or study your way into heaven. In fact, I would say that even if we tried to improve ourselves and not sin, we'd fail because we're human. It's impossible to achieve what Buddha teaches, and since we are neither Buddha nor God, what is impossible remains impossible. On the other hand, what seems impossible to us as humans can become possible with God."

She tapped her chin with a finger, then paused. "I never thought of it that way, but what you say seems right. It seems impossible for people to become perfect. You've given me a lot to think about. One thing is for certain. I feel a lot better after talking to you."

Perhaps there was some hope for their future together. A love for her far deeper than anything he had ever known tugged at his heart.

12

The Train

Arcadia, California – August 24, 1942

While waiting at the train station, Tad reflected on the three months they had lived in a smelly horse stall. Over half the people were stuck in them. The overcrowding, noise, lack of seating in the mess halls, and shortage of toilets were just a few of the dehumanizing conditions. Additionally, only 150 showers were available for close to 19,000 people.

Tad caught himself complaining and knew it didn't please God. He shifted his focus on the blessings, like being able to find work at the camouflage netting factory in the grandstand area. Over two-thirds of the people at Santa Anita didn't have jobs. Although it only paid $12 per month, working six days a week, it helped cover a small portion of their living expenses.

In his spare time, he taught Sunday school like he did back home, and he played softball on one of the many teams.

Lily cooled herself with a folded newspaper she used as a fan. "I'm so glad we're finally leaving this place. Did you ever find out where they're sending us?"

"I have no idea." Tad scanned the *Santa Anita Pacemaker* camp newspaper and read about how to wash your hair when there was no shampoo. The article recommended using soap flakes to lather and rinsing with lemon juice.

He lifted his head and watched a platoon of scowling soldiers positioning themselves about every twenty yards around the perimeter of the train station. *We're not trying to escape!*

Perhaps the raging battle on Guadalcanal, half a world away, flared the soldiers' hatred toward them. Ironically, many Nisei had cheered while watching a newsreel of US warplanes sinking Japanese aircraft carriers when the Americans successfully thwarted the invasion force from the Midway Islands.

Cardboard tags with serial numbers hung from the lapels or sleeves of peoples' clothes. Some sat on their suitcases and stared into nothingness.

At 2:00 p.m. the rear cars of a long train backed in from the east. Hydraulic brakes whooshed and springs screeched as it eased to a stop.

"Listen up!" A dour-faced sergeant scanned the crowd. "Pick up your belongings and file in. You'll be searched for contraband and weapons."

Tad rolled his eyes. Not again. Weekly, the inspectors searched their mattresses calling it a "sanitation inspection." Some people had their valuables stolen during these inspections. If they reported it, the authorities did absolutely nothing. Maybe it was just an excuse to harass and steal from them.

After ninety minutes, a corporal gestured to the Omuras. "Over here." Tad and his family shuffled to the designated spot.

"Spread out your arms and legs," the soldier said to Tad. He patted down his clothes, limb-by-limb. "Now open up your suitcases."

Tad complied.

The corporal rummaged through their neatly folded clothes. "Sergeant, looks clean." Next he approached Lily.

He better not touch my wife.

The corporal peeked inside Lily's purse and another small bag. "Okay, you can board."

Tad relaxed his stance and let out a sigh.

Soon Mama was cleared and they waited for Danny.

A soldier patted down Danny's trousers but stopped halfway. "What's inside your pocket?"

"It's just my little pocketknife." Danny stuffed his hand in his pocket to protect his possession.

"That's contraband. I have to confiscate it."

Alarm shot through Tad. He moved toward the inspection area, but a guard blocked him with a rifle.

Danny took two steps backward and turned away. "I'm allowed to carry a little pocketknife if it's less than four inches."

The soldier's face hardened. "Hand it over." He stepped forward and reached for it.

"But I'm allowed to carry this." Danny gave him a shove on the shoulder, sending him back several steps.

Another guard charged over and slammed his rifle butt into Danny's abdomen.

Danny doubled over and dropped to the ground.

The crowd gasped.

Rushing forward, Tad found a rifle muzzle an inch from his nose. His mouth opened, but no sound came out. The unexpected threat left him breathless—the danger real.

"Back off!" the soldier barked at Tad.

Panting for air, Danny held his abdomen and groaned.

Two more soldiers pushed their way through the crowd and pulled him to his feet.

One soldier shoved his hand down Danny's pocket and yanked the knife out. Then they dragged him away.

"All right! Everybody settle down," the sergeant yelled. He locked his eyes on Tad. "You—get on the train."

For a few seconds, Tad stood immobilized, then turned to board the train. He plopped down next to Lily and Mama. "How stupid to fuss over a dumb little pocketknife. Probably not worth more than two bits."

Tears trickled down Mama's sunken cheeks. "Danny *wa doko e tsuretekaretaka?*"

"I don't know where they took him."

* * *

Slumped in his chair, Danny glared at the two men in suits hovering over him. "Who are you guys?"

"FBI," said one man with an edge in his voice. He flashed his identification badge in Danny's face. "I'm Special Agent Chambers, and this is Special Agent Jones."

"You pulled a pretty stupid stunt out there," Jones said.

Danny sneered. "So, where's your badge?"

Jones bared his teeth. "You know, I don't like your attitude."

"I don't like yours either. You arrest innocent people, take away our homes and belongings, throw us into horse stalls. And now you want to talk to me about my attitude? Boy, you've got a lot of nerve."

"Don't get cute with us, kid. You'll wish you were never—"

"Bill, show him your badge," Chambers said.

Jones glowered at his partner, then shot an indignant glare at Danny and flashed his badge. "Okay, here, wise guy."

"So, can I go now?" Danny fidgeted and looked away.

"You think this is some kind of joke, don't you?" Jones loosened his tie and took off his suit jacket, revealing biceps as thick as tree trunks. Strapped to his bull-like torso was a side-holstered revolver.

"That guard had no right to take away my pocketknife."

"Rights? You want to talk about rights!" Jones crossed his brawny forearms. "I'd say you have no rights. Not while your bucktoothed cousins are taking potshots at American GIs on Guadalcanal."

"I'm an American!" Danny tightened his grip on the arms of his chair.

"You look like a Jap. You smell like a Jap. You are a Jap." Jones laughed, then frowned.

"Hey, Bill, go easy," Chambers said.

"This kid is asking for it."

So that's what the Hakujin really think. To them, Japanese Americans weren't Americans. All that stuff they taught in school was a bunch of bunk.

Chambers combed through his salt-and-pepper hair with his hand. "Listen, you assaulted an American soldier. You could go to jail for this."

"Assaulted? I was the one being manhandled. I was only defending myself."

"Don't give us guff." Jones leaned in, his face inches from Danny's. "We'll put you in the slammer and throw away the key."

"What's the difference? We're already in jail." Danny pulled his face away from him. He wasn't going to let this guy intimidate him, FBI or not. As far as he was concerned, he had done nothing wrong, and he was determined to make that point. But if they were going to send him to jail, he'd let them.

Jones aimed fierce eyes at Danny. "Kid, you don't know how good you have it. These camps are like country clubs compared to real prisons like San Quentin or Fort Leavenworth."

Maybe it was all bluff. Danny angled his body away from Jones. "You ever seen the inside of a country club or prison?"

Jones lunged at Danny and lifted him from the seat by the collar. "Hey, you keep giving us lip, and we'll put the fear of God in you." He shoved him back down.

"Ow!" His abdomen still smarted from the earlier blow, and ached even more after being dropped into the chair. If God was on the side of these bozos, Danny didn't want anything to do with him.

* * *

The slap of the railcar door jolted Tad. He rubbed his eyes and saw a guard stepping into the next car. Lily and Mama sat quietly in their seats. Still no sign of Danny.

People around him read newspapers, conversed in quiet tones, or slept. Babies screamed with loud cries. Children asked, "Where are we going?" or "When are we leaving?" only to be hushed by their parents.

At ten past six o'clock, some passengers were pointing outside and murmured. He looked out his window to find two tall soldiers grasping Danny's arms and escorting him along the platform.

Lily turned toward her window. "Look, it's Danny!"

They marched him up the railcar steps. At the door of the compartment, Danny proceeded to an empty spot in front of Tad and Lily. He slunk into the seat and buried his head in his hands.

Good thing Danny wasn't thrown in jail. Tad stood up and moved next to Danny. "Are you all right?"

He didn't respond and kept his eyes covered.

"What happened?"

"I don't feel like talking. Leave me alone." The family gathered around him, but Danny turned away from them.

The locomotive chugged away at 6:30 p.m., blowing its horn periodically. People fanned themselves, seeking relief from the intolerable heat.

A gruff-faced soldier stood at the head of the railcar. "All passengers, close your window blinds, and do not raise them until we reach our destination."

"What do they think we're going to do? Send signals to spies outside?" Tad mumbled.

The world had changed so drastically in less than a year. Things couldn't get much worse. Maybe Danny was right. His older brother Akira might be better off in Japan.

Finally, they were on their way—destination unknown.

13

Jilted

Kumamoto, Japan

Hidden behind the stone wall, Hiroshi waited outside Emiko's house, his eyes glued to a small photograph of her that stared back at him. The marriage go-between hadn't asked him to send it back, and he held it in his palm.

In the last month, he called her almost daily, but her aunt who moved in to live with her answered the phone each time. She told him she'd relay the message, but Emiko never called back. He even sent a few letters, but he received no response. Perhaps a more direct approach would work.

While waiting for her in the sultry heat, Hiroshi relived the humiliation of the engagement party. How could she choose that low-class plebeian over him? He could provide her with luxurious clothes and exquisite jewelry, extravagant champagnes, and the finest foods. And, of course, a stately mansion. Many women fought hard to capture his heart, but not Emiko. Maybe that was why he wanted her even more.

Hiroshi was about to give up and go home for the day when the front door slid open. He peeked through the gate as Emiko stepped out, wearing a peach summer kimono that accented her striking looks and classically sloped shoulders. No other woman's eyes could sparkle like hers. No face could come so close to being perfectly formed. Good thing he hung around. He carefully placed the photo back into his wallet and shoved it in his pants pocket.

Emiko turned back toward the house. "Auntie, I'm going to meet a friend in town."

"While you're there, please pick up some eggplant and *nappa* cabbage at the market."

"All right."

Backing away from the gate, Hiroshi slinked around the corner. The footsteps grew louder, and he leaped out to intercept her.

"*Konnichi wa.* Good afternoon, Takata-san." Hiroshi bowed, keeping his eyes transfixed on her.

Emiko gasped. "Yamada-san, you scared me!"

"How have you been?"

"Excuse me, but I have a previous engagement." She edged around him and walked away briskly.

He wasn't about to let her go. Bolting forward several steps, he caught up to her. "Emiko-san, please reconsider my proposal. I can offer you so much—"

"Yamada-san, I will never marry you, so please don't contact me anymore." She resumed her march away from him.

Hiroshi wasn't going to allow her to humiliate him again. He vaulted ahead and cut in front of her. "No, you can't just leave me like this. I can't live without you—"

"Please stop following me." Emiko tried to maneuver around him, but he quickly blocked her path. She turned in the other direction, but he shifted to impede her.

"Yamada-san, I think I've made it very clear to you that I have no desire to see or hear from you ever again." Her eyes blazed like fiery embers. "Now, let me go!"

No one spoke to him like that. "Wait! I have something to say to you."

"I don't want to hear it. I need to go." She looked past Hiroshi and smiled brightly at someone and waved her hand. "Over here."

Hiroshi twisted around to see a tall young man in a white, open-collared shirt and beige trousers approaching them. So, this was the friend she planned to meet—Akira, the one who barged in at his engagement party—his junior teaching colleague. Hiroshi clenched his teeth so hard his jaw began to hurt.

Akira grinned cheerfully at her, and then he turned toward Hiroshi, expressionless.

An awkward minute went by.

Emiko looked at Akira, then at Hiroshi. "I believe you two know each other."

Taking a cue from her, Akira bowed low to Hiroshi and addressed him as a person of higher rank. "Good day, *Senpai.*"

Hiroshi shifted his gaze to the ground, unable to return the greeting. "I was talking to Takata-san."

Emiko took hold of Akira's arm. "Shall we go?"

Her words sliced into Hiroshi like a samurai sword. He squeezed his hands into tight fists, digging his nails into his palms.

Akira nodded slightly to Hiroshi, then turned away.

They would both pay for the humiliation. Hiroshi's blood seethed through his veins, and fire ignited in his belly. If he couldn't have Emiko, neither would Akira.

* * *

In his bedroom, Hiroshi downed a shot of Yamazaki whiskey and slammed the glass on his persimmon wood desk. He buried his face in his hands. Humiliation ate away at his gut when he reflected back on Emiko's public refusal at the engagement party. Seeing her with Akira on the street today caused him to burn like a wildfire.

He would be an important man one day, and Emiko could be useful to him. Educated, graceful, and pleasing to the eye, she would be a showcase wife to parade among the social elite.

If any other woman had done that to him, Hiroshi would have roughed her up and defamed her as a slut. Somehow he couldn't do that to Emiko. No other woman's appearance could come so close to her's, and the lovely lines of her graceful neck truly exemplified Japanese beauty.

After the engagement party debacle, he had tried to find out everything he could about Akira. The man was a peasant. He had gone to an obscure local teachers' college. An inconsequential fellow who would spend the rest of his life teaching high school—no future, no money. The man wasn't even fit to be his rival, and yet she preferred this nobody to him.

As he contemplated the unfairness of it, a thought niggled at the back of his mind. On paper, Akira seemed so harmless, so beneath him. Yet, something was strange about him. He couldn't put his finger on it, but he'd find out.

He opened his wallet and pulled out the photo of Emiko and gazed at it again. She was a fool. He hated her, yet desired her.

A knock on his door shook Hiroshi out of his reverie. "Are you in there?"

"Come in." He continued staring at her photograph.

His father entered the room. "Still moping about that girl?"

He swiveled his chair away from his father and avoided making eye contact. The old man never sympathized or offered a kind word to him. "So, did you come in here to humiliate me even more?"

His father issued a guttural chuckle. "*Shikkari shiro!* Get a hold of yourself! There are plenty of pretty girls you could have."

"Not like Emiko."

His father harrumphed. "If you want her so badly, what do you plan to do?"

"Can't you have our lawyers enforce the stipulation in the uniform contract so she'd marry me?"

"That's no longer possible."

"Why not?"

"We no longer have leverage against them. Her uncle sold the factory to another businessman. That's what I came to tell you."

Hiroshi swallowed hard. "What am I going to do then?"

"I didn't raise my son to be weak and stupid. Figure it out yourself." The elder Yamada sneered. "Or give her up." He walked out of the room and closed the door.

"I'll show you," Hiroshi muttered to himself. He poured another shot and let the fiery liquid drain down his throat.

He stared into the empty glass. Perhaps he could find out if Emiko's family had some outstanding debts she couldn't pay. Or maybe he could find out something unsavory about Akira's background or family. There had to be something.

An idea came like a flash. He set the shot glass down on the desk. Picking up the phone, he dialed. "*Moshi, moshi*, Uncle, this is Hiroshi."

"Hello, Hiroshi. How are you doing?"

"I need your help."

"Oh? With the Takata woman?"

His uncle seemed to always be a step or two ahead of him. "Yes. How did you know?"

"Don't forget. She made a fool out of me as well. At least her father saved face by dying. So how can I help you?"

"Some time ago, you mentioned you could get me into the *Kempeitai*."

"I have some influence with the prefecture commander. Have you reconsidered my offer?"

"Yes, I'm definitely interested. Please recommend me to the commander. I'll be eternally grateful." When his uncle made the offer a year ago, Hiroshi had been promoted to the head of the political science and social studies department and ingratiated himself with the vice principal. It seemed like a more promising career back then.

Time to change plans.

No doubt his uncle would want some favors in return, but Hiroshi wasn't worried about that. If he belonged to this elite organization, he would have access to personal information on practically anyone. He could gather more data on Akira and Emiko and use it to his advantage. Then he'd be able to craft the perfect revenge.

No one humiliated Hiroshi Yamada and got away with it.

14

Heart Mountain

Wyoming - August 27, 1942

Intense sunlight temporarily blinded Tad as the shades opened inside the darkened railcar. He rubbed his eyes and squinted. People rose from their hard seats and gathered their belongings. Children asked, "Where are we?"

A painted sign on a ramshackle hut next to the railroad tracks identified the place as Vocation, Wyoming. Tad held Mama's hand as she stepped off the train, then he assisted Lily while Danny fetched their suitcases.

Tad checked out his new surroundings. A large mountain to the northwest stood like a tall man wearing a fedora.

Beige and brown hues dominated the surrounding landscape with insignificant clumps of greenery. The foreboding starkness of the land suggested to Tad that they weren't welcome here.

In the basin below, the camp spread out like a vast cabbage field with neat furrows of barracks. Miles of barbed wire fences with guard towers spaced at even intervals formed the perimeter.

Danny hooded his eyes with the bill of his flat cap. "Look at this place. We're out in the middle of nowhere. There's no two ways about it—a real prison."

For once, Tad agreed with him. This desolate land might be their home for a long while.

"I overheard a guard say we were supposed to go to Manzanar, but they're filled up there," Lily whispered. "I wish we went there, so we could be with my parents."

A twinge of sympathetic sadness fell upon Tad as he gazed at his wife. It was bad enough being moved a thousand miles away from home. She probably wouldn't be able to see her folks until the end of the war, whenever that would be.

They hopped on the open trucks that transported them near the camp entrance. A large sign near the main gate read HEART MOUNTAIN WAR RELOCATION CENTER. The driver signaled all inmates to get off.

As Tad and his family stepped off, the guards hurled their luggage onto the ground as if they were throwing out trash. It crushed his heart to see a lady cry uncontrollably. Dirt swirled around and sweat poured through Tad's clothes, making him itchy.

A baby-faced army officer addressed the crowd. "Follow the signs to the administration office." He pointed to a low-slung building in the center that appeared larger than the surrounding structures.

Tad and his family, along with a herd of other Japanese Americans, plodded over there on the unpaved, dusty ground, hauling their suitcases. As they drew closer, spooky-looking barracks came into view. Lily covered her mouth and gasped while other women burst into tears.

"They're ugly shacks!" Danny scoffed.

After a long wait, Tad filed into a room where he waited in more lines. He filled out forms, had his fingerprints taken, and interviewed for jobs. Next he answered a series of health questions and waited for the doctor, who gave him a cursory medical exam. The laborious process reminded him of Santa Anita—long lines to eat, long lines to pick up mail, long lines to use the lavatory and wash clothes.

Two staffers led them between rows of long barracks covered in black tar paper. Tad counted ten windows on each side and noticed several of them were missing roofs.

No trees could be seen anywhere. When he looked down at his feet, his shoes were covered with dirt—the only thing that seemed plentiful.

After a twenty-minute walk, they arrived at their assigned quarters on block 17, barrack 14, room E.

Tad turned the door handle and pulled, but it wouldn't budge. "What's wrong with this confounded thing?" He widened his stance and yanked it open.

He stared at the single room that had no kitchen, dining area, or bathroom. A bare lightbulb hung from a fixture in the center rafter of the ceiling with a wire wrapped around and down a crossbeam.

Folded blankets lay on five army cots along the walls. In the corner, a broom, mop and bucket were provided for them.

"Look at this place. Our living room back home is bigger than this ugly shack," Danny said. "There's a layer of dust everywhere."

"I'm so tired of having no privacy." Lily tossed her hand in the air, and her bracelet flew off. "Oh, no! My bracelet fell through that crack in the floor."

Tad crouched down and peered into the opening. "Maybe I can find a stick and fish it out, or I'll lift the floorboards."

Danny slapped the wall. "There's gaps everywhere. Look how big they are. What a shoddy job."

Tad took a few steps to the old-fashioned, potbelly stove in the middle of the room. He placed his hand on the sheet-metal exhaust pipe that extended through the roof. He doubted whether this thing would keep them warm in the winter.

Voices sounded over the thin walls that didn't extend up to the ceiling. Neighbors were moving in. Babies cried and children let out loud screams that traveled from somewhere in the barrack. On the other side of their room, cigarette smoke drifted in.

Danny fanned the smoke away. "Oh, great. They'll be able to hear everything we say, and we'll hear them."

Lily opened her suitcase and looked around. "No closets?"

"Leave everything in the suitcases until we figure something out," Tad said.

The door flung open and a young boy ran inside with a startled expression. "Oops, I'm sorry. I'm in the wrong room."

Tad smiled at the lad. "Don't worry kid. They all look alike. See you around."

Danny stepped around the luggage. He unlocked a window and tried to open it. "Sheesh, this thing won't budge. It's so hot in here. We're going to suffocate."

"With all the gaps in the walls and floor, that won't happen," Tad said. "Danny, let's go find some wood and tools. Maybe we can patch up some of the holes and fix the window."

* * *

An hour later, Tad returned with some scrap wood, a box of nails, and some tools. "The block manager told me I can borrow the tools, but next time, I need to purchase them from the Sears Roebuck catalog."

Danny slapped the wall with his hand and the room shook. "We had to leave our tools behind. Now we have to buy everything to fix their shoddy work? That's ridiculous."

Tad ran ropes across the room to divide it into smaller quarters or to hang clothes and towels.

Mama and Lily entered the barrack fanning themselves.

"The latrine is all the way down the barrack," Lily said. "The bad news is the women's toilets are in an open room with no stalls. I'm so tired of this."

"How are the showers?" Tad asked.

"They're in a room with a bunch of shower nozzles on the wall with no partitions, like Santa Anita. There's not enough toilets or showers again and no privacy anywhere."

"Plenty of scrap wood out there." Tad gestured to Danny with his hammer. "Let's talk to our block manager to see if we can round up some men to build stalls."

"This is too much. Why should we have to do all that work? The government should be taking care of it. I'm going to the administration office to demand that they do something. They're violating our rights as American citizens." Danny threw a board down and stormed off.

Tad glanced at the women. "For late nights, we'll keep a chamber pot in our barrack, like we did at Santa Anita."

After he covered some of the visible gaps, he examined the sparse, unadorned habitation. Then he remembered the jammed window frame. By chiseling away some excess wood with the screwdriver, he was able to open the window halfway, bringing in hot air.

An hour later Danny stomped in with a dark frown.

Tad could guess the outcome. "What did they say?"

"The man said they couldn't get a work crew here for at least three months. It's just a pack of lies."

"We can't wait that long. I'll talk to our block manager."

"Are you going to let them walk all over you again?"

With clenched teeth, Tad glared at Danny. Picking a fight with his brother wouldn't accomplish anything. He bit his tongue and strode out the door.

15

Christmas

Kumamoto, Japan – December 25, 1942

Snow that rarely fell in Kumamoto dusted the ground. Akira poked his head out the stone gateway of Emiko's house and scanned the street in both directions.

No one appeared to be out on this wintry evening. He motioned to Emiko. "Quick, follow me."

The frightening consequences of being caught at a Christian prayer meeting sapped Akira's desire to attend. But a strong and unyielding resolve to hold fast to something good, hopeful, and solid in the midst of these troubling times propelled him to the meeting.

They carried small bundles containing Christmas gifts and trod down the narrow, dark street with only a half-moon lighting their path. Within minutes, Akira and Emiko arrived at the host's home. No light shone from inside.

Akira rapped his gloved hand on the door. "This winter has been so cold. I wonder if the little grebe birds will congregate at the mouth of the Kuma River." He hoped he had remembered the code words correctly.

A latch unlocked and the door creaked open. "Welcome! Quick, come in," the maid whispered in a faint voice.

As instructed, Akira and Emiko wore their shoes inside the house in case they had to escape. The first time Emiko was told that, shock registered all over her face—such a foreign concept to wear shoes inside.

The maid held a lit candle and led them down a hallway to the parlor in the large house. She took their outerwear and hung them on the coat rack. Ten other guests, men in suits and women in kimonos, greeted each other with smiles, bows, and Christmas blessings.

The host, Mr. Yasuo Matsumoto, a well-to-do merchant in his sixties, mingled with the guests, laughing and exchanging anecdotes and pleasantries. He approached Yoshida-san, his business colleague. "I'm glad you managed to tear yourself away from work."

"I heard you were serving *sushi*," Yoshida said, laughing. "I couldn't miss your party. And it's Christmas after all."

Akira smiled, thinking this was probably a new experience for Emiko. Most Japanese didn't observe Christmas, but they celebrated New Year's, visiting Shinto temples, praying for good fortune, and feasting on delicious foods. Children received colorful *otoshidama* envelopes filled with money from parents and relatives.

Tonight, trays decorated the table with expensive *sushi* made of white rice. What a rare treat to eat such fine food during this time of strict rationing when most people were eating coarse-grain, watery brown rice mixed with *daikon* radish. It was a wonder where Mr. Matsumoto had found such delicacies.

Another high school teacher, Mr. Suzuki, approached Akira and Emiko. "Omura-sensei, Takata-san. How are you two lovebirds?"

Akira chuckled. "We're doing well," he said.

Emiko covered her mouth and giggled demurely.

Matsumoto joined them. "Merry Christmas to the lovely couple here tonight. I'm so happy you could make it."

He addressed his other guests. "I'll say a word of thanks to our Lord, so you can start enjoying the food." He bowed his head. "We are so honored to celebrate this very special occasion of the birth of Christ. Thank you Father for sending Jesus who came to give us an abundant life infused with purpose and promise. Finally, we thank you for this food. Amen."

Emiko handed the guests bookmarks and other crafts she made from bits of colored fabrics and ribbons. She wove her way toward the host. "Matsumoto-san, please accept my humble gift."

"You're so talented, Takata-san." He held her gift and bowed. "*Arigato gozaimasu.*"

"You're welcome," Emiko said, then whispered in his ear.

Matsumoto's eyes grew wide, and his mouth transformed into a gleaming smile.

The host urged Emiko and Akira to follow him to the center of the room. "Ladies and gentlemen, I have an announcement to make. Takata-san has received Jesus as her Lord and Savior. Praise God!"

Everyone applauded. One by one, the guests came forward and congratulated Emiko.

Akira's mind drifted back to those long, difficult discussions he'd had with her over the past few months. It finally paid off. She drilled him about creation, salvation by grace, and a myriad of other topics. He didn't know whether she'd ever become a Christian, but it finally happened.

When she spoke those words to him, ineffable warmth bubbled up inside him as he embraced her and whirled her around. "I'm so happy you've made this decision." Akira's heart and feet danced in elation. Now there was no longer any reason why he and Emiko couldn't get married.

The maid burst into the room and scurried over to Mr. Matsumoto. "Master, *Kempeitai* officers are at the door."

The host's eyes bulged. "Military Police? Everyone, quick! Grab the food and your belongings. Leave through the back entrance. Hurry!"

All the guests scrambled, seizing the food and their coats and wraps, and fled down the hallway toward the back door. Akira and Emiko double-checked for any evidence of the party.

Matsumoto directed the foot traffic. "Cut through the alley to the road along the river. Teruko-san, go now!" When the maid objected, he shoved her toward the other guests, who led her away.

Akira spun around. "Mr. Matsumoto, you must flee!"

"Don't worry about me. I've dealt with the *Kempeitai* before. Now, hurry both of you."

Akira had heard the *Kempeitai* arrested and imprisoned Mr. Matsumoto for having meetings like this. What a sacrifice he was making to give everyone time to escape. Akira and Emiko rushed toward the back of the house.

Heavy footfalls echoed from the front. Emiko had one foot out the back door when Mr. Suzuki reentered the house.

Suzuki held out his hands, urging them to move away from the doorway. "Get back inside," he whispered. "The *Kempeitai* are in the alley. I ducked in the shrubbery and crawled back when they weren't watching."

"What happened to the others?" Akira asked.

"I think they got away," Suzuki said breathlessly.

With all apparent escape routes cut off, the sheer terror of being discovered loomed within Akira's heart. He needed to be strong and keep his mind clear to find someplace to hide. He spotted a dark hallway to the left and grasped Emiko's hand. "Come on, let's go this way."

The trio tiptoed through the hall and entered a room with silk partitions propped against the wall. Akira helped Emiko crawl under a stack, then took cover next to her. Suzuki dove under another pile.

Indistinct yelling from another part of the house jarred Akira's mind. Partitions shook from Emiko's quivering body.

Akira tightened his grip on her to calm her nerves and whispered, "Be perfectly still. We mustn't make a sound."

The voices grew louder and stomping sounds came nearer. Akira's heart pounded.

"Are you sure you saw them running away from the house?" a baritone voice asked. "Search the entire house. Some of them may still be inside."

"Yes, Captain."

Akira's heart double-timed at the sounds of glass breaking, fabric ripping, and loud thumping.

A flashlight beam pierced through the translucent silk above his head, and he heard the clack and rattle of partitions slamming on the floor. More partitions fell. Akira wanted to spring up and subdue the man, but he was no match for an armed policeman, and others would hear the commotion and run to help.

The sounds stopped.

"Lieutenant, did you see anyone down there?"

"Nobody's back there, sir."

Akira released a lungful of air. Something about the lieutenant's voice sounded somewhat familiar.

"You didn't apprehend any of them besides Matsumoto?"

"I'm afraid not, Captain."

"Bring Matsumoto to me at once."

Heels clacked, and a few minutes later, faint groaning sounds and a noise like a sack of rice being dragged could be heard.

"Matsumoto, have you changed your mind about revealing the others?"

"What others?" Matsumoto coughed.

"Liar!"

Pounding fists and groans followed, making Akira's stomach churn like a cement mixer. Emiko's body jerked with every blow.

"Tell us who they are, and it'll go easier for you."

Silence loomed. Matsumoto groaned and coughed.

"You old fool! Don't you know that holding Christian meetings is an act of disloyalty to the emperor? You were warned the last time. This time you're going to pay."

"Captain, some suspects are reported to be hiding out a few streets from here."

"Get after them."

"What shall we do with Matsumoto?"

"Shoot him."

"Yes, Captain."

Emiko gasped.

Akira's adrenaline surged. He took a half step to spring out of his hiding place to rescue Matsumoto, but halted. How could he save Matsumoto without endangering Emiko and Suzuki?

A gunshot exploded.

Emiko's body went limp in Akira's grasp.

"Let's get out of here, now," the baritone voice said.

A door slammed shut. Voices and footsteps of the *Kempeitai* men grew faint and eventually faded.

Sweat beaded off Akira's face. He could hardly comprehend how this joyous evening had metamorphosed into a terrifying nightmare. He told himself to keep calm. "I think they're gone."

Emerging from his hiding place, Akira helped Emiko up, but she collapsed into his arms. He held her, not knowing how to console her.

Suzuki crawled out from his hiding place. "Let's find Mr. Matsumoto."

Akira released his grip on her. "Stay inside this room." He slowly turned and followed Suzuki to the parlor.

Mr. Matsumoto lay in a pool of blood with a gunshot wound to his head with his eyes wide open. Suzuki's brows squeezed together, and his mouth hung open.

Gripping the top of a chair to balance himself, Akira stared at Matsumoto's lifeless form. He crumpled to his knees and wept. "Oh, God, please stop this brutality!"

16

Injustice

Heart Mountain, Wyoming – January 20, 1943

Howling, icy winds roared down the slope of Heart Mountain, sifting the fine, sandy soil of the Wyoming high prairie through cracks, tiny gaps in window frames, under the door, and beneath patches of roofing material.

Tad rubbed his hands together and stood by the potbelly stove to stay warm. Earlier when he went outside to the latrine, the temperature had dipped thirty below zero. Flying particles pricked his face and dusted his hair. The powerful winds shoved him around as if he were a drunk staggering back to the barrack.

After the winds died down, Tad slapped the bare wood ceiling with an old T-shirt. Gray dirt rained down everywhere. Even though he spent the first two months plugging up holes and gaps, he was surprised about all the dirt and dust that still blew in.

He swept the fine particles into floorboard crevices, then gathered the blankets, sheets and damp towels that hung on the rope and shook them outside.

The temperature rose slightly in the afternoon. Tad stayed bundled up and ventured to the community garden. "Hi, I'm here to volunteer," he said to the person in charge.

"We can use your help," a man wearing a heavy muffler said. "Grab some tools. We're planting winter wheat."

Tad joined the others and began pounding the half-frozen ground with a pick. Anything was better than sitting around in this mind-numbing, demeaning place that had become his home.

He looked up and recognized a high school classmate. "Is that Ron Sano?"

Ron twisted around. "Tad! Good to see you. I didn't know you were at this camp."

"With over ten thousand people, it's difficult to know who's here."

"That's for sure," Ron said. "My wife and I are still looking for paying jobs. With our parent's bank accounts frozen, we're running low on cash."

Tad sighed. "I tried to find work at the camp motor pool, but they already had too many mechanics. And the cafeteria had enough people—even at fifty cents a day."

"The *Hakujin* workers have a lot of the jobs here and are making about ten times more than us doing the same work. It'll take years to recover our losses. We no longer own anything. My brother was just a month away from graduating UCLA but couldn't take any of his final exams. He was devastated."

"Sorry to hear that." Reaching for a shovel, Tad turned over the broken soil. "Lily and my mom occupy themselves making futon quilts and clothing with other women in our block. They sell a lot of it at the camp store, but don't make much money."

Later that day, Tad rested his achy muscles in the drafty barrack. The door flung open and Lily charged in.

"Danny's in trouble!" she shouted.

"What happened?"

"Jane Oda rushed into the sewing room and told us trouble broke out in the dining hall. They hauled Danny and some other guys away to the administration building."

"I'll go see what happened." Rushing out the door in his thick overcoat, Tad held the brim of his hat against the relentless dust storm that kicked up again. He slogged down F Street, the main thoroughfare, covered his face as the strong winds churned like a tornado. In the distance, Heart Mountain seemed to keep its ever-present watch over the camp.

Inside the building, Tad approached a middle-aged brunette at the receptionist desk. "Hello. I'm here to see Daniel Omura."

The brunette lowered her chin and glared at him over her reading glasses. "Are you related to him?"

"Danny's my brother."

"He's locked up in a holding cell. Check with Mr. Campbell, head of security. His office is down the hall, third door to the right."

Tad made his way over there and knocked on the door.

"Come in," a raspy voice called from inside.

Tad entered the room, which reeked of cigarettes. He stood in front of a desk where a pale man with thin gray hair sat hunched over some papers.

The man didn't look up. "Who are you?"

"I'm Tad Omura. Sir, I hear my brother Danny's—"

"Your brother and his cohorts attacked a white worker today, Ken Nelson, who's been treated for a sprained wrist and ankle and other bruises." Campbell lifted his head and glared at him through silver-rimmed glasses.

Despite his brother's quick temper and fresh mouth, Tad hadn't known him to be violent. Danny never even picked a fight with anyone at school.

Campbell opened the second drawer of the file cabinet. He pulled out a folder and examined the contents. "Your brother, I see, has a history of causing trouble. The incident at the Santa Anita train stop—"

"Mr. Campbell, Danny had every right to carry his pocketknife since it was less than four inches. He shouldn't have gotten into trouble for that. I'm sure he has a good reason for what happened today."

"Whether he does or not, I won't tolerate this kind of behavior." He snapped the folder shut. "It's a good thing Nelson's injuries weren't more serious. I would have turned your brother over to the authorities in Cody, and you know how they feel about you people in town. They'd railroad him to the prison in Rawlins or worse."

An image of a lynch mob seized Tad's mind. Danny wouldn't stand a chance.

"I'm holding him for three days, so he can think about what he's done. I'll let you see him now." Campbell scribbled on his monogrammed notepad, ripped off a sheet, and handed it to Tad. "Check in with the guard, and give him this note. Continue down the hall, first door on your right. Report back when you're done."

In the anteroom, a young soldier with a blond crew cut sat in a chair, smiling at a comic book. His rifle leaned against the wall.

"Excuse me, sir. I'm here to see Daniel Omura."

Grabbing his rifle, the guard jumped up.

Tad handed him the note.

The guard examined it carefully and retrieved a set of keys. He opened the door to the holding cell area. "You have fifteen minutes."

Tad entered the dimly lit room constructed with a crosshatch of cedar, rather than the vertical steel bars of a standard cell. Danny and another young Nisei sat against the wall. Another fellow lay on a double-decker cot bolted by chain links.

"Danny!" Tad called out. "What happened?"

His brother rose and shuffled to the front. "A kitchen worker, Nelson, was stealing meat, rice, sugar, and other items from our food supplies and receiving kickbacks. Haven't you noticed how little we've had to eat in the last month?"

"What proof do you have?" Tad asked.

"We caught him red-handed taking stuff out of the kitchen pantry and icebox and loading it onto a truck that goes into town. And we saw the driver hand Nelson a wad of cash. So we talked to him."

"Talked to him?" Tad said "You beat him up."

The other men in the cell crowded around Danny. One of them blurted, "He attacked us first."

Danny glanced at his friend who spoke up. "What Joey said is true. When we confronted Nelson, he claimed we were the ones stealing food. He threatened to turn us in, and he started swinging a kitchen knife at us. Nelson cut Ben in the shoulder. He was bleeding so bad, his brother took him to the hospital."

"Joey distracted Nelson, and I kicked the knife out of his hand. Then we roughed him up a bit."

"Did you tell the security officer about this?" Tad asked.

"Yeah, we told him, but he didn't believe us." Danny's face turned beet red and his eyes flared like kerosene lamps. "Nothing happened to Nelson. Instead, we were locked up."

The unfairness of it gnawed on Tad's gut. "I'll talk to the security officer and demand that he do something."

"Fat chance he'll do anything. They don't care about us." Danny jerked his head. "Hey Joey, tell my brother what happened to your uncle."

Joey gripped the cell door. "My uncle was locked up at the Topaz camp with his family. One day he got a little too close to the fence and a guard shot him dead. The army report claimed my uncle was trying to crawl under the fence. But my cousins inspected the scene and found a large bloodstain a good five feet inside the fence, which contradicted the report. As they were investigating, an army jeep came flying out and halted in front of them. The driver aimed a gun at them and yelled, 'Scatter or you'll get the same thing the other guy got.' The guard who shot my uncle was court-martialed, but pronounced not guilty."

Danny balled his fists and bared his teeth. "It's no different here."

Tad understood his brother's anger. He didn't know what he might have done if he were in his shoes. Maybe the same thing.

The guard entered the area. "Time's up."

With a hangdog look, Danny stepped backward and dropped onto the cot.

Back in Campbell's office, Tad waited patiently while the security officer cleared his desk and filed some folders. "Mr. Campbell, Nelson was stealing food and getting paid for it."

Campbell removed his glasses and wiped them with a cloth. "How do I know he's telling the truth?"

"There were several witnesses," Tad said.

"Swell, you mean his buddies?"

"Why else would they get into a fight with Nelson?"

"Don't ask me. The MPs who broke up the fight didn't report anything about Nelson stealing food."

"Mr. Campbell, I'd appreciate it if you investigate this further. I'm sure my brother can identify the driver who drove the truck into town and handed Nelson the money."

"Now, look! I don't have time to investigate every little incident. Nobody was hurt that bad, not even the person who was cut. He's all patched up with a few stitches in his shoulder."

Tad's blood boiled. He wanted to give Campbell a piece of his mind, but he kept his mouth shut.

On the way back to his quarters, Tad decided he would only tell Lily about Danny's situation, and remain quiet about Joey's uncle. It would only make her more upset and frantic.

At the barrack, Lily's jaw dropped. "I can't believe Mr. Campbell won't even look into the food pilfering. Isn't there any justice?"

Tad shook his head. "Somehow, we need to gain their respect."

17

Quandary

Kumamoto, Japan – January 27, 1943

A brassy, military song blared through the empty classroom, jarring Akira as he graded essays on the Meiji Restoration of 1868. He tucked a pencil behind his ear and stepped toward the frosty window.

He gazed at a panel truck decorated with fluttering military flags. The music stopped, and a man's voice bellowed over the crackling loudspeakers. "Attention, all subjects of the emperor. Attention! Our brave soldiers and sailors continue to beat back the enemy on every front. We have the American and Australian armies bottled up in New Guinea and the British stymied in Burma. Our superior navy continues to inflict huge losses on enemy fleets." The announcer's voice boomed louder and louder. "Japan is winning the war!"

More propaganda. Akira rolled his eyes and buttoned his heavy winter coat. He returned to his desk and opened his lunch box and ate one small rice ball. Then he chewed on a piece of pickled cabbage, which left him still hungry.

If Japan were winning the war, the government wouldn't be allocating such tiny portions of rice, and he wouldn't have to use safety pins to keep his suit pants snug around his waist. There'd also be enough fuel oil to heat the classrooms, and he wouldn't have to move his feet around and tap dance to stay warm.

He chuckled, recalling the time when he and his students could no longer withstand the numbing cold. Akira had stood in front of the room and started tap dancing, stamping his heels and toes on the floor in quick succession, shifting his weight and flinging his arms around. The students laughed, rose from their chairs, and joined in. They begged, "Please teach us tap dancing, Sensei. We want to do this every day."

"Okay. Arrive ten minutes early, and we'll begin, but this little secret stays inside our classroom." Bright smiles broke out on their faces, and their feet pattered on the floor.

Now all alone in the room, his thoughts drifted back to the war. Afternoon classes had been cancelled with students diverted to textile factories.

One student had told him, "All we do at the factory is load these large reels of a nylon-like thread on to whirring machines that get woven into a yarn that is further processed into *orimono,* a fabric for airplane wings. Each of us operates five or six machines at a time. Whenever the thread breaks, we mend it, and we have to thread the machines over and over again. It's so boring. We'd rather be in class."

Other students constructed balloons to carry bombs across the Pacific. Some made bandages, uniforms, and meal kits. Furthermore, his male colleagues were called to serve in the military one by one. All of these facts made the announcer's declarations all the more ludicrous.

He started to write comments on a student's essay when a sharp knock sounded on the door. Akira didn't think anyone else would be in the building so late in the afternoon. "Come in."

A man in a military uniform with red and gold insignias swept into the classroom. He toted a service pistol in a holster on his hip.

Akira snapped his pencil in half. *What is he doing here?* He scooted his chair back and shot up.

The officer doffed his cap, placed it on a student's desk, and faced him. "Good day, Omura-sensei."

"Yamada-sensei. I didn't recognize you." Perhaps Hiroshi was seeking revenge from Akira for disrupting his marriage plans. "Have you joined the army?"

"No, not the regular army. I am now a full-fledged member of the *Kempeitai*." Hiroshi took a seat even though Akira hadn't offered it.

Akira suppressed an icy shiver that coursed through his body. The horrific events of Christmas night came back to haunt him. He told himself to remain calm and not act surprised. "I heard you resigned your teaching position for another opportunity, but I didn't know where."

"I went to Tokyo for a few months of training. After completing it, I received a lieutenant's commission, and now I'm in charge of security and defense preparedness for three districts in our city."

"But how did you—"

"My uncle knows some of the top officers in the region. He was in the same university class as the commander for Kumamoto Prefecture."

News that his former colleague had joined the *Kempeitai* left a bitter taste of rising bile in Akira's throat.

"I came to offer you the same opportunity. Since you're my friend, I can talk to my uncle, and I'm sure he can get you in."

Friend? Akira's mouth went dry. "Thanks for the offer, but I have my students to think of."

"Omura-san, it's just a matter of time before they call you into the army. They'll put a rifle in your hand and send you to an infantry unit on some godforsaken island in the South Pacific. Would you want that?"

If he joined the *Kempeitai*, perhaps he wouldn't have to fight against Americans. But he remembered the brutal killing of Mr. Matsumoto. Plus, after what had happened at the engagement party, Hiroshi's offer to help him made no sense whatsoever. "Thanks for the opportunity, but I enjoy teaching and want to stay with my students."

"Don't be a fool, Omura-sensei. Come join me now while you have a chance."

Heat wrapped around Akira's shirt collar as he struggled to be respectful. "Yamada-san, thank you, but I'd rather teach."

Hiroshi's upper lip curled. "Here I am, offering you a great opportunity to do something prestigious, and you're looking at me as if I've insulted you."

Akira couldn't understand why Hiroshi acted as if nothing ever came between them—like old times, when he monopolized Akira's time in between class sessions and after hours.

Is Hiroshi over Emiko?

"Very well then." Hiroshi stood up, crowned his head with his cap, and pivoted toward the door. He marched out of the classroom without another word.

* * *

Emiko unlatched the sliding door and smiled. "Akira-san, you're here early."

Warm smile marks formed around Akira's eyes, and his luminous smile deepened his dimples. "I couldn't wait to see you, darling. I thought I'd stop by your house to see if there's anything I could help you with to prepare for tonight."

"Most Japanese men would never say something like that. How thoughtful of you."

He kissed her on the cheek. After he removed his shoes and coat, he carried worship song sheets to a low table covered with a *kotatsu* mat. A ground heater lay underneath. "Are we ready for tonight?"

"I believe so. How many people are coming?" She asked.

"Only four. The rest are too frightened. Are you sure you really want to do this?"

She didn't answer immediately. "Yes, I want to."

"You've only been a Christian for a short time, yet you're so strong in your faith."

Emiko couldn't believe that. Perhaps she was only putting up a brave front. Nobody knew who the informant had been. An image of Mr. Matsumoto's cheerful face skittered across her mind. If he were still alive, he would want the prayer meetings to continue. "How was your day at school?"

Akira's smile evaporated, and his face darkened. "Hiroshi Yamada visited me today."

Her hands shook, and she nearly dropped the teacup. His name always raised the hairs on the back of her neck. But even a man like him needed God's grace and forgiveness. "What did he want?"

"He joined the *Kempeitai*."

All the sentiments she experienced for the man an instant ago vanished in a flash.

"He wanted me to join him."

Her eyes widened. "You didn't say *yes*, did you?"

"Of course not. But there's something else. I didn't think of this before, but when I saw him in his uniform today, all the pieces came together. I can't be sure, but I thought I recognized his voice on Christmas night."

She gasped. "What?" Emiko froze and thought back to that night. Now that Akira mentioned it, she recalled the eerily familiar voice. The veins inside her iced over.

18

Victim

Heart Mountain, Wyoming

Brrr, it's cold. Freezing headwinds whipped through the camp and pierced through Danny's jacket as if he were only wearing a T-shirt. He dug his boots into the squeaky, light snow that had fallen the night before and tromped across camp to fetch aspirin for his mother, who had fallen on an icy patch in the middle of the night on the way to the latrine.

Danny missed the balmy temperatures in California that rarely dipped below fifty degrees Fahrenheit. Last week he learned the hard way not to leave the communal showers with wet hair after washing it. A block of ice had formed on his head on the way back to the barrack. It took a long while warming himself by the stove to thaw it out.

Plodding to the corner, he heard kids screaming, "He-elp!" Following the cries, Danny rushed to a playground where five boys surrounded a crying boy who flailed his arms—his tongue stuck to a steel pole. No doubt the victim of a foolish dare. They looked to be about eight or nine years old.

"Stay still, and I'll be right back." Danny sprinted to the nearest mess hall and excused himself with the people waiting in line to bring back a cup of warm water.

Returning to the pole, Danny poured the water on the victim's tongue to loosen it. He tossed the remaining water on the ground and glared at the others. "Who put him up to this?"

The other kids hung their heads and looked away.

"Come on, who did it?"

Finally, one boy pointed his gloved finger at the person next to him. "It was him."

The second child shoved his accuser. "No, I didn't. We all made him—"

"All right, guys. Knock it off." Danny squatted eye-level with the weeping child, who looked to be younger, maybe around seven. "What's your name?"

"Gar-wy." The boy mumbled between snorts, his red nose running. "Hurt."

Addressing the others, Danny barked, "One of you, go tell Gary's parents I'm taking him to the hospital." For emphasis, he frowned at them and shouted, "Go!"

The boys scattered in the direction of the north end of camp.

Danny offered to hold Gary's hand, but the little boy seemed determined to tromp alongside without any help.

They sauntered past an ice skating area crowded with children and young adults who glided across on ice skates. Some Nisei men created the ice skating area by flooding the ground with fire hoses and letting it freeze. Danny had heard the Quakers had spearheaded a gift-giving drive for Japanese children locked up in camps. Some churches and individuals donated Christmas gifts, which included ice skates. Others purchased them from the Sears Roebuck or Montgomery Ward catalogs. He wondered how families could afford them with the limited jobs and low pay.

"Gary, have you ever ice skated?"

The little boy shook his head.

"Me neither. But it looks like fun."

A blast of warm air greeted them inside. People coughed and wheezed as they waited to be seen by a camp doctor. Danny hoped he wouldn't catch anything while they waited.

The hospital for inmates opened at the end of August and was always packed. As winter approached many people caught the flu or pneumonia and some died. Chickenpox, mumps and measles quickly spread throughout the camp among children. His friend's father who worked there as a surgeon only made $19 a month—the highest pay an inmate could make and only a fraction of what the Caucasian doctors made. Even the Caucasian nurses were paid $150 a month. The unfairness of it grated on Danny's nerves.

A strange notion entered his thoughts. In some ways, his family and all the people in the prison camp were like the boy with the stuck tongue—victimized, captured, and helpless— except it wasn't a game. They couldn't venture outside the confines of the barbed wire fences without permission and an escort. If they even made an attempt, guards would open fire.

A blonde nurse greeted them. Danny explained the incident.

The nurse shook her head. "What naughty boys." She leaned toward Gary. "Open wide. Let me take a look." She examined Gary's tongue. "I'll get some medicated rinse."

"Gary! Gary! Are you all right?" another woman's voice called from behind them.

Danny turned and shifted uncomfortably. A young woman with large, upturned eyes approached them. She probably turned a lot of heads and his heart quickened. During the five months he'd been at Heart Mountain, he met a lot of new people, but had never run into her before.

She stooped down in front of Gary. "Are you okay?"

Gary started to nod, then shook his head.

She rose and turned her attention to Danny. "The boys told me what happened. They were really sorry. Thank you so much for helping my little brother."

Danny's tongue suddenly stopped working, as if he had been the victim with a tongue stuck to the metal pole. "Y-You're welcome."

The nurse returned with a small bottle of amber liquid and smiled at Gary. "Okay, let's rinse your mouth with this." She took the boy over to the basin and poured him a cup.

Danny glanced at the young woman again, still trying to figure out what to say. "Hi, I'm Danny Omura."

"I know who you are. I went to the same high school as you. You were on the football team."

He could feel a modest smile form across his mouth with the recognition. "Yeah, that's right."

The young woman removed her mitten and extended her hand to Danny. "I'm Mary Wada."

He shook her hand gently, all the while commanding his brain to figure out whether he really knew her back in school. "Hi, Mary."

The nurse returned with Gary in tow. "He'll be fine. Don't give him anything hot to drink for the next few days." She looked at the two young adults. "Are you his parents?"

"No, we're not." Mary blushed. She placed her hand on Gary's shoulder. "I'm his sister."

"Sorry about that." The nurse smiled and waved good-bye.

Mary glanced his way. "Danny, you don't remember me, do you? It's okay since we hung around in different groups."

"Of course, I remember you." He tried to sound convincing. Danny stood there, berating himself silently for not recalling who this pretty girl was. He froze with sudden recollection—that bookworm-ish girl with glasses, one year behind him—Spanish club, Scholastic Honor Society. It couldn't be.

"Thanks again for helping Gary," Mary said.

"It was my pleasure."

"I'll see you around." She looked at her little brother. "Let's go."

Danny watched Mary and her brother leave the hospital. He definitely wanted to get to know her and hoped she didn't have a boyfriend.

Daydreaming, Danny returned to his family's barrack. When he stepped through the threshold, he did an about-face. He'd completely forgotten about the aspirin for his mom.

19

Kempeitai

Kumamoto, Japan

Hiroshi laughed to himself as he strode to the prefectural headquarters of the *Kempeitai*. He knew Akira would never accept the opportunity, but he only wanted to see his reaction. If Akira accepted his offer, he would have made up some excuse. Anybody else would have jumped at the chance.

Father's words played like a broken record in Hiroshi's head. *There's no future in teaching. You'll always be poor and struggle. Only accept a prestigious job in business or with the government where you can advance your career.* As much as he hated to admit it, his father was right.

He paused for a moment at the entrance of the *Kempeitai* office. Hiroshi could make things happen in this position with the power he now wielded. A squad of military policemen stood ready at his disposal at all times. At last, he had found his true calling.

That evening, Hiroshi stepped inside a restaurant favored by *Kempeitai* officers. While other restaurants frequented by the general populace lacked quality food, this one was always well provisioned.

"Welcome, Lieutenant Yamada. Can I serve you today's special menu—cuts of fresh horsemeat sashimi, fried oysters and your usual Kuro Junmai Ginjo *saké*?"

"Yes, please, Keiko-chan." He knew she had a crush on him, and he winked at her, making it seem as if he liked her.

After Hiroshi finished his sumptuous meal, he had a final swig of warm *saké*. He glanced at his watch. Eight o'clock—two more hours of work at the office. He put on his overcoat and sauntered out of the restaurant.

A few blocks from the office, a howling dog drew his attention. Strict rules about maintaining silence were enforced throughout the city during the nighttime curfews, as if pilots flying in American bombers could hear barking dogs. But rules were rules. He stepped up his gait to investigate.

A small *Shiba-ken* backed up on its haunches, barking at Hiroshi.

He scowled at the annoying little dog, then lurched toward it. "*Urusai na. Shizuka ni se!*"

The curly-tailed animal ignored him and continued growling.

Hiroshi removed his service pistol, cocked it, and aimed squarely at the dog's head.

A young boy came running after the *Shiba-ken* and scooped it up into his arms. "No! No! Don't shoot my Chibi-chan." He muzzled the wriggling dog with his small hands.

If Hiroshi didn't take care of this troublesome animal now, it would probably happen again. But if he tried to shoot it, the bullet might hit the boy as well.

Taking a closer look at the dog, Hiroshi noticed it had the same fawn coloring of the *Shiba* he'd had as a child, only this one was smaller. His also barked a lot. He remembered how his father grabbed the dog by the nape and put it into a cage. "Hiroshi, you can't seem to control your dog. We're sending him away."

"No, Father. Don't take Goro away. I promise to keep him quiet."

"You've said that time and again. This time, I'm taking him away."

Tears had rained out of Hiroshi's eyes as he begged at his father's feet to keep the dog, but the next day when he woke up, Goro was gone. He never saw his furry best friend again.

The little boy's crying brought Hiroshi out of his memories. He lowered his pistol and put it back in the holster. "Boy, there's a war going on and everybody, including dogs, must keep quiet during the nighttime curfews. *Wakattaka?*"

The boy sniffled. "Yes, I understand."

What had happened to Hiroshi's dog twenty years ago still gnawed on his sense of well-being. In a symbolic rebellion against his father, he resolved not to let it happen to this boy. "Make sure your dog doesn't cause a disturbance again or next time I'll shoot." Hiroshi buttoned the holster and marched away.

* * *

Akira stepped into the principal's office and wondered what he wanted. If the principal had found out about the tap dancing, he would be in deep trouble, especially with the ban on American movies, music, and dancing. Perhaps he would tell him he was leading the students in calisthenics. "Good morning." He bowed low.

"*Ohayo*, Omura-sensei. Please be seated. You may have heard Hosokawa-sensei was drafted into the army last week. With one-third of our faculty now serving in the military, we're forced to reshuffle the classroom assignments again. We need your help in leading the daily drills and marches."

On top of teaching triple the number of students in his classes, Akira and the other teachers were required to dig *bokugo*—trenches all around the city for people to jump into during air raids. He also helped stuff cotton into heavy *zukin* hoods used to protect people's heads from flying debris to wear inside the *bokugo*.

Many times Akira had watched Hosokawa lead the drills through his classroom window. Boys and girls lined up in blocks of twenty, shouldering bamboo sticks with sharpened points. On Hosokawa's command, the little faux soldiers lunged with their weapons at tied thatches of straw, mounted on wooden stands. These children might soon be called upon to kill Americans.

Akira leaned forward. "Sir, there are more qualified teachers with military training who would be better suited for this task."

"This is not a request. This is an order." The principal fixed a piercing stare at him. "The time has come when everyone must prepare for the defense of our homeland. You are among the few male teachers under age thirty left at this school. Frankly, I'm surprised you haven't been drafted yet. Until that time, I want you to lead the exercises."

"Yes, sir."

On the way back to his classroom, the principal's words kept ringing in his head. It was only a matter of time before he'd be forced into the military. Akira stared at his hands, wondering whether he could hold a rifle with a bayonet and jab it into the belly of a fellow American.

He reflected back on Hiroshi's offer. Having to fight his own countrymen would be dreadful, but joining the *Kempeitai* would be unthinkable.

20

Loyalty

Heart Mountain, Wyoming – February 8, 1943

Tad peered out the window at the deadness of winter that mirrored the monotony of camp life, while Lily altered trousers donated by a gentleman with a waist eight inches wider than Tad's. She had ordered him a new pair of trousers from the Montgomery Ward catalog, but it would take several weeks for delivery.

"Sorry it's taking so long, dear. It'd be a lot faster if I could use a sewing machine, but none are available at the sewing hall right now. If I didn't sleep in, I would have had your trousers ready by now."

"Take your time. We all lost sleep after Yoshiko Harada screamed in the middle of the night again. This time, a mouse ran across her bed. Last time, it was a spider crawling up her arm. Her mother deeply apologized to everyone who was awoken this morning."

Lily looked up. "That poor girl. If that happened to me, I would have screamed too."

"Later today, I'll stop by the Haradas' barrack and plug up some of the knotholes and cracks for them. I think that's probably how they're getting in," Tad said. "Hey Danny, can I borrow your denim overalls to wear to the wood shop?"

"Go ahead." Danny wadded up the *Heart Mountain Sentinel.* "I can't believe the reporters write such trash. They side with the government on everything."

"Then why waste your time reading it?" Tad slid on the denims and readied himself. "Come on, when are you going to finish that coat rack?"

"Honey, I like your idea of carving cherry blossoms on the storage chest," Lily said. "I know you'll do a great job since you're so good with your hands."

Tad smiled, then glanced at Danny. "Come on, let's go make ourselves useful."

"All right. Hold on, let me get my jacket."

After receiving suitable pieces of pine from the block manager, they plodded across camp and entered the empty wood shop. Everyone was probably in line for lunch.

"Tomorrow we have that interview with the government." Danny pulled out sheets of paper from his shirt pocket. "Did you read it?"

"I did."

Danny unfolded the papers. "How are you going to answer question 27, 'Are you willing to serve in the armed forces of the United States on combat duty wherever ordered?' "

Tad shrugged. "I'm not sure."

"You're not going to answer *yes,* are you?"

"Maybe that's what we have to do to gain their trust."

Danny stood nose-to-nose with Tad. "You got to be kidding. The questionnaire's a joke. Here they lock us up and expect us to fight for them."

"I'm not saying you're wrong. I'm just saying nothing's going to change unless we show them we're loyal Americans."

"They're insulting us!" Danny's voice rose an octave. "Question 28 asks whether we'll reject our allegiance to the emperor of Japan. We never had any allegiance to begin with. Mom and Mas weren't allowed to become American citizens. And now, they have to give up their Japanese citizenship too? That's ridiculous!"

Tad agreed with Danny but remained silent. He put on safety glasses and turned on the lathe. When the piece of wood started to spin rapidly, he pressed the blade against it.

Danny slapped the kill switch.

"Hey, what are you doing?"

Stepping around the lathe, Danny waved the papers in his hand. "How can you support this?"

"I belong to this country, not Japan."

"This country doesn't want you. They hated us before the war, and they hate us even more now."

Tad removed the safety glasses and set them down. "You think we'd be better off if we were in Japan? Answering *no* could mean being sent there. Do you want that?"

"At least we wouldn't be treated like we don't belong."

Tad shook his head. "You don't know what it's like to live there. My classmates used to make fun of my accent and called me *batta-kusai*."

"What does that mean?"

"Stink like butter. When the Americans and Europeans first came to Japan, they brought butter, cheese and milk. The Japanese didn't like the smells. It's just like being called a Jap."

Danny picked up a hammer and pounded nails into a pine board. "I guess Akira's used to it. He's better off in Japan."

"Akira had an easier time than me, because he picked up the language quickly. Girls adored his good looks and brought him food and gifts all the time. But I never felt like I belonged there, and I hated living there."

"Why didn't they lock up the Germans and Italians living here? Why only us?"

Tad reached for a chisel. "The FBI picked up some of them."

"But only some." Danny pulled out sandpaper from the supply cabinet. "You know the real reason—they're white and we're not."

Danny had a point. The Japanese were treated differently, but the government wasn't about to change its mind. "It's tough to make any sense of this, but we have to prove we're loyal Americans. Otherwise they might deport us to Japan."

"You're willing to risk your life for a country that treats you like trash? Are you nuts? If they send you to the Pacific, you'd be killing your own kind. And what about Lily? You're going to make her a widow?"

"If we fight for our country, maybe they'll treat us like full-fledged Americans."

"Fat chance that'll ever happen." Danny's eyes shot bullets at him. "We have a word for people like you—*inu*. I can't believe it. My own brother—a dog!" He kicked the door open and nearly knocked it off its hinges, then stomped out.

A lot of what he said made sense, but much of it was out of pure anger. A miter saw couldn't have cut deeper than Danny's words.

* * *

While waiting in line outside the dining hall, Tad's fingers and toes grew numb even with wool mittens and socks. After twenty minutes, he entered the building, relishing the warmer air inside. Toward the middle, about a dozen makeshift booths were erected with plywood and canvas.

Men were being called up one by one.

"Hey, Tad," a familiar voice called from behind.

He spun around to see his friend Bob Miyazaki from his high school gymnastics team.

Bob breezed up and excused himself with the people in line. "It's been a while since I've seen you in camp. How're Lily and your folks?"

"We're surviving. How are you?"

"Same here." Bob's eyes shifted to the booths. "What do you think about the government getting us to volunteer for the army?"

"The war's getting really bad in Europe and in the Pacific. Maybe they finally realized they need us."

"I don't mind doing my part, but what irks me is being confined in this scrubby sagebrush prison. If they let us return home, then I'll consider fighting."

"That's not going to happen."

"You're going to answer *yes* to those questions?"

"I think so."

Bob grimaced. "You'll regret it. They'll give you some crummy job in the army and won't respect you any more than they do now. If they send you into battle, you might end up dying for a country that doesn't care about you one iota."

If Tad got stuck with some meaningless job, at least he'd be serving his country and return home alive. "Nothing's going to change if we don't do something."

"Don't do it! We're trying to convince everyone to answer *no* to these questions. Then maybe they'll listen to us."

"I honestly don't think that's going to happen."

"I thought you were a friend." Bob's words sounded more like a snarl than a statement.

"Look, you make your decision, and I'll make mine."

Bob stalked away. He'd never been like that before. They used to hang out together. A lot had changed since those days.

A clerk called Tad into a room, where he took a seat across a table from a young brown-haired army officer.

The expressionless officer accepted the questionnaire from Tad. "We're going to skip to questions 27 and 28 first, then return to the other ones later."

Tad shifted in his chair. "Sir, I'd like to know what would happen if I answered *no* to either question."

"Answering *no* could result in renouncing your American citizenship, and you could be deported to Japan. Even if you're allowed to stay here, you'll probably be subject to prosecution under the provisions of the Selective Service Act."

"But don't you think it's a bit unreasonable for us to say *yes* when we've been denied our rights as American citizens?"

"The fact is, you people are a security risk. The—"

"Excuse me, but if we're a security risk, why are we being asked to serve in the army?"

"You didn't let me finish. When I said 'security risk,' I meant security and protection for you people."

Tad couldn't believe his ears. How could he address them as *you people!*

The officer's face softened. "I know it's not fair, but there's not a whole lot we can do about what's happened. But there's something you can do for the future of your people." The recruiter leaned forward. "Last month, President Roosevelt and top army brass authorized the creation of an all-Japanese-American combat unit. The official unit tag will be the 442nd Regimental Combat Team. They already formed a nucleus with a battalion out of Hawaii, but they're looking for volunteers from the mainland as well."

"Won't we get drafted into this unit anyway?"

"Eventually. But if you volunteer, you'll be proving your loyalty to America, and you'll be remembered for serving your country in a time of crisis."

Tad remained silent. The officer's words resonated with him, and he had been praying about this for the last several weeks.

"While you're thinking about that, let's move on to question 28. 'Will you swear unqualified allegiance to the United States and faithfully defend the United States from any or all attack by foreign or domestic forces, and forswear any form of allegiance or obedience to the Japanese emperor, or any other foreign government, power, or organization?' "

Tad pondered the question. "I've never had any allegiance to the emperor."

"So your answer to 28 is *yes*?"

He nodded.

"Okay, let's go back to question 27. Are you willing to serve in the armed forces of the United States on combat duty wherever ordered? What is your answer?"

"My answer is *yes*."

21

Ambition

Kumamoto, Japan

Hiroshi leaned back in his chair, tapping a pencil against his chin and pondered how he could advance his career. His boss, Captain Morita, sat across from him, puffing on a wood pipe and burying himself in a newspaper. Two of the captain's assistants sat next to him, one on each side.

Lieutenant Uchida, a young man with a pockmarked face, rose from his seat and leaned over. "Captain, let me refill your teacup."

Morita set the newspaper down and nodded.

The lieutenant returned and poured steaming hot tea for him. Before Uchida took his seat, the other assistant, Lieutenant Murakami, struck a match. "Captain, your pipe. I'll relight it."

Hiroshi wanted to vomit.

Uchida fanned the smoke away with the file he should have been working on.

Fools—all of them. Ruthless and tough *Kempeitai* officers but fools nevertheless.

Morita had bungled the raid on Matsumoto's secret prayer meeting in December, allowing nearly all the suspects to escape. The captain left the unfinished business of killing Matsumoto to Hiroshi, who had never killed anyone before.

While the thought of carrying out the execution initially struck him with fear, Hiroshi pulled the trigger like a dutiful soldier. But the captain didn't even give him a commendation like the other men who participated. The unfairness of it gnawed at Hiroshi's gut.

Uchida handed Morita a file. "Captain, this is worthy of your review."

Morita frowned at Uchida and opened the folder. "What's this? Seven draft evaders from the same high school?"

"Yes, they're all about eighteen or nineteen years old. They received draft notices a month ago, but they never showed up at the induction center."

Captain Morita threw the file on his desk. "Another bunch of cowards to chase down, as if we didn't have enough to do around here. We'll get to it later this week." He rose and put on his uniform cap. "How about lunch at Sumi's Cafe? Murakami, Uchida, let's go." He glanced at Hiroshi. "And you, Yamada, are you coming?"

"No thank you, Captain. I've got some errands to run during lunch and an appointment with city officials this afternoon."

"Suit yourself." Morita strode out with the other officers.

Hiroshi reached over to Morita's desk and lifted the file. He didn't fear Morita. Rumor had it that the prefecture commander wasn't happy with the captain and wanted to replace him. Perhaps this was the perfect opportunity to make a good impression on the commander.

While examining each of the profiles, Hiroshi jotted down pertinent information in his notebook and paid particular attention to Keiji Takano. After graduating from high school, Takano had worked at his uncle's shoe factory until a month ago, and then he vanished.

Top student . . . captain of the soccer team . . . led several student clubs . . . voted most popular in the senior class . . .

It surprised him that a boy like this would be a draft evader. He probably recruited the other young men involved.

Hiroshi snapped the folder shut. If he could crack this case and bring in Takano and his friends, the commander would surely put him in for a promotion. He donned his cap and hastened out the door.

At the shoe factory, Hiroshi interviewed several employees Keiji worked with, then inquired at his high school, and learned about the places the young man frequented. He followed up each lead but found nothing. Hiroshi reexamined his notes. There had to be some clue. Lieutenant Uchida had already questioned his parents, but they claimed they didn't know what happened to their son.

That night, Hiroshi hid inside a gateway of the house next to the Takano residence. Around midnight, he heard someone leaving the suspect's home. He poked his head around the gatepost. A woman carrying a large bundle hastened down the street. Hiroshi abandoned his observation post and followed at a safe distance.

Air raid wardens had the streetlights turned off and ordered everyone to drape windows with dark curtains. Even so, the moonlight reflecting off the white inner fabric bordering the collar of her dark kimono allowed Hiroshi to keep the woman within sight.

She swiftly turned her head in both directions and kept a steady pace up the inclines and down the slopes until she came to the entrance of Suizenji Park. She proceeded about a hundred meters along the perimeter, then turned and disappeared into the brush.

Hiroshi scurried forward and found the narrow opening in the thick foliage she had passed through. The passageway led to a clearing and a small wooden structure that looked like a temple. He had never seen this place despite his many visits to the park. Creeping behind a mulberry bush, Hiroshi spied on the woman who stood in front of the entrance.

She knocked on the door. "Keiji."

Hiroshi had found him. He strained to hear over the rhythmic cadences of frogs croaking and chirping crickets. He inched closer. The door squeaked open, and a young man appeared.

"I brought you some food to last a few days," she said. "I'll be going now." The woman turned to leave.

"Mother, is everything ready for tomorrow night?"

She looked back at her son. "Yes, Uncle will take you and the others to Morotsuka."

Hiroshi knew exactly where they were going—a small mountain village about one hundred kilometers to the east. These criminals would be difficult to track in such a remote area.

He pulled his pistol out of the holster and released the safety. A second later, he recalled some *Kempeitai* officers were attacked and severely injured in recent fugitive hunts. He'd get some help and return in the morning. Hiroshi secured the pistol, placed it back into his holster, and tiptoed away from his hiding place.

At five o'clock in the morning, he rousted six military policemen out of bed and marched them to the park as the faint pinkish glow of dawn appeared. They surrounded the temple grounds while he crouched behind the foliage. At Hiroshi's hand signal, the men advanced with bayonets affixed to their rifles. He followed behind them. A policeman kicked the door open and charged in.

Several young men were asleep on the floor. One officer trained his rifle on them. They woke up with bulging eyes and gaping mouths.

"Saburo, Keiji, run! It's the police," shouted one boy. A policeman clubbed him in the face with a nightstick, and he toppled over.

Within a few minutes, Hiroshi and his troops had rounded up all seven of them. "Corporal, take them outside and have them line up."

Hiroshi followed the prisoners, and two policemen carried the unconscious boy out. He sneered at the boys as he paced in front of them. "So, how did you think you could get away with it? We would catch you eventually."

The boys trembled and squirmed.

"You were called to fulfill your duty to the emperor and your country, but you shirked your responsibility." Hiroshi pointed his pistol in the air. "I could have you executed, but I will give you one chance. Reveal the names of the people involved in this escapade, and I will let you off with a light punishment and allow you to join the army." If he frightened them, they'd spew out the truth.

The youths looked at each other, and a few of them started crying. Another one spoke incoherent words.

Hiroshi approached the boy. "Yes? You're about to say something?"

"Shut up! Don't say anything," shouted a fellow on the end. A policeman punched him in the face.

"We're not playing games." Hiroshi stared at the others and cleared his throat. "I want an answer, and I want it now!"

The boy who had started to answer spoke up. "It's Keiji's uncle. He was going to take us to Morotsuka."

"Which one of you is Keiji Takano?"

The lad in the middle of the line held up his hand halfway. "I am."

Hiroshi scrutinized the tall, broad-shouldered youth. "I hold you responsible for convincing everyone here to run away. I'll see to it that your punishment is more severe than the others. Your mother and uncle will go to prison."

Keiji lowered his eyes and said nothing.

"What will happen to us?" asked the boy who had snitched. "Are you going to let us go?"

Hiroshi ignored him and sniffed. He turned to the squad leader. "Corporal, place these men under arrest."

The policemen bound the prisoners' hands, waist, and ankles with rope.

"You will be sent to the army induction center for immediate processing," Hiroshi said. "You will serve your country and emperor. If any one of you disobeys your commanders or shows cowardice, you will be executed and your families will be thrown into prison."

22

The Gift

Heart Mountain, Wyoming

Danny brushed another coat of varnish on the lid of the pine jewelry box he had been working on for the past few days. Placing his hands on the edges, he held it up to the light and checked for brush marks in the gleaming finish.

With a satisfied smile, he set it down on the workbench. He'd sand it down once more before giving it to Mary Wada for her eighteenth birthday this Thursday. She was ten months younger than Danny. Ever since he'd met her two months ago, he couldn't stop thinking about her. If he could make her his girl, he'd be content forever. A quick look at the wall clock told him he'd better get in line for lunch. He'd finish up later.

Inside the dining hall, Danny scanned the bustling room and spotted Mary in the far corner, sitting at a table with two girlfriends. She was laughing heartily about something, looking especially fetching with her silky hair swishing around. Every time he looked into her lovely, dove-shaped eyes, he'd melt. He headed toward her and cleared his throat to catch Mary's attention.

A bright smile broke out on her face. "Hi Danny. Grab a seat."

Mary's friends waved their good-byes and left the table.

"How are you doing, Mary?" Danny seated himself across from her and told himself he'd better not flub asking her to this Saturday's Starlight Dance and Ice Cream Social.

She beamed. "My brother told me you've been teaching him how to play football."

"He's learning how to run a double-reverse and rush . . ." Danny could see in her eyes that she was getting lost in the details.

"I appreciate you spending time with him. It's so sweet of you."

"Gary's a good athlete." Danny needed to stop stalling. "Um, Mary, I purchased tickets to this Saturday's dance. Will you come with me?"

Her smile faded. "I'm sorry, Danny. I have other plans." She opened her mouth as if she was about to say something but closed it.

Danny's hopes deflated like an inner tube with a gigantic hole. "Oh, I see." He mentally kicked himself for not asking her earlier.

She averted her eyes. "Maybe next time."

He nodded. If there'd ever be another one. Not knowing what else to say, he forced a smile and stood up. "I have to run. See ya." He walked away quickly without looking back.

* * *

On Thursday, the day of Mary's birthday, Danny's hopes buoyed again.

With a cerulean sky overhead, the head-like summit of Heart Mountain seemed to smile at him today. Maybe if he gave her the birthday present, she'd change her mind about Saturday and go out with him after all.

He searched all over camp for wrapping paper and a ribbon. But he could only find orange construction paper and brown twine in a classroom and used them to wrap her gift.

Danny wanted to take Mary somewhere special—somewhere they could be alone. But no such place existed. Tucking the gift under his arm, he headed toward the library where she'd recently started working as an assistant librarian.

Rounding the corner, Danny came to a sudden halt. In the distance, Mary was talking to some guy with his back toward him. His ears perked up, but he could only make out bits of what they were saying. Her animated facial gestures and hand movements told him she enjoyed this fellow's company. Danny retreated behind the corner of the nearest building and watched them. The guy shifted his weight and turned partially. *Mickey Ogasawara.*

Mickey was a year younger—same class as Mary. He remembered him from the varsity football team. Danny and the other first-string players barely paid attention to benchwarmers like Mickey, but the fellow played half-decent basketball. Mickey also served as the president of the honor society that Mary belonged to.

Danny's eyes focused on them ambling side by side, talking and laughing, toward the opposite side of the building, their silhouettes growing smaller in the distance.

Too restless to go home, Danny wandered aimlessly around camp for over an hour. Then he staggered into the deserted wood shop. He turned on the lights and tossed Mary's gift onto the nearest workbench like yesterday's newspaper. It slid across the surface and nearly toppled over. He wouldn't have cared if it had.

His hands clutched the edge of the workbench like a pair of vise grips. What did she see in that Mickey? Danny spun around, opened the tool chest drawer, and drew out a large claw hammer. With one crushing blow, he could transform the jewelry box into bits of scrap wood. He shuffled toward the gift and raised the hammer high.

Suddenly Mary's face appeared in his mind's eye, her eyes radiant with a luminous smile. He loosened his jaw and set the hammer down. Even though he no longer had a reason for giving her the gift, it'd be a shame to destroy it. With eyes moist with tears, a bitter sob escaped him.

After indulging in self-pity for a few minutes, he pulled himself together. No sense moping. He left the gift on the workbench, shut off the lights, and exited.

He dragged himself past the playground with his eyes focused on the ground. Boisterous chatter and shouts of boys broke out.

"Over here, over here."

"Get him."

Mary's brother came charging toward him to catch a pass. The football bounced off Gary's outstretched hands and tumbled end-over-end on the dusty field, stopping near Danny's feet. He bent down and picked up the ball. "Gary, keep your eyes on the ball and watch it all the way into your hands." He demonstrated the motion, then tossed the ball to Gary, who promptly raced back into the game.

"Hi, Danny."

He recognized Mary's voice and circled around. "Hi." Not wanting to talk to her, he turned his head and quickly looked away in Gary's direction.

"Thanks again for coaching him," she said.

Danny nodded. "I didn't see you come."

"I came to watch Gary play." She drew in a deep breath. "Danny, about the dance Saturday night—"

"You're going with Mickey, right?"

"No. Whatever gave you that idea?"

"You're not?" The tension in his shoulders relaxed a bit.

"No."

"I assumed—"

"He's just a friend." A mischievous smile formed on her face. "When you asked me out, I didn't have a chance to tell you the reason."

"Oh, sorry." Danny averted his eyes, a bit embarrassed.

"I promised some people I'd help out with the church welcome party. Some churches donated Bibles, hymn books, and even a piano. Afterward we're planning to bake cookies in the mess hall."

"I see. I didn't know you were active in church."

"Danny, I want to invite you to come this Sunday. We meet in the elementary school building at ten o'clock."

Back at Santa Anita, he had made it clear to his family that he never wanted to attend church again. He couldn't worship a God who allowed innocent people like them to suffer in these prison camps. Of all the girls who attracted him, he had to choose her.

"So, will you come?"

His mouth tightened. "Ah no. Uh maybe . . . um, all right." For Mary, he'd go to church, but he wouldn't make it a regular thing. Good thing he didn't smash the gift.

23

Unveiled

Kumamoto, Japan

Hiroshi strutted about town with his head held high, chit-chatting with merchants.

One merchant handed him an envelope and bowed low. "Lieutenant Yamada, here are some complimentary meal and drink tickets for you at Kumamoto's finest cabaret."

"Thank you." Hiroshi peeked inside the envelope and found a stack of yen bills under the tickets. A broad smile stretched across his face.

City officials bowed deferentially to him, and regular army officers stepped aside for him. All it took was scratching his neck with his forefinger, and nonchalantly pointing to the *Kempeitai* star emblem on the collar tab of his crisp uniform.

This morning, the important work of finding eligible men for the Imperial Japanese Army demanded his attention at the public records office. Hiroshi enjoyed his job because of the influence he had over people, and he wouldn't have to risk his life on the front lines.

"Good morning, Lieutenant Yamada," the young clerk said, showing him to the largest office in the building. "Here are the files you requested, including that special one."

"What took you so long?" Hiroshi snarled.

"I apologize, Lieutenant. It was misfiled."

"Don't ever let this happen again, or I'll talk to the manager about this." Hiroshi brusquely dismissed the clerk, then combed through the stack, searching for the file he was most interested in. Finding it at the bottom, he seized it and scrutinized his rival's profile.

Name:	Akira Omura
Date of Birth:	1916.05.07
Current job:	High school teacher
University:	Keijo Teachers College
High School:	Fukuoka First High School
Junior High School:	no record
Elementary School:	no record
Address:	5-2-2 Asaka-dori, Kumamoto City
Previous:	no record
Parents:	no record
Guardians:	Tetsuo Nakamoto (uncle, deceased)

So little information about Akira. This was inexcusable. If he could find the miserable clerk who had prepared this sparse entry, he'd make sure that person received discipline. Hiroshi examined the rest of the record, noting other bits of missing information, like his childhood medical and dental records.

Tomorrow he'd take a trip to Fukuoka, where Akira attended high school. He remembered the prefecture commander had several urgent dispatches that needed to be delivered to the Fukuoka *Kempeitai* office. Normally this duty would be given to an enlisted man, but all of them were out on special training.

What perfect timing. Perhaps he found another way to please the prefecture commander, Colonel Nakano, in addition to taking him out to Kumamoto's best *geisha* house that evening.

If Hiroshi could ingratiate himself like this, he'd replace Captain Morita in no time and work directly for the colonel.

After a night out with the colonel, Hiroshi returned home and staggered to the bathroom. He had a mild hangover from drinking *saké* and carousing with kimono-clad beauties.

He struck a match to light the kindling under the deep *ofuro* tub. Usually the maid heated the bath water, but she had left early. After steam started to rise, he scooped a bucketful of water and washed and rinsed himself outside the tub. Then he dipped himself into the steaming tub and soaked in the muscle-relaxing water. Tomorrow could prove to be an interesting day.

* * *

The cool drops of the morning rain invigorated Hiroshi as he strode to the train station.

He boarded a camouflaged train bound for Fukuoka and his uniform allowed him free access to a first-class compartment.

As he stared blankly at the countryside, Emiko's lovely form and face saturated his thoughts. With the disastrous engagement party and her father's death, he had given up hope of pursuing her—almost.

About three hours later he arrived at the bustling Hakata Station in Fukuoka. Hundreds of uniformed soldiers scurried about from platform to platform and climbed aboard trains.

Hiroshi hiked to the *Kempeitai* office and delivered the dispatches. There he hailed a taxi and rode to Fukuoka First High School. Once again his cab ride was free of charge.

Soon, he arrived at a large multistoried concrete building and entered through the main doors. Students crowded the hallways—boys in black uniforms and girls in white sailor tops with neckerchiefs and black skirts. This place reminded him of the high school where he used to teach.

Hiroshi stopped a student. "Where is the principal's office?"

The student pointed. "It's over there."

He made a beeline for it and knocked on the door.

"Come in."

He entered the small office and approached a middle-aged man seated behind a large desk. "Excuse me sir. I'm Lieutenant Hiroshi Yamada of the *Kempeitai*." He bowed.

The man froze for a moment, then rose from his chair and returned the bow. "I'm Sato, principal at this school. Please have a seat. What can I do for you?"

Hiroshi doffed his cap and placed it on the desk corner. "I'm running a background check on a former student, Akira Omura, who has applied for a government position. I believe he enrolled in this high school about ten years ago. Any transcripts and disciplinary records you have will be helpful."

Sato sat back, his brows knitted and his mouth half-opened. "This is highly unusual. In all my years as a school administrator, I've never had the *Kempeitai* pay a visit like this."

Hiroshi smiled. "It's for a sensitive and important position. I'm not at liberty to disclose its nature."

"Those records are archived, but I'll have someone retrieve it immediately." Mr. Sato summoned his secretary and gave her instructions.

While they waited, Hiroshi engaged in light conversation, mentioning he had been a teacher. He glanced at the obligatory wall portrait of the emperor and empress, and two paper banners hanging beside it with patriotic slogans: "Drive Out the Western Invaders!" and "Japan will never be defeated!"

After fifteen minutes, the secretary brought in a file.

Sato opened it and perused the papers inside. "Akira Omura. Matriculated in 1931. I see he was an excellent student. I don't see anything unusual."

"May I take a look?"

"Be my guest." Sato passed it across the desk to him.

Hiroshi studied the information. "Principal, there is no record of his junior high school and elementary school. Nor anything on his parents. Isn't that a bit unusual?"

"Our admissions policy has always placed a higher emphasis on the entrance examination than on the schools they attended. Regarding his parents, I don't know why there is no data."

Hiroshi squinted as he focused on the file. "Now this is strange. The record says Mr. Omura was placed in a remedial Japanese language class." He glanced at the principal. "Why would an excellent student be in such a class?"

"I'm sorry, but I'm at a loss as to why. Does the file say who the instructor was?"

"It says Shizue Yoshikawa."

"She still teaches here."

Hiroshi's head jerked up. "May I interview her?"

"Yes, of course. I believe she may be free now since it's lunch time. I'll escort you to her classroom."

They climbed the steps and ambled down a long corridor, passing more patriotic posters hanging on the walls. At the far end, Mr. Sato knocked on the door.

"Come in." Mrs. Yoshikawa sat at her desk inside the empty room with a stack of papers. She looked up through spectacles, her graying hair in a taut bun.

"Excuse me, Yoshikawa-sensei. A guest is here to see you."

The woman looked surprised momentarily, then she rose and bowed. "Please have a seat. How may I help you?"

Sato turned toward Hiroshi. "I'll be leaving now." He bowed.

"Sensei, I am Lieutenant Hiroshi Yamada of the Kumamoto *Kempeitai* office." He settled into a chair and put on his most charming smile. "If I may have a few minutes of your time, I'd like to ask you about a former student of yours from about ten years ago. His name is Akira Omura."

She sat back down and set her spectacles on the desk. "Oh, yes. I remember him well. What is this about? Is he in some kind of trouble?"

He waved his hand in a reassuring manner. "No, not at all. We're considering his application for a sensitive government post, and a background check is necessary."

She nodded and smiled. "I see. He was a fine young man. One of my best students."

Hiroshi leaned forward. "I see he was an excellent student, but why was he assigned to a remedial Japanese language class?"

"Akira quickly mastered the necessary language skills, and we sent him into the regular curriculum."

"But my question is why. After all, isn't it odd that such a student would be in a remedial class in the first place?"

"No, not at all for those children who came from America."

Hiroshi straightened. "He's from America?"

"Yes, there were quite a few *Kibei*, born in America and sent here to be educated. Some could hardly speak Japanese and were put in classes one or two grades behind. In Akira's case, he spoke Japanese well enough but had not learned the sophisticated nuances of a native speaker. He was bright and motivated. After a short time in the remedial class, we promoted him into the regular curriculum. Furthermore, he became the only student to skip a grade."

Hiroshi forced himself to keep his expression neutral. Akira never told him he was born in America. No wonder he seemed lukewarm about Japan's successes and reluctant about joining the *Kempeitai*.

It made sense. With the anti-American sentiments of the past decade in Japan, a *Kibei* like Akira would want his background concealed. The *Kempeitai* kept several *Kibei* families under constant surveillance. One more to add to the list.

He thanked Mrs. Yoshikawa for her time and caught a cab to the train station.

As he boarded the train, Hiroshi pondered the mystery he had unraveled. So Akira's an American. Everyone seemed to like him. He was the most popular teacher at Kumamoto Senior High School. Maybe he was an American spy.

* * *

Before sunrise, Akira rose from bed and slipped on his coat and boots. He went outside and sidled to the back corner of the apartment building. Carefully sliding his fingers under a loose plank, he extracted a paper note and dropped it into his coat pocket. After stepping back inside, he shuffled to his desk and switched on the small desk light that couldn't be seen through black air raid curtains.

He read the note. Dates of the prayer meetings were always communicated in this fashion—never by telephone or mail.

Ever since the Christmas party raid, they had started using code names. The watch on his desk that Papa gave him showed

4:30 in the morning. Since he was wide awake, he reached for his leather-bound Bible and read the book of 1 John.

After reading five chapters, Akira meditated on two verses: "God hath given to us eternal life, and this life is in his Son. He that hath the Son hath life; and he that hath not the Son of God hath not life." As a young boy, Mama had him memorize one verse weekly.

How he wished he could worship God freely as in America, where he made a decision to follow Jesus at age ten.

Kneeling down, he lowered his head and prayed. "Father God, I commit this day to you. Please watch over Emiko and everyone in our prayer group, and my family back home. Also I pray that the people of Japan will find you and know you, so they, too, can experience your love, hope and eternal life—"

A rap on the door shattered Akira's thoughts.

"Omura-sensei, it's me, Suzuki."

Akira rushed to the door. "Suzuki-sensei, what's wrong?"

"The *Kempeitai* arrested Yoshida-san late last night. His neighbor notified me."

Akira's heart seized like an engine running without oil. "What happened?"

"Don't know. It's probably due to his business dealings with Matsumoto-san."

The noose around the prayer group was gradually tightening.

24

The Dream

Heart Mountain, Wyoming – February 15, 1943

For the past three nights, Tad broke out in night sweats and had been losing sleep. Tonight was no different. He stared at the ceiling planks, then flipped onto his stomach in bed. Danny's syncopated snores, along with the neighbors', disrupted the stillness of the night, and Tad wished he could sleep as soundly. He rolled to his side.

"What's wrong, dear?" Lily whispered. She snuggled close to him.

His restlessness had awoken her. Should he tell her? He had to at some point, but he'd been looking for the right time. They scooted up in their bed—not a true bed but two cots shoved together. Lily pulled the blankets over her shoulders.

Tad wrapped his arm around her. "This is going to sound crazy, but I've had the same dream for the past three nights. I keep dreaming about Moses like in the book of Exodus."

"Moses?"

"Yeah, I hear God calling, 'Moses, Moses, I am sending you to Pharaoh to bring my people out of Egypt.' Then I see myself in his place, leading a group of people, and they look Japanese."

"We're not Israelites, and we're certainly not in Egypt. What do you think it means?"

Tad released his arm around her. "We're held captive like them." He didn't know quite how to tell her. "You know I answered *yes* to the two loyalty questions, don't you?"

"You told me."

The next words were difficult. "It means—I'll be joining the army."

She gasped. "You didn't tell me that. How could you?"

"Lily—"

"No, please don't go. I don't want you to leave me. What if you get killed or injured?" Her tears seeped through his pajamas to his chest.

"I think it's the only way to gain respect from our government, so they'll treat us like Americans."

"Why do you have to go? Why can't some of the single men go?" Lily placed her hands over her face and wept.

He feared this would happen. If anything could break his heart, it was seeing Lily suffer.

"Are you people still up?" His mother's voice sounded from the other side of the sheet partition.

* * *

The next morning, hail mixed with sleet pelted Tad's ears and face as he left the administration building after examining the job billets. Once again, he found nothing. He passed the dry goods store toward his barrack. Every step became heavier as mud stuck to his boots. Soon, the hail and sleet subsided.

A short, stocky Nisei man moved toward Tad, and another Nisei, tall and slim, closed in from a perpendicular direction. A third man with a scar across his cheek came from behind.

The first man stuffed his hands inside his coat pockets and asked, "You're Tad Omura?"

"Yeah." The way they cornered him made him uneasy.

The slim man hooded his eyes. "We heard you answered *yes* to those questions."

"So what if I did?" Tad was taken aback. He hadn't told anybody besides his family and high school friend Bob Miyazaki.

"You shouldn't have done that." Scarface lit a cigarette and threw the match on the wet, snowy ground where it fizzed out.

"That's none of your business. Besides, who told you?"

"Word gets around," the stocky man answered. "We're trying to get all the men to say *no*, so the government will leave us alone. Go back and tell them you're changing your answer to *no*."

He didn't want a fight, but he feared he didn't have a choice. Tad looked around, but no other people were in sight. He could take any one of them, but not all three.

The slim man cocked his head. "You think it's right that they throw us in prison and now they want us to fight their war?"

"No, it isn't right. Nor is it right for you to tell me what to do."

"We all have to be in this together," Slim said. "Otherwise, the government isn't going to listen."

"Do you think they're going to listen if we all answer *no?*" Tad sidestepped around Slim but Scarface blocked his path.

"Where do you think you're going? We're not done talking."

"Look, you have a right to your opinion, and I have mine. Now move out of my way!"

"*Inu!* You stinking traitor!" Scarface shoved Tad on his shoulder and spun him around, then pushed him to the ground.

Tad recoiled to his feet, his fists held high. Somebody rabbit-punched him on the back of his neck, and he whirled around and connected with an uppercut to the left side of his attacker's face. The contact with the man's jawbone stung Tad's knuckles.

Scarface tackled Tad around the ankles, sending him into the muddy ground again.

Tad fought off kicks and punches with his legs and rolled to his knees. His back exploded with pain, and he turned around to see the slim man rearing back with a large wood stick aimed at his head.

Someone grabbed the man with the stick and threw him down. "Get off him!" It was Danny.

Slim peeled himself off the ground. "Hey, what are you doing?"

"Lay off him. He's my brother."

The stocky man faced Danny. "Your brother? Why is he supporting the *Hakujin*?"

Danny shoved the stocky man away from Tad. "You guys clear out!" As the three men left, Danny extended his hand to Tad, who lay on the ground. "You okay?"

"Yeah." Tad pulled himself up with Danny's help. Panting heavily, he rested on his brother's shoulder until his breath returned to normal. "Thanks for your help." He hobbled alongside Danny toward their barrack. "What are you doing hanging out with those thugs?"

"They're not thugs."

"Could've fooled me."

"Be careful from now on. I may not be around to help you next time," Danny said. "How're you going to explain this to Lily?"

Tad rolled his tongue inside his aching cheek. She was already upset about his enlistment. This incident was bound to cause her more anxiety. "Don't worry about Lily. I'll figure something out, but let me do the talking."

"Whatever you say, big brother."

* * *

Lily gasped when Tad entered through the door. Droplets of blood leaked out of Tad's nose and his swollen lip. She rushed toward him and assisted him into a chair. "What happened to you?"

"Three guys jumped him outside of Block 15." Danny flung his cap on his cot. "They didn't like the way he answered the loyalty oath questions."

She shot a look at Danny. "So, they beat him up on account of that?" While she knew his answers wouldn't be popular, she couldn't imagine something like this happening.

Tad gave Lily a wry smile. "I'm okay."

"You always say you're okay, even when you're hurt." Lily helped him out of his mud-splotched coat. Then she poured water from a pitcher into a bowl and added a shot of rubbing alcohol. She opened the storage chest, pulled out a clean hand towel, and dipped it into the water. Then she gently dabbed the welts and cuts on his face.

"Ow!" Tad grimaced and jerked his head away.

Who would do this to her husband? She glared at Danny again. "Did you know them?"

"I've seen them at the meetings."

"And you didn't stop them—"

"Honey, Danny broke up the fight and told those guys to scram."

"I'm sorry, Danny. Thank you for helping Tad." Lily finished cleaning Tad's wounds and carried the basin to the door to empty the water outside. She returned and took a seat on the cot. "Danny, can you fill up this pitcher on your way back tonight?"

"Sure."

Moments later, Mama came in through the door. Her forehead creased with wrinkles, and her mouth formed an oval when she saw Tad's face. "*Ittai, nani ga okotta no ka?*"

Before he could answer, Lily explained to her mother-in-law what had happened.

Mama fixed her gaze at Tad. "I don't understand why you want to join the army. What would happen to Lily if you die or become crippled?"

"If I fight for America, then maybe they'll start to treat us like Americans."

Danny harrumphed. "Yeah, sure. If you want to keep kidding yourself, go ahead." He rose from his chair, grabbed the empty pitcher, and plopped on his hat. "I'll see you later."

Tad rotated in his chair toward the door. "Hey, thanks for your help today."

Danny's mouth formed a crooked half-smile as he left.

"Mama, I don't want Tad to go either." Lily choked out a sob. "If anything should happen to him, I don't know what I'd do. But I pondered and prayed about Tad's dream."

"What dream?"

Lily explained the dream and what it might mean.

Mama turned her attention toward Tad. "You had the same dream three nights in a row?"

"Yeah. It was really strange."

Mama's face crinkled and a dull glaze covered her eyes. "What will happen if you change your mind?"

"The recruiter told me I could get drafted anyway."

"If you feel God calling you into the army, I can't stop you," Mama said. "Pray about it some more and do what God wants."

Lily looked into Tad's eyes. "If only you could prove your loyalty another way. But if God called you to go, who am I to say you can't?" Her voice started to crack. "Maybe you're meant to lead your people to freedom."

* * *

The cot squeaked, and Lily opened her eyes. The faint light of the outdoor lamp seeped through the curtains, illuminating the alarm clock that showed quarter to three in the morning. That dreadful day had finally arrived. Angst stabbed her in the heart as she longed to cling to her husband and never let go.

Tad threw on his shirt and slipped into his trousers. He reached under his cot and pulled out his duffel bag.

She sat up and tucked the covers to her chin.

"I'm sorry. I didn't mean to wake you," Tad whispered.

"You didn't wake me. I couldn't sleep."

He sat on the bed, cuddled next to her, and gently kissed her. "I love you, sweetheart. Don't ever forget that."

"I love you too."

"Tell Mama and Danny good-bye for me."

Tad made her promise not to tell anyone when he was leaving. Lily hated to be so secretive, but it was better this way. She didn't want him to have any more trouble with the "No-No Boys"—men who answered *no* to the two loyalty questions. It made her laugh the first time she heard the nickname—but it was no longer funny. They meant business, and news of escalating violence circulated throughout the camp.

Lily pressed her head against Tad's heart and gripped his hand, unsure of whether she could let go. She couldn't keep him from going, especially if God called him.

"Oh, dear Lord," she prayed softly, "please go with my husband. Give him the same protection you promised Jabez. Have your hand upon him and keep him from harm so he will be free from pain." Lily had come across this prayer yesterday in 1 Chronicles. It seemed to fit. Her tears turned cold in the freezing barrack.

"Jesus, please look after Lily while I'm gone. Be her husband in my place. Strengthen her and encourage her. Keep her healthy, and watch over our families. Thank you, Lord."

They unlocked their embrace, and she cupped her hands around his face. "Promise me one thing."

"What's that?"

"That you'll return to me when it's over."

"I will."

After one last kiss and hug, Tad slipped out into the cold night.

25

Treachery

Kumamoto, Japan – April 20, 1943

Hiroshi tossed Akira's dossier on his desk after scrutinizing it again for any bit of incriminating information. Ever since he discovered Akira's American origin, he had every reason to be suspicious of him. But to implicate him as a disloyal dissident, or better yet, as a spy, he needed solid evidence.

The telephone rang, and he snatched up the receiver after the first ring. "What's the situation?"

"Lieutenant, the suspect has left his apartment."

"I'll be there shortly. Which way is he headed?"

"Toward the main street."

"Follow him, and don't lose sight of him." Hiroshi donned his cap and stalked out of his office. Finally, he could take some action instead of stewing behind his desk. A thorough search of Akira's apartment could reveal some proof he could use against him.

Outside Akira's flat, Hiroshi looked side to side to make sure no one was watching. Then he reached into his trouser pocket and pulled out a penknife to jimmy the lock. He inserted the blade into the keyhole and jiggled it until the tumblers clicked. Grabbing the handle, he pushed the door open.

Stepping into the small apartment, he glanced around at the tidy room and stepped toward a desk with sheets of paper piled on top. He flipped through mail and student essays. Nothing. A thick, black book on the corner of the desk caught his eye. He lifted it and read the cover: *The Holy Bible*. Hiroshi had heard about this book but knew nothing about it. Cracking it open, he started to peruse it. He snapped it shut and gazed at the front cover again. Was Akira a Christian?

Strictly speaking, Christianity wasn't illegal. His colleagues in the *Kempeitai* office watched a few authorized Christian churches in the area closely. The government allowed them as long as the members revered the emperor as the supreme god. However, renegade groups like Matsumoto's that refused to accept the emperor's ultimate divinity had to be stamped out.

He set the Bible down on the desk and moved toward a bookcase across the room. Maybe it would yield something of interest. After scanning scores of history and literature textbooks, he searched other books and periodicals. Not a shred of evidence. There had to be something he could use that would ensure Akira's execution with his name blotted out with shame and disgrace forever.

Of course, he would be careful not to implicate himself in the arrest or execution. Then he could slowly try to get back into Emiko's life, showing kindness in her time of grief. He could ply her with extra food rations and gifts.

Frustration mounted inside him, and his temples throbbed. His eyes settled on the Bible again, and he returned to the desk. Hiroshi lifted the book, held it above his head, and riffled through the pages. A piece of paper fluttered to the floor. He stooped down and picked it up.

DECEMBER 25. MATSUMOTO. 8:00 PM.

His eyes bulged, and his heart pulsated. "Got him!" It had to be the same Matsumoto whose house they raided last year. If Captain Morita hadn't botched up the operation and sent men to cover the rear of the house, they could have caught all the attendees. This new discovery changed everything. Akira could be one of those radical Christians, which would be grounds to have him arrested for treason.

Hiroshi's jaw relaxed into a broad smile. Tapping his fingers on the desk, he contemplated his next move. The only wrinkle would be Emiko. She would never forgive him if she found out he was behind it. That meant he would have to forgo the pleasure of arresting Akira himself. Another officer could do that part as long as Hiroshi planned every detail. He could offer Emiko comfort after Akira's arrest. Yes, that would work even better.

Running his finger down the spine of the book, Hiroshi considered Emiko's possible reactions. Surely she couldn't be a Christian too. He had seen her at the Fujisaki Hachimangu shrine earlier last year, praying to a Shinto god, like any good Japanese person. At any rate, he wouldn't worry about that right now.

Hiroshi placed everything back exactly where he found it, but he kept the meeting note as evidence. He engaged the lock on the door handle and closed it behind him.

Revenge would certainly be sweet.

26

Kotonk

Camp Shelby, Mississippi – June 6, 1943

The scorching Mississippi sun beat down on Tad's back as he
sauntered toward his barrack to take a quick shower during
his afternoon break from medic training. His shirt, moist with
sweat, clung to his body in the sweltering heat. Around the
corner, a large circle of boisterous Nisei soldiers yelled, cussed,
and crowded around two shirtless combatants.

Private Okimoto, a wiry and muscular Hawaiian, raised and
shook his dukes at Private Ikeda, who hailed from Sacramento.
Ikeda, a slightly taller and huskier man, circled around Okimoto
and spit on the ground.

The Hawaiian lowered his suntanned shoulder and lunged
into Ikeda's midsection.

With raised fists, the mainlander pounded Okimoto's back
and neck like a drummer in a swing band.

"You stinkin' *kotonk!* You tink you mo betta den us!"
Okimoto whirled around and threw him.

Ikeda wobbled backward but quickly caught his balance.
"We are better than you! You dumb pineapple!"

Charging toward Ikeda, the young Hawaiian took him down
and landed some hard punches into Ikeda's side.

Ikeda laid his knee into Okimoto's chin and pushed off.

The spectators joined the fracas, Hawaiians pairing up
against mainlanders with fists flying and a lot of shoving,
grappling, and grunting. Tad dropped his medical kit and double-

timed toward the group. He jumped in to pull the brawlers apart but only succeeded in catching a few body punches. This senseless violence had to stop.

A whistle shrilled above the din, signaling the arrival of the military police. The MPs waded into the crowd swinging nightsticks. "Break it up! Break it up!" Sergeant Williams bellowed. "Hawaiians gather on my right. Mainlanders to my left. Now!"

Men crisscrossed and scrambled to their sides. Others limped a few steps over with blood dripping from noses and cut lips.

With a beet-red face, the sergeant paced between the two groups, slapping his baton repeatedly into his hand. "When are you Japs going to learn to get along? How are you going to fight real Japs, or the Nazis, if you can't stop fighting among yourselves?"

Japs? Real Japs? Tad and the other Nisei turned their bristling faces at the military police. In the electrified air around them, the Nisei and the MPs eyed each other.

The sergeant was right. A verse echoed inside Tad. "Every kingdom divided against itself is brought to desolation; and every city or house divided against itself shall not stand."

"Okay, fun time is over. If it were up to me, I'd haul all of you into the stockade, but the colonel wants you to work things out among yourselves. So cool off!" Sergeant Williams clipped his nightstick to his belt and looked at Tad. "Medic, take care of the injured."

Tad was training to treat bullet and shrapnel wounds, but this afternoon, he'd be fixing broken noses and bandaging scraped knuckles.

* * *

Later that evening, Tad entered the recreation hall and picked up a paddle to play table tennis with a fellow medic trainee, Jim Hori. After twenty minutes of whacking the ball vigorously back and forth, they each won a match. In the rubber match, Jim won a string of three points to take the lead. He delivered a hard-spinning serve, and Tad, determined not to lose, successfully returned it. Following a wild flurry of rallying across the net, Jim slammed a low top-spin shot past Tad.

"Good match, Jim. You got me." Tad grabbed a towel from a stack nearby.

"You put up a good fight for an old man."

"Hey, twenty-three isn't that old. I'm just one year older than you." Tad chuckled.

"I'll be back in a minute." Jim left the area.

Tad began to make his way toward the water fountain.

A guy wearing an Aloha shirt called out to him, "Heh, wanna cum play crap wit us?" Three other Hawaiians were sitting down, tossing dice next to him, bantering rapidly in pidgin—their fists clenched with wads of greenbacks.

Tad faced the Hawaiian. "No thanks."

"What, you no like play crap?" said another guy who peeled off a few bills after throwing the dice.

"No."

The Aloha-shirt guy stood up and cocked his head. "You no like us?"

"Yes—I mean, no." A minute went by.

"What wrong wit you, man?"

"Nothing's wrong with me. I just don't want to play." Tad didn't want the situation to turn ugly. He wasn't about to gamble away his hard-earned, GI wage of $21 a month—not when he sent a good portion of it back to Lily and his family at Heart Mountain. They needed money to buy household items and other necessities.

Jim returned and came alongside Tad. He flashed a big smile at the Hawaiians. "Hey boys, my friend Tad—" He pointed his index finger at his temple and made a spiral motion.

The Hawaiians busted up laughing. "Aw! Lev'um alone. He just one more *kotonk,*" the first Hawaiian said. They continued on with their craps game.

"What did you do? Tell them I'm crazy?"

"Look, there's four of them and only two of us."

Tad shook his head. "Let's get some water." On the way to the fountain he asked, "What's a *kotonk*?"

"It's the sound a hollow coconut shell makes when it drops on the ground. The Hawaiian kids who live in LA call us that, because they think we have hollow heads."

"Half the time, I can't figure out what they're saying."

"Pidgin's like a combination of English, Japanese, Chinese, Polynesian, and maybe some Portuguese. The Hawaiians think we speak English too well and we're uppity, and we think they're speaking pidgin to exclude us, but that's just how they talk."

"The government only locked up a few Japanese people in Hawaii," Tad said.

"That's 'cause there's too many of them. Their economy would collapse."

"So that's why they could gamble their money away." Tad earnestly hoped for a quick resolution between the warring groups.

27

The Proposal

Kumamoto, Japan – June 12, 1943

Akira scampered down the park path while gradually letting out kite string. A spring breeze cooled his face, and he lifted his head to watch the red and gold *koi*-shaped kite climb higher and higher into the incandescent sky. It had been a long time since he'd flown one, the last time about ten years ago on Boys' Day.

His pulse pounded in his ears. He couldn't remember when he'd been so nervous. Eight months had passed since Emiko's father died. He hoped she'd be ready for what he wanted to say to her. Good thing he arrived at the rendezvous site before her.

"Akira-san, Akira-san."

He glanced in the direction of her voice and observed Emiko gazing at the kite with a cheerful grin.

"You're always full of surprises. I never expected to see you flying a kite."

"Why not? I thought it would be fun."

"But you're wearing such a nice suit and tie. It's such an odd combination."

"Emiko-san, look at the kite and read what it says." He lowered the flapping fish kite to make the painted words more readable.

Her eyes traveled skyward and she mouthed, "Please marry me!" She gasped and embraced him, placing her head against his chest. "Oh, Akira-san!"

"Emiko-san, I love you, and I want to spend the rest of my life with you."

A smile that could brighten the darkest night stretched across her face. "Darling, nothing would make me happier than to become your wife."

His passion shot through the clouds. He twirled the kite and held it against the wind. With his free hand, he reached into his suit pocket and retrieved a little box. "Emiko-san, please accept this humble gift as a token of my love for you."

"You have a gift for me?" She opened the little box and gasped. Her eyes grew wide. "It's beautiful!" She pulled out a silver band with a mounted Mikimoto pearl and slid it on her ring finger. "I love it!"

"I'm sorry, it's not a gold ring with a diamond, but it's the best I can do for now."

"Akira-san, thank you so much. I know the government forbids the sale of fine jewelry because of the war. I'm surprised you were able to purchase this lovely ring. I'll treasure this for as long as I live."

"You probably shouldn't wear this ring in public or the police might confiscate it."

"I'll only wear it inside the house." She held up her hand, admiring the ring, then she carefully placed it back into the box. "Do you remember when we were standing right here and you made a heart with cherry blossoms?"

He grinned. "Of course, I remember. That was about a year ago."

"I remember that day like it was yesterday."

As the wind dwindled, the kite began to descend near some trees. "Ah, excuse me." He sprinted toward it to keep the kite from getting tangled in the branches.

Out of nowhere, a squad of *Kempeitai* policemen surrounded him with guns drawn.

"What's going on here?" Akira spun around.

Emiko scurried toward him, but a policeman blocked her path.

The commander aimed stern eyes at him. "Akira Omura, I hereby place you under arrest for treason against the emperor."

"Treason? What have I done?" He looked side to side, not comprehending his sudden predicament.

"There is evidence linking you to a radical religious group."

"What are you talking about?"

"We have reason to believe you attended the subversive Christian meetings at Yasuo Matsumoto's house. This group is bent toward the overthrow of the emperor."

Memories of that terrible night flooded his mind as he struggled to keep his face impassive. Matsumoto would never have been involved with plotting treason. He didn't want to say anything that would implicate Emiko, so he kept his mouth shut.

The officer pulled a white cord from his pocket. "Put your hands in front of you."

Akira dropped the kite spindle, and the fluttering kite caught the branches of a tree. He glanced at Emiko, who looked as though someone had stabbed her in the heart. His spirit plummeted like the kite that had fallen from high in the sky. This wasn't how the day was supposed to turn out. They should have been celebrating.

The officer tightened the cord around his wrists and gestured to the troops. "Let's go."

Emiko's safety was his number one concern, but now, he stood absolutely helpless. Guards held her back as she cried out to him. He craned his neck for one last look at her, stretching his roped hands toward her while the police dragged him away.

A strong gust released the kite from the branches and swept it higher and higher until it disappeared.

28

Reconciliation

Camp Shelby, Mississippi – July 14, 1943

Tad had taken only two bites of his lunch when the sergeant yelled, "At-ten-hut!" Immediately Tad and the soldiers around him stood to attention.

With piercing eyes set below knitted brows and a wide forehead, Lieutenant Colonel Melton stepped through the front entrance, exuding an air of command and control. "At ease, gentlemen."

Soldiers relaxed their stances and clasped their hands behind their backs.

"Starting tomorrow morning at 0-600 hours, men of Hawaiian origin will be visiting the War Relocation Authority camps in Arkansas, either at Rohwer or Jerome. Mainlanders with relatives in either camp will also be allowed to attend." The lieutenant colonel cleared his throat. "You'll spend the day observing a camp and return in the evening. Your company commanders will have the specific assignments, and you'll report to the assembly area near the entrance."

The Hawaiians looked at each other puzzled.

"Any questions?"

Private Okimoto raised his hand.

"Yes, Private."

"How cum we gotta go, but mos' mainland boys no need go?"

A murmur echoed in the assembled crowd.

Melton waited until they settled down. "It's because most of them are from the camps. The Hawaiians need to understand the mainlanders better. But let me make one thing very clear. Colonel Perry expects everyone to behave like gentlemen. One report of misconduct, and you'll all be denied weekend passes for the next two months. Clear?"

"Yes, sir," they answered. Everyone stood to attention until Melton left.

Tad sat down, and Chaplain Yukawa grabbed a seat next to him. Tad let out a smile. "What a great idea."

The hulking thirty-year-old chaplain chuckled. "Actually, I passed the idea up the line through my company commander after praying for a resolution between the quarreling groups. One day, it just came to me. I believe God gave me the idea."

"It's brilliant." Tad forked a cold slice of ham and chewed.

"My commander wants me to go tomorrow and asked me to bring a few trusted men to keep an eye on things. Why don't you come?"

"Sure," Tad said. "I'll be there bright and early."

The following morning, the golden sun peeked over the horizon. The Hawaiians hopped on board the convoy of buses with their ukuleles and guitars.

During the four-and-a-half-hour ride north along the US Highway 65, the rambunctious Hawaiians laughed and talked boisterously, and some strummed their instruments. Tak Nakada from Hilo belted out a rendition of the popular "Song of the Islands" in his fine tenor voice.

A couple of Hawaiians next to Tad chatted.

"Dem mainland girls, dey pretty, eh?"

"Some, dey okay."

"No can wait."

The music and casual banter stopped as the buses lumbered up the bumpy gravel road to the entrance of an isolated, swampy marshland near the Mississippi River. Jerome looked a lot like Heart Mountain, with a high barbed-wire fence and watchtowers looming above the enclosure.

Rows of long barracks covered in black-tar paper and unpaved grounds also reminded Tad of Heart Mountain. But the sticky-hot weather differed from the drier climate of Wyoming, and the spiny holly trees with clotheslines strung between them sharply contrasted with Wyoming's desolate scenery.

The Hawaiians eyes widened as they stepped off the bus. Unsmiling Caucasian guards kept watch over the residents.

At the entrance, a welcoming committee greeted the troops. Joe Sakamoto and a young woman led them on a tour. They first visited the living quarters of Sam Takahashi.

"Please come inside," Sam said, holding the door open.

White sheets draped over clotheslines, dividing the room into miniature sections. The Hawaiians whispered among themselves and pointed at the tiny room.

"How many stay in dis room?" Private Okimoto asked, fanning away buzzing mosquitoes.

"My son, his wife and two children, and me and my wife. Six of us. Twelve families live in one barrack," he said.

Next, the tour guides bypassed the line for the latrine. It consisted of a row of toilets placed about two feet apart with no partitions.

At the communal shower room, an eight-by-ten concrete slab held eight nozzles with no dividers or curtains.

The Hawaiians emerged from the facilities with long faces.

Pangs of loneliness rippled through Tad's chest as he wondered how Lily and his family were faring. He couldn't wait to see them during his furlough, but that wouldn't be for a while. The look she gave him before he left continued to haunt him.

The group sauntered across the camp, taking in the sights.

"Watch out for the snake!" shouted the tour guide.

A Hawaiian soldier jumped back after nearly stepping on it. Other Hawaiians and Tad quickly moved away from it.

"That's a coral snake—very poisonous," Joe Sakamoto said. "You can tell by their red, black, and yellow colors. Good thing it didn't bite or you'd be dead in a few minutes."

The Hawaiian looked as though he had seen a ghost.

Joe Sakamoto, the tour guide, stepped away to a nearby storage shed, then returned with a hoe. He hacked the snake several times, and the reptile continued to convulse even after being struck.

A young woman who accompanied the group grimaced. "They better not put snake on the menu again."

"It's not that bad. Tastes like chicken." Joe chuckled and turned toward the guests. "This camp was the last to open. It's in the flood zone of the delta and water had to be pumped out. This past winter, we've had heavy rains and flooding so there's a lot of snakes, chiggers, and mosquitoes."

"What are chiggers?" Tad asked.

"They're tiny red bugs—young mites. When they bite, they leave reddish spots like mosquitoes, but itch far worse."

At noon, the guests were ushered into a large mess hall. Ribbons and flowers made of colorful paper decorated the walls.

The hostesses adorned themselves in pretty dresses or pleated skirts with matching blouses and faces made up with rouge and bright red lipstick. Even in the midst of war, some things remained the same.

Servers carried trays of *musubi* rice balls with spam to tables along the wall. The aroma of barbeque chicken wafted in the air.

Men scrambled to the buffet line with their mouths watering, after eating months of tasteless army food.

Tad made a plate and sat with Chaplain Yukawa. "Wow! We never had a treat like this when I was at Heart Mountain." He sank his teeth into a crunchy potato croquette. "The food's delicious."

"It is. I like how the rice is cooked so perfectly, Japanese-style—not like the way army cooks make it." Yukawa called out to a hostess. "Hey, make yourself a plate and eat."

"The food is for you." The girl averted her eyes.

Yukawa lowered his chopsticks. "You can eat too."

"There isn't enough for everyone," she answered. "We saved our rations for you."

"You don't have enough for yourselves?" Yukawa asked.

Tad stopped in mid-chew. Other Hawaiians who heard the comment all froze. A murmur spread among the guests, and even the big eaters began to refrain from taking too much food.

"Why aren't you eating?" asked Joe Sakamoto.

"We neva know you saved dis food fo us," a Hawaiian said. "Tell everybody cum eat."

"No," Sakamoto said. "You boys are serving our country and making us very proud. We wanted to give you this party."

The Hawaiians waved the hosts and hostesses over. "Cum eat."

But the camp people refused.

"Look, our ladies spent hours preparing this lunch," Joe said with exasperation. "We're insulted that you're not eating."

Hearing this comment, the men resumed eating, but in a quieter, more sedate manner.

After lunch the guests mingled with the residents. Tad wandered around the mess hall. The interaction with the internees seemed to have a warming effect on the soldiers.

In the late afternoon, the hosts cleared the tables and made space for a dance floor. A teenage boy placed a 78-rpm record on the phonograph turntable and flipped the switch on. He gently set the needle onto the spinning record, and the soothing tones of Glenn Miller's "Moonlight Serenade" permeated the room.

Some Hawaiians struck up conversations with the hostesses, and a few couples took to the dance floor. The usually raucous Hawaiians seemed subdued even when the livelier songs, like "In the Mood" and "Chattanooga Choo Choo" played.

Private Okimoto and his partner glided over the dance floor in a foxtrot step. The roughneck was surprisingly a good dancer. His equally graceful partner resembled Lily in many ways—her slender figure, hair parted smoothly on top with long straight tresses to her shoulders, but it wasn't Lily. How he missed her.

At 7:00 in the evening, the men thanked their gracious hosts and hostesses and bid them farewell. They piled back onto the buses and took one last look at the incarcerated people. The convoy trundled southward on the highway toward the state line.

Tad noted a real contrast between the rides to and from Jerome. The young men who were so boisterous in the morning spoke that evening in hushed tones.

"I no can believe they live like dat," one Hawaiian said.

"Yeah, was like one big prison," said another.

"Da mainland boys . . . dey came from camps like dis?"

"Boy, I wonda if I would have joined up if my family was locked up like dat."

Deep in thought, Tad settled back in his seat. Hopefully the Hawaiians understood the mainlanders better now, and the 442nd Regimental Combat Team could truly gel into one harmonious unit.

29

Tribulation

Kumamoto, Japan

A hard fist whacked Akira's mouth like a brick and yanked his head as he sat tied to a chair with cords. Savage pain racked his jaw as he turned toward his tormentor.

The burly *Kempeitai* lieutenant who struck him glared at him. "Omura, if you don't want any more beatings, tell us the names of all the people who attended Matsumoto's party on December 25."

Akira remained tightlipped as warm blood dribbled down his chin.

"Why don't you talk? Do you want to spend the rest of your life in prison?"

No matter what happened, Akira couldn't divulge the names—especially not Emiko's. For all he knew, she might be detained in a similar jail for women.

The lieutenant smashed another punch to Akira's face, and everything around him blackened. Then the splash of cold water jarred him to consciousness. He hung his head and wouldn't talk.

"It's no good. Take this traitor back to his cell."

Two men picked Akira up and draped him over their shoulders. They dragged him along the hallway, opened the cell door, and threw him on the floor.

Faint light poured in through the small window of the dark cell. His face throbbed and stung as through it had been pounded with a meat tenderizer. He dragged himself to the back wall, where he made out the silhouette of his cellmate leaning against the corner.

"They beat you again?" Professor Kawabe whispered.

He nodded.

"Lieutenant Uchida does that to everyone the first two weeks, especially if you don't confess."

When they first met, Kawabe told him he had been a philosophy professor at Kyushu University. When relations between Japan and the United States started to deteriorate, the professor tried to publish articles in a Kumamoto newspaper, criticizing Japan's aggressive military stance and petitioning the government to pursue negotiations. That's when the *Kempeitai* arrested him.

Akira's thoughts drifted back to his arrest. Did Yoshida cave under pressure after his arrest? And if he did, was Emiko taken into custody? God forbid. If anything happened to his beloved, he wouldn't be able to live with himself.

* * *

Emiko fell to her knees and cried bitterly, as she often did ever since Akira's arrest. She had heard nothing about his fate, and her phone calls to every police precinct in Kumamoto had been fruitless. He might have been taken outside the city, but where?

The one person who might be able to help, Hiroshi Yamada, was someone she'd never ask, especially if that monster killed Mr. Matsumoto. She'd rather be dead than ask him. No, she'd find another way.

She clasped her hands and prayed. "Sweet Jesus, I'm consumed with grief and fear. Life is so hard, and I'm so afraid for my Akira-san." Her voice cracked. "Please give me courage and help me to find him."

After pouring her heart out, she wiped away her tears. Golden sunrays streamed through the window. A thought came to her.

She shuffled to the desk and dialed the phone number of one of her *ikebana* students. "*Moshi, moshi*, Mrs. Katsumoto. This is Emiko Takata."

"Ah, Takata-*sensei*, what a pleasant surprise. How are you doing, dear?"

"I've been fine." Emiko tried to mask her true feelings. "How are you?"

"Are you going to put on any floral exhibitions soon? I'd like to participate."

"I'm sorry. I'm rather busy with personal matters, but I'll keep you informed." Emiko paused, trying to figure out how to ask the next question. "Mrs. Katsumoto, I need to ask you for a favor."

"What is it, Takata-*sensei*?"

"I remember you mentioned your husband is an officer in the army judicial corps."

"Actually, he's the *Kempeitai* commander for the southern region. Why do you ask?"

The mere mention of *Kempeitai* sent a slithery coldness through her and jangled her nerves. After a moment, Emiko gathered her composure. "Police officers arrested my fiancé two weeks ago, even though he hasn't done anything wrong. I'm sure it's some mistake, but I haven't heard from him since. I've been so worried."

"How terrible. Poor Takata-*sensei*."

"I don't know where he's being held." She cleared the lump in her throat as warm tears flowed down her cheeks like successive waves upon a beach.

"I'm not sure if my husband will listen to me, but I'll see what I can do."

"Thank you so much." Emiko recalled the time a pottery artist and reputed communist was arrested. Mrs. Katsumoto, an ardent admirer of his work, managed to secure the man's release through the influence she had over her husband.

* * *

Emiko's heart beat with excitement as she packed a lunchbox with some of Akira's favorite foods, which included broiled mackerel, chopped burdock, and eggs. She purchased a white shirt and khaki trousers from a clothing store that hadn't yet depleted its inventory, given the wartime diversion of fabric to military uniforms. She wrapped the folded clothes and food in separate bundles.

Following Mrs. Katsumoto's directions, she rode a streetcar to a nondescript three-story building on the outer edge of downtown. A man dressed in a military uniform left the building as she approached the entrance. Under the bill of his service cap, he smiled and winked at her, making her uneasy. She ignored him as she passed through the entrance and rushed down the main corridor.

A *Kempeitai* sign hung beside the first door on the right. When she entered, several officers looked her way with wide eyes and silly grins. One man swiftly moved his feet off the desk and rose, brushing wrinkles from his uniform. She approached the officer who seemed to be the oldest and highest-ranked.

The officer stared at her with suggestive eyes, and his mouth formed a beguiling smile. "May I help you? I'm Captain Morita."

Mrs. Katsumoto recommended not disclosing her true relationship with Akira. "Captain, I was told that my brother, Akira Omura, is being held in custody here." Her voice came out steady, but a twinge of guilt pricked her conscience. "I would like to see if he's all right."

His lip curled upward, and he turned away from her momentarily. Then he fixed his gaze on her in a way that made her skin crawl. "It's a shame a traitor like Akira Omura has such an uncommonly beautiful sister. He isn't allowed visitors."

Heart pounding, Emiko calmly placed her bundles on the floor and kept her hands steady. She handed the captain a piece of paper.

Scanning the letter, he stared at Emiko and frowned. "You seem to have favor with our illustrious commander. Are you his woman?"

"How dare you ask me such a thing!" His question curdled her stomach.

He studied the paper again and shrugged. "All right. I'll permit you to see him for ten minutes." Retrieving the keys out of the desk drawer, he smiled smugly and headed toward the door. "Come this way, Miss Omura."

Emiko lifted the bundles and followed him. As she neared the door, a nameplate on a desk jumped out at her—Hiroshi Yamada. The blood in her veins froze. Thankfully he was away from his desk. Although he wasn't one of the arresting officers, she couldn't help but wonder whether he had something to do with it.

They entered a dimly lit, dank room with multiple jail cells. The stale odor of perspiration hung heavily in the air, and Emiko breathed through her mouth.

Three prisoners sat against the back wall of the first cell. Listless and downtrodden, the prisoners seemed to barely notice their presence as they passed. Captain Morita stopped in front of the last cell where two men sat next to each other in the corner, talking in quiet tones.

"Prisoner Omura, you have a visitor. Your younger sister is here to see you."

The man on the left lifted his head and stared in their direction. His matted hair hung below his ears, and a coat of dark whiskers covered his lower face. He slowly rose with a confused expression. "My sister?"

As he approached them, Emiko gasped. Bruises discolored his face, and a dry scab lined his lower lip. "Oh my! What have they done to you?"

"Emiko-san, how did you find me?"

She immediately noticed Akira's faux pas in calling her Emiko-san with the honorific *san*, rather than *you* or Emiko. She hoped Captain Morita hadn't heard. "My brother, I'm so happy to see you. I brought you some lunch, a new shirt and trousers."

The other prisoner stirred at the mention of food. Emiko regretted not bringing more to eat. At her request, Captain Morita opened the cell door for her. She handed Akira the lunchbox and fresh set of clothes.

"A home-cooked meal and new clothes? Thank you so much, Emiko." Her name came out of Akira's mouth haltingly.

"You're welcome. How long will they keep you here?"

"I don't—"

"Don't expect him to be released any time soon," Captain Morita said.

Emiko glared at Morita, anger tempered with helplessness. She wanted to slap him.

The touch of Akira's fingers melted the last bit of self-control she had, and tears welled in her eyes.

Akira wiped away her tears with his fingers and held Emiko tenderly. "Don't lose hope. Someday I'll be reunited with you. I know I will—"

Captain Morita sniffed. "Don't count on it."

The captain's words slammed into Emiko, but she fought to maintain her composure.

Akira looked deeply into her eyes. "Don't lose hope. I'll see you again. I know I will—"

Morita jingled the keys. "Time's up. Let's go."

"Already? That couldn't have been ten minutes," she said.

"Yes it was."

Emiko slowly turned away from Akira and reluctantly left the cell, not knowing when she'd be able to see him again.

Morita closed and locked the cell door behind her.

She turned and grasped Akira's hands on the bars until he peeled her fingers off. "I'll come see you again." Emiko dragged her feet toward the exit.

Back in the office, Morita proceeded to his desk and returned the keys to the drawer.

"Captain Morita, I'm appalled at how you've treated my brother, beating him and leaving him in that awful jail cell."

"That's what criminals deserve."

"My brother is not a criminal. I'm going to come back and check on him again. And if he's not treated any better, I'll, I'll—"

"You'll what? Ask for another favor from the commander?" He raised his eyebrows and waited for her response.

Emiko gritted her teeth. She couldn't let the captain have the upper hand. "Yes. Why not?"

"All right, if you want to see your 'brother' again, I'll expect another letter from the commander."

She hung her head, and her lips pursed tightly together. Emiko didn't know whether she could prevail on the good graces of Mrs. Katsumoto again.

Captain Morita chuckled. "Or if you have dinner with me tonight, I may be inclined to change my mind."

As much as she wanted to see Akira again, Emiko couldn't see herself socializing with this scoundrel. She walked quickly out of the office.

30

Furlough

Heart Mountain, Wyoming – October 1, 1943

On a blustery autumn day, Tad sat on the edge of the car seat, eager to see Lily and his family during his ten-day furlough. After enduring long train rides from Mississippi through the heartland of America, a bus from Cheyenne, and a shared taxi from Cody, he spotted Heart Mountain in the distance. His heart leaped with excitement.

The dry, thin air of the Wyoming plateaus parched his throat, and he craved a cold glass of ice water. What a contrast between this place and the lush green plains of the Mississippi Gulf.

He surveyed the camp as the cab drove over the bumpy, dirt road, kicking up clouds of dust. A few new buildings had been constructed, but everything else looked pretty much the same.

Exiting the cab, Tad passed through the main gate and quickly spied Lily's gleaming smile among the small crowd. He sprinted toward her with his heart palpitating. He set his duffel bag down, scooped her in his arms, and gave her a big smack on her bright-red lips. "How's my beautiful doll?"

She squeezed him tightly. "I've missed you so much."

With Lily's arm looped inside his, Tad moved toward Mama and hugged her.

Lily beamed at Mama. "Doesn't Tad look handsome in his uniform?"

"He looks good," she answered nonchalantly.

"Have they been treating you well?" Lily asked.

"Okay, but the fifty-mile hikes are exhausting. The food is a little bit better than here."

Lily's smile disappeared. "Do you know where they'll be sending you? You didn't mention anything in your letters."

"We're not supposed to write information like that. Our top commanders don't know what to do with us yet. They weren't certain how we'd perform in combat, but the 100th Battalion is fighting quite well in Italy, so we might go there. Or maybe they'll send us to the Pacific."

"Since you're going to be a medic, won't you be safer than the regular soldiers?" Lily asked.

He didn't know how to tell Lily without worrying her, but he decided to be honest. "Not necessarily. I'll be tending to the wounded near the front lines."

"Oh dear!"

The look on her face broke Tad's heart into tiny bits.

At the barrack, Tad looked around the room. "Yup, home sweet home."

"It's not like home in California," Lily said. "We're still crowded in this one room."

"Better than being crammed into the army barrack with twenty-five stinky guys." He chuckled and readied himself for lunch.

* * *

Someone snuck up from behind and blindfolded Tad's eyes with hands as he returned from the communal showers. "Honey, guess who's here?"

He recognized Lily's voice and chuckled. "Who?"

She forced his shoulders to turn left. "This way."

"Are we playing hide 'n' go seek?" Tad shuffled his feet in the direction she wanted.

"No, silly." She uncovered his eyes. "Ta-daa!"

Tad saw someone standing behind the sheet divider. "Mas! When did you get here?" He shoved away the sheet divider.

Mas smiled. "Thirty minutes ago, I come from Bismark, North Dakota."

"Bismark?" Tad said, taken aback. "We thought you were still in Montana. What were you doing in Bismark?"

"They move us. I lock up in jail again."

"Good thing they finally released you," Tad said, giving him a bear hug.

With a glint in her eyes, Lily gushed, "I ran into Mr. Murata, the JACL president, this morning. He told me Dad was released only because you are serving in the army."

Tad smiled, thinking that enlisting in the army was making a difference after all. "Does Mama know?"

"She's at her embroidery class. Danny went to get her."

Tad patted Mas on the back. "It's so good to have you back. As you can see, it's not much of a place."

"Better than Bismark," Mas said, scanning the four corners of the room.

"It's better than the horse stall in Santa Anita too. It was so smelly and crowded there." Lily pinched her little nose. "And the food has gotten better here ever since the Japanese took over the kitchen."

The door burst open, and Danny and Mama rushed in.

"*Anata!*" Mama swept over to Mas and embraced him. Tears poured liberally from her eyes. "*Yokatta neh,* so happy you okay. I pray for you every day."

Tad and Lily circled their arms around Mama and Mas and joined in the chorus of tears.

* * *

A few days before Tad's furlough ended, he and Lily joined other young couples on an escorted hike on a rugged trail in a hilly area outside the barbed wire.

Over time, camp administrators had eased up a bit and started granting resident prisoners some latitude and allowed them to take periodic trips outside the camp, escorted by guards.

Tad gazed at the craggy outline of Heart Mountain with the morning sun casting gray-purplish hues on its slopes. "Right now there's no other place on earth I'd rather be than here with you." He wrapped his arms around her neck and kissed her gently on the lips.

She rested her head in the crook of his shoulder. "I wish this day would never end."

From the opposite direction, Tad's high school gymnastics teammate Bob Miyazaki approached them with a friendly smile. "Hi, Tad, welcome back. Good morning, Lily."

Tad forced a smile. "Hello, Bob. Good day."

Lily's dark eyes flashed. She nodded and looked away.

"Tad, I've been wanting to tell you I had nothing to do with you getting beat up. Our argument isn't with you, but with the government."

Stepping in front of Tad, Lily placed both hands on her hips. "But aren't you the one who told everyone how Tad answered the loyalty questions?"

"I told a few people, but I didn't think they'd attack him."

Tad didn't want the touchy situation to escalate, so he sidled next to Lily and faced him. "Bob, I forgive you." He flung his arm around Lily's shoulder and nudged her. "We forgive you."

"Thanks, I appreciate that." Bob lowered his head then looked up.

Tad moved to a flat area and crouched down, placing both hands on the dirt. He lifted his legs high into a handstand like he used to do in the gymnastics team competitions. "Hey Bob, join me."

Bob chuckled. "You can still do it." He came alongside and hoisted his legs into a handstand as well, except his legs were straighter and his arms steadier.

Soon, Tad's legs began to sway, and he could no longer balance himself. His feet dropped to the ground while Bob maintained his handstand without a hitch.

"I'm out of practice," Tad said. "You're still the champion. I remember all the team competitions you helped us win. "

Bob flipped back onto his feet in perfect form. "Not just me, you too. Those were the good old days. Have you seen the new gymnasium?"

"They were still building it when I left for training camp. I'll check it out before I leave."

A smile spread across Lily's face.

That night, Tad sat up in bed. With slivers of light sneaking in through the curtains from the rotating searchlights, he could make out the silhouette of Lily lying next to him. Within a few months, he'd be shipped overseas. This could be the last time he'd see her for a long time, or even forever.

Lily stirred. "Tad, is everything okay?"

"Sorry, I didn't mean to wake you."

"I couldn't sleep anyway." She raised herself and sat with her knees against her chest. "In a few days you'll be gone again, and I'm going to miss you so much."

"I'll miss you, too." Tad pressed her head against his chest and lifted her chin and kissed her tenderly. Then they both reclined.

Their intimate times couldn't be spontaneous. Conversations, laughing, crying, and every kind of sound could be heard through the thin barrack walls. They had to be deliberate and quiet. However, long months of separation and uncertainty of the future overrode all prudence and restraint.

If she became pregnant, and if the war lasted a long time, she'd have to raise a baby inside camp. Or if something were to happen to him, the baby might not have a father. Terrible thoughts quickly dissipated in their passionate embrace.

* * *

Lily clung to Tad's arm like deadweight as they plodded to the camp's main entrance. She remained in deep thought. This time she wasn't just sending her husband off to training camp, but to war. She didn't know when or where, but soon her husband would be sent even farther away and into harm's way. She tried to be strong. With quivering lips and vision blurred with tears, she looked into his dark brown eyes. "Darling, I'm so afraid for you. Please don't die."

"Honey, don't worry about me. I'm coming back as soon as this war is over."

Lily knew he couldn't guarantee his promise. She couldn't understand what caused men to want to go to war and why they couldn't be content living peaceful lives as husbands and fathers. He could be killed or wounded. Nobody knew when this war would end.

Perhaps that's where faith came in.

She admired Tad for being a man of principles and deep convictions. Even if she could, it would be wrong for her to hold him back. Danny was so diametrically opposed in his political views but equally forthright and strong in what he believed. Right now, the army only accepted Japanese American volunteers, but sooner or later, the government would draft men from the camps. That's what everyone said. Danny would have to enter or make his stand. The two brothers were so different, yet so similar. She wondered what Akira was like. Lily shook loose from a trance-like state when Tad nudged her gently.

At the gate, she kissed him passionately, oblivious to her surroundings. All the tears she held back until now flowed liberally from her eyes, as if they could stop him from going.

Then he was gone.

31

Scheme

Kumamoto, Japan

The sneer on Colonel Nakano's face told Hiroshi his plans had backfired. He didn't know what he needed to do to salvage them and keep from incurring his superior's wrath.

"Yamada, just because you have reason to suspect this man of disloyalty doesn't mean I can order his execution." The colonel pulled a lighter out of his desk drawer and lit a cigarette dangling out of his mouth.

"But sir, he's a member of a radical Christian organization."

The colonel shrugged. "So what? I have bigger problems to worry about. The army is pulling my men away, and I can no longer guarantee internal security."

"But he's an American, a *Kibei*."

"Many *Kibei* live here. That doesn't mean they're disloyal. Have you found any solid evidence of espionage?"

Hiroshi lowered his eyes, knowing his personal vendetta wouldn't count as hard evidence. "Nothing conclusive."

"I promoted you to captain because I thought you were a competent and thorough investigator. Don't disappoint me now. Either find some evidence or forget it. One execution requires more time, energy, and paperwork than I can afford right now." He took a long drag of his cigarette and exhaled slowly. "How long has Omura been in custody?"

"About six months."

"Let's release him."

Hiroshi gulped. "Release him?" He couldn't allow his plans to vaporize like smoke.

"Yes, we'll release him into the army infantry. The fighting in the tropical islands is becoming desperate, and the army can use another strong back to dig tunnels and trenches. Chances are he won't survive."

Perhaps his superior was right about Akira meeting his end on some remote island, but things had a way of going wrong in a war. He would have to devise a solid plan to ensure Akira was out of the picture for good. Only then would he be able to make Emiko his—no doubt about that.

* * *

Inside a local *geisha* house, Hiroshi and the Kokura army base commander, Colonel Michio Abe, squatted on the *tatami* around a low table in a *zashiki* private room.

Three alluring young *geisha*, faces painted with pure-white makeup and cherry-red lipstick, attended them.

Yukie, the prettiest with high cheekbones and large eyes, gracefully pushed away the flowing sleeve of her floral kimono to pour *saké* out of a ceramic flask into matching cups for Hiroshi and the colonel. The scent of camellia perfume floated in the air and aroused Hiroshi.

Another girl, Tsuru, dressed in a sky-blue kimono with a burnt-orange *obi* sash, brought in a tray of mouthwatering appetizers, which included broiled cuttlefish, skewered *yakitori* chicken, and cucumber pickles.

The third *geisha,* Shizu, in a maroon-and-silver kimono, strummed and plucked a three-stringed *shamisen*. The tinny sounds resonated a popular melody.

After serving them, the other two rose to their feet and danced to the music with gilded fans.

Hiroshi and the colonel clapped to the cadence of the music. Wearing a broad smile and jovially prattling with the *geisha*, the colonel certainly seemed to be enjoying himself. Hiroshi hoped the merriment would put the colonel in the right mood for what he was about to ask.

After an hour of dancing and music, Yukie poured the colonel some more *saké*. "General, how many men are under you?"

"Yukie-chan, I have two thousand men in my command, and actually I'm only a colonel."

"Oh, but you'll be a general soon. I'm sure of it." Yukie covered her mouth and chortled. The other two *geisha* also chuckled.

Hiroshi and the colonel joined in the laughter. With a lustful grin, the colonel ogled Yukie's exposed neck as she reached over to fill Hiroshi's cup.

The alcohol did its job in loosening up the colonel, but Hiroshi couldn't risk getting him too drunk. "Ladies, please leave us for a few minutes. We have some business to discuss."

They frowned and complained. Hiroshi knew the *geisha* were just acting, because when he stepped out to go to the toilet earlier, he had overheard two of them say Abe was ugly with his bald head and broad pug nose. Sure enough, as they rose to leave through the sliding *shoji* door, their faces morphed into smiles and giggles.

Colonel Abe shifted his eyes to Hiroshi and scowled. "Yamada, make this quick. What's on your mind?"

"It's about a man we're about to draft into the army."

"Since when does the *Kempeitai* track the affairs of a single conscript, let alone one who hasn't even been drafted yet?" The colonel downed another cupful of *saké*.

"It's a matter of national security. The man is a member of a secretive Christian organization. We can't allow him and others like him to undermine the patriotism of our people."

"Why not just execute him and be done with it? It shouldn't be difficult to arrange."

"It's not that simple. If we execute him, like-minded Christians will make him a hero. That's not what we want." Hiroshi had spent considerable time crafting this story, and he didn't want to mention that his commander already rejected the idea of execution. He hoped he sounded convincing.

"So you think we should draft him into the army and send him to the front lines?"

"Yes. We'll take care of two concerns that way. First, Akira Omura will demonstrate his loyalty by subjugating his Christian faith to the glory of the emperor. Second, the likely scenario of his death in battle will put an end to any further influence he may have over his local constituency of believers."

"I can't say I understand your logic," the colonel said. "But I'll do you a favor since you're paying the bill."

He sure was—more than his captain's pay could afford. Good thing his father set aside a special fund for Hiroshi to use in situations like this. "Where do you think the fighting will be the heaviest?"

"That's hard to say. We could send him to China, the Philippines, or any one of a dozen islands in the Pacific. Maybe the Marianas Islands, where we expect to form a major line of defense."

Hiroshi had heard the same thing from another source. This was it. He wanted Akira sent there. "Can you make sure he is sent to the Marianas?"

"I can't guarantee it. Besides, Imperial General Headquarters doesn't really know where the Americans will concentrate their attacks. Our forces will be deployed according to the decisions made by our top strategists."

"But can't you send him to the most treacherous battlefield at any given time?"

Colonel Abe shook his head. "Armies, divisions, regiments, and battalions are deployed to specific areas, not individual men—certainly not anybody of his low rank. Think of the logistics involved. Would we send this one private on a special transport plane or ship to a far-off island under attack by the Americans?"

"How about transferring him to a unit slated for action? Surely, there must be several troop movements planned soon."

"But that's a guessing game at best. Last week I would've said that Formosa was most vulnerable to attack, but this week, our intelligence people say it will be the Marianas."

Hiroshi slammed his *saké* cup on the table. "What can you guarantee?" He began to regret spending all this money on him. Insufferable man.

"Remember your place, Captain. I'm still your superior." The colonel downed another cup of *saké* and lifted the empty cup for Hiroshi to fill. "Look, I'll see what I can do. Now, send the girls back in."

32

Prelude

Heart Mountain, Wyoming – December 1, 1943

For the past several months, euphoria filled Danny, and he couldn't be happier having Mary by his side during social nights, mealtimes, and even church. He held her hand as they exited the Block 28 mess hall. "I'll treat you to ice cream later tonight."

"I'll buy this time. You haven't found a job yet."

"You don't have to treat me, but thanks Mary. I'll drop by to see you after the committee meeting."

"You're going to another meeting?" she said in an edgy voice.

"An important one. We're getting ready to stand up against the Selective Service when they come."

"I hope you're not getting involved in any violence. I heard the No-No Boys have been attacking people who support the Japanese American Citizens League."

"Not me. I may not agree with the JACL, but I don't believe in beating people up." His association with the three No-No boys who roughed up his brother didn't help his case.

Mary withdrew her hand from his, her eyes lacking their usual liveliness. "Danny, we never pray together, and you seldom go to church. What happened?"

She was bringing it up again, and he wondered what excuse he'd make this time. "I'm too busy with the committee work."

"That's not a good reason for putting God aside."

How many times had he heard that from her? He blew out a deep sigh, not wanting to delve into it. "I don't see the point. As far as I'm concerned, God abandoned us. We've lost our freedom, rights, and dignity. I'm not sure if he even cares about us."

"Don't blame God for that. Things may look bleak right now, but God is faithful. He'll deliver us from these circumstances."

"I don't want to wait four hundred years for that to happen." Even though he wanted to say more, he bit back the words.

A single tear glistened as it traced its way down her cheek. "It's not good to think that way Danny. I think you're spending too much time with the committee."

"But it's everything I believe in. What's wrong with standing up for your rights?" he asked. "Instead, do you want me to join the army for a government that treats us like enemies?"

"No, that's not what I mean. God is a big part of my life, and I need someone who shares my faith."

"What's the big deal? I live a decent life and try my best to do the right things."

"That's not enough." With glassy eyes, her mouth collapsed into a frown, and she choked out a cry. "I don't think we should see each other anymore."

Her quiet words hit him like a sucker punch in the gut. "What? Why not? I thought you liked me." He wasn't about to let her go so easily. "But I love you."

She dabbed her eyes with her hand and slowly regained her composure. "I love you too. I'll still be your friend. But—"

"But what?" If she loved him, why was she giving him such a hard time? Of all the girls he'd ever known, Mary was the only one he could openly share his deepest feelings with. Her buoyant personality put a spark in his life and drew him close to her like a magnet. He never expected to be released from this relationship.

"You have to understand that I need someone who'll put God first. I can't be your girlfriend any longer." Mary's sobs drowned out her voice.

Her words jolted Danny, and he turned away. Now he'd lost the one and only bright spot in his otherwise dreary existence.

Mary couldn't possibly leave him, not now, not ever. Heels clacked, and he twisted around to see her scamper away.

Maybe she'd calm down in a day or two. Her melancholy face burned in his memory. He'd deal with it later. He looked at his watch and hurried to the Fair Play Committee meeting.

Danny entered the mess hall and found almost all the folding chairs occupied. He spotted an empty seat near the far end of the last row and trotted over there.

For the first few minutes, Danny couldn't shake Mary's words and stared into space. His heart tripped over itself. He shook his head and turned his attention toward the speaker.

Mike Murata of the Japanese American Citizens League stood behind the podium, addressing the crowd. "A few months ago, the 100th landed near Salerno. They advanced against strong enemy resistance to take Benevento, an important rail center and road intersection."

Danny had heard of the 100th Battalion that consisted of mostly Japanese Americans from Hawaii.

Murata looked at his notes. "Then they crossed the Volturno River, against heavy enemy machine gunfire and rocket launchers before driving the Germans even further north toward Naples—"

"We already know all that!" Tom Okada rose and yelled in his husky voice. "We've seen the newsreels. Get to the point."

Murata held up his hand. "Let me continue. They've won the respect of General Ryder, the 34th Division commander."

A smattering of applause echoed across the hall.

"Of course, the success was achieved at the cost of high casualties. But I'm here to urge you to get behind this noble cause to rid the world of fascism and help the enslaved people of Europe win back their freedom."

"That's fine and dandy, but what about our freedom?" Okada hollered.

Murata wagged his finger at the crowd. "The 100th Battalion is fighting hard to win back your freedom. And the all-Japanese American 442nd Regiment will be joining them. You know some of the men from this camp who signed up."

Danny couldn't convince his brother not to join the army, but that was Tad's choice, not his.

Amid other interruptions, Murata declared, "I'm here to tell you that the JACL urges you not to resist the draft."

Easy for Murata to say. At his age, there's no way he'd be drafted. Danny rose. "Sit down, Murata!"

The JACL man fixed his narrowing eyes at Danny. "Resisting the draft is a serious offense. If you fail to report, you could go to prison."

The crowd booed.

Bob Miyazaki sprang to his feet. "It's a joke that you call yourselves the Japanese American Citizens League when your views don't represent our people—only what the government wants."

"Look, I'm in this camp just like you, and I don't like it one bit either. But at least I'm trying to do something about it. You guys are asking for trouble."

More than half the men in the room stood up and roared in unison, "Down with JACkaL! Down with JACkaL!"

"How could you look at yourself in the mirror and call yourself a Japanese American?" Danny blurted to Murata. "Don't you see, most of us oppose the draft? You're nothing more than the government's lapdog."

Murata gave Danny a dirty look and stepped away from the podium. A few supporters rose to leave the mess hall with the JACL representative.

Boos and catcalls followed them out the door.

33

Imperial Soldier

Kumamoto, Japan – March 21, 1944

Emiko lifted her hand, adoring the iridescent pearl ring Akira gave her for their engagement. Its perfect spherical shape reminded her of the complete happiness that filled her heart whenever she reflected on their love for each other. She pictured his princely eyes and charming smile and prayed that he was safe and eating well.

Glancing at the wall clock, she removed her ring and placed it inside the jewelry box. She grabbed her purse and rummaged through it, looking for General Katsumoto's letter. When she found it tucked safely inside her purse pocket, she let out a deep sigh. She couldn't afford to lose the second letter of permission, as it wasn't easy to obtain. Mrs. Katsumoto had mentioned her husband flat-out refused the request twice until she reminded him it was her father who secured his position, and she would hate to tell him about the general's frequent dalliances with other women.

Snapping her purse shut, she gathered the lunchbox she had prepared for Akira, this time with extra food for the other inmate, and she dashed out the door.

She entered the *Kempeitai* office but found no one at their desks. Emiko proceeded to where she thought Captain Morita's desk had been. The desktop had been cleared. How strange. No nameplate, ashtray, files, nothing. She set the lunchbox down and checked the other desks with nameplates, including Hiroshi

Yamada's, but none belonged to the captain. She glanced at the entrance to the jail area. It couldn't hurt to see if the door was unlocked.

Emiko tried the knob, but it wouldn't turn. Hoping an officer would be inside, she pounded on the door several times, but no one came. Her throat tightened at the thought that she wouldn't be able to see her beloved.

Perhaps she'd wait around until someone returned. Minutes later, footsteps echoed down the hallway, and she hurried to the entrance, hoping to find Captain Morita.

The door opened, and Emiko froze, then backpedaled when she saw who it was. A desk blocked her retreat.

"Miss Takata, what a pleasant surprise to see you here. How have you been?"

Hiroshi's presence chilled her to the marrow. He wore a smile that reminded her of a viper ready to pounce on its prey. "Where's Captain Morita?"

"He no longer works here. I'm the ranking officer now. May I help you with something?"

It had been unnerving to deal with Captain Morita, but now, having to work through this blackguard was nearly enough for her to leave. How she wished the earth would crack open and swallow him alive. "I'm here to see my fiancé."

"Your fiancé?" Hiroshi glanced at her hand. "No ring?"

"Lieutenant Yamada, you—"

"That's Captain."

"Captain Yamada, you know the regulations against the public display of fine jewelry. Anyway, I have a letter from General Katsumoto." She opened her purse and pulled it out.

Hiroshi reached over to take the letter, his rough fingers making contact with hers.

She jerked her hand away.

He kept smiling while examining it. His gaze glided up from the paper to her eyes. "I see you have permission to visit Mr. Omura."

"Yes, I do."

"And I'm told the last time you were here, you passed yourself off as his sister. Why?" Hiroshi returned the letter to her.

She wanted to tell him it was none of his business, but Emiko hesitated, knowing he held the power to determine Akira's fate. "Just in case visiting rights were restricted to the immediate family."

"I see. All right. However, there is one problem."

"Problem?"

"He's been inducted into the army."

"What? The army?" Emiko suffered a temporary bout of vertigo and grasped the desk behind her to hold herself steady. "When did this happen?"

"About two weeks ago."

Akira had discussed with Emiko the likelihood of being drafted, but she didn't expect this to happen while he was in jail. Not even time for a final good-bye. She fought to control a tremor, not wanting Hiroshi to see her distraught. "Why wasn't I notified?"

"In situations like this, only the immediate family is notified. However, in this case, his family couldn't be identified. Even though you say you're engaged to him, you are not family."

She lifted her chin, determined not to be bullied by him. "Where was Omura-san sent?"

"I have no idea." He shifted his eyes away from her. "Captain Morita processed the induction before he left."

Gnawing doubt entered her mind. "Is there no record? Are you sure you don't know where he is?"

"Miss Takata, he could have been sent to any one of over twenty army bases in Japan."

She searched his eyes. "Are you telling me the truth?"

"Are you calling me a liar? Do you think I have him locked up in our jail?" Hiroshi stepped toward his desk, opened a drawer, and pulled out a ring of keys. He moved toward the jail area and unlocked the door. "Come, have a look for yourself."

Emiko moved toward the cells and peered inside. A few men sat cross-legged on the floor, but Akira wasn't among them. She proceeded to the next cell, which was empty, and finally to the cell on the end where Akira had been. A couple of men stood with their hands on the bars but no sign of Akira.

Not knowing what to do next, Emiko drew in a deep breath to keep the tears at bay. Turning abruptly, she brushed past Hiroshi to the office, picked up the lunchbox, and marched toward the exit.

"Don't leave just yet. I want to talk to you."

"I have nothing to say to you." His hand grasped her elbow from behind. "Let me go!" Emiko yanked her arm to escape, but his grip was too strong.

"Akira Omura is as good as dead." He sneered.

His words punctured her heart. "What do you mean?"

"We usually release prisoners to the front lines. Chances are he won't survive."

"I don't believe that." Before doubt crept into her mind, heels clacked down the hallway. Two uniformed men walked toward them.

Hiroshi released her arm, and Emiko ran past the two men and out of the building.

* * *

The Japanese flag fluttered from the pole high above the parade grounds where Akira and his unit of the 32nd Imperial Japanese Army practiced their battle formations.

Sergeant Kameda struck a thinly built soldier in the jaw, knocking him to the ground. "Private Saito, I've told you countless times to keep up," he yelled at the young recruit who lay sprawled on the ground groaning. "Get up, you weakling!" The sergeant planted a heavy boot into Saito's buttocks.

Akira cringed. No person deserved treatment like that. When Kameda turned his back, Akira broke ranks and dashed over to Saito. He squatted down and helped him into a sitting position.

"Get away from him!" Sergeant Kameda yelled, charging toward them. He punched Akira in the ear, making him tumble to the ground, and propelled a stiff kick to his backside. "*Baka yaro!* Fool!" The sergeant's husky frame loomed over him.

Bright lights spiraled in Akira's eyes, and loud ringing grated his eardrums. In all his life, he'd never encountered anyone so vicious. "I was only trying to help Private Saito."

"Who do you think you are Omura? Florence Nightingale? Get up!"

Akira expected another blow, but the sergeant wheeled around and faced the platoon.

"Men, do you know why I'm being tough on Saito and Omura?" Sergeant Kameda removed his field cap and wiped sweat off his close-cropped head.

No one dared to say anything.

"I'm being tough because you cannot afford to fall out of step in real combat. When you fight for your life, you'll find out how important it is. Otherwise, you're dead."

Akira gingerly rose to his feet, still reeling from the wallop.

The sergeant picked up an *Arisaka* rifle and aimed it at Saito, and then he pointed it at Akira. "Shoot accurately and throw your grenades with precision. And don't hesitate to stab with your bayonets." He held the muzzle and grounded the rifle. "If you lose your weapons, fight with sticks, rocks, and even your bare hands. The Americans will not be merciful. They'll gouge your eyes, tear out your hair, and at the end, murder you."

The sergeant's words didn't ring true to Akira. From what he could remember from living in America, most of them were fair-minded, although there was no telling how they would act in the heat of war.

"You think I'm making this up? Think again. I fought in Manchuria and later faced the Americans in the Philippines. I know what war is really like, so listen carefully." The sergeant continued down the line.

"I'm preparing you to become strong soldiers so you'll be able to fight and win. Then you'll be thanking me for being strict. Finally, never surrender, even if it means taking your own life. This is your duty to the emperor."

In the late afternoon, Akira scrubbed non-flushing, floor-level toilets in the officers' latrine. He held his breath to avoid the overwhelming stench and rose for air every thirty seconds or so. He had six more days of this extra duty, all because he and Saito caught the sergeant's wrath.

On his way to the janitorial supply cabinet, Akira ran into Saito.

"I'm so tired, I can't go on," Saito said. "I was never meant to be a soldier."

"You can't give up. You must endure."

"Shhh! Not so loud." Saito scanned the area. "I can't believe we're stuck with the most iron-fisted and meanest sergeant in the entire battalion. Do you know why Kameda's that way?"

"No," Akira whispered.

"I've heard rumors that he was born in America, so he thinks he has to prove himself by being super patriotic, super Japanese. They also say he was rejected at the officer training school because of his American origin."

That comment gave Akira a start. A Japanese American like him. Yet they were on opposite ends of the political spectrum.

34

Resistance

Heart Mountain, Wyoming – March 22, 1944

Loud pounding jarred Lily awake as she turned sideways in bed and squinted at the alarm clock perched on the storage chest. Seven in the morning.

She had awoken earlier when the baby kicked inside her abdomen but was too tired to get up. Mom and Dad were probably finished with their early-morning prayer meeting and halfway through their walk around the camp. Only Danny slept, snoring on the other side of the sheet divider. He had come in during the wee hours after another late-night meeting. Lily tightened her robe and shuffled to the door. "Who is it?"

"United States Marshals. Is Daniel Omura there?"

She stiffened. *Oh, no. Is he in trouble again?* "Just a minute. He's asleep. I'll wake him."

Lily padded a few steps and pushed the bed-sheet partition out of the way. Danny slept on his side with his back facing her. With a firm shake on his shoulder, she woke him up. "Danny, US Marshals are here!"

He rolled over and opened his eyes halfway. "What do they want?"

"I don't know."

He dragged himself out of bed, stretched his arms, and yawned.

Lily pulled the sheet back so he could get dressed. His lax attitude confounded her. She went to the door and opened it.

Two men, dressed in black overcoats with metal badges on their lapels, stepped across the threshold, bringing in the frigid air. The marshal to her left removed his hat. "I'm Deputy Marks, and this is Deputy Tuttle."

Danny emerged from the other side of the partition.

The taller marshal, Tuttle, stared at Danny with piercing eyes and a deep frown.

"Daniel Omura, you're under arrest for failing to report to your preinduction physical," Marks said.

Lily gasped. She knew the Fair Play Committee organized protests against the draft, but she didn't think they'd be arrested.

Danny rolled his eyes. "They sent the two of you to get me? Oh, brother!"

Marks wagged an index finger at him. "Don't get smart with us."

Lily turned to Danny. "You didn't tell us anything about this."

He flashed a half-smile at her. "It's okay. I'll be all right."

"This is serious. They're arresting you." She turned away from Danny and pivoted toward the men. "Where are you taking him?"

"The administration building," Marks said.

"Give me half an hour, and I'll report in." Danny combed his pachuco hairstyle with his fingers.

"No, you have to come with us now," Tuttle said.

"Can't he even say good-bye to his parents?" asked Lily.

Tuttle shot her a cold stare. "No dice. We have orders to follow."

"What are you guys afraid of?" Danny sneered. "It's not like I can escape or anything."

With fingers balled into tight fists, Tuttle lurched forward and towered over Danny. "You're going to be sorry you said that."

Lily bit her lip. If Danny would only keep his mouth shut.

Danny didn't give an inch. "At least let me throw some extra clothes in a bag."

"Not necessary," Marks said. "Just bring a jacket or coat."

Danny submitted to frisking before having handcuffs slapped on his wrists.

Marks opened the front door and led Danny out with Tuttle following.

Lily collapsed onto a chair dazed, shaken by the callousness and rudeness of the US Marshals. She worried about how Danny would fare.

* * *

Mary Wada ate at the crowded mess hall on block 17, hoping to find Lily. She hung around after eating and waited.

While she periodically ran into Lily across camp, she didn't speak with her much—not since the breakup with Danny—just quick exchanges of small talk. Several times Lily asked how she was doing, but Mary always responded vaguely and cut her off. She knew it was wrong, but she couldn't bring herself to talk to anyone with a connection to Danny. It hurt too much.

Today was different. Mary had heard the authorities rounded up the men who refused the draft. Danny was probably one of them, but she wanted to find out for herself. She spotted Lily and moved toward her table. "May I?"

Lily smiled. "Of course, have a seat. How are you?"

"Fine, I guess." The truth was she had been a basket case ever since the breakup. She seated herself next to Lily. "I heard you're pregnant. Congratulations."

"Thank you, Mary. I'm so excited."

Mary didn't know how to broach the next thing on her mind, but she was dying to find out. "I hope you don't mind me asking, but did they arrest Danny?"

"Yes, the marshals arrested him early this morning and took him to the administration building." Lily's smile evaporated.

Although she wasn't surprised, the news stung Mary as if a scorpion bit her. She could hardly breathe. Every time she'd seen Danny, she wanted desperately to run into his arms. But a strong sense of knowing what God wanted kept her away. One look in his eyes told her Danny still cared for her. But their encounters started and ended with a brief, "Hi," and that was it.

"The camp director is going to let the families say good-bye to them at three this afternoon by the front gate. I suppose we'll find out more then."

Tears threatened to spill out of Mary's eyes. "It's all my fault."

"What's your fault?"

"If we hadn't broken up, I may have been able to convince him to stop protesting, and he wouldn't be in the trouble he's in now."

Lily shook her head. "Oh, no. Danny's decision to side with the Fair Play Committee had nothing to do with you. He made up his mind a long time ago."

Mary cast her gaze onto the floor. Perhaps Lily was just trying to make her feel better.

"You were right to take a stand and make your expectations clear to him."

"Oh? I thought you'd be upset with me."

"When you two broke up, I was upset—but not at you. I was mad at my boneheaded brother-in-law." Lily dabbed her mouth with a napkin. "You're the best thing that's ever happened to him, and I let him know it, too."

"I thought I could handle it, but I do miss him. Maybe he doesn't show it very often, but he does have a sweet side to him."

"Danny misses you a lot, too. He doesn't say much, and he just mopes around. I can tell he regrets what happened."

As hard as she tried, Mary could no longer contain her pent-up sorrow. Fresh tears clouded her vision and cascaded down her face. Lily's words brought such great comfort and soothed her ragged up-and-down emotions.

Lily slipped a handkerchief to her.

"Thank you." Mary sniffled. She blotted her eyes and held the cloth to her cheek.

"Do you love Danny?"

"Yes, I do, but I believe God has other plans for me." She had promised herself she wouldn't cave in to her feelings, but every time she saw him from a distance, she'd forgotten everything she promised God. Her throat tightened and choked her whenever this happened. Then she would silently pray for forgiveness.

"Any time you want to talk, Mary, I'm here for you."

"Thank you. You've always been like a sister to me. Do you think it'd be all right if I join you at three?"

"Certainly."

"I'll be there."

35

The Letter

Kokura Army Base, Japan – May 14, 1944

Something was wrong. Akira had penned four letters to Emiko since he arrived at the base and received nothing back from her. Why hadn't she written? Did something happen to her?

Maybe today, he'd hear from her. After finishing his extra duties, he rushed to the barrack to see if any mail had arrived for him. Some men were asleep. A few sat against the wall with bored looks, smoking cigarettes. Others played *Karuta tori* card games.

"Fellas, I'm sorry to interrupt your game, but was there any mail for me?" Akira asked.

Private Hoshino shook his head. "They didn't call your name."

Akira's hope fizzled out like a spent flare. "Nothing came?"

"Maybe your mail got mixed up with someone else's. Check with the base post office." Hoshino looked at his watch. "If you hurry, you might be able to catch them before they close."

Akira sprinted to the post office with a mixed sense of anxiety and anticipation. He panted for air as he rapped on the door, hoping somebody would still be there.

The door creaked open, and a middle-aged corporal appeared at the threshold. "I was about to close for the evening."

"I'm sorry to bother you, but I couldn't make it to the mail call. Do you have anything for me?"

"Name and unit?"

"Private Omura, Akira. First Battalion, Sparrow Company, Third Platoon."

The corporal shuffled back to his workstation behind the counter and searched through a bin. "There's nothing for you, Private."

Akira hung his head. "Thanks for checking." Why hadn't she written? Maybe she didn't know where he was. Perhaps she was ill. Her neighborhood may have suffered damage from American bombings. Worse yet, the *Kempeitai* may have arrested her.

* * *

Kumamoto, Japan

Emiko's hand slipped while pressing a cherry branch into the metal spike holder of a circular vase. "Aah!" A spot of red spread on the back of her forefinger. She grabbed a handkerchief from her kimono sleeve and wrapped her bleeding finger.

Mrs. Katsumoto hurried to her side. "Sensei, you're hurt."

"How careless of me." Emiko smiled to reassure her student. Her mind had been so preoccupied, having heard nothing from her fiancé. Hiroshi's words, *Akira Omura is as good as dead,* kept coming back to haunt her.

"Let me take care of that." Mrs. Katsumoto rushed to another room in her mansion and returned with a bottle of iodine and gauze. She bandaged Emiko's injured finger.

"Thank you so much." Emiko watched numbly, thinking she should be searching for Akira instead of teaching *ikebana* to five rich ladies. Yet she was grateful to earn some money and shoved her troubled thoughts to the back of her mind.

After class, Mrs. Katsumoto gathered the flower arrangement supplies and placed them in Emiko's bundle. "Sensei, you seem worried. Have you heard from your fiancé yet?"

Holding back tears, Emiko shook her head.

The hostess placed her hand on Emiko's shoulder. "It's a common refrain these days. Our young men are sent to war, and their women are left behind to worry and wait. Some never hear from them again."

The frankness of Mrs. Katsumoto's words stung like a bee. Her vision blurred, and she braced herself on the edge of the table to balance herself. The thought of Akira never coming home sent tremors through her.

"Sensei, I'm sorry. I didn't mean to upset you. It's just that— wait a minute. When was your fiancé drafted?"

Emiko made her voice sound normal. "About two months ago."

"Then, chances are he is still stationed in a training camp."

"But where?"

"I don't know for sure, but men from this area are being sent to the large army base in Kokura. Why don't you send it there?"

"Thank you for that suggestion." She drew in a deep breath infused with hope.

* * *

Early in the morning, Emiko folded another letter to Akira, slipped it into an envelope, and wrote the address of the Kokura army base. Mrs. Katsumoto's husband had confirmed Akira was sent there.

Yet, after three letters to the base, she received no response. Maybe Akira was injured or ill.

In the desk drawer, she found a postage stamp and moistened it. A thought occurred to her. Maybe she could take the morning train and deliver the letter in person. Placing it in her purse, Emiko grabbed a sweater and rushed out of the house.

She rode the train to Kokura and arrived in the afternoon. There she inquired with the stationmaster for directions to the base. He directed her to the trolley lines and recommended a *jinrikisha* buggy cab for the last portion, due to the hilly streets.

Once she arrived at the base, a young sentry intercepted her.

"Excuse me, sir. I have a letter for Akira Omura, who is stationed here." She retrieved the envelope out of her purse.

The guard stared at her with a puzzled look and accepted the envelope. "Thousands of men are stationed here. Why didn't you use the postal service?"

"I've sent many letters to him, but I haven't received a single response."

"This is highly irregular. Wait here. I'll contact the sergeant." He strode to the sentry station.

After a few minutes, the guard came back and returned her letter. "Ma'am, someone will be with you."

"Thank you so much." She breathed out a sigh of relief. Finally, her letter would get through. Better yet, perhaps she could actually hand it to Akira directly.

Standing in the warm sun would have normally depleted her energy, but the thrill of being able to contact Akira made it well worth it. She pressed her lips together to contain her excitement.

A rugged soldier swaggered to the security post. He spoke with the sentry for a minute and then came out to meet Emiko. The sergeant smiled broadly, exposing a gold front tooth. He gave her a curt bow. "I'm Sergeant Takeshi Kameda."

Emiko returned the bow. "I'm pleased to meet you, sir."

"What can I do for you?"

"Sergeant, would you be kind enough to see that this letter gets delivered to Akira Omura?" She offered it to the sergeant. "I've written to him several times but received no replies."

"We've had periodic disruptions in the mail service due to bombings of our highways and rail lines. You're not the only person having trouble with the mail delivery."

"Would it be possible for me to see him, if he's available?"

"I'm sorry, that's not possible. He is on training maneuvers at a distant site and will be gone for several days. But I'll see to it that he receives your letter."

A breath escaped from her lungs as she dropped her gaze. At least she had consolation, knowing where Akira was, and he would receive her letter. "I appreciate it very much." She bowed. When she raised her head, she caught a glimpse of his leering expression, making her ill at ease.

* * *

Hiroshi picked up the ringing phone at his desk. "Hello, this is Captain Yamada."

"Abe here. I have some news for you. A woman came to the base today to deliver a letter to Private Akira Omura. Sergeant Kameda told me she's a very fine-looking woman."

This development caught Hiroshi by surprise. "Uh, well . . . yes, she is . . . Colonel." His mind started to churn, trying to figure out what was going on.

"Is this what it's all about?" Abe chortled and coughed.

"Well, no, it's like I told you. We suspect the person she was trying to contact is a radical Christian and—"

"Yamada, you don't have to playact with me. I appreciate beautiful women as much as you do. Anyway, I don't care what you do as long as you pay me."

"Colonel, what did she write in her letter?"

"That she's moving to a relative's home in the country."

"Did she say when? Or where exactly?" It would be more difficult for Hiroshi to pursue her if she moved away and lived with relatives.

"The letter doesn't say."

"When is Akira Omura scheduled to be deployed? And where?" Hiroshi asked.

"Okinawa, sometime later this month. The fighting will likely be intense when the Americans invade."

"Thank you for the update, Colonel. I'll send you your next payment."

Hiroshi put down the receiver and tapped his fingers rhythmically against the desk. His well-thought-out plan had been forestalled by some unidentified cog in the bureaucracy since Akira hadn't been deployed yet. He didn't want to make any direct overtures to Emiko until Akira was out of the way. But now, with her plan to move away, Hiroshi could no longer wait. It was time to visit her.

36

Jail

Laramie, Wyoming – June 5, 1944

Inside the county jail, Danny awoke bleary-eyed and squinted at the diffused sunlight seeping through the small frosted window caked with dirt. He sat up on the thin mattress atop a steel-spring bed. Only two working lightbulbs out of four lit the dim hallway. Dirt and grease marks were smeared across the wall opposite his cell. Peeling paint and water stains marred the ceiling directly above his head.

What a contrast between this place and the clean, modern Casper jail where he and the other dissidents spent the first month before being transferred here. This place probably hadn't changed much since the days of the Old West.

Pounding, shouting, and clanging tin cups had kept Danny up most of the night until early morning when he passed out. He couldn't see anyone and sat alone in a cell sandwiched between boisterous strangers. At least at Casper, his buddies were nearby, where they conversed with each other. Here, he called out to his friends, but no one answered. The isolation was the worst part of being in this jail.

At noon, a deputy passed a food tray through the horizontal opening in the cell door. Danny grabbed the tin tray and hunkered down on his bunk—famished since he missed breakfast. He scooped a spoonful of baked beans into his mouth and spewed it out. *Yuck! How awful.* Chewing on mud would have been better. He jabbed his fork into a piece of rubbery meat and kept chomping on it but finally spit that out too. Undissolved mashed potato flakes stuck to the roof of his mouth. He left more than half of his lunch untouched.

An hour later, heavy steps traveled down the hall. The deputy came to collect his tray.

"That was the worst meal I've ever eaten. The potatoes weren't even fully cooked." Danny passed him the tray.

The deputy smirked. "I thought you Japs liked your food raw."

Danny choked the bars of the cell door. "Don't call me that! I'm every bit an American as you."

"I'll call you anything I want."

Crude words almost flew out of Danny's mouth, but he held back. The foul aftertaste hung inside his mouth, and he ran the tip of his tongue along his front teeth. "Hey, can I have a toothbrush and some toothpaste? I haven't brushed since yesterday."

"Nope. You should have brought them from Casper."

"They wouldn't let us bring anything here. Can you send somebody to the store?"

The deputy chuckled. "Would you like a comb and some candy too? There's a bar of soap on the sink. Use that with your finger." He snickered and disappeared down the hall.

Danny couldn't believe they wouldn't even provide him with the basic hygiene supplies. He stomped to the sink, and in one motion, he scooped up the bar of soap and hurled it.

* * *

"Hey, Jap. Wake up!" the deputy yelled. "You have visitors."

Danny pushed himself off the mattress. "I keep telling you, I'm not a Jap. I'm an American citizen."

"Yeah, whatever you say."

Two men, a Nisei and a Caucasian, walked up to the cell. Danny recognized the JACL president who addressed the Fair Play Committee, but he didn't know the thin Caucasian who swam inside his double-breasted suit.

"Hello, Daniel Omura. My name is Mike Murata—"

Danny crossed his arms and stared at him. "I know who you are. You're the JACL man who sold us out to the government."

"We're not here to talk about me, but about you." Murata turned to his right. "This gentleman is Mr. Paulson, a government attorney."

Paulson nodded. "Mr. Omura, how are they treating you?"

"Like trash. I consider it cruel and unusual punishment. Look how filthy this place is. They won't even give me a toothbrush and toothpaste. My teeth are going to rot."

The lawyer scrunched his bushy eyebrows. "I'll speak to the administrators about that."

"And another thing, they won't give me anything to read or do around here. All I get is thirty minutes a day in the exercise yard."

"I'll talk to them," Paulson said, taking notes. "Anyway, Daniel—if I may call you that—we're here to give you another chance to reconsider. If you resist the draft, you'll be facing three to seven years in prison."

"Three to seven years?" Danny breathed deeply and looked away for a moment. "Mr. Paulson, as a lawyer, you must know what makes sense and what's fair."

"Unfortunately, in this case, fair has nothing to do with it. We're at war, and all able-bodied Americans are being called to serve whether they like it or not. There's no doubt that racism and prejudice has played a major part of our country's history. You know how the Negroes have been treated, yet they're not exempt from this war. They even fought on both sides of the Civil War."

Danny rolled his eyes. "Enough with the speeches. I'm not changing my mind."

The lawyer heaved a sigh. "I've laid the facts out for you. I don't know what else to say. You'll have to decide. And one more thing—conditions inside a federal prison are likely to be far worse than here."

Spending years in a place worse than this was unthinkable, but he steeled himself against this possibility and remained silent.

"If you change your mind, let the guard know," Paulson said, tucking his little notepad inside his suit pocket. He turned to Murata. "Let's go see the next one."

Murata reached inside his coat pocket. "Before I forget, here's a letter from your family." He passed it through the bars.

Receiving a letter was like a ray of sunshine pouring into the dreary dungeon. "Thanks." Danny waited for them to leave, and he sat on the edge of his bunk, eager to swallow any morsel of news from the outside world. He tapped the end of the envelope and tore it open, pulling out several sheets written in Lily's neat handwriting.

The first few words inquired about his health. The family was well and making do. Lily had written about Mama's entries in the handicraft fair contest and Mas's work in the community vegetable garden. Ordinarily, Danny would have grown bored reading about such things, but now each word drew strong memories. He pictured his mother crocheting colorful patterns and embroidering intricate artwork and his stepfather hoeing straight furrows in the soil.

Lily also mentioned she received a letter from her parents in the Manzanar relocation camp in the Southern California desert. They had written that her fourteen-year-old brother and a friend snuck out beneath the barbed wire at night to go fishing for trout at George Creek in the Sierra Nevada. They returned two days later and shared the delicious trout. What rascals! If the guards had spotted them going even close to the barbed wire, they'd open fire and shoot them dead.

She also wrote how embarrassed she was waddling around camp. For baby names, she had picked Janet for a girl and Brent for a boy.

Danny shook his head. He was going to become an uncle—a jailbird uncle.

The subject changed to Tad's deployment overseas. Lily didn't know where he was sent, just somewhere in Europe. Although she never mentioned the possibility of Tad getting killed or hurt, Danny could sense fear and sadness in her words.

His mind reflected on the arguments with Tad last year. But now those things didn't matter anymore.

For one frozen moment, Danny wondered if he'd done the right thing. Things might have been different if Akira returned home to America and if Tad hadn't signed up for the army. Danny made a choice too. They all had to live with the choices they made.

As he turned to the last page of the letter, he noticed another sheet of paper in a different handwriting.

May 24, 1944

> *Dear Danny,*
>
> *How are you doing? I hope you're safe and healthy. I can't imagine what it's like to be in jail. How are they treating you? Is the food okay?*
>
> *As for me, I'm doing well. I'm still working in the camp library. We finally have enough books. Imagine that. I enjoy helping students research their term papers.*
>
> *I get together with Lily almost every day and help her get around. We've become such good friends, and we pray for you daily.*
>
> *Please remember that no matter how bad things get, the Lord is with you. Open up to Him. I hope you'll find your way back to Him.*
>
> *Love,*
> *Mary*

Danny read Mary's letter again. He scolded himself for the way he had treated her, putting the Fair Play committee ahead of her.

While he didn't want to go to church just for her sake, he could've been more sensitive. When she came to see him off, they didn't have an opportunity to talk, and he couldn't tell how she felt about him.

Boy, do I miss her. He didn't see this coming. Danny could handle the hardships of being in jail but not his loneliness.

Maybe it was for the best that they broke up. Even if he got out of prison, Danny couldn't imagine what kind of life he could offer her with a prison record.

Danny folded the letters, put them back into the envelope, and placed it on his bunk. He covered his eyes with his hands and wept bitterly.

* * *

The Heart Mountain draft resisters murmured among themselves as they waited in the exercise yard for the lawyer who was already a half-hour late. Danny seated himself on a folding chair in the front row while guards circled the perimeter.

Tom Okada counted the draft resisters. "There's about thirty here," he said to Danny. "Casper and other jails make up sixty-three total."

"Is that all? Over a hundred guys used to attend these meetings."

"Used to," Tom said. "But some of them buckled under the pressure by the camp director and FBI."

"So we're the real McCoy." Danny glanced around.

At 2:35 p.m., keys clanged and the steel gate screeched as the guard opened it. A thickset Caucasian man stepped into the yard in front of the assembly. He dropped his leather briefcase on the ground and draped his gray suit jacket over the back of a wooden folding chair. He loosened his necktie and cleared his voice. "Good afternoon. I'm Attorney Samuel Meyer, out of Denver," he said in a booming voice. "The Fair Play Committee has retained my services."

"Are you from the ACLU?" asked Shig Fujii.

"No, but I have represented clients of the American Civil Liberties Union on numerous occasions. I fought for Negroes and Mexicans who were victimized by greedy white factory owners and farmers in 1935 and won. I even defended Communist party workers accused of taking over labor unions in the meat-packing plants in Chicago and got them acquitted."

The young men looked to each other and nodded their assent. Finally, someone to fight for them.

"Let me assure you, I will do my utmost to have you cleared of all charges."

The man next to Danny whispered, "Do you think we can trust this guy? I heard when he met with our leaders, all he talked about was money."

That didn't sound promising. Danny wished he could have been involved in the negotiations.

Meyer cleared his throat. "I want to go over a few things before the trial, which begins in a few weeks. First of all, look neat and presentable. The sheriff's office arranged for a number of barbers to cut your hair. Also, people in the surrounding communities donated clothes—"

"They don't fit," someone in the back row shouted.

Meyer took a quick look around the audience and seemed to understand. He reached into his briefcase, took a notebook out, and scribbled.

"I'll send word back to Heart Mountain and have clothes shipped here."

Some men chuckled.

"Okay, now that we got that out of the way, let's get into the particulars." Meyer scanned the men from side to side. "You have a choice. Do you men want to have a jury trial? Or do you want the judge to be the sole arbiter?"

The men turned toward each other and whispered.

Danny didn't know what would be better.

"Now, I'll tell you what I recommend." Meyer reached into his briefcase and pulled out a newspaper. "I don't think a jury trial will work in your favor." He let the comment sink in. "Here's why. The people in these parts aren't likely to be sympathetic to your cause."

He held up the front page of the *Wyoming Gazette*. "The headline says, 'JAP DRAFT DODGERS TO STAND TRIAL.' "

A cacophony of indignation erupted.

"That's what you're up against. The jury pool would be drawn from people who read this newspaper."

Bob Miyazaki rose. "Do you think the judge will be fair?"

"That's difficult to say. Judge Blake will preside. He's a tough, old-school judge who's been serving on the federal circuit for a long time. To my knowledge, he hasn't presided on a single case involving the Selective Service. But I'm sure that the outcome will depend upon the evidence and how well both sides present their cases."

Danny blew out a breath. It didn't seem like the guy was giving them any straight answers. No matter what happened, he wanted to make sure their voices were heard. "Will we be able to testify?"

"That all depends on how the trial progresses. The first thing I'm going to do is move for acquittal on grounds that the prosecution's case is a violation of your freedom of speech. Judge Blake is very strong on constitutional law."

The men nodded to each other and buzzed in low whispers.

"Frankly, I'm not sure that the motion will be granted. Blake is known as a strict constructionist, which means he has a tight definition of what he thinks is freedom of speech. To him, it may mean ensuring such things as freedom of the press and the right of lawful assembly. I'm not sure his definition includes civil disobedience, which is what your actions amount to."

Danny picked up on Meyer's uncertainty. "So, if the motion doesn't work, what's going to happen?"

"Then we proceed with the trial. We'll present our arguments and hope for the best."

Bob Miyazaki stood up and turned to face the other men. "Let's vote. How many of you want a jury trial?"

No hands went up.

"Okay. I guess we all want the judge to decide, right?" Bob said. "Put up your hands to make it official."

Every man raised his hand. Danny pushed his hand up halfway, still unsure of this guy.

While the vote was being taken, Danny sat quietly, taking in what he had heard thus far. He wasn't sure he understood everything. A question occurred to him, and he stood up. "Would we be able to represent ourselves?"

"No, that would imply separate trials for each of you. The court has already decided to try you as a single group. Besides, it isn't advisable for you to defend yourselves. You're not lawyers. The judge and the prosecutor will eat you alive."

Easing back into the chair, Danny wondered whether Meyer was saying that just to keep this job. How hard could it be to stand up and state what was fair and right?

Bright smiles broke out among the other men, who seemed encouraged that this lawyer could get them out of jail and show everyone the justice of their cause.

But Danny wasn't so sure he could put his faith in this man. Meyer reminded him of a used car salesman, only with big, fancy words. They didn't have many alternatives. For now he'd go along and see what would happen.

37

Thwarted

Kokura Army Base

Time was running out for Akira. The 44th Independent Mixed Brigade of the 32nd Imperial Japanese Army, would be deployed overseas soon.

He dreaded having to fight against the country of his birth, but now he had no choice. If he refused to serve, he would likely be sent to prison or executed. Worst of all, he feared for Emiko if something were to happen to him.

Still no word from her.

Despite earlier reports that the rail lines to Kumamoto had been bombed, mail was going through now. Surely she must have received one of his many letters. Something must have happened to her. After weeks of insomnia and breaking out in night sweats, he could no longer avoid asking Sergeant Kameda for help.

Akira entered Kameda's office, stood to attention, and saluted. "Sergeant, may I have a word with you, sir?"

"Omura, what you do want?" Kameda reeked of alcohol.

"Do you know what might be happening with the mail? I haven't received any since I've been here."

"How should I know?" The sergeant poured himself a shot of whiskey.

"The other men from Kumamoto are receiving letters from their families."

"Maybe your family forgot about you." Kameda laughed derisively.

If Akira didn't mean anything to Emiko, she wouldn't have accepted his marriage proposal or visited him at the *Kempeitai* jail. "Sir, please ask the officer in charge of the mail service to investigate."

"You want me to see Captain Kajiwara and tell him that his operation is losing mail? Are you crazy? He'll have my head." The sergeant's complexion turned even redder, and the vein in his throbbing temple looked ready to burst.

"Sir, then will you allow me a few days' furlough to investigate the situation back home?"

"Omura, there are men serving in China and the Pacific islands who've been separated from their families for five years. And you want me to grant you a leave after a few months?"

"But sir, something is wrong—"

The sergeant grabbed Akira by the front collar and shoved him back. "Get out of my office!"

He should have known better. Akira bowed stiffly to Kameda and left. Overwhelming despair hovered over him like an ominous dark cloud. He'd find another way to contact her.

38

Deployed

Civitavecchia, Italy - June 11, 1944

Early in the morning, Tad opened his eyes and sat upright inside his bedroll in the bombed-out ruins of an old church. He rubbed the sleep from his eyes and peeled himself out of his bedding. His companions hadn't yet stirred from their slumber.

Fog blanketed the sky above the church's half-destroyed ceiling—a good indication that perhaps today might bring some relief from the sweltering Mediterranean sun. Ever since they had arrived in the Italian seaport of Civitavecchia five days ago, temperatures hovered around eighty-five degrees Fahrenheit.

He opened a C-ration tin and spooned himself roast beef hash, chasing the meaty mouthfuls with swigs of water from his canteen. Not exactly the most appetizing breakfast, but at least it would keep his stomach from growling. In the background sirens blared.

A fellow medic John Sasaki flung the door open. "Tad! Tad! They're calling all medics to report to the field hospital on the double. Wounded coming in."

Tad threw on his uniform and snatched his medical kit. "Yikes, we're actually going to treat real patients this time."

Young men wailed and howled like wild animals as Tad carried dozens of stretchers with John and other helpers from the field ambulances.

The metallic smell of blood hung in Tad's nostrils, and he fought a battle with queasiness, seeing so many men writhing in pain with severed arms and legs, dangling tendons, and exposed organs.

A young soldier bellowed, "It hurts! Oh God, it hurts!"

The putrid stench of a festering laceration overwhelmed Tad as he leaned over the soldier who was screaming and crying. "We're going to get you cleaned up while you wait for a doctor. Hang in there."

John held down the soldier while Tad unraveled the bloody gauze and gently sponged antiseptic on a fist-sized wound. He deftly applied pressure bandages to stanch the blood flow and taped them down.

Semi-digested hash rose in Tad's throat, and he covered his mouth. "I'll be right back." He ran outside and could no longer hold it in and vomited on shrubs just outside the treatment area. *Jesus, please help me to get through all this. There's no time for a weak stomach. Also please ease the pain of these soldiers.*

When Tad returned, he hastened to a man with large gaping holes in his abdomen, requiring treatment beyond his capability. All of the lectures, medical manuals, and training mannequins hadn't prepared him adequately. *Lord, please guide me. I have no idea what to do.* The soldier spoke deliriously and went into hyperventilation. Tad lightly placed clean bandages on the damaged area and prayed for a doctor to arrive soon.

Corpses began to pile up on one side of the room to clear the path for triaging the wounded. Next, he injected morphine into a victim who was bawling with second- and third-degree burns. Tad's stomach twisted as he dabbed saline on the patient's leg.

Another patient lay unconscious with a head contusion. He cleansed the wound and said a quick prayer. One after another, Tad tried his best to treat each individual, not knowing whether they'd survive.

After a long shift, he washed up and reported to the assembly area where the 3rd Battalion soldiers gathered to receive mail. The truck from the supply ship was late. Lily was probably close to having the baby, but he most likely wouldn't read about that until next time since sea mail took about a month. The thought of becoming a father brought a smile to his face. In her last letter, she also mentioned that Danny had been arrested and his case would go to trial. Tad feared this would happen.

His friend Jim Hori snuck up from behind. "Hey, Tad, the good guys landed in Normandy last week and are pushing toward Paris. We're coming up the gut through Italy, and with the Ruskies pouring in from the east, this war could be done in no time."

"That's great news, but let's not get ahead of ourselves." The bloody wounds of soldiers carted into the hospital and the scores of dead bodies at the collection area awaiting burial told a different story. In one day, he'd seen enough death and gore to last a lifetime. If it were possible to go home to Lily and his family, he'd be the first in line, but that wasn't likely to happen. Not until they licked the Germans.

The mail truck finally rolled in, and men waited in eager anticipation. By the time Tad's name was called, most people already collected their letters and drifted away. A few milled around joking and laughing. Tad received his mail and slit the envelope with a penknife when another group of soldiers poured into the area. Their shiny helmets and pressed uniforms told him they were new arrivals.

"Get a load of this," said a tall private with a Southern drawl. "Jap soldiers."

A beefy soldier who looked like an offensive lineman smirked. "Yeah. Who would have thought?"

Tad forced a breath through clenched teeth. *What nerve! They're supposed to be on the same side.* This type of attitude was the very reason why he enlisted in the army in the first place. Tad and his people were every bit as American as these yokels, and he wanted to prove it.

The tall private turned to his companions. "Y'all better watch yourself around them. They may join their Nazi pals and shoot us in the back." He and the others laughed.

"Aah, they're just a bunch of buck-toothed monkeys." The offensive lineman waddled about in a circle caricaturizing a monkey, scratching his right shoulder with one hand and the left underarm with his other hand.

"Hey, which side are you on?" yelled the tall Southerner.

Two Nisei, Okimoto and Ikeda, spun around in boxing stances, ready to take on the white soldiers.

Okimoto's eyes blazed like flaming torches. "Who you calling monkey?"

"You Japs!" another white soldier shouted.

Not another fight. Tad pocketed his letter. He didn't raise his fists, but neither did he back away.

A stout, tow-headed Caucasian lieutenant stepped in and squeezed between the two groups. He approached Okimoto, who stood with his dukes up.

"Is this how you stand in front of an officer?"

Okimoto straightened and stood to attention. "No, sir."

The lieutenant turned to the white soldiers who were also standing at attention. He strode in front of the tall private. "What action have you boys seen so far?"

"None, sir."

"Uh-huh. A bunch of greenhorns. Is that correct?"

The private winced. "Yes, sir."

"I'm Lieutenant Mark James of the 34th Division. I've been fighting this war since the beginning of '43. We chased Rommel out of North Africa and Sicily."

The lieutenant's chiseled face hardened as he scanned the men on both sides. "Then at a mountain village outside Salerno, the Krauts had us pinned down with three machine-gun nests, one on each side and one directly above us. Couldn't call in aerial or artillery, because my radioman had been killed. Bullet holes peppered the walkie-talkie on his back. Crossfire picked off a couple of runners I tried to send back to our lines. I lost over a third of my platoon."

His description reminded Tad of the wounded and dead soldiers he had seen earlier in the day.

Lieutenant James took a step toward the white soldiers. "That's when I first met the men of the 100th Battalion. They came out of nowhere and charged up the hill, taking out all three machine gun nests, and killing over fifty enemy troops. They lost a lot of men doing it. But I wouldn't be standing here today if it weren't for them. That wasn't the only time. At Anzio and Cassino, they proved themselves again and again."

Smiles formed on the faces of Okimoto and Ikeda, and their chests puffed out a bit.

Lieutenant James glowered at the tall private. "And do you know who the men of the 100th are?"

The young man's eyes shifted from the Nisei to the lieutenant. "No, sir."

"They're Japanese Americans, just like them." He pointed to Tad. "Japs, you call them. For my money, they're among the bravest men ever to wear American uniforms. So, before you continue to insult them, I want to see you charge up a hill and take out some Germans just like they did."

The lieutenant turned his attention to the Nisei soldiers. "Keep up the good work." He pivoted and strode to his jeep.

The tightness in Tad's chest disappeared, and his mouth stretched into a wide smile. What perfect timing. The lieutenant's vote of confidence reassured him that joining the army was worth it after all.

At last someone had stuck up for them.

39

Deceit

Kumamoto, Japan

Emiko continued demonstrating *Hana-isho* techniques to her *Ikebana* students. "Insert several stems at different points along the outer circle and point the tips outward. This creates a spiral sense of movement."

At the conclusion of the lesson, Mrs. Katsumoto ushered her into the anteroom. Her sudden action puzzled Emiko. "What's wrong?"

"Sensei, have you heard anything from Akira-san yet?"

"No, I haven't." The question deflated her like air being let out of a balloon.

"He didn't respond to the letter you delivered to the base?" Mrs. Katsumoto's forehead wrinkled, and the corners of her mouth turned downward.

Emiko shook her head slowly. "Maybe he never received it."

Mrs. Katsumoto peeked into the living room where the other ladies fashioned their arrangements, then looked at Emiko. "I don't know whether I should tell you this, but Mrs. Endo wants to introduce her son to you." She wore a mischievous smile and handed Emiko a photograph. "He's a handsome man."

"Why?" Emiko didn't bother looking at the photo. She couldn't possibly meet another suitor, not when her heart belonged to Akira. Hadn't she made that clear to her?

"Mrs. Endo has taken a liking to you. Her son's wife passed away three years ago and left him with a young daughter."

"But doesn't she know I'm engaged?"

"I never told her." Mrs. Katsumoto lowered her gaze. "Her son is a major in the army, evidently highly placed on General Yoneda's staff."

"Who's General Yoneda?"

She displayed a scheming smile. "I met the general and his wife at a party. He's chief of Army Operations. His office maintains all personnel records, so he can probably find out where Akira-san was sent."

"You want me to meet her son so he can help me locate my fiancé?" Emiko shook her head.

"You can tell him Akira-san is your cousin."

Emiko's breath caught in her throat. "I can't do that." Mrs. Katsumoto might be trying to help her, but Emiko couldn't get involved in something so manipulative. Passing herself off as Akira's sister was bad enough when she visited him in jail.

"I understand how you feel, but—" Mrs. Katsumoto glanced toward the living room, then back at Emiko. "What's the harm in just meeting him? Mrs. Endo is a good friend of mine, and I'd hate to disappoint her. Besides, you're not promising anything at this point."

"But what if he's expecting to start a courtship? I can't give him a false expectation." Emiko reflected on her father's words about meeting Hiroshi. *Why can't you at least meet him? If you don't like him, then you don't have to marry him.* What a disaster that turned out to be.

"If your engagement doesn't work out, I can think of worse things than being married to this fine man."

Her bluntness left Emiko speechless. She wouldn't stop at anything, but now, Emiko needed to derail her. Emiko tried to make her understand her reservations without offending her. She couldn't afford to have Mrs. Katsumoto think badly of her, not when she helped her gain students for her *ikebana* classes.

"If you don't want to continue seeing him after the initial meeting, I'll explain it to them," Mrs. Katsumoto said.

"I'm not comfortable doing this."

"Sensei, Akira-san could be deployed to the battlefront any day now. What if you never see or hear from him again?"

* * *

Emiko tried not to stare across the table at the dashing figure of Major Endo in his uniform. His large, dark eyes, square jaw, and straight set of pearl-white teeth reminded her of a slightly older version of Akira.

Underneath his commanding aura, she sensed something gentle about him. Perhaps it was his polite manner or the tender words he used to describe his wife who died of cancer.

A waitress brought a teapot, matching cups, and light appetizers of dried persimmon and rice cake wafers on a tray. The major stayed silent as she served them piping-hot tea, placed the appetizers in front of them, then bowed and left the private dining room.

"My daughter, Ayako, is like an orphan now. When I talk about her mother, she says she misses her, but I don't think she really remembers her. I'm called away to Tokyo so often that she hardly recognizes me when I periodically return to Kumamoto."

The major reached into his uniform jacket and retrieved his wallet. He pulled out a photograph and handed it to Emiko. "This is my daughter."

Emiko peered at the photo, which showed a smiling young girl in her school uniform. "How old is she?"

"Seven." He paused. "Fortunately my mother looks after her and is raising her to be a proper young lady."

The photo and his words brought back her own loneliness and sense of abandonment when her mother died when she was eight. Her heart ached for the little girl.

Major Endo sipped his steaming tea. "I don't mean to spoil this evening with my problems."

She returned the photograph. "Your daughter is very pretty."

A glint of a smile appeared on his face. "Thank you for saying so. She takes after her mother."

Emiko held the teacup to her lips and tried to calm her emotions. She savored the bitter taste of *gyoroku-cha* tea. Had it been another time under different circumstances, she might have easily fallen for this decent and sweet man. But his uniform reminded her that her beloved Akira also served as a soldier somewhere in Japan or on the battlefield in a distant land.

"Mrs. Katsumoto mentioned you're trying to find out where your cousin has been stationed. You haven't been able to contact him?"

Guilt bit into Emiko's conscience, and she tried to keep her hand steady. Mrs. Katsumoto had fabricated the story, and now she could not dishonor her by correcting him. Emiko nodded.

"Perhaps I can help locate him." Major Endo pulled out a little notebook and fountain pen from his uniform pocket. "What is his name and when did he enter the army?"

"Akira Omura. He was drafted about three and a half months ago. I've sent several letters to him but haven't received a single reply."

"You must be very close to your cousin." He jotted down notes. "These are chaotic times. The Americans have stepped up their bombing raids, and the fighting is fierce in the southern Pacific islands." Setting his pen down, he turned his eyes toward her. "But it is odd that you haven't heard from him."

Emiko sucked in a breath and released it. "Yes, I . . ." She glanced at the floor, trying to make the words come out, but she couldn't go through with it. She looked up at him. "Major, I'm afraid I haven't been truthful to you. He's not my cousin, but rather my fiancé."

"Your fiancé?" He sat back in his chair, and his eyes widened.

Emiko's face grew hot, and she lowered her gaze. "Yes. I'm so sorry that I lied. I want you to know the truth."

"The truth? You knew this was a meeting for a marriage match, yet you had no intention?" His brows drew together, and his forehead formed deep lines.

"Please forgive me."

He closed his notebook, capped his pen, abruptly rose, and strode out of the room.

All her hopes and intentions had crumbled in the space of a minute. Shame and regret thrashed her conscience. Emiko buried her face in her hands and cried. Akira's whereabouts would remain hidden from her, perhaps indefinitely.

40

Day in Court

Cheyenne, Wyoming – June 12, 1944

Danny and sixty-two other resisters sat crammed behind the attorneys' tables. He twiddled his thumbs and turned his head toward the gallery but only recognized Mike Murata and another JACL person. Attorney Meyer had told them no relatives would be allowed to attend for security reasons. Reporters with press badges occupied the rest of the seats, ready with pencils and notepads.

He never imagined the trial would be such a big deal. His gaze slowly moved across the marbled walls and traveled to the high ceilings. The seriousness of the case began to sink in.

Just before ten o'clock, the door on the left side of the bench opened, and a balding judge with remnants of white wispy hair entered with an unsmiling expression.

"All rise," the bailiff called. "The honorable Thomas Blake presiding."

Danny rose and scrutinized the deep frown that seemed to be permanently cemented on the judge's face.

After everyone sat down, a clerk handed the judge some documents that he reviewed for a moment.

The judge addressed the audience with a stern look. "This trial is the only one in the docket and is expected to last no longer than a week. I see the defendants have elected not to have a trial by jury." He cast his eyes at the defense counsel. "Mr. Meyer, I assume your clients fully understand the implications of the election, and the decision I will make is final, pending any further appeal."

Meyer stood up. "Yes, Your Honor."

Danny's focus shifted from their attorney to the judge. Their fate depended only upon the ruling of one man. He wasn't sure whether they had made the right choice.

Judge Blake turned to the court clerk. "Let the clerk read aloud the specifications."

"In the case of the United States versus Shigeru Fujii, et al, defendants from the Heart Mountain War Relocation Authority facility are charged with violating the Selective Training and Service Act of 1940, Title 50 United States Code, Section 311. The specified charges include failure to register with the Selective Service Board and submit to military preinduction medical examinations, thereby constituting evasion of the requirements of the law."

The judge then addressed the federal prosecutor. "Mr. Stacker, you may proceed with your opening statement."

Carl Stacker rose. "Thank you, Your Honor. This is a case where the defendants have knowingly and willingly violated the provisions of the said section of the Selective Service law. This much is beyond dispute. At issue here is the simple question as to whether there has been compliance with the law or not."

Stacker extended his hand toward Meyer. "My esteemed colleague for the defense will attempt to argue that the law is unconstitutional, in light of the special circumstances of the emergency relocation of a certain ethnic group to which the defendants belong. While those circumstances deserve to be examined in an appropriate legal forum, the time and place is not now. The court should confine itself to the examination of the facts pertaining to—"

"Mr. Stacker, I will decide what the court will or will not confine itself to." Judge Blake shot him a dirty look.

The audience laughed, prompting the judge to pound his gavel and yell, "Order! I say order in the court! Or I'll clear the gallery."

Stacker's face flushed slightly. "Your Honor, I apologize for my presumption. I have no further comment. Thank you." He sat down in his chair.

Danny stared at Stacker and smirked. He turned his head from side to side, smiling at his companions. What a clown the prosecutor was. Maybe the judge wasn't so bad after all.

"All right. Mr. Meyer, do you have an opening statement?"

Samuel Meyer rose. "Yes, Your Honor."

"You may proceed."

"Thank you, Your Honor. Mr. Stacker states that the motivation for my clients' actions is of no consequence. He doesn't seem the least bit curious about it. And I find that very curious."

The crowd, including Danny, laughed, prompting Judge Blake to use his gavel once again. When silence returned, the judge said, "Continue."

"Your Honor, I would argue that the motivation—the reason for my clients' refusal to comply—is the very heart of the matter. Our country was founded on such an issue. The colonists first stood up to protest King George's unfair and burdensome stamp and tea tariffs and later took up arms against the redcoat soldiers who were sent to enforce their collection. If the issue then was a matter of simple compliance to the king's edicts, our ancestors would have never risen up and united as a country. We would still be British subjects."

Meyer turned over a page of notes. "I also submit that it is a matter of perspective. From the British view, we were breaking the law. But from an American point of view, there was no cause for trying the acts of disobedience against the old system of law. In fact, the essence of every act of civil disobedience is in that motivation."

He extended his arm toward Stacker. "Therefore, Your Honor, I beg to differ with Mr. Stacker. It is not just the simple question of whether the defendants disobeyed the law. The real issue is whether there were justifiable reasons for that act of disobedience—"

"Very eloquent, Mr. Meyer. But where are you going with this line of argument?" The judge's voice came through crisp and clear.

"Your Honor, the defense moves for dismissal of all charges on the basis of special circumstances, namely the abridgement of civil rights for the families of the defendants. Their resistance to the Selective Service Act is a legitimate protest against that abridgement and is an expression of the defendants' freedom of speech."

Danny wasn't sure what all the fancy words meant, but he got the gist of it. Their lawyer sounded good.

The judge turned to the prosecutor. "Mr. Stacker, any rebuttal?"

"Yes, Your Honor. The counsel for the defense makes an interesting case, but I never thought he would bring our founding fathers and King George into the fray."

Laughter burst out among the people. Even Meyer broke out into a big grin.

"Order! I say order! There will be no further outbursts. Gentlemen, levity has no place in my courtroom. I strongly recommend you adhere strictly to the business at hand." He wrote something down while the rest of the court remained quiet.

Judge Blake looked squarely at Meyer. "I happen to subscribe to the belief that the First Amendment does not apply to the flagrant disregard for other provisions of the law. Therefore, motion to dismiss is denied."

The defendants made a loud and collective groan.

Danny turned to Tom Okada and said, "What's wrong with the judge? Doesn't he get it?"

"Order! I say, order!" Judge Blake again pounded his gavel and narrowed his eyes at Danny. "I will not tolerate disrespectful behavior in my court. If I hear another disturbance, I'll throw you Jap boys back into your cells and hold the defense in contempt. You got that?"

The epithet stung Danny. He didn't think the judge could hear him. It was one thing to be called a Jap by some no-account on the street, quite another to be slapped like that by a federal judge. A knot jerked tight in his stomach. He began to doubt this would be a fair trial.

"Mr. Stacker, are you ready to call your first witness?"

"Yes, Your Honor." Stacker scanned the courtroom with a thin smile.

* * *

During recess Danny and a few men gathered around their attorney in an adjacent room guarded by five sheriff's deputies.

"Mr. Meyer, what do you think our chances of winning are?" Kaz Tokuda asked.

"We've been dealt an initial setback with the motion to dismiss, but I expected that. Judge Blake is a tough old bird. He's hardworking and knows the law." The men groaned, but Meyer held up his hand. "But I think we can turn him around."

Danny stood in front of the attorney. "Looks to me like our goose is cooked. He called us 'Jap boys' in there."

Tom Okada glowered at Danny. "And whose fault is that?"

"I'll be careful from now on." Danny swiped his mouth with his thumb and forefinger to zipper it shut.

"Don't give up hope," Meyer said to them. "This trial just started, and we have a long way to go before it's over."

Air whooshed out of Danny's lungs. "If you ask me, the judge's mind is already made up."

The other men standing nearby hung their heads.

"Fellas, this is what we'll do," Meyer said, drumming his fingers on the table. "In the next few days, we're going to do a full-court press. We'll call up witnesses who will attest that none of you have a disloyal bone in your body and show them you're protesting the ill treatment the government has meted out to you and your families. And that protest, my friends, is an unalienable right of every American."

"But he's already denied the motion on the freedom of speech," Kaz Tokuda said.

"Boys, we're going to demonstrate to the judge how unfair the government has been. If the rule of law is based upon anything, it is the principle of fairness to all citizens. Once we're through, I don't believe the judge will be able to deny it."

Sounded like a lot of doubletalk, but maybe this lawyer really knew what he was doing. Danny relaxed his stance. He would give him a chance before dismissing him completely. "Okay, Mr. Meyer, we're with you all the way."

* * *

Danny ran his fingers through his crew cut. He had never worn his hair this short. From his usual seat in the front row, he scanned the other resisters. At least two-thirds of them also followed Meyer's suggestion to have their hair cut short.

"Mr. Meyer, please call your witness."

"Yes, Your Honor. The defense calls FBI Special Agent James Farber to the stand."

Danny vividly remembered the ill-humored G-man who had interrogated him on the day of his arrest.

After the oath of witness, Farber took his seat.

"Special Agent Farber, you were called to the Heart Mountain War Relocation Authority facility on March 22 to process the arrests of the defendants. Is that correct?"

"Yes."

"When you arrived, did you notice if the camp was surrounded by barbed wire?"

"It was surrounded by wire, but I didn't notice whether it was barbed or not."

Laughter erupted among the defendants. Even the prosecutor cracked a smile.

Judge Blake gaveled them to silence.

Meyer smirked at Farber. "Surely you couldn't be suggesting that it could be anything but barbed wire in a prison camp?"

"Objection, Your Honor," Slacker said. "Heart Mountain is a War Relocation Authority facility, not a prison camp."

"Sustained." The judge scowled at the defense attorney. "Mr. Meyer, care to rephrase your question?"

"Could you not see that it was barbed wire?"

"It was dark already. I couldn't tell whether it was barbed."

Danny rolled his eyes and forced air through his teeth.

Meyer flipped a sheet on his legal pad. "Personal opinions aside, we'll accept that statement. Special Agent Farber, you were involved in questioning many of the defendants—Thomas Okada, Shigeru Fujii, Daniel Omura, to name a few. Do you recall interviewing these men on March 22?"

"Yes, I do."

"Can you identify the three men I just mentioned?"

Farber thrust his head forward and scanned the resisters, his squinting eyes moving left to right, and back again. Silence reigned as the agent repeated the process. "No, I'm afraid I cannot," he mumbled.

Meyer cupped his left ear toward the witness. "I didn't hear your response. Please repeat it so we can all hear."

"No, I cannot identify them."

"The average length of each interview was thirty minutes. You must have gotten a good look at each of them. Are you sure you cannot pick out any of them?"

"It was three months ago. I interviewed twenty-five of them."

"Please answer the question—yes or no?" Meyer's tone grew louder.

"No, I can't."

"Are those really the reasons why you can't remember? Or is it because all Orientals look alike?"

Danny now realized why Meyer had suggested they get crew cuts. Their attorney was clever, but could he win the case?

"Objection!" Stacker interrupted. "Defense counsel is leading the witness."

"Sustained." Judge Blake focused his frown on Meyer. "Mr. Meyer, where are you going with this line of questioning?"

"Your Honor, I insist that the charges against my clients be dropped. The agent cannot even identify the alleged perpetrators."

Judge Blake sneered at Meyer. "No! The defendants identified themselves at the time of their arrests. They signed their names on fingerprint cards. That is adequate identification, Mr. Meyer. Your request is denied."

Danny's companions on both sides wore glum expressions and hung their heads with their backs hunched. The judge had derailed every argument Meyer could muster.

"Mr. Meyer, I order you to desist from any further theatrical ploys and clever antics. I want you to get down to serious legal work. Otherwise, I will hold you in contempt of court. Is that understood?"

"Yes, Your Honor. I have no further questions for the witness."

Danny's hopes deflated like air being released from a tire.

41

Gambit

Kokura Army Base

A heavy breath escaped Akira's lungs as he stood in formation with other soldiers on the parade grounds. General Hideki Soma stepped behind the podium wearing a full-dress uniform. Numerous medals pinned to his tunic glinted in the sunlight. He addressed the division. "The time has finally come for you men to perform your duty to the emperor and your country. Even though the enemy has stepped up its attacks on our homeland, we will ultimately be victorious. Throughout our history, we have proven that the indomitable spirit of our soldiers cannot be defeated."

On cue, several thousand men raised their arms and shouted, *"Banzai! Banzai! Banzai!"*

General Soma cleared his throat. "We know that the gods are protecting our homeland. That was proven when they called down the *kamikaze* winds to blow apart and sink the Mongol invasion fleet in the thirteenth century. Today we honor a special group of young men who volunteered to serve in that same spirit and have been undergoing intensive aircraft training for several months. They will become our main line of defense against enemy ships and other targets." He motioned to an officer nearby. "Lieutenant Colonel Yamaguchi, have the *kamikaze* trainees come to the platform."

A column of over fifty men filed in from the far side of the assembly, wearing impressive uniforms with distinctive wings on both shoulders and blue *sakura* insignias.

"Let's give them a rousing cheer!" General Soma yelled.

All the men raised both arms above their heads and shouted, "*Banzai!*" five times.

Akira mouthed the words and participated in the ritual so he wouldn't be suspected of disloyalty.

The crowd died down, and the general continued. "For the rest of you, I expect no less. Work hard, fight hard, and die for your country if necessary. May the gods be with you."

Die for your country—which country? And these gods were not the *one* and *only* God Akira knew and served.

Recently he had been thinking a lot about the possibility of dying in the war or coming back maimed for life. His gaze drifted to his boots. It had been four months since Emiko visited him in jail. What could have happened to her? More than ever, he had to trust God for her safety and well-being.

Late last night, Akira prayed fervently for some way of contacting her and penned one more letter. During the prayer, he sensed God telling him not to mail the letter but couldn't understand why.

He remembered a teaching from his church. God sends us a helper—the Holy Spirit—who is like the wind that propels us like a sailboat when we seek his guidance.

Beside him, Private Saito whispered, "Do you know what the *kamikaze* pilots' missions are?"

Akira understood the historical reference but not how it related to these young pilots. He looked at Saito. "Not exactly."

"They've been trained to fly planes loaded with high explosives and crash them into enemy ships and die in the process. That is why they receive the best food, the nicest-looking uniforms, and a night with the prettiest *geisha*."

Akira gazed at the young pilots. What a waste of lives. It was in line with the samurai *Bushido* ethic—fighting to the last man and committing suicide to preserve honor.

The general saluted and left the platform.

"Everyone! Line up and board the trucks to the transport ships," bellowed Sergeant Kameda.

Akira and his unit prepared to climb aboard a truck. About ten meters away, two young women wearing pretty kimonos caught his eye. How strange for them to be on base. Perhaps they were the *geisha* prize that would be given to the pilots.

Sergeant Kameda inspected the line and marched past everyone.

The moment Kameda was out of sight, Akira stole another look in the direction of the *geisha*. Now only one woman stood there. An idea flashed in his mind.

He glanced at the line and paused. If this notion was from God, Akira needed to act quickly. Just as he was about to climb aboard, he wheeled around and ran toward the woman.

Akira pulled the letter out of his uniform shirt pocket. "Excuse me, miss. Could you do me a great favor and see that my fiancée receives this letter?" He placed the letter and money in her hand. "Please do not mail it. Instead, have it hand-delivered by someone you trust. Here's one hundred yen for your trouble."

The young woman's eyes bulged. She made no attempt to return the letter or money.

A moment later, hands grabbed Akira's collar from behind and yanked him away. "What are you doing, Omura?" Sergeant Kameda blared. "It's no time to flirt. Get into the truck."

As Akira stepped onto the flatbed, he turned his head toward the woman. The sergeant was talking to her, but Akira couldn't hear what they were discussing. He didn't see her hand Kameda anything, nor could he tell whether she hid the letter.

Had God really told him not to mail the letter? The young woman didn't know him and certainly had no obligation to him. She could easily discard the letter and keep the money. Worse yet, she could hand it over to the base authorities. But something about the way she looked at him gave him a glimmer of hope.

The engine rumbled and exhaust fumes floated in the air as the truck lurched toward the gate. Akira watched the woman who stood there alone, staring back at him. She became smaller and smaller and finally disappeared from his sight.

Please God. Please have my letter delivered to Emiko.

42

First Blood

Civitavecchia, Italy - June 18, 1944

Looking around the bustling mess tent, Tad set down his breakfast tray between a Hawaiian and a mainlander. It pleased him to see the two groups intermingling a lot more ever since the Hawaiians' field trip to the internment camps. But two weeks ago, a fight had broken out between Kawakami from Honolulu, and Terada from San Francisco. Trouble must have brewed from the listlessness caused by the long wait at Newport News and the endless voyage, zigzagging across the Atlantic.

"Good morning, fellas," Tad said.

The mainlanders and the guys from the 100th Battalion returned his greeting with warm smiles.

"Hey Tad, you hear dey gonna join us wit da 442 and change our name to 1st Battalion?" a Hawaiian said. "I no like dat."

Tad glanced at the blue and white insignia patch with the motto, "Remember Pearl Harbor" on the Hawaiian's sleeve. "I understand why you want to keep the 100th unit tag. You guys fought really hard and proved yourselves in battle at Salerno, Anzio, and Cassino. You deserve to keep it."

The men of the 100th let out proud smiles. Tad had bonded with many of them, treating the wounded and greeting their buddies who visited the field hospital. They laughed, jabbered about friends back home, baseball standings, and Italian girls.

After breakfast, Tad reported to the assembly area of his fighting unit—the 3rd Battalion, I Company. Boots clapped to attention and grins disappeared when Lieutenant Sadaichi Takechi appeared in front of the group. He was one of the few Japanese American officers in charge of a rifle company.

"Good morning, men," the ruddy-faced lieutenant said to them. "The 2nd and 3rd Battalions have been given orders to move out. We're going northeast to a place called Belvedere. There's a crack German battalion holed up in the hills above town, and they're controlling the coastal highway to Sassetta. We have to take them out. It won't be easy because they're a motorized SS unit with tanks, half-tracks, and artillery."

An eerie silence hung in the air, and a rush of adrenaline quickened Tad's pulse. It would be the first time he and his unit would be sent into battle. His chest tightened thinking about how many of them wouldn't make it back.

A broad smile stretched across Lieutenant Takechi's face. "You guys had one of the best training records in the States, and we're very proud of you. Now, let's show them what we're made of." The smile gave way to a serious look. "Any questions?"

Corporal John Ishii stepped forward. "Sir, is the 100th going to lead the way?"

"No, Corporal. The boys are being held in reserve this time. Now it's your turn."

The troops of I Company remained quiet and still.

"All right, be ready to saddle up tomorrow at 0-800 hours." The lieutenant pivoted and exited.

Tad swallowed hard and glanced at the men around him. Color drained from their faces. Perhaps their stomachs were also somersaulting like his.

Lily's plea echoed in his thoughts. *Why do you have to go? Why can't the single men go?*

He had no way of knowing if she had given birth and whether he would ever see his baby.

A verse came to Tad's mind. *Be strong and of a good courage; be not afraid . . . for the Lord thy God is with thee . . .*

* * *

A thunderous boom of a German 88-millimeter cannon blasted and pulverized the earth and rocks around the beleaguered men of I and K companies. Tad and his compatriots huddled in depressions, behind rocks or anything that gave them cover from the murderous enemy fire and flying debris. By midmorning, two soldiers had been killed and a dozen wounded. He crouched next to Lieutenant Takechi, waiting for his order to tend to the casualties.

Between volleys of artillery blasts and constant machine gun bursts, wounded men moaned and cried hysterically, twisting Tad's gut. He started to move toward them, but the lieutenant grabbed Tad's shoulder and held him back.

"Omura, it's too dangerous. I can't send you out yet."

It was as though Tad were in a boat, watching men drown and not being able to help.

When the shooting died down, Lieutenant Takechi signaled to Tad. "Go!"

Tad crawled to the ridge with his head low to the ground. Bullets from a German machine gun whistled by and punched holes into the dirt embankment above him. He froze with death seemingly only inches away. Heart pounding, Tad continued his inexorable creep for several yards until he reached a young man whose leg had been blown off. He palpated the soldier's neck and found no pulse. Reddish mud smeared Tad's shirtsleeves as he reached into the dead soldier's shirt for his dog tags—PETER TAKESHITA.

He closed Peter's eyes and crawled to the next downed trooper lying a few yards away. The young soldier wailed and grimaced in pain. "My shoulder."

Cutting away the right sleeve of the uniform, Tad examined the raw flesh and bone fragments. "I'll get you patched up." He broke open a packet of sulfa antiseptic and sprinkled it on the wound and dressed the shoulder with gauze. "Put some pressure on this with your other hand and lie still. Help is on the way."

Tad continued his triage, tending seven more men, and he dragged one of them back to Lieutenant Takechi's position.

"What's the status out there?" the lieutenant asked.

"Five dead, eighteen wounded. Not sure about casualties down the ridge or on the other side of the hill."

"Good work, Omura. I've radioed battalion HQ. All companies are reporting heavy enemy fire, and we can't advance against them. Only good news is the cannon company's knocked out two German tanks. HQ is calling the 100th Battalion back in. Pass the word to the other medics."

"Yes, sir." Poor guys in the 100th. They get no rest.

Later that afternoon, gunfire and mortar explosions moved toward the eastern flank of the enemy's line.

"It's the 100th. They're here!" one man shouted.

Lieutenant Takechi emerged behind large boulders and motioned. "Let's go."

They slowly slipped out from their hiding places.

Deafening explosions rocked the earth beneath Tad, as he and another medic, Yosh Hamada, crawled toward the loud cries for help.

Soon enemy gunfire tapered off, and the task of retrieving the wounded became easier.

By four in the afternoon, the artillery explosions and gunfire had ceased.

At a rendezvous point up the hill, Lieutenant Takechi spoke into a walkie-talkie, then turned to his men. "The 100th has taken the hill. They've whipped the Krauts!"

The men cheered and slapped each other on the back.

Yosh Hamada wiped sweat from his forehead. "Man, those guys in the 100th are good. They know what they're doing."

Tad grinned. "Yeah, they're good. We have a lot to learn from them." He thanked God for the victory. Yet, he knew there would be many more battles to fight.

43

The Visitor

Kumamoto, Japan

Emiko's fingers flew gracefully across the piano keys as she practiced playing Chopin's lively "Fantaisie-Impromptu" for the tenth time. After finishing, she rested her hands on the grand piano, pleased to get through such a difficult piece.

She rose and picked up a photograph of Akira from the shelf and lovingly held it close to her heart.

An unfamiliar woman's voice sounded from the front of the house. *"Gomen kudasai.* Hello, is anyone home?"

Setting the photograph down, Emiko padded to the foyer and opened the door. An attractive young woman with lustrous hair arranged in a traditional coiffure stood smiling. She wore an elegant midnight-blue kimono with an ice-pink chrysanthemum pattern. A silver *obi* wrapped around her thin waist. With wartime shortages, such fine apparel was rarely seen these days.

Emiko glanced down at her homemade *mompei* pants, then raised her eyes to her visitor. "Hello. What can I do for you?"

The woman bowed. "I'm sorry for disturbing you, but are you Miss Takata?" A fragrant gardenia scent wafted in the air.

"Yes, I am." Emiko returned the bow.

"My name is Okoto Harigae. I have a letter for you from your fiancé."

"You do?" Emiko's heart leaped for joy, but her momentary elation fell like a dead leaf. Did Akira fall for this young lady? Could this be the reason why she hadn't heard from him? She tried not to doubt him and set aside these anxieties. "Please come inside."

Okoto stepped inside the foyer and removed her *geta* sandals.

Emiko beckoned her guest into the living room. "I'm sorry, but I have nothing to offer you except a little tea. It will take me just a minute to prepare."

"Oh, no, please don't bother. I won't be able to stay long." Okoto gracefully kneeled and sat on the *tatami*. She reached inside her sleeve of flowing silk and pulled out a flat package, neatly wrapped in a *furoshiki* scarf. "Here's the letter."

"Thank you." Emiko couldn't wait to read it, but for the sake of good manners, she refrained. "Miss Harigae, how is it that you know my fiancé?"

"Actually, I don't know him. We only met briefly."

The response puzzled Emiko, and a myriad of questions swirled in her mind.

"I was at the Kokura army base to say good-bye to my fiancé, Shigeru, who was being shipped overseas. Your fiancé ran up to me and gave me this letter. He asked me to arrange delivery for it and gave me money."

Emiko could hardly believe what she was hearing. "How was he? Was he well?"

"He looked fine."

"I'm happy to hear that." The news brought Emiko a little reassurance. At least Akira didn't have bruises like the time she visited him in jail.

Okoto smoothed the kimono fabric on her lap. "I thought, 'Who is this man? And why did he give me this?' His voice sounded so urgent and sad. Then I saw in his eyes a look I'll never forget. They showed a deep love for someone—for you."

To hear of Akira's love from a stranger was more than Emiko could bear. Her eyes watered, and a teardrop slid down her cheek. She slipped her hand into her *mompei* pocket, pulled out a handkerchief, and dried her eyes.

"He specifically asked me not to send it through the post office and wanted me to arrange an alternate delivery." Okoto's thin eyebrows arched. "I thought, 'What a strange request. Why wouldn't he use the postal service? One hundred yen is a lot of money, far more than is needed to hire a special courier.' But he caught me by surprise, and I didn't know what to do."

A strange request, indeed. Perhaps something was interfering with the delivery of his letters. Emiko unwrapped the scarf and lifted the envelope, recognizing Akira's writing. A hundred yen bill lay underneath. Her eyes met Okoto's again. "I haven't received any mail from my fiancé since he left for the army in March, even though I've written him a dozen times."

"No?" Crease lines formed across her forehead. "That's very strange."

The concern on Okoto's oval face certainly looked sincere. It seemed safe for Emiko to confide her fears with someone going through the same separation from a loved one. "At first, I thought American bombings had disrupted mail service between Kokura and here. But my neighbors said they were receiving letters from that area. I waited to receive mail from him, but nothing ever arrived. Finally I went to the army base to hand deliver a letter to him."

"Then your fiancé must have received it."

"A sergeant told me Akira was out on maneuvers, but he assured me he would give it to him. But no letters have arrived from him."

"Perhaps that's why your fiancé asked me to bypass the mail service."

Something odd was happening. Emiko couldn't fathom why the sergeant would withhold her letter from Akira.

"Miss Takata, I'm sorry it's taken me this long to visit you. For days, I wrestled with my own loneliness and fear. But then I started thinking about your fiancé. Here was this handsome, yet sad and desperate man. I couldn't shake the look in his eyes, and I finally resolved to do something to help him."

The words were too much for Emiko to bear. She chided herself for doubting Akira earlier. He still loved her and cared for her.

"Miss Takata, I know nothing about you or your fiancé, but I do know how deeply he loves you. He risked severe punishment by running to me."

"What happened?"

"After he spoke to me, his superior grabbed him by the collar and ordered him back onto the truck. Once they left the base, I never saw him again."

"They left? Do you know where they were sent?"

"Okinawa."

Emiko gulped. "Okinawa?" A tight knot formed in her throat. Akira might be in grave danger.

Okoto pulled out a handkerchief from her sleeve and dabbed her wet eyes. "I almost sent your letter by courier service from Fukuoka, but my curiosity was killing me. I had to find out for myself about your fiancé's circumstances and who you were."

"You traveled all this way? I deeply appreciate it. Please keep the money. You took the time and expense to come all the way over here from Fukuoka."

"No, I can't accept it."

"Please, I insist."

"If you insist, I'll leave immediately." Okoto started to her feet.

"I'm sorry to offend you." Emiko rose and reached for Okoto's hand. "I will humbly accept your kind gesture."

Without warning, Okoto's face blanched, and she started to cry. "I'm so scared for my Shigeru. I'm afraid I'll never see him again." She patted her tears with a handkerchief.

Emiko nudged closer to comfort her guest, who shared the same unbearable grief she had.

Okoto glanced at the wall clock. "My, I didn't realize how long I've been here, taking up your time."

"No, not at all."

Emiko wanted to do something for her but didn't have a gift she could offer with half her belongings packed away in boxes. A thought came to her—she would pray for Okoto. Normally, Emiko didn't disclose her faith to just anyone, in case the person was part of some elaborate *Kempeitai* trick to entrap Christians. But this young woman's story seemed plausible, and the handwriting on the envelope was Akira's. "Miss Harigae, before you leave, may I pray for you and your fiancé?"

"Oh, that's very kind of you." Okoto looked around in the room. "Where is your *butsudan?*"

"I don't have a Buddhist altar. I'm a Christian."

Okoto raised her eyebrows. "A Christian?" Her surprised expression melted into a winsome smile.

Her smile looked genuine, and it was too late to take back what she had offered. "Yes."

Emiko clasped her hands and closed her eyes. "Sweet Jesus, my new friend, Okoto, and I pour out our hearts to you. As you know, both of our fiancés have been sent to Okinawa. Please protect them and keep them from harm and bring them back to us safely. I know you love us deeply and care for us. Your Word says even the hairs on our head are all numbered. We ask all these things in your precious name. Amen." Emiko opened her eyes and lifted her head.

"I've never heard a prayer like that, nor experienced such calmness like this."

"You're experiencing God's love for you. He gives us peace even when life's circumstances are difficult. When we pray to him, it's like talking to a close friend, which is so different than chanting Buddhist sutras."

"I don't understand everything you said, but I'm encouraged. Your God is wonderful." Okoto glanced at the clock again and rose. "I really must be going now. Thank you so much."

"You're welcome. Thank you again for coming all this way to deliver the letter." Emiko lifted herself off the *tatami* and reached for a piece of paper. She wrote down her name and uncle's address. "I'll be moving to Takeo soon. Please, let's keep in touch."

"I'd like that very much." Okoto reached for the note. She stepped down into the foyer and slid her feet into her *geta* sandals. A radiant smile lit up her face, and she bowed deeply.

They exchanged pleasantries again, and Emiko followed her out to the gate. Then she hurried back inside, anxious to read Akira's letter. Warmth coursed through her body as she picked up the envelope and kissed it gently. She eased herself down on the *tatami,* slit the envelope and started reading.

June 12, 1944

> *My Darling Emiko,*
>   *How are you, sweetheart? Is everything okay? I've been so worried about you since I haven't heard from you. I've written to you at least ten times.*

Ten times? Emiko hadn't received any letters. Her throat tightened, and her hands shook. She checked the date—June 12. She had written hers on the fourth and delivered it to the army base on the fifth. Emiko couldn't believe that seven days after her visit, Akira still hadn't seen hers. The sergeant had lied to her.

> *I thought about how much I miss strolling through the park with you. It was there that we shared our hearts and dreams together, laughed and cried, held hands and smiled. And it was there that we parted from each other.*
>   *I'll always cherish the fond memories I have of you—your loveliness, vibrant spirit, and soft caresses.*
>   *But just in case something happens to me . . .*

No, Akira. That can't happen. You can't die.

> *I pray God will protect, provide, and comfort you. Loving you for all eternity.*
>   *Your devoted,*
>   *Akira*

While having received a letter from Akira elated her, his words about possibly not surviving the war sent her spiraling into utter despair.

Her strength vanished. Just a little while ago, she had been so brave, comforting Okoto. But now she was alone—truly alone. Emiko had quickly forgotten the uplifting words she spoke to her new friend a few minutes ago. She needed to believe them for herself and trust God.

The letter slipped from her hand and fluttered to the floor.

44

Predetermined

Cheyenne, Wyoming – June 23, 1944

A dismal cloud of gloom loomed over Danny on the final day of the trial. The judge had shunted each tactic their lawyer used, declaring his arguments irrelevant or without direction. Meyer's red complexion and audible sighing told Danny they were in a losing battle.

Danny gazed at his companions seated around him, their eyes no longer showing any zest or fire, but only listlessness and despair.

Yesterday, Meyer had won a minor victory when he argued that their rights as American citizens were violated with the relocations. The prosecutor jumped in with an objection, but the judge overruled him.

That gave Danny a crumb of hope, but other than that, the prosecutor seemed to have the upper hand. At this point, Danny just wanted the trial to end.

"Mr. Stacker, proceed with your closing argument and please be brief."

"Thank you, Your Honor." The prosecutor stood up and smiled at the gallery. "Throughout the course of this trial, the defense counsel has questioned the government's justification for relocating the Japanese population from the West Coast military zones to the WRA facilities. The government's actions were necessitated by the threat posed by the armed forces of the empire of Japan. The relocations significantly reduced, if not eliminated, the real possibility of sabotage and espionage by people having sympathies for the enemy."

Danny fidgeted in his seat, and his heart burned with fury. He couldn't listen to any more lies. Their lawyer said nothing to refute them. Danny's initial impressions of him had been right. As long as he got his money, Meyer didn't care about the outcome.

Stacker pointed toward the defense counsel. "Mr. Meyer has also suggested, according to unconfirmed reports, that the WRA facilities are similar to the Nazi concentration camps where the Jews are being persecuted. Even if those reports are only half-true, I, as an American, am personally offended by such a ludicrous comparison."

The prosecutor faced the press corps and paused. "Unlike what's happening in Europe, the defendants are being amply fed, housed, protected, and cared for. Under these circumstances, they are costing us valuable taxpayer money."

The prosecutor's whitewashing of the prison camps made Danny's body heat rise from hot to searing. Stacker completely ignored the testimonies by several defendants that described the devastating losses of jobs, their hard-earned possessions, homes, and businesses. Not to mention being caged in like animals in the middle of nowhere with armed guards pointing guns at them.

Stacker continued. "At the same time, they say they will not fight for this country, yet they want freedom. Is that freedom to send signals to the submarines of the Imperial Japanese Navy? Or is it just an excuse?" He accentuated his last word with a hiss.

Pumping with adrenaline, Danny wanted to burst out of his seat and denounce Stacker's claims as a pack of lies. But Meyer had warned them to remain calm no matter what happened during the closing arguments.

The prosecutor turned and faced the judge. "In either case, the defendants have made a stand against the duty and moral obligation of every decent American. On that basis alone, these men should be convicted of the charges levied against them. I have nothing more to say, Your Honor."

The judge motioned to the defense counsel. "Mr. Meyer, your turn to summarize."

The defense counsel busily scribbled notes on a pad of paper.

"Mr. Meyer, I'm waiting."

He looked up and slowly rose without the vitality he had shown on the first day. "I'm sorry, Your Honor." He inhaled a deep breath. "Throughout the entire proceedings, including the closing argument, my esteemed colleague for the prosecution has pointed out that the relocation of the Japanese Americans from the West Coast was necessary to guard against the possible threat of sabotage and espionage. Yet there has not been one reported incident in Hawaii or—"

The judge slammed his gavel. "Mr. Meyer, it's not my habit to interrupt counsel in the middle of a closing statement, but in this case, I must." Blake frowned. "I remind you that during a military crisis, any such incidents would likely be withheld from the press due to security reasons. Therefore, your assertion is without merit. Please continue."

Danny aimed a hot stare at the judge. His opinion of the man was now complete.

"Yes, Your Honor." Meyer swallowed hard and looked down at his notes. For the first time during the trial, he seemed to be at a loss for words.

Blake directed a stern look at the defense counsel. "Mr. Meyer, do you have anything else to say?"

"Yes, Your Honor. I'm sorry, but I was just trying to collect my thoughts to make the most cogent argument possible."

"Well, hurry up collecting. We haven't got all day."

Meyer tugged on his tie. "During these proceedings, the prosecution has sought to prove disloyalty on the part of my clients. Nothing could be further from the truth. A serious miscarriage of government policy has been imposed upon them and their families, and if it weren't for that, my clients would have gladly entered the military and served—"

"Mr. Meyer, does my memory serve me correctly, or do I recall that over a thousand other Japanese Americans have volunteered to serve in the military despite the fact that their circumstances are identical to those of your clients?"

Tad's decision to join the army was being used against them. Meyer should've thought of that.

Their lawyer shuffled papers on the table then raised his head. "Your Honor, I feel as though I'm being cross-examined and not allowed to complete my closing argument."

"Mr. Meyer, it's not my normal practice, but I will step in if I feel that the closing argument is misleading or false."

It was over. Danny could see it in the faces of his compatriots that they all knew the outcome.

Meyer's face turned scarlet, and he shut his eyes, then opened them. "Your Honor, I have nothing more to say." He crumpled into his chair.

Danny's gut tightened like a lemon squeezed of its last drop of juice.

Judge Blake tidied his loose papers into a neat pile. "This marks the end of the evidentiary phase of the trial. I'll take all that has been presented under advisement. We will adjourn until next Monday, when I announce the verdict." He pounded his gavel.

The bailiff called for everyone to stand as the judge exited.

Meyer turned to face his clients. "We gave it our best shot. All we can do now is hope for the best."

The defendants' faces wore the pall of defeat.

Danny stood in front of Meyer, glaring. "Best shot, huh? You're getting your money, and we're going to prison."

* * *

June 26, 1944

Unlike the other mornings when they were herded into the courtroom, Danny and his fellow defendants kept their mouths shut. They had discussed all the possible scenarios and penalties and could only wait for the inevitable.

Five minutes before ten o'clock, the left side door opened, and Judge Blake entered the courtroom.

The judge smiled, something Danny didn't think he was capable of doing. But the smile quickly transformed into a frown in one continuous movement. "Before I declare the verdict, I'd like to say a few words. Then you'll understand my decision."

Danny leaned forward in his chair, his ears burning to hear the verdict, yet dreading it.

"First of all, this trial has lasted too long. Some arguments were irrelevant and a ridiculous waste of the court's time. We could have dispensed with the verbose oratories by both the prosecution and the defense."

Stacker and Meyer sat impassively as they received their scolding.

The judge's eyebrows furrowed, and his crow's feet lines darkened. "Since the founding of our republic, brave men have taken up the mantle of defending our country during perilous times of conflict. It was their God-given duty to set aside their personal freedoms and sacrifice time with their families and friends to fight our wars. They didn't think twice about whether it inconvenienced them or their families."

Judge Blake was twisting the truth. Danny shook his head.

"We're faced with dangerous enemies on both sides, and we've taken decisive action to counter the advantage our enemies may have had. The reason for relocating the Japanese from the West Coast was the strong possibility of invasion by Japan."

The judge stared daggers at Danny and continued. "The move greatly reduced the threat of clandestine activities by a minority who might have been sympathetic to the empire of Japan. In addition, the Japanese were brought to the WRA camps for their own safety. They've been housed, fed satisfactorily, and humanely treated in all other respects."

Whoa! Danny couldn't believe what he was hearing and his fingers balled up into tight fists. Blake completely whitewashed their dilapidated living conditions. Just five minutes from their flimsy barrack, a cemetery was built where they buried all the people who had died in camp. It kept expanding in size. Many died, especially the elderly who couldn't withstand Wyoming's extreme weather conditions and succumbed to heat strokes, hypothermia, or other illnesses.

"The defendants made a serious mistake in formulating their conclusions, which brought about these proceedings. They erroneously thought loyal citizens should protest in lieu of performing their duties in the cause of our national defense." Judge Blake motioned to the bailiff.

"Defendants, please rise," said the bailiff.

Danny and the others complied.

The judge sipped his water then set the glass down. "In the case of the United States versus Shigeru Fujii, et al, I find each defendant guilty of draft evasion according to the provisions of the Selective Training and Service Act of 1940, Title 50 United States Code, Section 311."

Danny aimed a flaming stare at the judge that could burn holes through him.

Without a flinch, the judge turned his attention toward the other Nisei. "You're sentenced to three years in a federal penitentiary at either Fort Leavenworth, Kansas, or McNeil Island in Washington State. You are remanded to the custody of the United States Marshals, who will make arrangements for your transportation."

Judge Blake's final words knocked the wind out of Danny, and he nearly doubled over. It didn't take a law degree to see how unfairly they were being treated. The trial had nothing to do with logic or law, but everything to do with prejudice.

Something inside Danny burst like a ruptured fire hydrant, and he shot up from his seat and approached the bench. "Your Honor! You can't do this—"

Judge Blake hammered the gavel furiously. "Bailiff, seize that man!"

The bailiff and a sheriff's deputy rushed over and grabbed Danny's arms and clasped his wrists in handcuffs. They dragged him toward the door.

As he was being escorted out, Danny snatched a look back at Blake. "You're not a fair judge!"

The judge directed a stark gaze at Meyer. "I warned you I would not tolerate such outbursts in my courtroom! I want to see you in my chambers immediately."

* * *

An hour later, Danny and the other prisoners milled around in the holding area. Some men slept on wooden benches along the walls. Others slouched forward and stared into space with clasped hands under their chins.

Jail was bad enough, but the thought of being locked up in a real prison for three years with hardened criminals flattened Danny like a steamroller.

Danny paced in front of a group of men. "What was the point of the trial? The judge's mind was made up from the beginning."

"Yeah, what a joke," Okada said with a livid face.

The door swung open, and the imposing figure of Samuel Meyer appeared.

"Hello, boys." Meyer set his briefcase down and loosened his necktie. "I'm sorry the trial didn't turn out the way we wanted."

Danny crossed his arms. "The judge had it in for us. Can't you do something?"

Meyer lit a cigarette and took a drag. He blew out the smoke through his nose. "It did appear that the judge had preconceived notions. Under normal circumstances, it might be enough to petition for a mistrial, but these aren't normal times."

Danny gritted his teeth at Meyer. "I can't believe we're going to prison for three years!"

"You're lucky it's not longer." Meyer turned his attention to Danny. "The judge was furious with your display of defiance, and he wanted to lengthen the sentence—not just for you, but for everybody. I had to plead with the judge and told him it was just an emotional outburst, and you meant no disrespect. After I apologized profusely, he finally agreed."

All eyes glowered at Danny, and before anyone lashed out at him, he looked away.

"Isn't there anything that can be done?" Tokuda asked. "What if the war ends soon?"

Meyer took another drag. "Even if the war ends, that may or may not have an effect on the length of time you spend in prison. But I can file an appeal, so don't lose hope. I'll do my best to get you guys out."

More empty words from their lawyer. Danny kicked a bench over.

45

The Unthinkable

Kumamoto, Japan

Taking a seat on the *tatami* next to a low table, Emiko thanked the Lord for a simple meal. With the strict food rationing, the government only allocated tiny portions of rice every month. To make it last, she mixed in *daikon* radish, *nappa* cabbage, and potatoes. Emiko picked up a piece of radish with her chopsticks and began chewing. A sharp rap at the front door broke into her thoughts. She blotted her mouth with a napkin, then rose.

"*Konnichi wa*," a deep male voice called out. "Is anyone home?"

She tried to place the vaguely familiar voice as she shuffled to the foyer. "Who is it?"

"Captain Hiroshi Yamada."

Emiko nearly jumped out of her skin. The very man she hoped never to see or hear from invaded her life again. Without opening the door she asked, "How may I help you?"

"I'm here on official business. Please may I come in?"

"What official business would I have with you?"

"I received a report from the commander at the Kokura army base that you were having problems with the mail. I've conducted an investigation and would like to report my findings."

Tension mounted as she considered sending Hiroshi away, but she needed to know what happened to Akira's letters. Biting her lip, she unfastened the latch and cracked the door open partway.

The bright afternoon sun shone behind Hiroshi's capped head, creating a corona around it that hid his face in the shadow.

"Please come in." She stepped back as he removed his boots.

Hiroshi entered the living room, sat on the *tatami,* and doffed his peaked cap next to him. "Emiko-san, how are you doing? It's been a long time."

She squirmed inside, uneasy with his familiar tone, but she maintained a calm facade. "I'm sorry, but I can't offer you any tea. My ration has run out."

"That's quite all right."

Her ration hadn't really run out, but she hoped to make his visit short. She wanted to forgo any more small talk. "What can you tell me about the mail delivery?"

"A sergeant at the base reported your visit."

She looked away and drew in a deep breath. Hiroshi seemed to know everything as though he had been spying on her. How unnerving. Emiko returned her attention to him. "I wasn't aware that the *Kempeitai* would trifle with something like this."

"We are responsible for investigating all suspicious activities involving civilians and military personnel, including private mail."

"I see. Then you know I'm having problems receiving letters from my fiancé?"

"Yes. From him."

Hiroshi's use of the familiar *him* with a hint of disdain, instead of the more proper Omura-san, told Emiko all had not been forgotten. She began to regret having this conversation. Hoping to hurry it along, she tried a more direct approach. "What can you tell me about your findings?"

He smiled. "Our investigation revealed that, except for temporary disruptions, your letters have gone through, but the other party hasn't mailed any."

The letter Akira smuggled through Okoto contradicted his words. Emiko concealed her shock by glancing down at her hands. She struggled to keep her face impassive as anger mounted inside her. "How can that be?"

"For security reasons the base post office logs all incoming and outgoing mail for every soldier." Hiroshi sat back on his haunches, expressionless, his eyes aimed straight at her.

As much as Emiko wanted to unmask his lie, she refrained and bit her tongue. She could get her new friend Okoto in trouble and would be no closer to finding out Akira's whereabouts. Emiko rose and bowed. "Thank you for bringing me the news."

But Hiroshi stayed seated. "You're still as beautiful as I remember."

Indignation flamed through her. The nerve of this man. She searched for words to respond politely, but firmly. "Captain, please remember I'm engaged to be married. Your comment is inappropriate. I'm sorry, but I must ask you to leave."

"So soon? But we're old friends. Is that how you treat your friends, push them out the door?" He patted the space beside him. "Sit down and tell me how you're getting along these days. I haven't seen you in a long time."

"Please, I insist." Before she could back up so he could pass, Hiroshi's fingers wrapped around her arm like a spider latching on to its prey. Emiko wanted to scream and forced herself not to wince from his tight grip.

Without warning, he yanked her closer to him. "You don't know how I've longed for you."

"No, please let go of me!" Her protests didn't deter him. She jostled her arm to break free, but his firm grip wouldn't release.

"I've always loved you." He drew a finger across her cheek.

She jerked her head back. "Let me go!" His hungry cat eyes made her skin crawl.

"Don't be like this. You belong to me, not to Akira. He doesn't care about you. That's why he hasn't written to you."

Her arm broke free. "That's a lie!" She pounded her fists against his chest.

He grabbed Emiko's shoulders and rolled her onto her back, pinning her to the floor while lowering his head with pursed lips.

"No, don't! Get off of me!" Emiko flung her face to the side so that his lips grazed her hair.

Hiroshi flicked his tongue like a viper and tried to kiss her again, but she yanked her head to the side. His lips glided across her neck like a slithering snake. Pulling back, he grasped her chin and pressed his mouth to hers.

The slobbery sensation of his lips on hers made Emiko want to gag, but his fingers digging into her jaw made it impossible to stop his kisses. She bit his lip and spit in his face.

He slapped her across the cheek and pressed his knee against her chest so she couldn't move or breathe.

Gasping for air, she struggled to expel his heavy body. Her heart seemed ready to burst and her lungs burned as she sucked in air and screamed, "Jesus! Heelpp!"

His clammy hand pressed down over her mouth, muffling her cries.

Dread squeezed her heart like a python. Emiko's tears fell uncontrollably as his other hand unfastened the buttons of his tunic and pulled his suspenders off. Her anger melted into utter desperation and sheer horror. Just when she lost all hope, indistinct voices sounded outside. Her ears perked up.

Hiroshi paused, cocking his head as he, too, listened. He turned and momentarily uncovered her mouth.

Before she lost her chance, Emiko yelled as loud as she could. "*Tasukete!* Help!"

* * *

Hiroshi quickly smothered Emiko's outburst with a cushion over her mouth. He hoped no one had heard her, but he couldn't take the chance.

Every fiber of his body hungered to continue the liaison, and the terror in her eyes only magnified his desire to possess her completely. First, he would have to take care of the disturbance.

To silence her, Hiroshi pulled Emiko onto her knees, and using a technique he learned in *Kempeitai* training, he struck her neck to render her unconscious. Her body went limp, and he let her down on the floor. He slipped on his suspenders, refastened the buttons of his tunic, and crowned himself with his cap. Creeping to the foyer, he jammed his feet into his boots, then tiptoed to the front door.

Hiroshi unsnapped the button of his holster, pulled his sidearm, and cocked the slide. Before he could reach the handle, the door slid open. The sudden infusion of light temporarily blinded him. When his eyes came into focus, a tall, uniformed man was pointing a pistol at him.

"Put the gun down on the floor," the man said.

Hiroshi stood frozen. "Who are you?"

"Never mind. Just do as I say."

He slowly set the pistol down and caught a glimpse of the man's uniform, which had the insignia of a major. Perhaps he could try to intimidate him with his *Kempeitai* officer's position. Regular army officers, even of superior rank, were often afraid of the military police. "Major, I'm Captain Hiroshi Yamada of the elite *Kempeitai*—"

"Shut up!" The man gestured with his gun. "Keep your hands where I can see them. Now!"

"The *Kempeitai* has jurisdiction in all domestic matters. I insist—"

"You'll insist on what? I'm Major Ichiro Endo of Imperial General Headquarters."

A bolt of fear struck Hiroshi, having come face-to-face with an officer from army headquarters. Had the major been from a regular army unit, Hiroshi could probably wiggle out of his predicament. He had no choice but to obey the command.

The major kept his weapon trained on Hiroshi while grabbing the gun on the floor. He released the bullet magazine. "Captain, what were you doing with the woman of this house?"

Hiroshi's mind raced as he tried to formulate a plausible excuse. He bowed his head to display as much dismay as possible. His explanation better work or he'd face a court martial, imprisonment, and perhaps worse. "Major, I don't know how to explain this, but it's quite embarrassing. I'm having a love affair with the woman of this house."

A middle-aged woman stepped inside the foyer and stood next to the major. "Liar!" she shouted. "Emiko-san would never do such a thing."

Hiroshi didn't know who she was, but he could swear he'd seen her before. He had to salvage his innocence as best he could. "No, it's true. I swear, I'm telling—"

"Mrs. Katsumoto, please stay behind me," Major Endo said.

Ignoring the request, the woman arched an eyebrow. "My husband, the general, will certainly hear about your disgraceful behavior."

General Katsumoto? The regional commander of the *Kempeitai*? No, it couldn't be. The punishment for something like this, especially a charge brought forth by an officer from army headquarters and attested by the general's wife, could certainly spell the end of him.

The major turned to the woman. "Mrs. Katsumoto, please go check on her."

She wove her way around Hiroshi and entered the living room. Within moments she let out a loud shriek. "Emiko-san!"

"Captain, I'm placing you under arrest for sexual assault and conduct unbecoming of an officer," the major said curtly.

Sweat dribbled down Hiroshi's forehead. "Major, you're a man, and you have your needs—"

"Shut up!" The major scowled.

Mrs. Katsumoto returned to the room with piercing eyes that could drill holes into Hiroshi. "You despicable animal!" she said, baring her teeth.

The major turned to the woman. "How is she?"

"Unconscious. I'll get help."

"Please notify the authorities as well."

"I certainly will." The woman pointed a finger at Hiroshi. "I hope you rot in prison! Or better yet, I hope you are executed."

As the woman traipsed around Hiroshi, something warm and wet splattered on his face. He blinked.

All the hard work Hiroshi put into his well-crafted plan had gone awry. With Akira deployed to Okinawa, his campaign to reclaim Emiko as his woman should have gone without a glitch. Blocking the mail should have convinced her to give up on Akira. But he let his physical passions take over, and he couldn't have foreseen the untimely visit by the general's wife and this major.

Now, disgrace and ruin loomed before him. His career, his privileges, and even his life might be forfeited.

46

McNeil Island

McNeil Island Federal Penitentiary – July 10, 1944

From the fifth floor of the "Big House" main prison, Danny scanned multiple tiers of drab cells that overlooked a cement floor about sixty feet below. He longed to go outside for some fresh air.

"Hey Danny, what do you think of our new digs?" Joe Akamatsu said, climbing to the upper bunk.

Danny gazed at the dreary cage that contained bunk beds for six inmates, a metal sink, two spigots, and a toilet. "This place reminds me of those prisons in the gangster movies with George Raft and James Cagney. I thought it would be much like Heart Mountain, but it's so different."

Joe rolled over his squeaky bunk. "The claustrophobia is killing me. But you know what I miss the most? Women."

"Me too. The only one here is that grouchy old nurse in the infirmary." Danny yearned to be with Mary and missed her vivacious personality, glistening smile and warm eyes.

Loud shouts rang out in the neighboring cell. Danny could hear banging, grunts, and punches. "Not again. Another fistfight next door."

A loud metallic clank echoed down the hall with heavy footsteps.

The neighboring cell grew quiet.

A burly guard stopped in front of Danny's cell and faced him with a beady glare. "Hey, you Japs! Shut up in there!"

"That wasn't us." Danny jerked his head toward their neighbors.

The guard slammed the cell bars with his nightstick, and his face twisted into an ugly scowl. "Listen, I don't care who it was. It's bad enough that you're Japs, but you're draft dodgers to boot. Show some respect or you'll wish you were never born."

Danny almost erupted like a volcano, but he held back his angry words, figuring they wouldn't have any impact on this moron.

The guard turned and stormed off. The steel door slammed shut.

With his cheeks flaming hot, Danny slammed his fist into his bunk bed.

* * *

With nothing but time on his hands, Danny reread a tattered newspaper that must have passed through a hundred pairs of hands.

Tak Ito called out to everyone, "Hey fellas, Kaz is organizing a dominoes tournament tonight in his cell. Anyone interested in playing?" He looked from left to right and counted. "Okay, four of us. Anyone else?"

Danny chuckled, knowing the domino games were cleverly disguised poker games. The warden had made it clear that gambling and any form of card playing was strictly forbidden. "You guys are so sly using domino tiles as cards."

Tak held a domino tile between his thumb and forefinger. "Kaz thought of coloring the dots to represent the club, spade, diamond, and heart suits and using the number of dots for ace through queen, and no dots for kings. Danny, you in?"

"Nah, don't think so." No point in playing for cigarettes since he didn't smoke.

"Then can you be a lookout for the guards or swap cells with a player after dinner? The guards don't know the difference."

"Sure. Have fun."

* * *

The arrival of new prisoners caused a constant reshuffle of cell assignments. Danny now shared a two-man cell with a muscular black man, Will Jackson.

"What you in here for?" asked Will.

Danny raised his eyes from a *Life* magazine. "Refusing to serve in the army." He returned to his reading material.

"You scared of being shot or something?"

The implication grated Danny's nerves, and he wanted to issue a sharp retort. But no hint of malice appeared on Will's face. "I'm not scared. The government locked up my family in a prison camp all because we're Japanese. That's why I'm not serving."

"They think you're going to help the enemy?"

"It's because we're not white."

Will cracked a smile. "I know all about that. No job, no money. The white man don't give us no chance."

"How about you? Why are you in here?"

"I used to be in prizefighting. I was the Washington state champion from '38 to '40 in the featherweight division. When the war broke out, matches dried up. Couldn't find steady work. One day I got caught heisting hubcaps off a car. They threw me in the can for a year, but when I got out, it was still the same—no job, no money. Had to steal to survive, so this time, I'm back in here for five to seven years."

During mealtime, Will introduced Danny to some of his black friends. They gradually warmed up to him after he shared cookies and other goodies Lily and Mary had sent. One time, four white prisoners cornered Will, hurled epithets at him, and beat him like a punching bag. Danny came to his aid and took a pounding until the guards broke up the fight.

When the cell assignments were about to change again, Will shook Danny's hand. "We're brothers. If any white boys give you any trouble, let me know. We'll take care of them."

Danny knew what he meant.

* * *

A few months later, favor smiled upon Danny and most of the other resisters when the warden transferred them to a work camp known as "the Honor Farm" a few miles from the main prison. No guard towers overshadowed the compound, but it was still a prison.

Danny and Joe Akamatsu were assigned to a work gang to cultivate strawberries.

Joe set his shovel down and blew out a deep breath. "It feels so good to be out of that birdcage and do some real work."

"Yeah, we're no longer rotting away in our cells." Working at the Honor Farm reminded Danny of the happier times, planting, nurturing, and harvesting berry and fruit crops on the family farm. "And the guards aren't that strict here. I don't even have to button my shirt collar at mealtimes anymore."

"Too bad the guys who said they're going back to Japan are still in the Big House."

As fervently as Danny believed in the cause, he never once thought of going to Japan. He looked out across Puget Sound to the Washington mainland. "The Honor Farm isn't so bad, but I sure want off this island."

47

Unexpected Encounter

Okinawa

Something like a seismic wave reverberated up Akira's arm with every blow of the handpick, which broke off only fragments of the hard rock. Akira and numerous soldiers dug a vast network of tunnels and caves running east to west across southern Okinawa for camouflaged gun emplacements and thousands of troops.

Taking a shovel, Akira scooped up heavy pieces of crushed coral and limestone and piled them into a wheelbarrow. Even though he didn't believe in the Japanese cause, he worked hard to avoid Kameda's wrath.

Despite the backbreaking work, Akira whistled a merry tune. Last night, after months of waiting, worrying, and praying, Akira finally received a letter from Emiko. He had devoured every word like precious morsels of scarce food.

"Hey, Akira, it's lunchtime," Saito said, grinning as if he were about to attend a sumptuous banquet. "I heard your pretty fiancée wrote to you."

"Yes. I'm so glad to hear from her. I was so worried about her." He shoved the wheelbarrow aside, and they descended the long, crowded tunnel leading to a mess hall chamber.

The cook's aide scooped a half cup of watery rice, a tiny piece of broiled fish, and pickled cabbage into Akira's tin plate. "Thanks," he said, but wished for more. In the last two months, the quantity and quality of food had worsened with thousands of new soldiers arriving and American bombs disrupting the food supply chain.

Akira and Saito carried their plates and wandered toward a spot where several men from their platoon sat waving at them. They plunked themselves down next to the young men.

"These long workdays are killing me," Hoshino said. "The officers work us so hard and feed us a few miserable grains of rice. I sure miss the good foods we ate before the war like *sukiyaki* and *sushi*."

Saito's mouth watered. "I miss *okonomiyaki*—"

Suddenly, Sergeant Kameda marched in with two officers. Akira dropped his chopsticks, and his eyes stretched wide. No, it couldn't be.

"Attention!" Sergeant Kameda shouted.

Boots clacked, and Akira and the men around him rose.

Captain Mayeda slapped his riding crop on his hand. "Men, this is Lieutenant Hiroshi Yamada. He is your new platoon commander and my adjutant. I order you to give him complete respect and support. Reporting to him is Sergeant Kameda." He escorted Hiroshi down the line of men who stood at attention. "That is all." The captain excused himself and stalked off.

Hiroshi strutted in front of the assembled platoon. "Men, I just arrived here to undertake the great privilege of stopping the American invaders. I'm told you helped build impregnable defenses. With Sergeant Kameda's assistance, I'll look at our strengths and vulnerabilities to come up with ways to make our unit even stronger. That, combined with the heroic sacrifices by our *kamikaze* pilots, will lead us to victory for our great nation. We will fight to the very end and if need be, die for the emperor. I'm counting on your support in this great endeavor."

What is he doing here? Somehow Hiroshi appeared different. His words didn't sound as arrogant, and his steps lacked the swagger of old. Hiroshi looked his way but didn't acknowledge him.

* * *

Hiroshi surveyed the platoon of twenty-five stiff-faced men standing before him. When his eyes met Akira's, he froze for a moment, then quickly looked away. Tension coiled in his chest.

Continuing down the line, he pretended to be unfazed. Hiroshi knew he might run into Akira in Okinawa, but he didn't expect to meet him so soon, nor did he expect Akira to be under his command. He wondered whether Emiko mentioned anything to him about his visit.

The events of the past few months crowded Hiroshi's mind. He swallowed hard as he remembered that day when he had stood before Colonel Ito, head of the military tribunal.

"Captain Yamada, you are found guilty for sexual assault and for lying to a superior officer in the commission of that crime. What do you have to say for yourself?"

"Your Honor, I apologize for my actions." Hiroshi parroted the words his father's lawyer had advised him to say. "I have no excuse, except to say I let my passions for the woman rule over me that day, clouding my good judgment. I admit my guilt and acknowledge my dishonorable behavior."

"Captain, your offenses would normally carry a prison term of three years. Since you've served your country admirably prior to this incident, and because you expressed remorse, I'm going to commute your sentence to time already spent in the stockade."

The tightness in Hiroshi's chest released.

"However, effective immediately, you are expunged from the *Kempeitai* and are assigned to the 32nd Army infantry division. Furthermore, you are reduced in rank to second lieutenant with a commensurate reduction in pay and privileges."

"Yes, Your Honor." Hiroshi dropped his head to show shame, but it was a feint. How fortunate to get off with a light sentence.

His father's influence-peddling had paid off once more. Even so, Hiroshi's hand began to shake, and he placed his other hand on top to steady it and hide his fear. As an infantry officer, he would likely be sent out to some island where he would face flying bullets and exploding bombshells.

Sergeant Kameda's loud reprimand of a private in the first row jerked Hiroshi back to the present. He pivoted, stepped toward the middle of the line, and spotted Akira again. Hiroshi carefully observed him to see if there was any reaction. If Akira was angry about what had happened with Emiko, he didn't show it.

For now, he would keep his distance, and only speak to Akira if he had to. Even if he knew something, a lowly private couldn't do anything to him anyway.

Now, Hiroshi would devise a new plan to reclaim Emiko. The field postal service was beyond his span of control, so he could no longer stop the mail between Akira and Emiko.

This time he would have direct control over the situation and wouldn't have to rely on greedy, parasitic men like Colonel Abe.

He vowed he wouldn't rest until Akira was dead.

48

Medic

Biffontaine, France – October 22, 1944

Tad dove behind an old church as machine-gun bullets whistled by his head and peppered the church exterior in a frightening, high-pitched staccato.

Pieces of glass and stone chips scattered in his direction. His heart beat wildly, and he inhaled air heavy with gunpowder and smoke.

Earsplitting cannons blasted, shaking the earth beneath him. With fingers wedged in his ears, Tad raised his head and could see ominous shadows from crumbled buildings in the late afternoon sunlight. His hand jittered at the constant fear of being shot or blasted to smithereens, but he had a job to do in this remote mountain village in eastern France.

From a distance, Lieutenant Kogawa signaled him to back away from the church.

During a lull, Tad scurried to where the lieutenant had taken cover and waited for further instructions. "Omura, any more wounded soldiers up there?"

"No, sir. We got them out."

"Good job." Kogawa sighed. "It looks like we're trapped. No one expected this counterattack."

The possibility of being taken prisoner added to Tad's tension. "Lieutenant, I'll go check on the wounded." Nearby, another spine-shocking, artillery shell detonated, rattling his nerves.

Tad moved cautiously from stretcher to stretcher and froze when he came upon the fifth man. *No, not Jim Hori!* Stooping down, he reached for his buddy's vital signs. The faint pulse worried him, and he lifted a bloody gauze on Jim's chest and neck. Tad checked the lacerations most likely caused by shrapnel. He winced and hooked Jim up to a bag of plasma.

The cheerful medic he met during training always had a funny quip for anyone within earshot, but now he looked somber and pale. In a photograph he had once seen, Jim's pretty wife resembled Lily in many ways, and their son was born about the same time as his.

"Jim, Jim, can you hear me? It's Tad."

He gazed at Tad and blinked twice.

"Jim, I have something very important to say to you," Tad said, taking his friend's hand. "We all have a priceless soul that lives forever. God has a special gift for each of us—an eternal home in heaven, where streets are made of pure gold and city walls are decorated with precious stones. We enter this wonderful place through Jesus, who died for us and rose again. Jim, do you understand? Jim—"

He closed his eyes and stopped breathing.

Tad checked his pulse and knew he was gone. Pain burst inside him like an exploding grenade. So many young men had died before his eyes, but losing Jim was like having a limb chopped off. He crumpled to his knees and wept and hoped Jim had silently accepted Jesus into his heart.

With evening approaching, gunfire and explosions ceased.

Diesel engines began to throb beyond the defense perimeter—German Tiger tanks for sure. Tad's body quivered in sheer terror.

Crackling and thudding sounds came from a loudspeaker. "American soldiers," said a voice with a German accent. "Your situation is hopeless. You are surrounded. Surrender or you will be annihilated. You have ten minutes."

Images of Lily and his baby floated across Tad's mind. Would he ever see her again or meet his newborn?

During the interlude, the pall of death cast its shadow on the ashen faces of soldiers surrounding Tad. Another gruesome battle was about to start—ready or not.

Gunfire started up again, and explosions rumbled.

Lieutenant Kogawa moved toward Tad who was treating the injured. "We'll try to hold out until reinforcements get here."

"Sir, we have to get the wounded to a field hospital soon, or they'll die!" Tad said.

The lieutenant rubbed his chin. "Omura, just care for them the best you can until help arrives." Kogawa strode away without looking back.

Tad started to go after him, but it would probably be futile.

A moment later, a husky Nisei captain with a rugged face strode into the area. Tad was surprised to see a Nisei officer ranked higher than a lieutenant.

The captain gingerly raised his bloody right hand to Tad. "I caught a blast from a Kraut submachine gun. Can you take care of this?" He grimaced. "It hurts like the dickens."

Lifting the forearm, Tad noticed a bullet had torn through the palm. "I'll patch you up in a jiffy." He gently dabbed antiseptic on it and wrapped the hand with heavy gauze and tape. "I'm going to give you some morphine that'll make you woozy."

The captain glanced at the wounded men and turned his attention toward Lieutenant Kogawa, who had returned to the area. "Lieutenant, our boys are holding the line, but we have to evacuate the wounded. Get a detail ready to go before dawn and use some of the Kraut POWs to help you carry the litters."

Finally, someone who could make a decision. Tad injected a morphine shot into the captain's hand and eased him down onto a stretcher.

Lieutenant Kogawa pulled Tad aside while the captain rested. "You know who that is?"

"No, sir."

"He's Captain Young Kim—one brave son-of-a-gun. In Italy, he and another soldier crawled behind the lines and captured several enemy soldiers to gather intelligence."

Tad turned the name over in his mind. "Kim? That's not Japanese."

"He's Korean."

"I didn't know Koreans were in our outfit."

"Yeah. When he received his officer's commission, they assigned him to the 100th, thinking he was Nisei. But when they discovered he was Korean, his commander offered to reassign him, since Japanese and Koreans don't usually get along. Surprisingly, he wanted to stay with the 100th. 'We're all just Americans, fighting for the same cause,' he said."

Just Americans. Tad held his thumbs up and smiled.

That evening, gunfire intensified, and thick smoke from tank cannon blasts cloaked the air as the enemy inched toward them. It was like standing in front of a firing squad. Tad rushed from one downed soldier to another. Other medics who ferried the injured from the defense line filled him in on how the battle was raging street-by-street and house-by-house.

Before dawn, Lieutenant Kogawa followed Captain Kim's order to evacuate. He led the group in front while Tad brought up the rear. A team of six Nisei soldiers guarded about twenty German POWs, who were pressed into service as litter bearers to carry the wounded westward.

In the dim light of the awakening day, they escaped out of town into the dense forest. They made their way up the mountain path, following a route the medical detachment had taken a day earlier to get to Biffontaine. The line of men and litters stretched over a hundred yards with Tad walking alongside Captain Kim's stretcher.

The lieutenant raised his hand, signifying a halt.

"Oh, no!" Tad caught a glimpse of gray German uniforms pointing rifles at Kogawa and Nisei soldiers. His heart jumped out of his chest. "There's a Kraut patrol up ahead, and it looks like we're outnumbered," he whispered to Captain Kim. "Why haven't they started shooting?"

"Because we have their friends under guard," the captain said.

German litter bearers abandoned Captain Kim's stretcher and ran forward to join their compatriots. Other POWs followed suit.

Captain Kim extended his left arm to Tad. "Help me up. I'm not going to surrender."

"Sir, you're not in any condition to run. You've lost too much blood."

"Never mind. Just do it. With all the commotion, I think we can slip away."

Even dosed with morphine, the captain was very alert. Tad tucked his arm under the officer's back and pulled him up. From the corner of his eye, Tad could see Nisei guards holding out their rifles while raising their free hands. One by one, the former POWs began to yank the rifles away from the Nisei at the front of the line.

Captain Kim braced himself on Tad's shoulder. "The Krauts aren't looking. Let's go!"

Pumped with adrenaline, Tad hooked his shoulder under the captain's left arm and widened his stance for better leverage. In the distance, he caught a glimpse of Kogawa and the other Nisei with their hands on the back of their helmets. No telling what would happen to them. Tad stepped off the trail with the captain and disappeared into the dark forest toward the American lines.

* * *

Belmont, France

Tad counted his blessings, having escaped Biffontaine with Captain Kim three days ago. Maybe he'd live to see his newborn after all and return home to Lily.

After nine intense hours of cleaning and bandaging wounds, Tad sauntered toward a bombed-out building along a stone wall where exhausted men from his unit sat. "Hey fellas."

"Hi, Doc." A couple of soldiers scooted aside for him.

Feeling the autumn chill of the Vosges Mountains, Tad buttoned up his jacket and fanned away the acrid cigarette smoke that drifted in his face. It had been too long since he'd written his wife. He opened his field pack, pulled out paper, and placed it on his medical kit. Deep in thought, Tad pressed his pen down on the paper.

"Omura, we captured some wounded Germans," Lieutenant Miyamoto said, nodding in the direction of the far wall. "Around the corner."

Tad wished the lieutenant would have found another medic, but he folded the letter, placed it in his shirt pocket and rose.

Two Nisei soldiers guarded five POWs squatting on the ground. The Germans couldn't have been much older than eighteen. They stared at their captors as if they were confused by the faces of American soldiers who didn't look American.

Four of them had minor wounds, but the fifth was missing a hand. Tad crouched next to the handless prisoner and reached toward the bloody stump.

The blue-eyed youth jerked it back, uttering a torrent of German words. To protect their comrade, the other POWs crowded around Tad. The guards moved in with their rifles to keep them at bay.

Tad pointed to a temporary field hospital. He remembered the words for doctor and hospital from his high school German class. "*Arzt, Krankhaus*," he said, lifting his medical kit and pulling out bandages.

After a brief moment, the handless man's face softened, and he gently moved his forearm toward Tad to inspect it.

Someone had skillfully applied a tourniquet below his elbow. "This one needs to see the doctor right away," Tad said to the guards. He flexed his shoulders and returned his attention to the handless prisoner. "*Stehen Sie auf, bitte.*"

The prisoners smiled at Tad and helped their buddy to his feet.

Tad's few German words seemed to melt away their distrust.

One guard motioned to the prisoner and led him away.

Before applying antiseptic and fresh gauze to the other POWs, Tad noticed one of them wearing a cross on a silver chain under the unbuttoned tunic, similar to the one he wore. Tad pointed to the POW's cross, and then he pulled out his. "I have one too." They smiled at each other. How ironic. This man was the enemy, but at the same time he might be a brother in Christ.

After patching them up, Tad made his way back to the wall and dozed off for a while.

That evening, he scrubbed and rinsed off dirt and grime that had clung to his skin for over a week. What a treat it was to have access to a steaming shower at a Belmont hotel that survived the shelling.

Tad walked to the hotel's dining room, eager for a hot meal—his first in over a week. What a delightful change from eating C-rations, which, while filling, left a lot to be desired. Tad savored every bite of his cordon bleu and potatoes au gratin, along with every sip of French wine.

He plodded back to the scorched building where his unit was quartered for the night. Just as he settled into his cot, Lieutenant Miyamoto ordered everyone to assemble in the town square.

"What now?" Okubo, another medic, asked.

Tad shut his eyes and didn't want to open them. He pushed himself up from the cot and readied himself to go to the meeting place.

Colonel Perry and three officers entered the square, and all the men stood at attention.

The stocky, middle-aged colonel stepped forward. "At ease, men. Tomorrow at 0-300 hours, the 100th and 3rd Battalions will move out on a rescue mission, followed by the 2nd Battalion."

Fatigue and resentment showed on the Nisei soldiers' faces and their shoulders sagged.

The colonel glanced from side to side. "The 1st Battalion of the 141st Alamo Regiment is trapped in the mountains and surrounded by hundreds of enemy troops. Other units of the 141st tried to break through, but couldn't. The press corps got hold of the news and now stateside politicians are calling for a rescue mission for the 'Lost Battalion.' It's become a public relations nightmare, and we've been ordered to get them out of there."

Why them? More Nisei would die. Tad had already seen enough dead bodies. There was just no relief in sight.

The colonel paused and surveyed the assembled men. "Boys, I know you're tired, and we've had high casualties in the last round, but you're the best unit in the entire army. General Dahlquist has the highest confidence in you men and we're counting on you. Your company commanders will give your units specific orders. Any questions?" He looked side to side and waited, but no one spoke up.

With that, the colonel and his officers stepped away and moved toward a jeep.

As soon as the officers were out of earshot, the men turned to each other, many with livid faces. Private Okimoto shook his head. "I no can believe it. We jest came back."

Tad could always count on the irascible Hawaiian to complain about something.

"When will we ever get some rest?" Private Tamura's brows crinkled on his round face.

"Other units have been sitting on their behinds for weeks," Private Ikeda said through gritted teeth. "Why can't they send them?"

Okimoto smirked. "Cause dey *haoles.* Dey no care what happens to us."

Private Tamura broke into a wide grin and straightened his hulking frame. "What the colonel said about us being the best unit is true."

Okimoto slapped Tamura on the shoulder. "Hey, you can have da medals. For me, I jest like to get home."

Tad agreed. The savage firefights the 442nd had been thrown into were essentially suicide missions. The last few weeks had been hell, fighting against stiff German resistance in the French villages of Bruyeres and Biffontaine. Everyone selflessly gave more than 100 percent and lived up to their motto, *Go for Broke.* So many Nisei died or suffered life-threatening wounds.

Worst of all, Tad could hear the hysterical cries of downed soldiers that couldn't be described in words or the pitiful whimper, "Mama, help me!" that brought tears to his eyes. Often, he reached a soldier too late, and he could only make the dying man as comfortable as possible with extra morphine shots and prayer.

He snapped out of his thoughts when heavy transport trucks rumbled through the main street. Looking at his watch, it was time to finish Lily's letter and get some sleep.

49

Secrets

Takeo, Japan – October 27, 1944

The black, hairy legs of a giant spider pinned Emiko down on her bed. Its scissor-like pincers sheared back and forth as its fangs dripped venom. The sneering and prurient face of Hiroshi loomed over her, and she yanked her head to the side.

"No! Don't! *Yamete!*"

Hiroshi's massive palm descended toward her mouth.

Emiko screamed, and her eyes sprang open as she clenched the quilt in the dark room. Perspiration dribbled down her forehead, stinging her eyes. She wiped the moisture away with her palm and blinked several times to bring herself back to reality. Another bad dream. The hellish memory of Hiroshi's attempted rape seared her heart. She yanked on the chain above her head to switch on the light.

What a relief to stay in her own cottage, away from her uncle's house on the other side of the garden. Emiko hoped the distance was great enough to muffle the sound. If they had heard her screams, they never asked her about them, and Emiko never volunteered any information. Maybe Uncle Teruo and Aunt Shizuko were heavy sleepers. Ever since she moved here a month ago, she'd had four such nightmares.

A few hours later, the crisp morning air greeted Emiko as she slid open the *shoji*-screened door. Her nightmare slowly dissipated as she gazed upon the serenity of her uncle's garden. The luxuriant yellow, burnt-orange, and flaming red of the

Japanese maple leaves offset the green hues of azaleas, rhododendrons, and forest grasses.

While she could certainly enjoy this setting, Emiko needed to put away the bedding into the closet and help her aunt with chores.

Emiko washed the rice in a bowl and poured it into a wooden cooker that she placed over the open hearth in the kitchen.

Aunt Shizuko stirred a pot of *miso* soup and smiled radiantly. "We have a treat today, broiled *sanma* for breakfast. Uncle went fishing yesterday and caught a net full of them."

Emiko's mouth watered for the tasty morsels of mackerel pike. Before the war, she would never have considered eating *sanma,* which only poor people ate or used as bait. But now, eating it was like heaven.

After breakfast, Emiko gathered the laundry into a wicker basket and carried it outside. Dark cumulus clouds hung in the horizon. Hoping the rain would hold off, she quickly dipped the clothes in a basin with soapy water, scrubbed them, and rinsed them in a large bucket. As she hung them on the clothesline, Emiko reflected on the remarkable way God answered her prayer. Major Endo and Mrs. Katsumoto came to her rescue at the most opportune moment. She had told Emiko that the major was wanting to apologize for leaving the *omiai* abruptly, so she guided him to her house.

"Emiko," her aunt called. "A soldier is here to see you. He says he knows you."

"A soldier? Did you get his name?"

"He's such a handsome man, I forgot it." Aunt Shizuko's eyes twinkled as she chuckled. "I'll finish here, so go greet him."

Emiko's heart fluttered at the possibility that it might be Akira. Maybe that's why he hadn't written in order to surprise her. She dashed to her cottage, kicked off her clogs, and changed out of her work clothes into a simple but tasteful kimono.

To assume a veneer of propriety, she came through the side entrance of the main house. She slipped into her aunt's bedroom and looked into the mirror. Thank goodness, her face wasn't flushed, and her natural light complexion brought a smile to her face.

As good manners dictated, she knelt outside the parlor and quietly opened the *shoji*-screen door with her head down. Emiko entered the room, turned toward the door, and knelt down again to close it. She circled around to face her guest, who was seated next to the serving table, sipping tea. She drew in a quick breath. "Major Endo, what brings you here?"

"I'm sorry to startle you. I should have sent advance notice."

Emiko smiled to mask her disappointment. "Not at all, Major. It's good to see you again." She squared her knees on the *tatami* floor and bent low. "Forgive me for not properly thanking you for rescuing me." Before she left Kumamoto, Emiko had written him a letter expressing her thanks, but somehow it didn't seem adequate.

"Don't worry about that. I only did what any decent man would have done." A subtle but affable grin spread across his face. "I wanted to see how you were doing."

"Major, I'm forever indebted to you. I don't know how I would ever repay you."

"Seeing you safe and well at your uncle's house is payment enough for me." He smiled magnanimously.

"Also, thank you for providing me with the instructions on where to send letters to my fiancé."

The smile on his face faded, and he nodded slightly.

Emiko couldn't understand how anyone could be so gallant and selfless. "You came out of your way just to check on me?"

"I didn't have a chance to speak with you after the incident, because I was called back to my post in Tokyo."

"I see. Thanks again for all you've done." She couldn't put her finger on it, but there seemed to be more to it.

"You're quite welcome." His smile disappeared, and he lowered his gaze. "Today I took my daughter to my sister's home in Saga City. Since I was in your area, I thought I'd stop by."

"Thank you for visiting. Did Mrs. Katsumoto give you my new address?"

"Yes, she did."

Mrs. Katsumoto seemed determined to bring them together, although Emiko had made it abundantly clear that her heart belonged to Akira. She remembered what the woman had told her. *Besides, if your engagement doesn't work out, I can think of worse things than being married to this fine man.*

"She said to tell you hello." He sat back and blew on his steaming tea. "Tell me, have you received word from your fiancé?"

"No, I haven't."

"I'm sorry." The major lowered his eyes and looked away for a moment, then returned his attention to her. "By the way, Captain Yamada confessed to stealing your mail and implicated a sergeant at the army base."

"It doesn't surprise me. I only received the one letter from Akira, which was smuggled out of the army base."

"Captain Yamada will be court-martialed and sent to prison for all his offenses."

Emiko fought back tears as she relived that incident.

The major ran out of things to say, and they sat silently for several minutes. He straightened his uniform jacket. "I'd better be going. I'm sorry to have taken so much of your time."

"Oh, not at all. Thank you, again, for everything you've done." She bowed low to him again.

He rose and sat on the ledge of the lower foyer to put on his boots and uniform cap. Walking to the entrance, he pivoted and faced Emiko again. "If it's all right, I'd like to visit you from time to time."

Emiko didn't know what to say. Clearly, he wanted to continue this relationship. After all he had done for her, she couldn't tell him no. "Yes, please do."

Major Endo bowed. When he straightened, he flashed a one-hundred-watt smile. "*Ja, mata ne.* I look forward to the next time." He showed himself out and closed the door behind him.

Placing the teacup and kettle on the serving tray, Emiko carried them back into the kitchen.

Aunt Shizuko pounced on her. "How did it go?" Her wide eyes and eager grin underscored her curiosity.

"You surprised me."

"*Gomen nasai.* I'm sorry, but it's not every day a military officer visits us. Such a good-looking young man, too. Is he married?"

Aunt Shizuko and Mrs. Katsumoto both. All this talk about Major Endo wearied her. Emiko wanted to retire to her cottage to think and pray about the situation. "I don't want to talk about this right now."

Her aunt caught her before she left and handed her an envelope. "I almost forgot. This came for you today."

Emiko reached for it and examined the writing. It was from Akira. A wide smile stretched across her face, and elation bubbled up inside her. "Excuse me, Auntie. I'll be in my room."

Back at her cottage, Emiko opened the envelope and pulled out the letter.

> *Darling Emiko,*
>
> *At last, I received a letter from you. I've been so worried about you since I haven't heard from you. But now, I'm relieved. Also, I'm glad to hear you moved to your uncle's house. Conditions are probably a little better there than in Kumamoto. I'm sure your circumstances can't be easy . . .*

She paused and reflected on the trials she had endured, then continued.

> *My days in Okinawa are mostly full of physical labor. During the spring, I substituted as a high school teacher in Naha for a month. It was a refreshing break to interact with students.*
>
> *The blissful times we've shared together give me hope and fill my empty and dark days.*

Although life has no guarantees, and I have no claims on knowing the future, something whispers to me that I will return unharmed to you.

I can't wait until that special day we're reunited. Never forget how much I love you, my darling.

Your devoted,

Akira

Emiko clutched the letter and kissed it. She wavered about whether she should tell him about Hiroshi. Akira deserved to know, but somehow she couldn't bring herself to write about it. Perhaps—because of shame—she feared Akira might think she was culpable, even though nothing could be further from the truth.

One day she'd tell him, but not now. It would only cause him anxiety.

Neither could she tell him about Major Endo. The next time they met, Emiko would resolve this matter with the major as gently as possible.

She took a deep breath and returned to his letter to reread it.

* * *

Akira quickly penned a letter to Emiko. Between the backbreaking work of digging tunnels and Sergeant Kameda's orders for combat drills, he could only eke out a few minutes here and there to write. He still couldn't figure out why he had only recently started receiving mail from her. The timing seemed strangely coincidental with Hiroshi's sudden appearance in Okinawa. Why would a *Kempeitai* officer be here in the first place? It made no sense whatsoever.

Ever since Hiroshi arrived, not a word passed between them, which was fine with Akira. Perhaps he was following the proper protocol of officers not fraternizing with enlisted men. Their eyes had met a few times, but Hiroshi pretended not to see him.

If Emiko found out Hiroshi was in charge of Akira's platoon, she would worry, especially knowing he was there with the *Kempeitai* at Matsumoto's Christmas party. Also, any mention of Hiroshi would remind her of the *omiai* and the near-disastrous engagement party.

No. Akira wouldn't mention anything about him in his letter.

50

Lost Battalion

Vosges Mountains, France – October 30, 1944

Tad shivered in a foxhole and wiggled his toes in sopping socks inside damp boots. Rainwater seeped through a roof of cut branches. He'd better not get trench feet like some men already had. He needed to keep his feet dry. Many soldiers left them untreated and ended up getting gangrene that sometimes required amputation.

Incoming artillery shells screamed overhead, and thunderous explosions hammered the earth, shaking the ground like strong temblors. Single shots fired from M1 and Karabiner rifles punctuated the *rat-tat-tat* of American Browning automatic rifles and the *brrrp* of German submachine guns.

The last four days had been hellish for Tad and I Company in their mission to rescue the trapped men of the Alamo 141st Regiment. Dense fog, rain, and snow intermixed with smoke along with the thick canopies of evergreen branches reduced visibility to dusk-like conditions on steep hillsides pitched at forty-five degrees. The Germans couldn't have asked for a more defendable terrain.

Merciless gunfire and exploding mortar shells had killed and maimed numerous Nisei, including one soldier who completely disintegrated when a mortar shell landed on top of him. They couldn't advance forward without getting massacred.

Someone shouted, "We're moving out! Let's show 'em what we're made of!"

Tad shoved away tree branches and hoisted himself out of the dugout. Other men around him crawled out of their foxholes and began to charge uphill toward enemy lines, yelling, "Go for Broke!" The rallying cry resounded as more Nisei ascended, dodging between tree trunks, ducking behind ridges, and keeping an eye out for the camouflaged machine gun nests.

A hail of bullets whizzed past them, and countless Nisei fell like toy soldiers all around Tad. He dove to the ground, numbed at the gruesome sight. Nearby, Private Tamura toppled backward. Tad inched his way to Tamura and looked into his lifeless eyes. *Not Tamura too!* The bullet found its mark through the helmet, and blood gushed out of his temple. How he wished he could have saved the round-faced kid from San Jose. They'd collect his body later.

At this rate, Tad and the other medics wouldn't be able to treat all of the fallen men. The entire company could be wiped out.

Someone yelled, "Medic! Get your *okole* over here! Ikeda's hit."

Tad ran up a rise in the general direction of the shout and plunged into a thicket. From there he crawled on his belly through mud below the Germans' line of fire.

"Over here." It was Private Okimoto.

Ikeda had been shot through the left shoulder and chest ominously close to his heart. Tad cut away what remained of Ikeda's shirt, blotted excess blood, and examined his chest.

Okimoto leaned over to check on his friend. Back in training camp, he and Ikeda had squared off against each other in a silly fight. It warmed Tad's heart to see them like brothers now.

Bullets had poked holes through Ikeda's shirt pocket. To Tad's surprise, he found two silver-dollar coins inside. "Ikeda, this is amazing. These coins stopped the bullets from taking your life."

Ikeda heaved rapid breaths openmouthed and nodded.

Tad cleaned and bandaged Ikeda's shoulder wound. "You're going to be okay."

Okimoto smiled. "*Mahalo.*" The Hawaiian charged off.

Raising his head slightly Tad could see Okimoto and another soldier crawling into the shrubbery. They leaped out and hurled hand grenades. The blasts threw dirt and rocks into the air. When the smoke cleared, a few Germans lay slumped over their sandbagged nest.

With another enemy machine gun trained on him, Tad stayed put for a while, then continued crawling toward the loud cries. Nearby another medic was treating a frenzied soldier writhing in pain. "Let me help you," Tad said to the medic. "I'll give him some morphine."

"Thanks, Omura."

"Sure thing." Tad ripped open the morphine syrette and administered the shot. "You can take it from here."

Tad crawled ahead, looking for other downed soldiers. Private Terada and other Nisei aimed their weapons and opened fire. A loud explosion rocked the ground. When the noise settled, Tad noticed another machine gun nest had been obliterated. "Way to go fellas!"

By Tad's calculation, they had advanced less than one hundred yards in the last two hours. The Nisei had finally made some headway when a large contingent of German soldiers charged down the hill with guns blazing. Loud wails from downed Nisei tightened Tad's gut like a nut on a bolt that wouldn't budge.

Nearby, Captain Whelan barked into a walkie-talkie, "This is I Company. The enemy has launched a counterattack. Request artillery support. Over."

The walkie-talkie crackled, "I Company. We copy. What is your position? Over."

"About eight hundred yards above the large ravine."

"Copy that. Pull your men back. Over."

The I Company platoons withdrew carefully and quickly with the Germans firing at them. About twenty minutes later, they were safely below the ravine. Soon a violent blast shook the ground.

Keeping the field glasses glued to his eyes, the captain grabbed the walkie-talkie. "Spot it three hundred yards above the ravine. Over."

A second earsplitting shot pounded the hillside above them. "Fifty yards lower!"

Then a third blast exploded.

"Good. Fire for effect! Over."

A barrage of deafening artillery shook the earth beneath Tad and wouldn't quit. When the noise subsided, Tad looked up to see thick black smoke shrouding the entire hillside.

As the smoke began to dissipate, the captain spied out the target area through field glasses. A triumphant smile broke out on his face. "You got 'em fellas! You got 'em. Great shooting!"

Men around the commander whooped and cheered, and slapped hands with each other.

The remnants of I Company, shored up by K Company, began their slow ascent again. With the American artillerymen doing their job, they were able to fight their way up.

Tad slogged uphill, passing pieces of rifles, canteens, and dead bodies that littered the terrain. Every time he closed his eyes, the contorted faces of dying soldiers haunted him.

After five brutal days of constant fighting, they broke through the German defenses to free the trapped Texans.

Soon Tad and other GIs encountered the forward guard of the Texans in the afternoon.

"Boy, I'm glad to see you Japs," the guard said with a drawl.

Judging from the smile on the Texan's face, no offense was intended. Tad shrugged and moved past him.

As more Nisei clambered up the hill, the men of the Lost Battalion emerged from their hiding places. Tad received a weak, but sincere, hug from a rail-thin, pale-faced Texan. Other rescued soldiers cried openly and thanked them.

Nearby, Captain Whelan crouched on the ground with an Alamo officer. "Lieutenant Higdon, what happened here?"

The officer wiped his smudged forehead. "We were completely surrounded, low on ammunition, and hadn't eaten for days. The airdrops of supplies landed near the Germans or got snagged in the trees. We were losing all hope. You're a Godsend."

"Food will be arriving soon," Captain Whelan said. "How many men did you lose?"

"Sixty-four dead. Twice as many wounded."

Tad's rough count told him that the 442nd had suffered more than one thousand casualties while rescuing the Texans. No other regiment could achieve what the Nisei had accomplished. Victory came at a very high cost.

Into the early evening, Tad and the other medics continued the enormous job of treating hundreds of men in the makeshift aid station. About an hour later, he spotted Private Okimoto being carried on a stretcher and rushed over. "Not you, too!"

Okimoto groaned and opened an eye. "Got hit by a mortar blast. The bugga hurts lots." He wore his usual smart-aleck smirk.

Tad unraveled the blood-soaked bandages and flinched at the sight of the Hawaiian's upper torso.

"Am I going to make it?"

He didn't know how to respond. "You better."

"I no can figure you out, Tad."

"What?" Tad toweled blood off from Okimoto's left side, then cracked open a morphine syrette. He gently poked it near his chest. "Hopefully this will help ease your pain."

"You so calm all the time." Okimoto took short breaths. "Me, I ack tough, but inside, I really scared every time."

"I'm just as scared as anybody, but I believe God is faithful. If I die, Jesus has a home for me in heaven."

"I neva believe that stuff." Okimoto grimaced with pain. "I'm a *buddahead* and all *buddaheads* are Buddhists."

"It has nothing to do with being Hawaiian, *haole*, or any color. But it has everything to do with making your peace with God. Jesus died to save us from our sins. He came back to life and is alive today."

"I neva know dat. I thought he jest die on da cross an go away."

Tad placed a hand to his own heart. "Jesus lives inside here, just as he lives in anyone who invites him to be their God."

"Das why you so calm, yeah?" Okimoto coughed. "You know, I loss so many buddies, and I been thinking dat I not going make it out of dis war. I not going to see Hawaii again."

"Tommy, do you want the same peace I have?" Tad asked.

Okimoto's eyes rolled up then down, as though he was thinking hard. He coughed, then looked at Tad. "Yeah, I like same ting."

"That's great. I'm going to lead you into a prayer. Repeat after me the best you can. 'Father God, I admit my wrongs and ask for your forgiveness. Come into my heart and fill me with your peace. Be my Lord and personal Savior . . .'"

Okimoto mumbled the words. After the prayer, his usual tough-guy smirk vanished. "Tad, I have peace. I no afraid no more."

Tad's heart soared like a signal flare. "That's swell, Tommy."

Later that night, Private Okimoto died. It deeply saddened Tad, but he took great comfort in knowing the Hawaiian went to heaven.

The next morning, Tad and the other medics set about the enormous task of collecting dead bodies. "Stay low," Tad said to John Sasaki as they readied themselves to collect a dead soldier lying in the meadow. "Watch out for the snipers in trees. They're hard to see with their camouflaged uniforms, and they don't always respect the big Red Cross insignias on our helmets."

Sasaki looked up in the trees.

Tad took a deep breath. "All right. Ready—go!"

They moved toward the fallen man when shots rang out. Tad dove to the ground and turned his head to see Sasaki sprawled on the meadow grass.

Several Nisei returned heavy gunfire into the trees where flashes of light had originated. A sniper fell from the tree.

Tad crawled over to John and checked his pulse. He had taken a bullet in the neck but was still alive.

A moment later, a Nisei rifleman crept over to help Tad.

"Let's get him out quick." Tad pressed a gauze bandage on Sasaki's neck, and then they placed him on the stretcher. Tad lifted the front end and turned slightly.

A flash lit up dark shadows in the trees, and a shot cracked through the silence.

* * *

In the cool autumn night, Lily rocked little Brent to sleep and set him down inside the crib. She buttoned her wool sweater around her shoulders and shuffled to the potbelly stove. She opened its door latch and troweled in coal from a storage box. Revolving searchlights beamed through the window curtain. She sat on her cot and read her Bible under the bare lightbulb that hung from the ceiling of the austere barrack.

Lily paused and glanced at the photograph of her husband on the wall shelf. "Lord, please look after my Tad. I don't even know where he is right now. Somewhere in Europe, I suppose. Why did he have to go to war?" She blinked hard to stem the warm tears that began to form. "Keep him safe and out of harm's way. I miss him so much."

Little Brent woke up crying. She sprang to the crib and scooped up her baby. "What's wrong, sweetie?" She kissed her son lightly on the forehead and continued praying. "Jesus, please bring Tad safely home to us. He has never even met his son."

The possibility of Tad never returning sent a hollow fear to her stomach. How terrible it would be for Brent to grow up without knowing his father. Lily tried to banish the thought. She needed to remain strong for Brent's sake.

Oh, God! Please help me to stay calm and trust you. Tad will come home. He will come home.

Holding her little baby, she returned to the cot. With her free hand she turned to Psalm 18:2. *The Lord is my rock, and my fortress, and my deliverer. . .*

51

The Major

Takeo, Japan – November 8, 1944

Emiko finished reading another letter from Akira. Now that his letters started arriving regularly, she missed him even more, knowing he was still alive. She held the letter close to her heart.

Aunt Shizuko entered Emiko's room. "Are you ready? Major Endo will be here any moment." Her lilting voice carried an exhilarating expectation that troubled Emiko.

Ever since his first visit, her aunt couldn't stop raving about him. On the other hand, Emiko dreaded the coming of this day. Although Aunt Shizuko knew about her fiancé, she never said anything about Akira, perhaps because they'd never met.

"Put on your finest kimono and come to the main house. I have to finish preparing the *sushi*." Aunt Shizuko rushed out.

Emiko resolved to tell the major that her heart belonged to Akira, and she couldn't continue seeing him. She should have never agreed to his visits, only to retract now. He was such a nice man, which made it even harder. Any other woman would gladly marry him. She neatly folded Akira's letter, placed it on top of the other ones, and tied twine around them. Then she put the collection away.

At exactly four o'clock, the doorbell rang. "*Gomen kudasai,* excuse me. It's Major Endo."

Emiko accompanied Aunt Shizuko to the foyer, where they bowed to their guest.

Her aunt's face lit up. "Welcome, Major. Please come in."

Emiko smiled but remained silent.

Out from behind him, a little girl made her appearance, clinging to her father shyly.

"This is my daughter, Ayako. I hope you don't mind that I brought her. My sister had to leave the house this afternoon, and I couldn't leave her alone."

Aunt Shizuko blossomed with sparkling eyes and an enchanting smile. "*Wah! Tottemo kawaii!* So cute! Of course, she's welcome."

"Thank you so much."

"It's quite all right, Major. Your daughter looks just like Emiko did when she was her age."

Major Endo nodded at Emiko with a quick grin. He stooped down to Ayako's height. "*Goaisatsu o chanto shinasai.*"

The young girl obediently followed her father's order to extend her greetings and bowed. "*Hajimemashite yoroshiku,*" she said with a sweet, innocent voice.

Major Endo reached into his inner coat pocket. He retrieved a small package and presented it to Aunt Shizuko.

Her aunt received it and examined the packaging. "*Wah!* What a treat. This *nori* seaweed is rare."

As if Aunt Shizuko needed more encouragement to be endeared to the major.

The major grinned diffidently. "It's just a trifle."

Uncle Teruo entered the room with a welcoming smile and greeted the guests. "So nice to meet you." He bowed.

Emiko took the major's coat, then helped little Ayako with hers. The girl was indeed pretty, but Emiko didn't think she looked anything like her at that age.

* * *

While the others gorged themselves, Emiko hardly took three bites of the feast Aunt Shizuko had prepared. Major Endo and Uncle Teruo conversed throughout dinner about his family, their mutual acquaintances, and they toasted each other with cups of *saké*. *"Kampai!"*

Emiko remained quiet for the most part, periodically smiling, making polite small talk, and trying to start conversations with the major's daughter. She kept minimal eye contact with the major, dreading what she was going to tell him later in the evening.

Aunt Shizuko lifted a dish of sautéed burdock and bamboo shoots and offered it to the major. "Can I serve you some more vegetables?"

"Thank you, but I've had quite enough of this delicious food. *Gochisosama deshita.*" He flashed a charming smile at Aunt Shizuko.

Her aunt lowered the plate. "I'm sorry that the food is so bad-tasting. With the shortages, I couldn't acquire all the ingredients to prepare it properly." She bowed her head slightly, in false humility.

Major Endo chuckled quietly. "On the contrary, it was fabulous."

Aunt Shizuko placed her hand over her mouth and muffled a giggle. "You're too kind."

Uncle Teruo grasped a flask and poured another drink. "Have some more *saké*."

Her aunt looked at her husband with concern. "*Anata*, you look tired. Why don't you get some rest?"

"One more drink, and I'll retire for the evening."

Emiko and her aunt rose and carried the dirty dishes to the kitchen.

Auntie nudged her. "After we go back, I'll have Uncle go to bed to sleep off the *saké*. And I'll take Ayako-chan to my sewing room to show her my *kokeshi* doll collection. This way you and the major will have a chance to talk together."

Emiko's heart beat in allegro tempo as she pondered what would happen next.

* * *

Although she had rehearsed numerous times, Emiko couldn't bring herself to start the conversation. Major Endo sat silently, sipping his green tea and staring off into space.

Emiko couldn't delay any further. "Major—"

"Takata-san—"

They both smiled at each other's attempt to speak at the same time. Emiko waited a moment to regain her composure. "Major, please go first."

"No, I'd like you to go first."

She sucked in a deep breath. How terrible it was to let him down twice, meeting him for the first time on the pretense of a potential marriage match, and now having to say good-bye to him. "Major, you've been so kind and helpful to me and my family these past few months, especially after all that I've put you through. But I . . . I—"

"Yes?"

"Major, you are an honorable man. You are a good father to Ayako-chan." She wanted to tell him so much, but she didn't want to ramble on. "I feel horrible. I deceived you, and then involved you with my troubles. You deserve so much better. And—"

"Stop." He lowered his glance. "Don't say anything more."

Emiko sighed, not knowing what to expect next. Rather than say anything, it would be best to let him speak.

He raised his head. "Takata-san, I assumed you started to hear from your fiancé, because you made no mention of the mail problem the last two times I spoke with you on the phone. I could tell by the tone of your voice that I made you uncomfortable. Tonight, I came to confirm it in person. You don't want to see me anymore."

"I'm so sorry. I should have told you earlier, but I didn't quite know how to."

"It's all right. I understand."

She could see the deep disappointment in his eyes.

The major clasped his hands together and lowered his chin. "I knew your heart belonged to your fiancé, but I was being stubborn. Please forgive me. I was secretly hoping you would never hear from him again." He looked away. "I'm such a fool."

Her eyes widened. This man whom she admired was human after all. Knowing that he would even think such a thing was a bit disappointing. Emiko lowered her gaze to the floor. The difficult part of delivering her message was done, but relief escaped her.

The major sat straight and let out a glum expression. "There's something else I need to tell you."

Emiko looked at him again, unable to mask her surprise that there was more. "Please, Major, go ahead."

"I'm afraid this isn't good news." He lowered his eyes and tightened his lips momentarily. "Hiroshi Yamada was released from custody last month."

"*Nandato?* How can that be?" A sudden coldness rippled down her back, and she shuddered. That monster—set free?

"I can't believe it either. I found out he was court-martialed but not sentenced to prison."

"When the prosecutor's assistant interviewed me, he told me Yamada-san would go to prison for at least three years. I don't understand how this could happen."

"I don't know all the details, but I heard he was reduced in rank to lieutenant and reassigned to an infantry unit."

"What shall I do? I'm frightened."

The major nodded slightly. "He doesn't know you're at your uncle's house. And chances are, if he's now part of the infantry, he'll be sent overseas soon, if he hasn't been already."

Her nightmare wasn't over.

52

Aftermath

Heart Mountain, Wyoming

Chinook winds blustered in from the Pacific, sweeping over the Rockies and warming the otherwise frigid air. Lily pressed her way against strong headwinds as she sauntered toward the camp post office to mail a package for Tad.

Three weeks had passed since she received a letter from him. Lily couldn't shake the ineffable feeling that something happened to him. Today she hoped to hear from him. A strange mixture of expectation, anxiety, and fear spilled over her as she entered the post office. She removed the scarf she wore over her braided hairdo.

"Hi, Lily. How are you and the baby?" her friend Ann Ito said.

"We're doing fine. Little Brent is such a good baby, and he sleeps through the night, unlike the infants three doors down."

They continued the small talk while inching along in line. When it was Lily's turn, she lifted the package onto the counter.

The postal clerk accepted it, stepped away for a while and returned. "Mrs. Omura, there's a letter for you." He handed her a thin beige letter with the familiar Victory Mail logo.

"Hooray. I've been waiting for this. Thank you!" Her heart flipped cartwheels as she stepped out of line. Lily tore the seal open and squinted at the tiny, one-page print. She wished she had the original since the V-Mail facsimile was printed from microfilm and hard to read. She understood why they compacted the letters, which saved space needed for more vital military cargo aboard the transport ships.

October 7, 1944

> *My Precious Lily,*
> *I miss you so much, it's unbearable. How are you and little Brent doing? I can't wait to see him.*
> *In my last letter, I mentioned how angry I'd been with Danny and felt he got what he deserved. Men here are scared to death and see their friends dying all around them. Yet, they rise each morning and battle the enemy. So it's hard for me to sympathize with him.*
> *But today, I sensed the Lord nudging me to forgive him. As hard as it was, I let go of my anger and realized Danny, too, was fighting for the same cause. It takes a lot of guts to do what he did. Also serving a prison sentence isn't easy . . .*

The tone of his letter struck her as uncharacteristic of Tad. He didn't seem to have that quiet confidence he had when he left Heart Mountain. Lily read the letter again, hanging on to each word with concern. Then she folded it up and placed it into her handbag. She wrapped the scarf over her head and stepped outside.

Battling the whipping winds on the way back to the barrack, She kept telling herself Tad was safe. After all, she received his letter today. *Tad will return to me and live to see his child.*

Inside the barrack, Lily took Brent from Mama and gently rocked him in her lap. "Daddy's letter came today."

"What did he say?" Mama asked.

Suddenly a rapid knock came to the door, and a woman's voice called from outside, "Lily, an army car is coming."

Panic jabbed her heart. She lifted Brent in her arms and rose abruptly. "Mama, please watch him for me."

Mama reached over to receive Brent, who protested with a squeal.

Lily rushed outside and skidded on a patch of ice, almost losing her balance. The winds had died down, and she dashed to the gate.

A small group had already gathered behind the fence in the shadow of a grim guard tower. Heads turned toward a drab-olive sedan with a white star painted on its side, making its way into the camp—a harbinger of tragic news. The engine's whine and scratching of tires on the gravel road broke the eerie silence.

She bit her lip, trembling, and stood alongside of other soldiers' loved ones. *Oh, Lord, please don't let it be my husband. Please, oh please, Lord, not Tad!*

The first time the army car had made its appearance, the names of the deceased were not released until the officials spoke to the families at their barracks.

Nevertheless, no one, including Lily, could bear to just wait and be surprised. It was a strange ritual of wait and see in the common area, followed by the families scurrying back to their barracks.

An army officer stepped out of the car and greeted the camp director, Robert Gilbertson. They conferred for a minute and disappeared into the office. A short while later, they left the administration building and strode down a row of barracks. The army officer held a folded American flag under his arm. People who had gathered in the common area dispersed like a flock of birds.

Lily rushed back to her barrack and waited outside.

The officials began to march toward her. Lily's diaphragm constricted, and she couldn't breathe. With widened eyes, she held her hand to her mouth. Her heart thumped like a kettledrum being struck harder and harder. *No, no, no!*

Closer and closer they came. *No! Not Tad!*

The solemn procession passed by and kept going.

The knot in Lily's throat released, and she relaxed her stiff shoulders. *Thank you, Lord, it wasn't Tad.*

At the beginning of the next block, the procession stopped. The army officer addressed the Shimizus standing in front of their barrack. It had to be their eldest son, Minoru. Lily bit back her tears. She covered her mouth and drew near them, but stopped short.

Mrs. Shimizu shrieked and wailed and collapsed into her husband's arms. He held her up with their younger son, Ken.

The officer patiently waited until the woman calmed down. Mr. Shimizu and Ken braced her as they walked into the barrack with the officer and camp director following them.

Guilt sliced into Lily. She couldn't lift her feet to join the others who waited for the officials to leave. What right did she have to console them when she secretly rejoiced in her heart that it hadn't been Tad? *Lord, forgive me and comfort the Shimizu family.*

* * *

Paris, France

The sound of clicking heels woke Tad, and a blurry light shone above his head. After blinking a few times, the overhead light fixture came into focus. He tilted his head and saw nurses scurrying about. On one side, a man wrapped head to toe in bandages lay next to him. Tad tried to lift himself upright, but burning pain flared in his chest, forcing him back down. He caught a glimpse of his chest wrapped in gauze with several flexible tubes protruding out.

A pretty brunette nurse approached him and smiled. "Hello, I'm Susan. You're Ta-day-oh Omyura?"

"I go by Tad. Where am I?"

"You're at the 815th Station Hospital Center in Paris." She lifted the clipboard attached to the bedpost then looked at him. "Dr. Harris operated on you a few days ago, and he said a bullet came within an inch of your heart, tearing up part of your lung."

The news completely astounded Tad.

"The chest wall had to be reconstructed, so we've had to keep you sedated for most of the time. How do you feel?"

"Groggy. My mouth feels dry."

"That's because you had a breathing tube down your throat and were connected to a ventilator to help with your breathing. We removed it a few hours ago. I'll bring you some water, but first, let's take your temperature." She placed a thermometer under his tongue, waited a few minutes, then pulled it out. "Good, no fever." She stepped away.

Little by little, Tad began to recall the rescue of the 141st, but he didn't remember getting shot.

Nurse Susan returned with a large cup of water and set it on the tray. "I'll prop a pillow under your neck." She raised his head slightly and slipped the pillow behind him.

"Thanks." Tad sipped the cold water and coughed. His chest erupted in excruciating pain.

"Are you okay?"

Tad nodded, trying to suppress his cough. He slowly drank some more until his cup was empty.

"I'll bring you some more water, but first, I need to take care of another patient, then I'll return. Dr. Harris will be stopping by to talk to you."

"Okay, thank you." With his head propped up, Tad could see dozens of wounded men in the ward. His mind drifted to Okimoto dying on the aid station cot. Then he remembered Sasaki was shot when they were collecting bodies. Shortly after that, he must have taken a bullet. If Lily saw him bandaged up with tubes hanging out of his chest, she'd fall to pieces.

A man in a white coat approached. A major's gold oak leaf insignia was pinned on his collar. "Hello, I'm Dr. Harris. You're a mighty lucky man. It's truly amazing that you survived."

"Yes, sir. I believe God kept me alive."

"You're probably right." Dr. Harris smiled. "When we operated on you, I saw how close that bullet came to taking your life. It's a miracle it didn't tear through your aorta or hit your spinal cord."

Tad's vision blurred with tears, remembering the countless men who had died and were strewn all over the forest. His comrades were still out there, fighting their way to the Rhine and into Germany. "Sir, when can I rejoin my unit?"

"You're not going back. Men with less serious wounds have been sent home. You'll be here for a few weeks. Then you'll be transferred to another hospital stateside for rehabilitation for a few months. After that they'll send you home."

"Home, sir?" Never in his wildest imaginations did Tad think he would go home before the war ended. "I can finally see my wife and my son."

"Congratulations. So, where's home?"

"A little town called Mountain View, near San Francisco."

"Nice. I'm from Chicago, but I've been to the West Coast a couple of times. So your wife and kids are waiting for you there?"

"Only one son. My family's in a Wyoming internment camp."

"Hmm. I've heard about those camps. It's a shame."

Tad wondered what would have happened if he and the other Nisei hadn't volunteered to serve. If this were a civilian hospital, would the doctors treat him cordially? "Thanks for looking after me, Dr. Harris."

"My pleasure. Oh, there's something else." He opened a folder. "Your regiment commander sent a report. It says you were the best medic in the detachment, and you saved numerous men in the line of fire without shying away from your duty."

"I just did what I had to do, sir. No more than anyone else."

"Be that as it may, he's put you in for a Silver Star medal. Congratulations, soldier!"

"I don't know what to say. Thank you, sir."

"You're welcome. Get plenty of rest, and I'll check on you again. Let the nurse know if the pain becomes unbearable." Dr. Harris flashed a genuine smile and walked away whistling.

Tad was going home to Lily . . . to his son . . . to a new life.

53

Impossible Mission

Okinawa – April 1, 1945

Inside the dimly-lit cave, Akira ducked as falling rocks broke loose, and debris flew about, pelting his helmet. The invasion of Okinawa had arrived. American naval guns blasted the island for hours, shaking the ground like powerful earthquakes.

Countless Japanese would die in this battle—innocent lives who had nothing to do with the ill-conceived decision to attack Pearl Harbor.

Now, he had to make a decision. He didn't know what he would do if he faced a kill-or-be-killed situation. Akira was torn between Japan and America, but he decided to stay loyal to his country of birth.

As the preinvasion bombardment decreased and halted later that day, Akira and his platoon scurried to the closest lookouts. Peering out through the cave entrance, he blinked hard at the ruins of the capital city of Naha below, spreading from the foot of Shuri Castle westward to the harbor. Much of the city lay flat with plumes of black smoke.

Sergeant Kameda surveyed the landscape through a pair of military field glasses. He handed the glasses and a clipboard to Akira. "Omura, I'm going to see what Lieutenant Yamada wants. Count the enemy landing craft, tanks and armored vehicles."

"Yes, sir." It seemed odd that Hiroshi hadn't said a word to him. When they taught high school together, it was Akira who had tried to avoid Hiroshi's annoying visits in between classes.

Through the powerful field glasses, Akira kept a watchful eye on Hagushi Bay. Beyond the harbor breakers, an immense American armada dotted the cobalt-blue waters.

Akira spotted small specks fanning out from the ships and streaming toward the beach. Ten, twenty . . . fifty amphibious landing craft loaded with American troops commenced their assault.

* * *

In the first five days of the American invasion, Akira's unit saw no action except a few reconnaissance missions. Other units had already engaged in bloody skirmishes with many lives lost. Sergeant Kameda ordered Akira to remain at his observation post.

Scanning the eastern horizon, Akira spotted a squadron of twelve Japanese planes speeding toward the American fleet. As they drew closer, fireballs erupted with loud pops from batteries of anti-aircraft guns on board the ships. Hundreds of black smoke puffs floated in the air, just ahead and below the attacking planes.

The planes banked into steep dives with their engines screaming. From the ships, machine guns opened up with successive tracer bullets, painting dotted lines of light across the sky. Flak disintegrated several of the lead planes and turned them into fiery comets that crashed into the sea. Flames flared on other planes as they lost chunks of their wings or tail assemblies and cartwheeled in the air and tumbled into the water. The Americans were knocking the Japanese planes out of the sky as if they were shooting skeet.

Akira tracked a single plane from the rear making a beeline for one of the larger ships. One wing caught fire, but the pilot seemed to be holding his line. It crashed into the superstructure of the ship, setting off a huge, thunderous explosion.

Another disabled plane slammed into the bow of a smaller ship.

Under a sky darkened by thick smoke, the battle subsided with no more Japanese planes in this attack wave, leaving the

American fleet relatively intact. What a tragic waste of human lives.

* * *

Sergeant Kameda lit a cigarette and took a drag. "The enemy is swarming below the lower ridge, and we're just sitting here doing nothing. I'm so sick of it."

A corporal from another squad saluted Kameda and handed him a note. "Sergeant, this is from Lieutenant Yamada."

Kameda read the note and looked up. "Omura, you've been given special orders. You're temporarily assigned to a rifle company in the 62nd Division."

"Just me?" Akira's palms became sweaty.

"It looks like you'll be seeing combat before the rest of us. I'll escort you to Tunnel 43, where you'll report to Lieutenant Honda. Be ready at 1930."

"Yes, sir." Akira circled the muzzle of the rifle barrel with his index finger, contemplating the choice he would soon have to make between his head and heart.

At 1930, Sergeant Kameda and Akira arrived at Tunnel 43, where a livid-faced lieutenant with a brush mustache was shouting at a subordinate.

Akira observed dozens of riflemen cinching up straps on their field packs. Some checked the actions on their weapons, while others attached hand grenades to their shoulder straps. Behind them, machine gunners draped belts of heavy-caliber bullets across their chests. If these men experienced the same spasms of fear he had, they didn't show it.

The lieutenant dismissed his charge and turned his attention toward Akira and Sergeant Kameda. "I've been expecting you."

They saluted. "Lieutenant, this is Private Omura."

"Sergeant, you are dismissed. Private, this way."

Akira followed him past stacks of rifles and mortar shells to a hollowed area that appeared to be a stub for an uncompleted tunnel.

"Tonight we're going to attack Yontan Airfield where the enemy's interceptor-fighter planes are stationed. We need to destroy as many aircraft as possible and kill their pilots and crew members. Otherwise our *kamikaze* pilots will be exposed when they fly over Hagushi Bay to attack their fleet."

Heart pounding, Akira flinched. *Why me?*

Lieutenant Honda aimed steely eyes at him. "We need to sneak past the outer perimeter before the enemy realizes it. Your company commander told me you grew up in America and speak English fluently. Is that correct?"

Akira blinked. "Yes . . . um, I do." How did he find out about his American origin?

"Your mission is to get us past the guard using your English to make them think we're American troops returning from patrol. We'll disguise ourselves by wearing uniforms and helmets we've captured. It'll be easier for you to pass as an American since you're taller than us. They won't be able to see your face in the dark." Honda tapped a cigarette out from its pack and stuck it in his mouth. "Any questions?"

Fear tightened Akira's throat. He had lots of questions, most of which would stay unasked. "Sir, if they challenge me and ask for my unit identification, what shall I say?"

Honda lit the cigarette and inhaled. "Be clever and make something up."

"I'm not sure that will work. Sir, I—"

"If it doesn't work, we'll start shooting." Lieutenant Honda took another drag and blew out smoke through his nostrils. "I'll warn you about one other thing. If you're even thinking about tipping off the Americans and going over to their side, just know that I understand some English. I'll have my gun trained on your head, so don't be stupid. Understand?"

"Yes, sir."

"Good. Now, report to Sergeant Nakamura. He has your uniform and helmet."

En route to the assembly area, Akira stopped in his tracks. Hiroshi must have found out about his background through the

Kempeitai. He could have selected Sergeant Kameda, an experienced fighter, who also grew up in America. Or maybe he was too short.

Akira reported to Sergeant Nakamura and recognized him as the subordinate Honda harshly reprimanded in front of everyone. Nakamura handed him the American uniform.

A sewn-over bullet hole and discoloration appeared in the fabric where the man's heart would have been. Akira fingered the mend, praying silently that another hole wouldn't take its place while he wore the uniform.

At 2100 hours, Akira sat with other men along the tunnel wall. Sergeant Nakamura marched down the line for last-minute preparations and squatted near Akira. "Omura, stay close to the lieutenant and me. Whatever you do, don't run toward us. We might mistake you for the enemy and shoot." He shouted to the other men. "It's time."

The platoon stole out of Tunnel 43 under a thin crescent moon that provided minimal light. They descended the rocky slope in single file, avoiding the large craters formed by artillery explosions. Akira's knuckles scraped a shard of rock, and he sucked back his groan to follow strict orders to be silent. Crickets that once sang on forest-covered hills couldn't be heard anymore. Only the crunching of rocky soil underneath their boots broke the hush.

The advance group—Akira, Lieutenant Honda, and three other soldiers—gingerly climbed to a low rise above Yontan Airfield. "Let's begin our attack," Honda said. "Be on your guard."

This could be the end. Emiko's lovely face invaded Akira's mind, and his heart plummeted like an airplane being shot down. Perhaps he'd never see her again.

A rifle cocked. Akira and Honda froze.

"Halt! Who goes there?" an American voice called out.

Akira's moment had come. He had to decide whether to go along with the plan. If he didn't, he'd take a bullet from his commander. "We're coming back from patrol."

"Patrol? Nobody's supposed to be patrolling beyond this guard post. What unit are you with?"

"First Platoon, Baker Company," Akira said.

"Baker Company? You guys are supposed to be out on the east side of the ridge. What are you doing here?"

"We got lost."

"Got lost? Who are you? Come out here where I can see you."

Akira had one last chance to change his mind. A desperate desire to warn the American begged to come out of his mouth.

"Where are the others?"

"The others?"

"Yeah, you said 'we.' Where are—ugh!"

The American crumpled to the ground with a hand muffling his mouth from behind. Honda yanked the knife out from the American's back. He turned to Akira. "Omura, let's go."

Akira followed Honda with a heavy heart.

The infiltrators made it to the razor-wire barrier surrounding the outer perimeter. Bright security lights illuminated parts of the runway with silhouettes of American planes.

Lieutenant Honda surveyed the site through binoculars. "There's another razor-wire fence we have to cut through," he whispered. "Beyond that, six sentries and two machine gun nests are guarding the main entrance." He panned to the right and halted. "There's a blind spot between the third and fourth guard positions on the other side. We might be able to sneak past them."

Private Tsuda snipped the bottom of the fence with wire cutters. A faint ringing echoed when the steel tension wire snapped back. Soon he had cut a semicircular hole about a meter wide. Lieutenant Honda crept in first, then motioned to Akira and the others to crawl toward the second fence.

Sergeant Nakamura followed about thirty meters behind with the support group. Scrub grass muffled the sounds of their boots and bodies as they slithered to their target.

Once the second wire barrier was breached, the advance group slipped in. They rushed behind a stack of large wooden crates, perpendicular to the machine gun's line of fire. About 150 meters ahead, Akira could see the American fighter planes parked on the tarmac.

"Private, let's move closer," whispered Lieutenant Honda. "I want to see how many planes there are. Walk erect and shoulder your rifle. If the guards see us, we have to look like Americans."

They slowly rose from behind the crates and marched toward the planes.

"Hey, what are you guys doing there?" an American sentry called out.

They stopped abruptly and turned to face the sentry, who stood about fifteen meters away. Akira couldn't allow another American to die in order to save his own skin. Apprehension and remorse exploded inside him. He could sense Honda glaring at him expectantly.

The American had his rifle pointed at Akira. "I asked you, what are you doing out there?"

"We're just taking a walk," Akira responded.

"Taking a walk? Are you nuts? Do you want to get your heads blown—"

"Soldier, it's a trap! Watch out!" Akira shouted.

Lieutenant Honda yanked his pistol out of his holster and took aim at Akira's head.

Akira shoved his rifle butt into Honda's pistol, causing it to fire askew. He slipped and fell to the ground. Several rounds of shots fired, and Akira raised his head slightly to see what was going on.

The commotion stirred the American machine gunner who sprayed bullets in their direction. The remaining Japanese soldiers opened fire.

Akira kept his head as low as possible. A loud explosion shook the ground, and he opened his eyes to see smoke rising and fire blazing where the American machine gun nest had been. A Japanese hand grenade had done its job.

Another American machine gunner opened up on the Japanese soldiers and sent several of them sprawling to the ground. Sirens blared. In the far distance, Akira spotted a large American contingent coming in their direction. Then someone touched his shoulder, and Akira jerked his neck.

"Omura, are you hurt?" Sergeant Nakamura and another soldier pulled Akira up. "Let's get out of here."

He wished he hadn't moved so he could be left for dead. Akira rose and made a mad dash with them through the inner fence, then scrambled through the outer perimeter wire. They hastened up the ridge above the airfield and disappeared into the night.

American mortars fired into the ridge and into the foothills. By then Akira and the others were safely out of range.

"Let's take a rest," Sergeant Nakamura said, panting heavily. He turned toward Akira. "Omura, what happened back there?"

Good thing Nakamura didn't seem to know anything about his betrayal. Catching his breath, Akira scrambled for the right words. "It wasn't dark enough to hide our faces, and the guard started firing."

"You're awfully lucky," the sergeant said. "Lieutenant Honda is dead, and so are the other three men you were with."

"It was a close call." Turmoil churned in Akira's stomach about the deaths on both sides. "Thanks for pulling me out, Sergeant." He'd continue the charade for now.

After they returned to the cave, Sergeant Nakamura removed his helmet and wiped perspiration from his forehead with an ashen face. "Omura, change back into your regular uniform and return to your unit tonight. I have to report to my superiors."

"Yes, sir." Akira didn't envy Nakamura, who had to report the mission as a failure. He'd wait for another opportunity to escape.

54

Homecoming

San Francisco, California – May 10, 1945

In just three more hours, Tad would be reunited with his family and meet his son for the first time. Unspeakable joy filled his heart. He watched some soldiers milling around the San Francisco train station two days after Germany's surrender—VE day. Many more would be coming home soon unless the top brass shipped them out to the raging war in the Pacific.

In her last letter, Lily wrote how thrilled she was to finally be home after three of the most demoralizing years of her life. They were among one of the first groups to leave Heart Mountain and had arrived at their farmhouse in April. Being able to leave early was truly remarkable. She attributed much of it to the patriotic sacrifices of Tad and others serving in the 442nd Regiment.

Tad ran his hand through his thick hair. It would be nice to get it barbered, so he'd look his best for homecoming. He glanced at the wall clock. Just enough time to get it cut and groomed if he could find a barbershop right away.

He checked his duffel bag into a locker, dropped a nickel into the slot, and exited the station.

A cool breeze blew in from the bay, and fog retreated toward the west. He buttoned up his uniform jacket to ward off the chill as he strolled along Townsend Street.

Tad scoped the storefronts on both sides of the bustling street. A half block up, he spotted a swirling red, white, and blue-striped barber pole.

When he reached the shop, he opened the door and set off tinkling bells.

A middle-aged, Caucasian barber stood braced against a push broom, staring at him.

"Hello," Tad said, removing his uniform jacket and cap.

"I don't cut Jap hair." The barber scowled.

"I'm not a Jap, and I just returned from the war."

The barber said nothing and stormed away.

"Hey, I need a haircut," Tad called out, but to no avail as the man disappeared through a back door.

What nerve! Here he was dressed in a US Army uniform with a Silver Star and Purple Heart dangling from his chest. He couldn't believe he had risked his life for someone like that.

Gathering his belongings, he stalked out of the shop, dazed. Tad stomped down the street for twenty minutes, too steamed to look for another barber. He glanced at his watch and headed back to the station.

The southbound locomotive clattered down the peninsula, passing through small towns and cities. Colorful matchbox houses dotted the green hills to the west and the San Francisco Bay sparkled on the east. The scenery brought back memories—driving the Bayshore Highway with truckloads of blackberries, cherries, and apricots to and from the farmer's market in the city—an eternity ago. He glanced at his watch. In less than an hour, he'd be reunited with his family.

After his discharge from Walter Reed Hospital, Tad had sent a telegram to Lily before leaving Union Station in Washington, DC. He wondered whether anyone would greet him at the station.

One stop from Mountain View, Tad reached for his duffel bag in the overhead compartment, but the residual pain from his chest restricted him from moving his right arm above his head.

A fellow soldier who helped heft the bag up had already disembarked. He turned to a Caucasian man sitting nearby.

Tad paused, uncertain about how this man would respond. "Excuse me, sir. Could you help me bring my duffel bag down? I was wounded in the war."

"Why certainly." The man rose and dragged the bag down.

"Thank you kindly." The stranger's helpfulness and friendly attitude pumped Tad with hope.

"My pleasure. Welcome home, soldier." He shook Tad's hand, smiled warmly and returned to his seat.

Tad surveyed the approaching platform for familiar faces. He put on his service cap and reached for the support bar as the train slowed to a halt with squealing wheels and hissing brakes. He made his way to the exit and climbed down.

* * *

Lily's heart skipped a beat and a joyous cry rang out of her mouth the moment she spotted her husband stepping off the train. She bolted toward him.

With a mile-wide smile, Tad set his duffel bag down and held out both hands.

She wanted to jump into his arms, but with his recent chest surgery, she refrained. Lily gently wrapped her hands around his neck, pressed her lips against his and kissed him passionately. "Oh, honey, I missed you so much." She burst into tears.

"I'm so glad to be home! You look pretty."

"Thank you." Lily released her embrace, wiped her eyes with a tissue and anchored herself to his elbow. An outpouring of joy that had been repressed with months of worrying, loneliness, and waiting, suddenly released inside of her. "Come on. It's time to meet your son."

They hurried down the platform where his stepfather and mother waited with a baby stroller.

Tears spilled out of Mama's eyes, and she hugged him. "Welcome home!"

Mas warmly greeted Tad with a firm handshake and smile.

Lily's heart beat with excitement as her husband stooped down to meet his son for the very first time. She bent down by Tad and gushed, "Oh, little Brent, Daddy's home. He's finally home for good. Look, Brent—Daddy."

Tad reached inside the stroller and held Brent's tiny hand. "I can't believe it—my son!" Tears dripped down his cheeks. "After all I've seen on the battlefield, there's something very therapeutic about seeing Brent and holding his hand."

Brent responded with an engaging smile. "Dah, dah." Then he gurgled.

"He did it! Good, Brent!" Lily could see pure ecstasy and wonderment in Tad's enlarged eyes, and she immediately recognized a resemblance between father and son.

"Come on, let's go," Mas said, limping with a cane. "We have to return Bill Johnson's Oldsmobile."

"That's so kind of Mr. Johnson to lend us his car, " Tad said.

"I'm so thankful about everything our neighbor did for us while we were gone," Lily said. "If it weren't for Mr. Johnson, we wouldn't have a home to return to. We'd be like many other people who lost everything. Some people refused to leave Heart Mountain because they had nowhere to go."

"Maybe there's something we can do to help them," Tad said. "Offer them a place to stay for a while."

Lily nodded and gazed into his eyes. Despite his amiable smile, she could see an undecipherable sullenness. No doubt the horrors of war had taken their toll on her husband.

As they ambled toward the parking lot, Lily took in a deep breath. The sky looked so blue, and the air smelled so fresh. In the distance, the tree-covered Santa Cruz Mountains crowned acres of orchards that exploded in pink and white blossoms. In a few more months, they would yield countless bushels of succulent plums, cherries, and apricots.

Today marked the beginning of her new life together with Tad and little Brent—full of hope, dreams, and promise.

55

Confession

Okinawa

From his dugout, Akira precisely aimed his rifle slightly above an American soldier's head and squeezed the trigger. The bullet hit dirt harmlessly behind the man. He pulled the bolt action back and fired a second shot, purposely missing another soldier.

Eight tanks and five half-track armored vehicles rumbled alongside successive waves of American infantrymen mounting their attacks up the slope, firing rifles, throwing hand grenades, and spraying fiery napalm.

When the American forces climbed within two hundred meters of the Japanese redoubt, Sergeant Kameda signaled to Saito and shouted, "Now!"

Saito waved the red-and-white flags to the four bunkers on his right.

Immediately the Japanese machine gunners started to mow down the oncoming troops with frightening accuracy, scattering columns of American foot soldiers.

A barrage of shells from Japanese 47-millimeter antitank guns bombarded the battlefield, destroying American tanks and half-tracks and setting napalm ablaze.

The Imperial Japanese Army troops shouted, "*Banzai! Banzai!*" and they lifted their rifles triumphantly.

Akira cringed and his heart sank over the hundreds of his countrymen lying dead below him.

* * *

Okinawa – May 30, 1945

The morning sunlight leaked through a crevice on the dugout wall inside the cave fortress underneath Shuri Castle while Akira and other soldiers took a break from shoveling rocks and debris into heaping piles.

Near the archway of an inner chamber, three officers conversed with each other. Akira listened with rapt attention.

"Why can't we send airplanes to attack their tanks?" asked an officer.

"Headquarters is reserving them for *kamikaze* attacks on their ships. We have no serviceable planes on the island."

"How about artillery?"

"Unless we can get radio communications coordinated between our spotters and gunners, our artillery can't zero in. Most of our repeater stations have been destroyed."

"What about the 47-millimeter antitank guns?" someone asked.

"We don't have enough."

Based upon what Akira was hearing, Japan was in a losing battle. By late May, just eight weeks after the American landing, they had taken a page out of the Japanese playbook, sending small squads of infantry sifting through crags and crevices. Scores of tanks trundled up the slope, blasting the Japanese pillboxes with enormous firepower.

Later that afternoon, Sergeant Kameda approached Akira. "Omura, empty your field pack and come with me."

Akira hesitated, then squatted down and shook the contents into his duffel bag. Some items fell to the ground, including his Bible. He palmed it quickly and stuffed it into the other bag, hoping Kameda hadn't noticed.

"Let's go," the sergeant said.

They arrived in a special underground chamber, where the other men in the squad were assembled. Kameda addressed the group. "Men, we're going to charge down the hill to blow up enemy tanks."

Akira had heard many Japanese units were completely out of ammunition and ordered to charge with their bayonets and swords, only to be gunned down.

Color drained from the young men's faces and their jaws dropped. Finally, a corporal spoke up. "Sergeant, we only have our rifles. How are we going to do this?"

Kameda picked up an empty field pack, then pried open a crate with his knife and pulled out a bundle of dynamite. Then he extracted a detonator with a short fuse from another crate. He turned and faced the men. "Place these explosives into your pack and attach the detonator like so. It's a satchel bomb." He placed his arms through the shoulder straps. "Crawl underneath a tank with the bomb strapped to your body. Then light the fuse."

The sergeant's voice faded as Akira's thoughts imploded. So the rumors were true. Akira swallowed hard in disbelief. His brain raced as he sought for a way out of this sadistic and hopeless act.

"The explosives will blow the steel treads off the tanks and immobilize them. Any questions?" Kameda looked around and no one answered. "Get your packs ready."

Desensitized by the sergeant's words, Akira picked up his field pack and silently prepared a bomb. The other soldiers did the same.

Kameda led the squad down the slope in a meandering line through the pockmarked soil for about two kilometers. An incoming mortar shell whined overhead. "Take cover!"

Akira dove behind an outcropping of large rocks. Within seconds an explosion near the rear rained down debris. Then another shell shattered a boulder and showered its pieces onto Akira's back and shoulders like a hailstorm. More shells exploded in quick succession.

Smoke billowed around him, and Akira couldn't see anything but his hands in front of him. When the air cleared, he crawled out to see what had happened. It looked like a mortar shell had fallen on a satchel bomb. Bloody arms and legs of Japanese soldiers lay strewn over rubble, dirt, and plants. Akira flinched at the horrific scene. His heart dropped to his stomach, and he ached for the dead soldiers.

Kameda led the remaining men farther down the slope into a ravine covered with prickly ash shrubs that provided adequate cover. Then he hiked to the top of a ridge and surveyed the area through binoculars. He turned and waved his hand vigorously for them to follow.

From the ridge, Akira peered down at five huge American tanks lumbering up the sandy plain, supported by scores of infantrymen. His heart beat rapidly.

"We're splitting into two groups." Kameda pointed. "Hoshino, Yamamoto, Tanaka, and Goto, take out the tanks on the left. Saito, Toda, and Omura, we'll attack the other side. Understand?"

"Sergeant, we have no chance against them," Private Hoshino muttered. "There're only eight of us."

"You're to fight until the very end," Kameda said glumly.

Akira knew this meant certain death for all of them. They would die carrying out their orders or be shot by Kameda if they refused. The thumping in his ears grew louder and louder.

The first group crept on their hands and knees and disappeared into a swale near the American tanks. A flame-throwing tank spurted out fiery napalm in their direction. Seconds later, an explosion rocked, and screaming men emerged with bodies aflame, reminding Akira of hell itself. He grew numb in disbelief.

No time to dwell on the tragedy. He could see the Adam's apples of Saito and Toda forcing their way down their throats in this no-win, diabolical situation. The end was near. *God if possible, please rescue me. Otherwise, let it be quick.*

Kameda watched a tank turn away from them. "Saito, your turn."

Saito sprinted toward the tank, but before he could get close, the turret of an American tank rotated and opened fire.

Noooo! Saito's lifeless body hurled amid a cascade of dirt and rocks, and his bomb exploded harmlessly, leaving a large crater.

Akira's heart intensified to a wild cadence. How he wished he could have helped his buddy somehow.

Kameda turned around, wearing a disgusted scowl as he stared at Akira.

Stiffening his upper lip, Akira prepared himself. But Kameda turned to Toda. "You're next!"

Toda cinched his helmet strap, grabbed his satchel, and dashed toward the tank.

Akira began to think Kameda was playing a cruel trick on him, making him go last. Suddenly, a flash blinded Akira, and a loud boom reverberated—then nothing.

* * *

When Akira regained consciousness, he found himself flat on his back. Other than a massive headache and a few scrapes, he seemed okay. He recalled a fiery explosion but nothing after that. Looking around, he spotted Sergeant Kameda lying still but breathing.

Now he had the perfect opportunity to escape and surrender. He raised his head and noticed the Americans had moved on. If he followed them in the direction they had been going, he might eventually catch up to them.

Something held him back. The words from the Bible echoed in his mind—*"Love your enemies, do good to them who hate you."*

Akira didn't want to obey these words. "Oh, God, please don't have me do this. I'm so sick of the fighting and killings." With anguish in his heart, he crawled over to Kameda.

Blood covered the lower right side of Kameda's chest. Akira searched the sergeant's body for his canteen and a found a flask of whiskey instead. He opened the flask and poured its contents on the wounds.

Kameda blinked and coughed. "Omura, is that you? Where are all the others?"

"Dead."

The sergeant groaned. "It hurts. Reach into my trouser pocket. I have some whiskey in there."

"I used it to disinfect your wounds."

"Blast you! I wanted to drink it." Kameda screwed his face.

"You need medical attention. Let's get you up."

"Just leave me here to die."

Akira was tempted for a moment, but an inner voice whispered, *Help this man*. He somehow knew God was speaking to him. Akira tore his own uniform shirt sleeve, rolled it up, and plugged Kameda's wound with it. Even with the makeshift bandage, blood seeped through.

"Sergeant, let's get you some help." He placed Kameda's left arm around his neck and lifted him.

"Omura, put me down. I need to rest."

Lowering Kameda into a sitting position, Akira gently placed him against a rock wall. He opened his canteen and held it up to Kameda's mouth.

"Why are you being so good to me? You must hate my guts for treating you so badly. Just let me die."

"I can't do that."

Kameda peaked an eyebrow and looked at Akira. "Why not?"

"God deeply cares for you regardless of what you've done."

For a long moment, Kameda stared blankly beyond Akira and said nothing, then he turned his head. "Omura, I was just following orders, but they don't mean anything to me now."

"Orders? I don't understand."

"Back in training camp, Colonel Abe ordered me to block your mail."

The news rocked Akira back on his heels. "Why?"

"At first, I thought the colonel had designs on your fiancée, but that wasn't it." Kameda coughed and motioned to the canteen.

Akira held it close to Kameda's mouth.

"I overheard the colonel talking to Hiroshi Yamada, and it turned out to be the lieutenant who had been scheming on her."

"What?" Akira had no idea Hiroshi would go this far. But what better way to drive a wedge between them, making it seem as though Akira didn't care about Emiko.

"Omura, you know that Lieutenant Yamada has been trying to get you killed, don't you?"

Akira paused for a moment. "I had a hunch."

"That mission he sent you on—you weren't supposed to come back alive. He could have sent me instead. He knew I spoke English."

Images from the past poured into Akira's consciousness. He flashed back to Hiroshi's indignant glare when he saw him near Emiko's house, and the dark look on his face when he questioned Akira's loyalty. And he must still be holding a grudge from the disastrous engagement party. It all made perfect sense now.

The sergeant wouldn't live much longer. Now wasn't the time to think about Hiroshi when eternity stretched before Kameda.

Akira remembered a verse from church. *For God so loved the world, that he gave his only begotten Son, that whosoever believeth in him should not perish, but have everlasting life.*

"Sergeant, I appreciate you telling me the truth about the blocked mail, and I forgive you for your involvement in this."

Kameda gazed at Akira with a startled look.

"I want to ask you something very important that involves your eternal destiny. We're all flawed in different ways, but God sent Jesus to die in your place to save you from your sins, regardless of what you've done. He made a way for you to spend an eternity in heaven. Do you want to receive Jesus as your Lord and Savior?"

After a long pause, Kameda nodded. "Yes." He closed his eyes, and his head lolled limply to the side.

56

The Old Man

McNeil Island, Washington

News about Mary contracting tuberculosis sucked the air out of Danny's lungs, and his pulse pounded in his ears. His hands trembled as he read Lily's letter. No wonder Mary hadn't written in a while. How he wished he could do something for her. More than ever, he longed to be by Mary's side. What if she died?

He had written to Mary once a week on the allotted single sheet of lined paper, and she usually responded just as often. Danny told her he loved her and wanted to marry her. She responded by sending her love, but never mentioned anything about marriage. He understood why. Time and again, Mary diplomatically coaxed him to reconsider his spiritual views. Often he had the urge to write the words she'd want to hear, but he couldn't do that just to please her.

The next day at the Honor Farm, Danny and a work gang seeded sugar snap peas in an open field on the west side of Still Harbor. A surge of adrenaline shot through him even though he had hardly slept, and he dug deeper and faster than the other inmates. The cogs in his brain spun like truck wheels at high speed. Somehow he'd find a way to escape off the island.

Kazuo Hashimoto, a husky Issei, dug alongside him, whistling a cheery melody. Danny couldn't understand how he could have such a pleasant demeanor while serving a life sentence. The sixty-year-old never talked about his offense, but

Danny knew he'd been in prison a long time. Perhaps Kazuo might know something about escaping. Danny had heard a few men had succeeded.

The morning dragged on, but soon the whistle blew for lunch. Danny made a beeline toward him. "Hi, Kazuo, do you want to grab a quick bite and take a stroll to the pier?"

He nodded. "Sure."

The lax security of the Honor Farm made it easy for inmates to wander about, unlike the main prison. Here they were even allowed to visit each other's cells until 9:00 p.m., when the guards enforced the nightly lockdown.

Danny and Kazuo wolfed down their sandwiches, then set out to McNeil Island Road. Others either napped or played dominoes on straw mats.

"Byu-tee-ful day, *ne?*" Kazuo said, wearing a cheerful smile.

From the ferry landing, Danny took in the hazy eastern horizon across Puget Sound to the town of Steilacoom and beyond to Tacoma. In the distance, snow-capped Mt. Rainier loomed large and majestic. "Kazuo, you've been here a long time, right?"

"Yeah, long time."

Danny looked him in the eyes. "Do you ever think of trying to escape from this island?"

"Escape? No-oo." Kazuo's pleasant demeanor vanished, and he turned away.

Puzzled, Danny circled around to face him. "Why not?"

"No, no. You crazy."

"What's so crazy about that?"

"Ferry boat, only way. Guard check everybody. This prison island." He shook his head. "No vacation place."

"How about other boats?"

"No other boat." Kazuo smirked.

Danny looked toward the water. "There's got to be some way off this island. Maybe I can swim across."

"No, no. Too cold. You swim, you die." Kazuo scratched his head. "Why you want escape? You only one or two more year."

"My girlfriend, Mary, is really sick with a high fever." Danny lowered his head. "She might die."

"Ahh-ah, *so omotta.* Woman, huh? Sorry. So, where she?"

"At Heart Mountain. The doctor says she has tuberculosis. I'm so worried about her."

"Oooh. No good. When I come Seattle from Japan, I get TB. Live dirty place, food bad." Kazuo feigned a cough and held out his palm. "Cough blood. Maybe die."

Danny remembered the flimsy barracks and inadequate food at Heart Mountain, conditions that caused many camp residents to become ill. "But you got over it, right?"

Kazuo looked down and shook his head. "Doctor give up. Say I dead."

"Then what happened?" Obviously, he was still alive. Danny's interest piqued.

"Nothing. I worse and worse. But Christian man *Hakujin* visit me. He pray for me." Kazuo put one hand on his forehead and the other on his chest. "I no understand. He say Jesus heal me." Kazuo paused with a wistful look in his eyes.

"So, what happened?"

"*To-to yokunatta.* Long time, but I better. One day, I get out bed and okay. No medicine."

"No medicine?" Danny stood there, staring at him in disbelief. "That's incredible."

Kazuo shook his head. "Den, I forgot man. Everything I forgot. I have good time. You know, drinking, girls." He reclined his head and pretended to hold a bottle and drink. "When I thirty-two, work farm, Tacoma. Den, trouble."

"What kind of trouble?"

Kazuo gazed out over the water, silent for a few minutes. It didn't seem as though he wanted to talk about it. He turned toward Danny. "Owner wife, pretty woman. She like me. I like her. Thirty years ago, I handsome boy."

Danny couldn't help but chuckle. He couldn't imagine this balding man with wispy gray hair on the sides and liver-spotted complexion as ever being handsome.

"She marry bad man. He hit her. All the time, she crying." Kazuo paused, his eyes brimming with tears. "I can't stand. He hitting her face. I so mad." He hung his head.

"That's outrageous!" Danny had heard about men who abused women, but he couldn't imagine ever striking one himself.

Kazuo lifted his fists into a boxing stance. "I fight him. He pitchfork." He made a lancing motion with an imaginary pitchfork, slapped his right thigh. "Argh!"

Danny grimaced.

"Den, he fall. I grab head." Forming a grappling hook with the crook of his right elbow, Kazuo demonstrated a hard yanking motion toward himself. "Den, urgh! Neck break. He die."

"So that's how you ended up here." The injustice of it bit into Danny. "But you were only trying to protect her."

"My lawyer say self-defense, but no work. Judge want me hang. Den, lawyer say I no plan kill. So, judge say, 'Okay, go prison. Never come out.' "

"But wasn't there something your lawyer could do?"

Kazuo cupped his left hand over his eyebrows and checked the position of the sun over the western horizon. "Come on, we go back. Lunchtime over."

* * *

At dinner, Danny looked for Kazuo but didn't find him. He plunked his tray down at the dining hall table, his soup sloshing around. Other men greeted him, but he only nodded. He left half his tasteless meal on the tray and rose when Kazuo sauntered by. Danny cracked a smile and sat back down. "Having a late dinner?"

"Yeah, I read Bible and pray."

"I didn't know you're a Christian."

"Yeah, after ten year, Christian pastor come here. He tell me Jesus love me. First, I no want to hear nothing. I kill man. But he say God forgive me."

"But you're still in prison."

The old man lowered his eyes and nodded. "*Sore wa shikata ga nai.* Can't help." Then he smiled and lifted his face to the ceiling. "I remember when Jesus heal me. Den, make sense. I well. I happy. When die, I go heaven."

"Mary is a Christian." He looked away from his companion. "I guess I sorta am." A pang of shame shrouded the second statement.

"Den, you pray for Mary." Kazuo bowed his head to say grace before shoveling a forkful into his mouth.

"I guess I should." Danny looked down at his shoes. "I haven't been praying much lately." He pushed some peas onto his fork. "It seems so useless to pray."

"After eat, you pray. Den come my cell."

Danny took a few more bites. "I'm done. I'll see you later." He rose and ambled to an empty cell. His cellmates had left for a poker tournament in a different block.

Kazuo's words, *You pray for Mary,* echoed over and over again. The old man's story of how he recovered from TB filled Danny with a twinge of hope. He would try prayer. After all, it would be difficult, if not impossible to escape from prison.

Near his bunk, he collapsed to his knees, joined his hands together, and bowed his head. "Dear God, it's been a long time." The cement floor hurt his knees, and he wanted to stop praying. "I'm sorry I haven't spent time with you. And I'm sorry I haven't read the Bible or gone to church. I don't know what's wrong with me." His words almost refused to come out.

"I've been so angry at you, blaming you for my troubles. Please forgive me."

Danny paused. "Anyway, I want you. I ask you—I beg you to heal Mary. Make her well again, God, please . . . please." He started heaving and sobbing uncontrollably.

After his tear ducts could produce no more, he collected himself. At the washbasin, Danny splashed water on his eyes and toweled off his face, then headed for Kazuo's.

On the corner of the block, Kazuo had a cell all to himself. He raised his head from the bunk and smiled.

Danny opened the door and entered. "Hi, Kazuo. I did it. I prayed for Mary to get well."

"Oh, good, good. You different now."

"Different?"

"Yeah, before I see angry man. Now, happy man."

"Happy?" Danny said. "I don't feel any different."

"Prayer work." Kazuo knelt down on the cell floor. "We pray now." While the old man prayed in Japanese, Danny lost himself in deep thought. *Kazuo's stuck in prison for the rest of his life, yet he has such great faith and joy.*

After Kazuo finished praying, he turned to Danny and urged him to pray.

Prayer came easier for Danny this time. Also the cement ground didn't feel so hard. He kept it short.

For the lights-out bed check, Danny shuffled back to his cell and dwelled on all that had transpired. His mind raced to and fro, contrasting Kazuo's assuring words about God's faithfulness with fearful visions of Mary's grave illness. She might be days away from dying.

Two weeks earlier, Bob Miyazaki learned his mother had passed away at Heart Mountain. Yet the warden denied Bob's request to attend funeral services. What chance did Danny have?

57

The Deal

Okinawa – June 18, 1944

Pelting monsoon rains soaked through Akira's uniform as he stood guard at his observation post. He spiraled into gut-wrenching despair, knowing he had blown his opportunity to escape to the Americans side when he was found by a Japanese patrol shortly after Kameda died.

Inside the cave, Akira shoved wet hair off his forehead and ambled to the assembly area. Captain Mayeda was speaking to several platoons—or the remnants that had survived—about fifty men. Akira stood at attention with them.

"General Ushijima has ordered you to continue fighting until the very end," Captain Mayeda said. "Your job is to keep the Americans occupied while our homeland prepares its defenses. When you've expended your last bullet, you can die a glorious death to the emperor and our country with honor and pride."

The general's message confirmed what Akira's gut told him. *We're dead men.*

The next morning, the sun peeked through thick layers of slate-gray clouds as Akira surveyed the terrain from a ridge. Innumerable Japanese soldiers had died, because undoubtedly, they were ordered not to surrender. Every dead soldier was somebody's loved one, and somewhere back in Japan—or in America—wails of grief would soon be heard.

Artillery shells screeched through the air and crashed with thunderous booms and fiery explosions. Piercing steel sprayed out from strafing American fighters, and bombs dropped from other planes.

The flanks of the Japanese defense crumbled before Akira's eyes. Successive waves of soldiers, who were out of ammunition, rose from their hiding places and charged to the American line, yelling, "*Banzai!*" American machine guns obliterated them before they could even get close.

Heavy rains returned in the afternoon, giving the Japanese troops a temporary reprieve. Akira suspected the attack would resume as soon as the weather improved, and the men of his new platoon could soon be ordered to their deaths. He crumpled to his knees and prayed. *Dear Jesus, I know the end is near. After I'm gone, please watch over Emiko and my family—*

"Private Omura, I wish to speak to you."

The voice sounded like Hiroshi's. Akira looked over his shoulder and was taken aback to find him standing there.

"Follow me." Hiroshi pivoted and headed toward an empty cave chamber.

Ever since Akira learned the truth from Sergeant Kameda, he had been tempted to put Hiroshi's head inside the sights of his rifle and squeeze the trigger. Akira clamped his teeth to contain his rage.

Hiroshi stopped and whispered, "Omura-san. I need your help."

The use of the honorific -san coming from a superior surprised Akira, but he knew it wasn't sincere. "My help?"

"In getting through to the north."

"So, you're making plans to continue fighting as the general suggested?"

Hiroshi's eyes darted side to side and he leaned forward. "What the general didn't say is a few key officers will return to the homeland on fishing boats and other vessels. They will be anchored in tiny coves along the northern shore. I've made arrangements for us to get on one."

How cowardly of him to flee while his men continued fighting. "What does that have to do with me? I'm not an officer."

"Omura-san, you're fluent in English. If we encounter enemy patrols, you can negotiate the best terms."

Although Akira couldn't trust Hiroshi, it might be a way off this island of death.

"Omura-san, if you try to escape on your own, you could encounter army officers who will shoot you as a deserter. If you surrender, the Americans might kill you or lock you up in a prisoner-of-war camp for who knows how long. But if you help me, I'll tell the boat captain you're an indispensable aide, and you'll be able to return to Japan. Will you help me?"

Perhaps it was another trap, but he simply couldn't let Hiroshi go back to Japan by himself—not with Emiko there. "All right, I'll help you."

Hiroshi nodded, and Akira detected relief in his eyes.

"Good. We leave tonight at midnight. Meet here and take some civilian clothes left by the workers. We'll change once we leave the cave. And don't discuss this with anyone."

As if Akira needed to be told that. If anyone found out, it would mean certain death for both of them. For now, Akira would cooperate with him. He never imagined traveling through the Valley of the Shadow of Death with the devil himself.

* * *

With palms slick with sweat and his heart pumping hard, Akira approached the designated spot at midnight.

Hiroshi stood waiting for him. "Did you find those extra flashlights and batteries?"

"Yes." Akira slid on his field pack and reached for his rifle.

"No, don't bring your rifle. We're supposed to be civilians. I'm only carrying my service pistol that I'll conceal in my bag and use only in case of an emergency."

An alarm sounded inside Akira. Nothing would stop Hiroshi from murdering him when they reached their final destination. Maybe he should back out of this now if he could. "I should have a weapon as well."

"I only have one pistol. If you don't like it, you can stay here and die with the others."

Akira remained silent. He'd find a way to snatch the pistol away from Hiroshi.

They slipped out from the back of the cave under a three-quarter, pale moon. Akira shivered with a strange combination of exhilaration and sheer terror. After traveling half a kilometer, they changed and hid their uniforms in the foliage.

Clouds began to obscure the moonlight. Two hours into their trek, the sound of nighttime bombardment ceased. Akira could hear ocean waves crashing, which reminded him of the time he and Emiko took a daytrip to the dramatic seascapes in Shimabara, near Nagasaki. During this trip, Emiko told him about her first impressions of him.

"When I first saw you on the crowded streetcar, I thought, 'What an attractive man.' I melted when I looked into your large dark eyes as you offered me your trolley strap. I felt so nervous standing next to you, I faced the other way. You were so kind to help retrieve the items that spilled out of my bundle when the streetcar jolted. When our eyes met again, my mind went blank momentarily. Your charming smile gave me goose bumps. When I stepped off the streetcar, I turned around for one last glimpse of you. I was so sad when I didn't see you. It thrilled my heart to run into you again when I was in trouble with the drunk. Somehow when you told me to run, I didn't want to leave you. You were so gallant."

Akira remembered how surprised he was when Emiko recounted this to him. He had no idea that she even noticed him.

The dreamlike memory seemed like eons ago and was so different from the world he lived in now. He might never enjoy a lovely outing like that again or Emiko's warm embrace.

The sweet remembrance turned bitter, knowing he was traveling with the man who had plotted to kill him and snatch his fiancée. Left to his emotions, he'd want nothing more than to strangle Hiroshi, but his faith forbade him. For now, he needed to concentrate on how to survive.

A peach sunrise blanketed the eastern horizon as the two of them navigated through the thick, subtropical forest. They kept their eyes peeled for the terrain's venomous *habu* snake and jabbed the ground with sturdy bamboo sticks.

When the sun rose well over the horizon, Akira marveled at the brilliant azure sea beyond the vast sugarcane fields and rocky cliffs. He prayed he'd soon be traversing it back to Emiko.

They arrived at the coast two hours later. Powerful waves slammed into rocks over fifty meters below. Akira turned around to see Hiroshi opening a meal pack.

"Here, have something to eat." He handed Akira a pack.

"Thanks." Akira couldn't believe he was sharing a picnic lunch with him. After eating one rice ball, he observed Hiroshi, who had finished both of his and sat with his back turned to him. Curiosity warred with fear and won. "Why did you leave the *Kempeitai*?"

Hiroshi kept his gaze on the ocean. "There was nothing left for me to do in Kumamoto, and I wanted something different."

That's a lie. He wouldn't leave a safe post to risk his life for this hellish fighting.

After the less-than-adequate meal, they set off again on the trail that hugged the rugged black and gray cliff's edge. Albatrosses rode the updrafts high into the pale-blue sky, making high-pitched shrilling sounds. In the distance, Akira heard a voice. He rounded a corner and signaled to Hiroshi, who came alongside.

A Japanese army officer about fifty meters away addressed a group of fifty or sixty people, mostly civilians wearing kimono tops and *mompei* pantaloons. The officer shouted over the crashing waves and howling wind. "You people have been loyal," his voice trailed away. "Barbaric Americans will enslave you . . . rape women . . . torture men . . . now fulfill your duty to the emperor . . . leap off this cliff."

The officer's words curdled inside Akira. How could this man order these innocent people to their deaths? Akira shouted, "Nooo! Don't!" but a gust of wind drowned his voice.

"Shut up, Omura!" Hiroshi aimed his pistol at him.

"We can't let them die." Akira didn't know whether the suicides shook him up more or the gun pointed at him. He took a step but halted when Hiroshi cocked the gun.

"You'll do as I say. Someone may go back and report seeing us. I can't take the chance."

It was too late. A man wearing a white shirt and dark pants vaulted off the cliff. Within seconds, his body impaled on the jagged rocks below. Others followed, including young women carrying babies, some pulling small children along, plummeting to their deaths. He couldn't bear to watch anymore and turned away. Akira's heart plunged like an anchor sinking to the ocean floor at the thought of so many precious lives lost.

A while later, Akira turned around to see the officer standing precariously near the cliff's edge, saluting and launching off yelling, "*Banzaiii!*"

Crushing oppression enveloped Akira and suffocated him. Patriotism was one thing, but this officer's overzealousness was pure insanity. How could people blindly follow orders and die like that?

Hiroshi put the pistol away. "Stupid fools. What a waste. All in the name of honor. I'd never do anything like that."

For once Akira agreed with him but for different reasons. He burned with fury at Hiroshi for not stopping the carnage.

* * *

At sunrise, they trekked north around the rocky cape of Kiyan Peninsula, the southernmost point of Okinawa. Cliffs plunged dramatically into the shimmering aquamarine water that foamed when waves collided with the rocks. Akira couldn't believe this lovely island could be the stage for such horrible tragedy.

Hiroshi took a swig from his canteen and rested under a mangrove tree. "In about an hour or so, we'll be in Itoman, where we'll be able to buy food."

In the last two days, Akira had eaten only two small rice balls and an unripe mango he plucked off a tree.

When they arrived, no place appeared to sell food of any sort. Thick plumes of smoke drifted from smoldering wooden houses. Akira squinted at the morning sun that cast a fiery glow on the eerie sight of flattened or substantially damaged buildings.

A ten-minute jaunt took them to the harbor. Hiroshi shook his head. "All the boats are sunk or listing on their sides. There's nothing here. Let's go."

The sun blazed directly overhead when they arrived in Naha, and Akira sweltered as if he were taking a steam bath. Only a few months ago he had walked the vibrant streets of this city when he substituted as a high school teacher. Now piles of concrete rubble and smoldering lumber littered the ground for blocks. Only a few houses and other small structures remained standing around the fringe of the city.

Lord, be with the families who lost loved ones, homes, and businesses. Cruelty in war was not the province of one side or the other.

"This place is crawling with Americans," Hiroshi whispered. "Be careful and blend in with the civilians."

"All right." Akira considered losing him in the crowd and surrendering, but he didn't want to be locked up in a POW camp while his nemesis sailed back to Japan.

They moved among multitudes of people crowding the narrow backstreets, avoiding major roads where American trucks and jeeps rolled through. The unmistakable stench of dead bodies hung in the air.

At the bustling harbor, Hiroshi scanned the area. "We're not going to find a boat here. Let's head back."

Akira pointed. "Look, there are people selling food."

They purchased dried fish, rice balls and seaweed at black-market prices from the vendors. After devouring some of the food, they saved the remainder in their bags.

* * *

As they traveled further north, Akira knew he'd have to somehow get the pistol, but Hiroshi always kept it close to his body, even while sleeping.

Hiroshi's face pinched as he gazed at the northern horizon. "We should be close to Hentona. There's a paved road leading north."

A rumble came from behind Akira.

"Take cover." Hiroshi pointed to a thicket of bamboo trees.

They dove behind the dense growth of green stems and peeked through them.

Hiroshi scanned the vehicle with his binoculars. "Looks like a truckload of Okinawan natives. Let's flag them down."

Emerging from their hiding place, they trotted to the middle of the road, waving their arms. The truck slowed to a stop.

Hiroshi nudged Akira. "Tell them we want to go north."

The passenger door opened, and a short Okinawan man jumped out. "We're fully loaded. We can't take anyone else."

"We have food to exchange for a ride to Hedo Misaki," Akira said.

The man conferred with the driver, then returned. "Okay, we'll give you a ride, but only as far as Hentona."

They squeezed into the back of the truck beside four well-behaved children. The vehicle lumbered along the narrow road under overcast skies that dulled the vivid sea colors he'd seen on sunny days. Akira glanced at his traveling companion, who napped with his head tucked into the corner of the truck's cargo area.

Forty kilometers to Hentona took over two hours through many detours and broken roads. Everyone climbed off the truck to stretch their legs.

"Thanks for the ride." Akira handed them some dried fish and seaweed.

Hiroshi pulled the pistol out from his pack and approached the driver. "Give me the keys to your truck."

The man shook with fear.

"You heard me. Give me the keys, now. Or I'll kill you."

Akira gritted his molars and stepped toward Hiroshi. "What are you doing? That's not right. You made a deal with these people—"

"We need to get to the rendezvous spot today!" Hiroshi waved the gun at Akira briefly, then pointed it back at the Okinawans.

The short man directed the driver to turn over the keys. The women screamed and cried, and gathered the children together.

Hiroshi handed the keys to Akira. "Drive."

* * *

Dark rain clouds hung ominously from the sky, matching Akira's gloomy mood in the pale light of the late afternoon.

Hiroshi studied the map. "We're at the northernmost tip of Okinawa. The boats are moored somewhere in this vicinity. Stop the truck and we'll find the rendezvous point by foot."

Stepping out of the truck, Akira viewed crests of seawater rushing into little inlets and punishing walls of sharp black rock in futility. Morbid images of men, women, and children leaping off cliffs invaded his mind, and he struggled to cast off the chilling memories.

Hiroshi jogged past Akira and opened his pack, pulling out binoculars. "Look! There it is in the next cove, I see it." He scampered around several boulders for a better look. "Yes, it's here."

Shielding his eyes from the sun peeking through the clouds, Akira rushed over. Down below in a protected cove, a dark-gray, cylindrical vessel undulated on top of the flowing swells.

"I didn't expect a submarine to take me home." Hiroshi chuckled. "I thought it'd be a fishing boat."

Akira gazed at the northern horizon toward Japan when a metallic click sounded. Turning around, he found Hiroshi pointing the gun at him.

58

Redemption

McNeil Island, Washington – June 20, 1945

Danny's back muscles ached after harvesting raspberries for seven long hours. But his physical exhaustion couldn't quell his strong desire to write to Mary. He couldn't wait to tell her everything that had happened. Perhaps it was wrong to broker a deal with God, but Danny believed if God was really listening, he could and would heal her.

He dropped into his bunk and grabbed a three-inch pencil stub and a sheet of lined paper. Danny jotted down his thoughts and held his hand steady to make his handwriting legible.

> *Dear Mary,*
>
> *I pray every day for your quick recovery. Yes, I've been praying.*
>
> *A month ago I would have never done that, but I sit here in my prison cell with a lot of time on my hands, and I've been doing a lot of thinking.*
>
> *In the past year, I've met people who showed me what I'm missing—the love of my family and friends.*
>
> *Somewhere along the way, I forgot to reach out and love these people back, including you. I've been insensitive to you, caring only about the cause I've been fighting for.*

So, I've stopped running from God and realized he cares about me. He's been with me all along.

I dropped down on my knees and prayed he'd forgive me and take me back. And I want you to understand that I didn't do it just for you, but for me. Now, I pray every day for your complete healing.

Love,
Danny

* * *

After two weeks of praying, hoping, and worrying, a letter arrived from Heart Mountain. Danny's jaw dropped when he recognized the handwriting on the envelope.

Dear Danny,

I hope you are well. I'm writing to let you know I'm doing fine.

The doctors told my parents I needed surgery. They were going to collapse one lung and give me medicine to see if the lesions would heal on their own. But they said this kind of operation doesn't always work.

Surgery was scheduled for the 20th, but three days before it, a blinding light woke me up in my dark room. And I sensed the powerful presence of Jesus. My fever dropped and my cough vanished.

The doctors had never seen anybody recover from TB so quickly. They were astonished and couldn't explain it.

But I know it was God who healed me. When you wrote in your letter that you had gotten on your knees and asked him to heal me, it thrilled me to no end. Nothing could make me happier.

Now, my heart is lighter whenever I think of
you, and I can't wait until the day I see you again.
Until then, I'm praying for you.
    All my love,
    Mary

Danny set her letter down on his bunk and wiped tears from his eyes with his shirtsleeves. Ultimate joy crowded out the sting of his circumstances. Jesus was there for him after all.

"Oh, Lord. Thank you! Thank you so much for healing Mary. You made her well for my sake. I know I don't deserve her. Please forgive me for thinking that I didn't need you, because I do. Jesus, I want to live for you and serve you all the days of my life."

59

Revenge

North Shore, Okinawa – June 24, 1945

Akira knew Hiroshi's proposition had been too good to be true. However, staying with his unit would have meant certain death, so he took the chance. *God, please help me!*

"You didn't honestly think I was going to let you go home, did you?" Hiroshi kept the gun pointed at him.

"Just what do you have against me?" He didn't dare take his eyes off Hiroshi. Maybe by keeping him talking, he could figure out a way to disarm him.

"Emiko would have become my wife, but you stole her from me."

"Stole her? We were in a relationship before you met her." Akira couldn't fathom the depth of Hiroshi's obsession, even after what Sergeant Kameda confessed to him.

"I would have convinced her to marry me."

"She would never have agreed to it."

"Oh no? She was very friendly to me when I visited her."

"Liar!" Akira bit down hard on his lower teeth. He wanted to charge after Hiroshi, gun or no gun.

"She didn't write to you about that?"

Emiko's letters seemed as though she was withholding something, but she didn't mention anything about Hiroshi.

Perhaps she didn't tell him so he wouldn't worry. He trusted her, but being separated for so long allowed uncertainty to crowd in. Pressure built up behind Akira's eyes.

A thin smile snaked across on Hiroshi's face. "Before I came to Okinawa, we spent a very pleasant afternoon together, reminiscing about old times. Emiko was a bit thin in the *mompei* she wore, but still had her lovely figure."

"I don't believe you're telling me anything remotely truthful."

"How can you be so sure?" Hiroshi let out a wicked laugh. "Prepare to die." He aimed the gun at Akira's head and pulled the trigger. A click sounded. "Huh?" Hiroshi stared at the pistol cockeyed.

Akira dashed forward and lunged into Hiroshi's midsection, taking him down. He grabbed Hiroshi's wrist and slammed it hard on the ground. A shot fired toward the sea.

Whoa! The gun must have been jammed. With resurgent energy, Akira slapped Hiroshi's hand against a rock surface, shaking the pistol loose. The gun skittered a half meter away.

Driving his legs, Hiroshi reached for the gun.

Akira pulled him back by the collar, then he dove forward, tangling his hand with Hiroshi's. The mad grab shoved the gun over the edge of the cliff.

With his knee, Hiroshi kicked Akira in the ribs and grabbed him by the throat.

The two men grappled and grunted, rolling over several times toward the cliff's edge.

With a loud growl, Hiroshi kicked Akira in the groin with his boot.

With excruciating pain, Akira staggered to his feet, gulping for air.

Hiroshi pulled out a dagger and lunged toward Akira.

Out of the corner of his eye, Akira saw him coming and dodged right. The blade slashed his clothes and a burning sensation striped across his chest. He grabbed Hiroshi's wrist and pushed firmly, keeping the blade away.

Hiroshi's leg wrapped around Akira's calf, taking him down. Then he pounced on Akira and pressed the dagger down against his face near his eye.

The sharp point cut into the skin above Akira's eyebrow. He resisted with all his might and managed to force the dagger up a notch. Hiroshi's face, a contorted mass of hatred, hovered only centimeters away from his. Akira spat into his eyes.

"Aak!" Hiroshi blinked several times then wiped his eyes with his other hand. He released some pressure on the dagger.

Within a split second, Akira smashed a hook into the left side of Hiroshi's face, causing him to roll off. Akira rose.

Once again, Hiroshi charged toward Akira, whirling the dagger and taking swipes. He reared back to throw it, forcing Akira to backpedal close to the ledge.

The dagger flew harmlessly above his left ear and over the cliff. Akira dove straight for Hiroshi's legs and landed short of his boot. The boot kicked Akira in the head and another powerful kick hammered his side. Grimacing in pain, he labored to his feet with his head throbbing. Blood flowed from the cut above the eye and obscured his vision. Through half-opened eyes, he saw Hiroshi hurtling toward him again, knocking Akira back several steps.

Hiroshi swung an uppercut that connected with Akira's jaw.

The punch caused Akira to lose his balance, and he plunged backward off the cliff. "Aaaaah!"

60

A New Life

Palo Alto, California

Tad maneuvered his truck around the circular flagstone driveway and parked in front of a massive, neoclassic mansion on University Avenue.

He stepped out of his vehicle, opened the tailgate, and rolled the lawnmower down a ramp when a sharp pain knifed his chest. "Ow!" He stood immobilized for a while, then caught his breath. Eight months had passed, but his wound still bothered him.

With Danny in prison, and his stepdad in poor health, he couldn't manage the farm by himself, not without his full strength. So he took a job as a gardener.

Tad moved slowly, not wanting to trigger another bout of pain. He unlatched the side gate and entered the backyard. Tad pushed the mower past the shimmering swimming pool to the expansive lawn. Just as he was about to pull the starter cord, an older Caucasian man seated inside the gazebo waved.

"You there," the man said. "Are you Japanese?"

Oh no. Tad girded himself against the insults and epithets that were sure to come. "Yes, I'm a Japanese American."

"I like Japanese."

Befuddled with the comment, Tad drew his head back. "May I help you with something, sir?"

"No, no. You're doing a great job." The man wore a cheerful smile. "I bet you're wondering why I said I like Japanese. Do you have some time to hear a story?"

Tad glanced at his watch. He had finished his morning rounds ahead of schedule, and the man's comment intrigued him. "Sure, I can spare a few minutes."

"Please have a seat. By the way, my name is Jakob Horowitz." He offered his hand.

"Tad Omura." He shook Mr. Horowitz's hand and settled on the bench next to him.

"Have you ever heard of Mr. Chiune Sugihara, a Japanese diplomat?"

"No, sir." The deep lines in Jakob's face, crowned with a shock of white hair, showed the wear and tear of a long life.

"I'm a Jew, and I immigrated to this country from Poland in the twenties. In late 1939, I went back there to visit my dying mother." He paused and cleared his throat of emotion. "The Germans and Russians had invaded our country. The Nazis proceeded to commit unspeakable atrocities against my people, and the Russians looked the other way."

He could see deep grief in the wrinkles around Jakob's eyes.

"My family and I escaped to Lithuania with many other Jews, but once we got there, we were trapped. Going west toward Germany was out of the question, and the Russians blocked passage to the east unless we had transit visas."

Tad hadn't heard anything about this.

"Only the Japanese and Dutch diplomatic missions remained open in the city of Kaunas where we were. The Dutch consulate adamantly refused to grant visas, leaving us with only one alternative. We gathered at the Japanese consulate and explained our situation to Vice Consul Sugihara. He petitioned the Japanese government officials in Tokyo three separate times, but they refused each time. You know Japan and Germany were allies."

"Yes, of course."

"We were devastated when we found out our requests were denied. We had nowhere to go. But one morning, news spread throughout the Jewish community that Mr. Sugihara was issuing transit visas. Naturally, a huge throng of people crowded the consulate." His eyes glistened.

"Mr. Sugihara signed transit visas from eighteen to twenty hours a day, risking his life and career to help us. With these documents, over six thousand Jews escaped and made it across the Soviet Union, into Japan, and then to China and other countries. My family and I took a freighter out of Shanghai and sailed to San Francisco. That is the sole reason why my family and I are alive today. We will forever be indebted to Mr. Sugihara—such a fine man."

"Wow! What a story. Now I understand why you like Japanese."

"Yes." His face lit up. "We owe that brave man our lives."

"Mr. Horowitz, why didn't the Japanese government turn you over to the Nazis?"

He shook his head. "I don't know. Perhaps it was some type of bureaucratic mistake." He stared at the pool with a wistful look. "I've always wondered what became of Mr. Sugihara."

"When I served in the US Army in Europe, I heard about the murder of the Jews. But the reality of it didn't hit me until my buddies in the 522nd entered the Dachau concentration camp and wrote to me about it. Their descriptions of bone-thin people, heaps of dead bodies, and incineration ovens turned my stomach."

"You were in Europe?" Horowitz's eyes flashed wide.

"Yes, I served with the 442nd Regiment."

"Why, you're a hero! I saw the newsreel about the 442nd." He patted Tad on the shoulder.

"I don't know about that, sir. I only did my part until I was shot in the chest. The doctor said it was a miracle that I survived. A lot of brave men fought in the war." Tad's voice began to falter. "And many didn't return."

Mr. Horowitz nodded in solemn agreement. "I'm sorry to hear you were wounded. I read that your regiment suffered very high casualties, yet achieved numerous victories. You fought valiantly for your country even though your families were exiled from their homes and wrongfully incarcerated, like my people were in the Nazi concentration camps."

"The relocation camps were bad, but probably not nearly as bad as the Nazi camps."

"Perhaps so." Horowitz stared at his feet with downcast eyes, then looked at Tad. "Did you kill a lot of Germans?"

"No, sir. I didn't carry a gun. I was a medic."

"A medic? Hmm. You know, I'm a retired professor of medicine from the University of Krakow and Stanford. I recently moved here to live with my son and his wife. He's a surgeon at Stanford Hospital and also a professor at the medical school."

"What an impressive background." Tad glanced at his wristwatch. "I'm sorry, but I've got to finish up and move to the next place. It's been a pleasure talking to you, Dr. Horowitz."

"Likewise. We'll talk again. I want to hear about your wartime experiences."

Over the following month, Tad and Dr. Horowitz conversed with each other weekly for as long as Tad could spare.

* * *

Jakob poured Tad a glass of lemonade. "How did you dress serious battle wounds?"

Tad sipped the ice-cold drink. "I did the best I could with antiseptic and bandages until we could get to a field hospital. Sometimes I applied tourniquets. Other times I could only give morphine shots and pray for them."

Dr. Horowitz shook his head. "You're a praying man?"

"Yes, I believe in God, and I have faith in Jesus. By the way, thanks for the lemonade. It's so refreshing."

"You're welcome." Dr. Horowitz rubbed his chin. "Come to think of it, Mr. Sugihara was a Christian. He told me so during my interview for the transit visa. Back then, I remember thinking how Christians talked about love all the time, but I had never experienced any genuine love from them. However, Mr. Sugihara was different. Both of you are fine men."

"It's quite flattering to be compared to Mr. Sugihara, but I don't come close."

"You're a war hero. Both of you fought against fascism in your own way."

The chats with Dr. Horowitz became Tad's bright spots in his mundane routine of mowing lawns, weeding, and trimming trees and bushes.

Perhaps he'd like to do something else with his life—but what? During his commute between job sites, he prayed with all of his heart. "Jesus, please guide my life. What is your will for me? I want your plans and purposes—not my own. You promise great things to those who follow you. Please guide me."

Tad arrived at the mansion early one afternoon and found Dr. Horowitz seated at his usual spot inside the gazebo. The trimming and weeding could wait a few minutes. He wasted no time greeting his friend. "Good afternoon, Dr. Horowitz. How are you, today?"

The doctor seemed to be deep in thought. Tad began to spray water on the lush lawn and vibrant flowers.

"What are you doing here?" Jakob asked.

What an odd question. Tad turned around and faced Dr. Horowitz. "I'm here to do the gardening like usual."

"No, that's not what I mean." Horowitz shooed the air. "Here you are a bright young man and a brave one to boot, working as a groundskeeper. You could be doing something more."

"Like what?" His ears itched to hear what the professor thought.

"You were a medic. Ever thought of becoming a doctor?"

"That would be like a dream. But I don't have any college credits, and I can't afford it. Plus, I have a family to support."

Dr. Horowitz was silent for a moment. "What if I help you?"

Tad had no idea what the doctor meant. "I have some money coming from the GI Bill, but I don't know whether I could get into college, let alone medical school."

"I've made some inquiries with people I used to work with at Stanford. You could take general education courses—some biology, chemistry, and physiology, and in a couple of years, you could get into the medical school. As far as the money is concerned, I'll pay for it, and I'll take care of your family's living expenses."

The surreal proposal floored Tad. He plopped onto the bench to collect his wits. "Dr. Horowitz, I couldn't possibly accept your kind offer."

"Why not?"

"It's way too much. How could I ever repay you?"

He cracked a smile. "Think of it as my way of repaying you. You fought in the war against the Nazis who persecuted and murdered my people. I was never able to contact Mr. Sugihara. By helping you, it's my way of thanking both of you. What do you say?"

"I'm overwhelmed."

"Mind you, it won't be easy. You'll have to study harder than the other students to catch up, but I think you can do it."

"I'd have to talk to my family about it." Tad's mind leaped with mental gymnastics.

"Do that and get back to me."

Tad couldn't wait to tell Lily and his family. He finished all his work before rushing home.

God, is this your answer to my prayers? Dr. Tad Omura . . . Tad Omura, MD.

61

Rainbow

North Shore, Okinawa

Hiroshi touched his left cheek and recoiled from the sharp pain—a parting gift from his rival. It didn't matter because Akira was dead.

He crawled over to the cliff's edge and focused on the cobalt waters fringed with white foam. About three meters below, a leaf-covered tree branch extended from the sheer granite face that plunged over a hundred meters to the water's surface. No one could survive a fall like that. He couldn't see any sign of Akira's body floating on the surface or on the rocks jutting out. The strong rip currents had probably dragged him under.

Finally, after months of scheming and planning, he could now head home to Japan. Nothing stood in his way of reclaiming Emiko. He chortled, happy to be rid of his rival, but it hurt to laugh. Bracing himself with his arms, he sat back and rested for a minute. Then he rose and staggered toward the submarine bobbing in the distance.

* * *

Akira opened his eyes, and dark spots floated around with flashes of light. He blinked hard and shook his head to regain clarity. A granite rock wall came into focus, which extended about five meters above him. He turned his head sideways and ran his bruised hand through a thick carpet of moss that covered the rock cleft he was lying in. Cuts and scrapes covered his body. Searing pain bit into his side and shoulder, and a salty, ferric taste of blood coated his tongue.

Images of Hiroshi's crimson face twisted with hatred flashed in his mind. The last thing he remembered was descending backward and walloping a tree branch or plant of some kind.

Heavy shrubs covered the cliff directly above him, and loud, crashing waves sounded below. The reality of the fall seized him, and he began to hyperventilate.

After regaining awareness, Akira stretched out one hand and grasped a small ledge. He braced himself with his elbow and slowly pushed himself into a sitting position. Looking below, he scrutinized the area but couldn't see where the submarine was moored. He didn't know how much time had passed. Perhaps Hiroshi already boarded the vessel and set sail for Japan.

The only way to find out meant he would have to climb to a vantage point that overlooked the cove. Akira cautiously rose and placed some weight on his left foot. Piercing pain ripped through his ankle. He winced and hoped it wasn't broken.

Thrusting his hand above him, he grabbed a small overhang and pushed himself up. Then he lifted his good foot onto a ledge and shoved it against the rock to balance himself. He patted the granite surface above him until his fingers slid into a notch.

Using all the strength he could muster, Akira lifted his injured foot and placed it into an indentation, while keeping his weight on his good foot. His fingers slipped, and he began to slide down, but at the last second, he grabbed a protruding rock. Terror coursed through every cell of his body as he imagined plunging below.

Negotiating this climb with no injuries was difficult at best, but in his condition, nearly impossible. However, he needed to stop Hiroshi.

Bowing his head, he pleaded in utter desperation. "Oh, God, my Creator, please give me strength to climb to the top!"

From the corner of his eye, he noticed the cliff surface had larger crevices and ledges to his right. If only he could reach it without falling. It would mean traversing a narrow overhang with footholds no wider than four or five inches over a vertical section. Nothing but air existed between him and the sea below.

Akira cautiously hugged the rock wall with his hands and moved carefully. Halfway across, a strong gust caused him to falter. He tightened his grip and dug in his toes as hard as he could to balance himself. Once the wind subsided, he proceeded.

While gingerly traversing the rocky surface, Akira rested his body, then inched along closer and closer. Before he knew it, he made it to the other side.

He dug his hands into the rocky surface and crawled upward. With five feet more to go, rain began to fall. The wet rock made the last bit even harder, but he managed not to slip. With his last scrap of strength, he lifted his sore body over the top and collapsed.

But he couldn't stop now. Akira shaded his eyes from the afternoon sun that poked through a rain-cloud-laden sky and squinted to see if he could spot the submarine. Struggling to his feet, he turned toward the adjacent cove and could see the submarine moored off the beach.

He hobbled as fast as he could. Akira couldn't bear to think what would happen if his foe made it to Japan before him.

On the beach below, two sailors shoved a rubber raft into the water. Someone who sat inside looked like Hiroshi. It was Hiroshi. He was going home.

"No-ooh! Dear God, no-ooh!" The howling winds gained momentum and the crashing waves colliding into rocks deadened Akira's yell. Nobody in the raft noticed him.

He stepped up his gait, no longer feeling sharp pain in his ankle.

Crewmen closed the hatches of the submarine, and the propeller screw started to churn. He wasn't going to make it.

Akira started climbing down when an engine revved, and he twisted his head to see the submarine ease out of the cove. He paused and burst out in a loud cry. "How could this happen, Lord? You brought me this far, only to have me fall short."

He climbed back up and stared at the submarine receding from the beach.

Emiko-san . . . His heart pounded like a jackhammer. "What am I to do? This can't be happening."

Moments later Akira received a distinct impression. *My grace is sufficient . . . My strength is made perfect in weakness.*

He considered those words for a moment, and peace stole over his heart. The wind whipped around him as he turned and the submarine cleared the end of an inlet.

From behind, a loud buzz caused Akira to whirl around, and two gull-winged aircraft zoomed in. The forward plane dove straight toward him, and he ran as fast as his bad ankle allowed toward an outcropping of boulders.

The plane spit bursts of fire from machine guns, missing him by a meter or so. The strafing plane with red, white, and blue emblems on the fuselage and wings flew past him—Americans.

Once that sight would have thrilled him, but now he could only hope his life would be spared. The engine roared and the plane climbed to rejoin the other one.

He wasn't sure if they were through with him, and he kept a watchful eye to the sky. The American planes circled overhead, then veered toward the water. Akira shuddered, knowing he had escaped a close call.

Beyond the cape of the inlet, Akira spotted the submarine heading out to the open sea. One plane accelerated and dove in at a steep angle with its engine screaming. At the last possible moment, it unleashed two whistling bombs before breaking off and climbing.

One bomb exploded near the front of the submarine, and the other fell toward the rear. Huge cascades of whitewater shot up with each explosion, rocking the vessel from side to side. The second plane came in on a shallow angle and dropped another bomb.

In a fiery blast, the submarine ejected airborne and snapped in two like a toy. Seawater spiked and dark-gray smoke billowed skyward.

Akira looked up as one plane waggled its wings. He shifted his focus below and the broken bow and forward hull of the submarine rose up before sinking into the white foam and churning water. The tightness in his chest loosened like a high-pressure release valve being opened.

For several minutes, the roaring planes continued to circle the sinking submarine like vultures.

Surely Hiroshi couldn't have survived those bombs. No lifeboats or men appeared floating on the surface.

After the planes flew off, Akira came out of hiding and collapsed to his knees. He fell facedown and broke into a flood of tears in a sudden release of suppressed fear, sadness, and joy. "Thank you, Lord, for sparing my life and keeping Emiko safe from Hiroshi."

When he lifted his head, his eyes met a brilliant rainbow arching across the sky. Truly God had given him a miracle today.

62

Released

McNeil Island, Washington—July 14, 1946

The razor buzzed over Danny's head as he sat in the barber chair for his final prison haircut at the Big House. On one hand, it elated him that he and the other resisters would be released eleven months early, but at the same time, doubts and fears crept in.

Of course, he wanted out. He missed his family and wanted to pick up where he had left off with Mary. In one letter, she mentioned she and her family left Heart Mountain last fall. Since they lost their house, they lived in a shelter for five months. Danny couldn't understand why they wouldn't move in with his family, even though Lily begged them to. Mary was relieved when she and her parents found work, and they eventually moved into an apartment.

It warmed Danny's heart to hear in Mary's letter that she would stick by him even without her parents' blessing.

When he found out her parents opposed their relationship, he understood their concerns and way of thinking. Nobody would want to hire a convict, and her parents would be concerned about how he could provide for her.

With the job market practically nil for Japanese Americans due to the still raw sentiments about the war, maybe he'd save himself the grief and work on his stepfather's farm.

Lily had mentioned in a letter that Tad was preparing for medical school and catching up on prerequisites. Good for him.

That meant Danny would have to do all the farming himself. Maybe that was a good thing; otherwise they'd probably kill each other.

He rubbed his hand over his crew cut and faced the barber. "Thank you." Before checking out, Danny changed into his suit and visited his former cellmate, Will Jackson.

"Good-bye, Will. It's been nice knowing you."

"You're all dressed up. You leaving?" Will rose from the floor and stepped toward the front, sliding his hand through the bar.

"Yeah, I'm leaving. The warden had these suits delivered to all the resisters. Hey, I'll be praying for you." Danny reached for Will's hand and squeezed it firmly. "Take care of yourself."

"Man, I wish I was leaving too. You take care, buddy."

The guard escorted Danny to the release office, where he waited to collect his personal belongings. On one hand, joy burst inside him, knowing he'd soon be a free man after two years in prison and two years at Heart Mountain and Santa Anita. On the other hand, it saddened him to leave behind some priceless friendships.

This morning's final meeting at the Honor Farm with Kazuo crowded his mind. Danny had gripped his hand and squeezed it. He blinked back tears and choked out words. "I'm really going to miss you. You've been my best friend here—like a father to me." Danny's real father died when he was five, and he could never call his stepfather "Dad" or "Father," but with Kazuo, it was different.

"Danny, don't worry. I okay. God will take care." Kazuo pulled away. "You go now."

"I'll come back to visit you."

Kazuo looked at him with eyes set in a no-nonsense, stoic manner—so typical of older, Japanese men. "No. Just live good life. I pray for you."

In those expressive eyes, Danny could see Kazuo's heart, strong and gentle. He wanted to say something more, but a lump formed in his throat. He knew he couldn't count on writing to

Kazuo, given his English limitations. "I'll be praying for you, too."

If it hadn't been for Kazuo, he more than likely would not have invited God back into his life, and Mary would have probably died. The lessons Kazuo taught him had been invaluable.

Danny turned and strode away quickly without looking back, because it would be too painful. His mind reflected on some recent news clippings Lily sent from home about the JACL trumpeting the victories of the 442nd. These Nisei veterans, including his brother, weren't likely to welcome draft resisters like him back into the community. He'd find out real soon.

He had nothing to be ashamed of. It was ironic that other prisoners, even Caucasians and some guards at McNeil Island, sympathized with the Nisei resisters. One person said, "If I were in your shoes, I would have done the exact same thing."

After waiting a few minutes, Danny received his wristwatch, jacket, and other personal belongings. The release officer's grim expression broke into a smile. "Prisoner Omura, you are hereby released. Here's some travel money for your trip home. We wish you the best."

"Thanks." With that, Danny stepped out of the building and walked through the gate, joining the other resisters who looked sharp in their suits. Before they departed, they posed for a group photograph.

He might be going home a free man, but part of his heart would always remain on this island.

63

Return to Japan

Sasebo, Japan—July 18, 1946

Smiling broadly, Akira stepped off a US Navy transport ship, his boots clomping down the ramp. He was finally returning to Japan with thousands of other Japanese soldiers repatriated from Okinawa, Saipan, Iwo Jima, and other battlefields in the Pacific.

It had been three long years since he had seen Emiko, and he couldn't wait to see her. His heart exuberated, but at the same time, he grappled with fear. Did she still love him and want to marry him?

The war had ended eleven months ago. Akira didn't know the date he'd be leaving, so he'd surprise her. He had hoped to return earlier, but he contracted malaria shortly before his capture by the Americans. It took six months in an American POW hospital before he fully recovered.

During his hospital stay, Akira was appalled to discover his US citizenship had been taken away from him for serving in the Japanese army. He was told if he served as a translator in Okinawa for several months, it would help convince the officials to restore his citizenship. Akira planned to return home to America one day and needed to get it back.

Considering what he'd been through, returning to Japan was a miracle. An American officer in the POW camp reported that over twelve thousand US troops, one hundred thousand Japanese soldiers, and one hundred thousand civilians died in Okinawa.

Roughly seven thousand Japanese were captured and taken to POW camps. Akira shuddered, thankful he was one of them.

Standing next to him, a young soldier muttered, "I should have died in Saipan."

Akira turned to him. "Why do you feel that way?"

He looked at Akira. "I can't face my mother and younger brothers as a defeated soldier."

"Despite the government telling everyone how honorable it was to die for the country, your family would never want you dead. Besides, do you think the outcome of the war would have been any different if you had died? God spared your life for a special reason, so don't look back. Live your life fully and help rebuild this country."

The young soldier wiped away tears. Akira prayed silently for him and hoped he had made a difference in his life.

A chilly sea breeze swept through the dock area as boat horns droned in the distance. As he boarded the truck to the train station, his heart grew heavy when he faced southeast, reflecting on the frightful new weapon that had obliterated Nagasaki.

On the train leaving Sasebo, Akira stared out the window and trembled at the widespread destruction of collapsed buildings and charred ruins. At train stops, scores of civilians flocked around detrained passengers with outstretched hands, begging for *gohan*, rice. The multitudes of starving people caused him to ponder whether Japan would ever recover.

At the Takeo station, Akira and two former soldiers said their farewells and stepped off the train. He spotted the stationmaster at the end of the platform and headed toward him. "Good afternoon, sir. Can you provide me with directions to this farmhouse?" He handed him an envelope with Emiko's return address.

The stationmaster examined the address and flipped the envelope over. He sketched a map and pointed northwest. "When you see a checkerboard of rice paddies, cross the footbridge over a small canal, then turn right. It's near the hot springs." He handed the map to Akira.

"Thank you for the directions." Akira bowed.

Along the way, three American GIs riding a jeep slowed down to negotiate a narrow street. Akira almost waved but decided not to when he met their cold stares.

Perhaps his tattered Japanese army uniform brought back bitter memories. Shortly before his capture, he had removed the uniform from a dead Japanese soldier, because his blood-stained, civilian clothes had been ripped apart during his fight with Hiroshi.

Farther down the road, the same soldiers stopped near a school. A dozen smiling Japanese school children encircled the army jeep. "*Chokoreito kudasai!*" they shouted. The Americans returned smiles and handed them the requested chocolate bars. The sight warmed Akira's heart.

Heading northwest brought him into the countryside where tall camphor trees lined the road and gave off a minty, pungent scent. Within a few kilometers, round emerald hills overlooking rice paddies came into view.

Breathing in the aroma of the fertile loam, he imagined in early summer, the seasonal monsoons flooding these paddies—a necessary process in cultivating rice. Up ahead, Akira spotted the footbridge, and he compared the landmark to the map and turned right. In this area, the plots of land were larger with fewer farmhouses.

Soon he encountered a bamboo grove with verdant leaves flocking hundreds of green and yellow shoots, and a large pond mirroring the brilliant sky. Next to it, white and lavender wildflowers flourished. Akira stooped down and picked up a bunch.

Yanking a loose string from his threadbare uniform, he tied the bouquet at the stem and placed it inside his bag with the blooms peeking out.

A short distance from the road, he spotted the name Takata on the entrance of a large, white house with a small cottage toward the back. "Bingo!"

* * *

Emiko splashed water on the *nasubi* eggplants when she heard footsteps.

"*Tadaima modorimashita,* I'm home. Emiko-san!"

Immediately she recognized Akira's voice and gasped. "Akira-san!" She dropped the bucket she held in her hand and turned around.

His arms drew her into a warm embrace, and Akira's lips tenderly kissed hers. Then he held her at arm's length.

"*Okairinasai!*" Tears welled in her eyes. "You're back! I prayed for you every day. Are you well? Not injured?"

"Darling, I'm fine." Akira opened his canvas bag and pulled out the flowers. He dropped to one knee and handed her the bouquet. "*Kekkon shite kudasai.*"

"Yes, of course, I'll marry you. I've waited four long years for you." She graciously accepted the bouquet. "These are lovely. Thank you." She sniffed the flowers and lowered them.

He flashed a luminous smile. "Thank you for waiting so long." Akira reached for her free hand, held it high, and clasped his other hand around her waist. "One-two-three," he counted. "Step forward with your left foot."

Emiko giggled. "What are you doing?"

"I'm teaching you the waltz."

"You're always full of surprises." She savored the moment. "It was well worth it."

"What was?"

"Waiting for you."

He stole a kiss from her and grinned. "Now, move diagonally with your right foot, then step together and back again with your right. Then diagonally with your left. Bring your feet together and repeat."

She followed his instructions and laughed. He lifted her up and twirled her around a couple of times. It was like floating in the air. When he set her down, they braided their fingers together and strolled toward her cottage.

EPILOGUE

San Francisco, California - June 4, 1955

The Super Constellation's propeller engines hummed as the airliner soared high above the Marin Headlands. Akira peered through the window and pointed. "Look, the Golden Gate Bridge and the city. And over there is the Bay Bridge," he said to his family. "Those bridges weren't around when I was a kid."

Twenty-six years after Akira made the long sea voyage to Japan at age thirteen, his dream of returning home to America finally came true. After flying over the tall skyscrapers of downtown San Francisco, the plane banked right and began its descent. The glistening blue waters of the bay transformed into a dull gray, punctuated with little white caps in the final approach to the airport.

After the plane touched down, Akira and his family exited down the steps onto the tarmac. He could see the golden sunburnt hills of the East Bay through the disintegrating blanket of fog. It thrilled him to see the somewhat familiar landscape. Akira couldn't wait to reunite with Mama and his brothers and meet their families.

Inside the terminal entrance, animated voices called out his name. He immediately spotted Mama and Tad waving their arms.

Joyous tears welled up in Akira's eyes. "Mama! Tad!"

Mama scurried over, eyes brimming with tears. "Akira-chan! I can't believe it's my Akira!" She rushed into his arms and squeezed him tightly.

After Mama released him, Tad greeted Akira with a bear hug and big smile. "It's good to see you, brother."

"Likewise." Akira brought his children to the forefront. "This is my seven-year-old, Yukio, and five-year-old, Kiyomi, and Emiko." He turned to the kids. "This is your grandmother and uncle."

Emiko and the kids bowed. "*Hajimemashite yoroshiku.* It's nice to meet you," they said.

Mama stooped down toward the children and wrapped her arms around them. "*Kawaii.* The kids are so cute." She rose to greet Emiko and embraced her. "It's so nice to finally meet you. I've heard so much about you."

Tad waved at the children. "Hi there. I'm Uncle Tad. You're such good kids and well-mannered."

Akira chortled. "That's not how they really are." He turned and looked outside the terminal window. "It's so good to be back home."

"Let's get your luggage and have you clear customs," Tad said. "Everyone's waiting to meet you at home."

* * *

Akira and his family stepped out of the guest room at Danny's house and entered the living room.

Lily set the appetizer tray down and approached Emiko. "Those are gorgeous kimonos you and your daughter are wearing."

"Thank you." Emiko smoothed her deep purple kimono with embroidered cherry blossoms.

Akira grinned, pleased that his wife had paid attention when they practiced English together.

Lily turned to Akira and Yukio. "Both of you look so handsome wearing matching charcoal blazers with bow ties." She turned around. "Please everyone, help yourself to some hors d'oeuvres."

Emiko sampled one. "*Tottemo oiishi desu.* Delicious."

In the dining room, they enjoyed a lavish dinner with *sushi, sashimi*, and other delicacies, along with American dishes of lasagna and barbecued short ribs.

Mama spoke to Emiko in Japanese at a rapid-fire, nonstop clip.

Both Danny's kids and Tad's boy immediately warmed up to their cousins. After dinner, the kids scampered to the family room to play board games. The Omura ladies congregated in the living room while the men remained in the dining room.

Akira scanned an old family photo with his real father and paused. "I wish Papa were here. You fellows were probably too small to remember him."

"No, we remember him," Tad said.

Akira shifted over and lifted a photograph of his stepfather perched on the hutch. "I wish I could have met him."

Tad came alongside. "Mas was a hard-working, good man."

Placing the photograph back, Akira turned toward his brothers. "Japan was in really bad shape after the war with so many homeless people living in the streets, under bridges, or in the train stations. Also, the yen devalued so much, people lost their life savings."

"We heard you had a child who died," Danny said.

"That was our first son, Yutaka, whom we adopted him from a Catholic orphanage near Nagasaki. He died of leukemia, probably caused by radiation from the atomic bomb. Our son didn't live to see his fifth birthday."

"That's so tragic." Tad shook his head. "The A-bomb has had a lasting effect."

"We miss him a lot. He would have been the same age as Tad's boy, Brent. After he died, Emiko was so distraught I had to force her to eat." Akira turned toward the living room where the ladies were. "Because of the McCarran-Walter Immigration Act, Emiko couldn't immigrate until this year. Actually, it worked out well with my job transfer here."

Mary entered the room and set a tray down on the table. She handed Akira a dish. "Have some chocolate soufflé."

"Thank you, Mary. What a treat." Akira glanced at the oak framed, beveled glass door as she left. "Danny, your house is beautiful and about four times larger than most homes in Japan."

He smiled modestly. "Thanks. After we got married, we remodeled the house and Mary did a great job decorating it."

Akira bit into the light, airy soufflé. "Mmm. Delicious. By the way Danny, thanks for letting us stay here until we get situated."

"Stay as long as you like."

"If Danny throws you out, you can always stay with us," Tad said with a hearty laugh. "But seriously, little brother's done an amazing job with this place, quadrupling the yield on the fruit trees and blackberries using the latest technology for soil testing and irrigation. And he donates the surplus crops to the poor."

"Impressive." Akira peered out the large window toward the fields faintly visible in the moonlight.

Danny shrugged. "Mas—I mean, Dad had the farm running smoothly before he passed away. I only made a few tweaks."

Akira smiled and turned to Tad. "And you've become a surgeon at Stanford Hospital."

"Incredible, isn't it? God led me down that path and provided." Tad let out a coy smile. "You've made quite a change yourself, from teaching to business management. Tell me about that company you work for."

"After the war, I worked for the occupation forces in Tokyo. One day, the supplier I worked with offered me a job."

"What company?" Danny asked.

"Tokyo Telecommunications Engineering."

Tad arched his brows. "That's a mouthful."

Akira chuckled. "My boss, Mr. Akio Morita, wants to change the name to Sony. It's the brand name of our latest product—a transistor radio as small as a bar of soap. He sent me here to generate interest with retail stores. If I'm successful, we'll be opening a branch office in San Francisco."

Tad cracked a smile. "Sony—now that's easy to remember. I want one of those little radios."

"Me too." Danny sipped his drink, then snapped his fingers. "Hang on a second. I almost forgot." He disappeared from the room and returned with a photo album. "Check this out."

Akira opened the album and stared at it openmouthed. "I don't believe it. My baseball cards!" He leafed through the textured pages, remembering vividly that day in 1929 on board the ocean liner when he handed Danny the wooden box packed with his cards. "This is great. You saved these?"

A half-smile sneaked across Danny's face.

Memories inundated Akira's mind as he turned the last page then gazed at his brothers. "We were so young back then." His eyes misted. "Each of us has been through so much. Tad, you were wounded in the war."

"Yeah, I still have pain every once in a while."

"I heard that the 442nd Regiment is the *most decorated* combat unit in the history of the US military. That's incredible!"

"We had something to prove, but we really paid a high cost for it with so many guys who didn't make it home."

Danny turned toward Akira. "Even President Truman highly praised their regiment and told them, 'You fought the enemy abroad and prejudice at home and you won!' "

"Danny, you also fought for our rights by standing up for what you believed in," Tad said. "Also you've caught a lot of flak for being a No-No Boy and even went to prison, where you could have been killed."

Akira wrapped his arms around Tad and Danny. "Each of us have faced many storms in our lives. But I suppose if it never rained, flowers wouldn't bloom so beautifully. God can take our darkest days and shattered lives and turn them into a kaleidoscope of hopes and dreams we never imagined. He is so good."

ACKNOWLEDGMENTS

Cherry Blossoms in the Storm would not have been possible without the team of people who spent countless hours on this project, reviewing and editing the manuscript, and making helpful suggestions.

Our deepest gratitude go to the members of the ACFW critique groups: Gail Sattler, Sarah Hamaker, Ginny Hamlin, Jennifer Uhlarik, Kail Harbick, Lee Carver, Linda Truesdell, Ruth Reid, David Longeuay, Mary Vee and others.

We also thank reviewers from Ethel Herr's critique group: Pam Chang, Stephanie Shoquist, Sandra Gutknecht, Adam McDonald, and all those who provided wise counsel, mentoring, and critiques at the ACFW and Mount Hermon Writers Conferences: James Scott Bell, Rick Acker, John Olson, Brandilyn Collins, Gayle Roper, Randy Ingermanson, and Nick Harrison.

Our heartfelt thanks goes to those who reviewed the full manuscript or provided resources and other useful input: Nana Nishida, Yuki Suminaga, Paul Tabe, Mabel Okamura, Barbara Kawamoto, Stan Date, Irene Hirano, Jimmy Matsuda, Sadie Yamashita Hutton, Doug Endo, Sets Tomita and others from Yu-Ai Kai and other Japanese community organizations.

We are grateful to our graphic artist, Lauren Kudo, and editors: Suzanne Lakin, Kelly Lee, Mabel Okamura, and Amanda Price.

Finally, a special thanks to Dr. Lynn Chang for reviewing the medical scenes and to all who prayed and participated in the birthing of this book.

ABOUT THE AUTHORS

Robert and Gail Kaku are Sansei—third generation Japanese Americans—with personal connections to this story. Robert's father, Shogo Kaku, was incarcerated at Santa Anita, California and Heart Mountain, Wyoming. Gail's father, Masao Nishida, was incarcerated at Turlock, California, Gila River, Arizona, and Tule Lake, California. Both mothers, Tsuyako Kaku and Nanako Nishida, lived in wartime Japan.

Robert is a graduate of the University of California at Berkeley and works as an information technology manager at a health care company. His hobbies include golf, alpine skiing, and traveling. Gail is a graduate of the University of Southern California and also has a background in information technology. She enjoys traveling, skiing, and being at the beach. They live in the San Francisco Bay Area.

Other Books by Bob and Gail Kaku

Popcorn Miracles

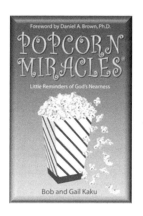

Fill yourself with fun, laughter, eye-popping inspiration and a potpourri of extraordinary stories. Then begin your journey of Popcorn Miracles.

Visit the book trailer at:
PopcornMiracles.com

Kernels of Hope

Give yourself a Kernel of Hope today. What are they? Kernels represents hard, difficult problems that burst under heat into amazing breakthroughs. Both the pops and kernels are awaiting you today.

Visit the book trailer at:
Kernels-of-Hope.com